TILLY

PATRICIA DIXON

Print ISBN 978-1-912986-48-4

In memory of Mum and Dad
The heroine and hero in the stories of my life
You were the centre of everything
And remain there in my heart always
Be happy in heaven
I love you

PROLOGUE

Dear Diary
Well, it's almost here, by this time tomorrow I will be in France and I suppose I will finally have to face up to the fact that I am doomed. There's no going back now and I'll have to live with the consequences of my actions forever. I know I'm a spineless, two-faced wimp and it's all my own fault, but we've been round the houses with this and there's just no way out. Everything is packed and ready to go, my ticket and passport are taunting me from the top of the sideboard and the 'thing' is in its box, wrapped with a stupid bow. Luke is downstairs watching the news while I'm up here committing what feels like treason, simply by writing these words to you. It's ironic, isn't it, that he doesn't even know about you? That's how compatible we are! He has no idea that I vent my soul most nights to an imaginary friend who knows my innermost thoughts and with whom I share my deepest feelings. If he did discover your existence I think he would most likely die of shock as he read the words on these pages. Anyway, it's too late now to change anything so I may as well go to sleep. Thank you for your patience and being such a good listener while I ranted on and explored the recesses of my addled brain. I'm glad you can't answer back because I dread to think what you would say – although I expect it's nothing I wouldn't

1

say to myself. I will update you when and if I have anything interesting or joyous to tell you, which is unlikely, so don't hold your breath. Night night, Diary.

CHAPTER ONE

The coastline of France appeared from beneath wispy, white clouds and Tilly's heart lurched while her brain lamented the fact that somewhere down below, her poor deluded parents would be zooming towards the airport, brimming with excitement and anticipation. She had made this journey so many times before and the contrast with how she felt on previous occasions was akin to torture. Every emotion she felt, every thought that zapped through her muddled brain reminded her that she was making a huge mistake, yet no matter how hard she tried to force it away, the truth returned to taunt her.

Her wedding dress hadn't helped, attracting unwanted attention as she boarded the plane. Everyone loves a bride-to-be so she'd bravely endured the well-meant questions and comments from fellow passengers and air crew as she tried to stuff the offending object inside the small, overhead compartment. Tilly half hoped they'd make her put it in the hold and then she could pretend it had got lost and redirected to God knows where, but she knew this wouldn't solve her dilemma. It would only create a huge crisis that would be averted and somehow solved by her unflappable mother.

Thinking of her mum, Freda, made Tilly want to cry.

She had put her heart and soul into this wedding and more or less organised everything single-handedly. She knew her mum was struggling with her health and had swept this aside to give her daughter the perfect wedding. All Tilly had to do now was put on her dress, turn up at the *Maire's* office and enjoy the day, was that really too much to ask?

* * *

It had been Freda's idea to have the wedding in France and at the time Tilly was thrilled, so she left it all to her mother who had done everyone proud. She'd found the venue for the reception at a beautiful countryside hotel called *Les Trois Chênes*. She'd arranged accommodation for the guests who were flying in from all over the place and sorted out the very complicated legal requirements that went hand in hand with all things French. As a consequence Tilly would be spending exactly two full weeks as a resident in France before the big day.

Being on good terms with the *Maire* always came in handy and as her dad played *pétanque* in the village team, they had managed to come to an agreement with regards to the nitty-gritty of French law. As her parents lived there permanently it qualified their daughter to be married by the *Maire*, however, either the bride, groom or both had to reside with them for a fortnight before the nuptials. Luke was busy at work and had to attend a conference so he would be driving over with the best man and her chief bridesmaid on the Thursday before; around the same time the rest of the wedding party would start to arrive.

There it was again, the stomach-churning reminder of yet another reason why she had to go through with this wedding. Everyone who Tilly held dear was making the journey over and for some it would be a monumental effort or an expensive long-haul flight. Scott, her brother, along with his wife, Susie, and Charlotte their gorgeous six-year-old daughter – and possibly the most excited bridesmaid in the whole world, were coming all the way from Brisbane.

They were combining the wedding with a month long stay in Europe, where they would also spend time in England with Susie's parents. The minute Tilly's engagement was announced they promised to attend the wedding and the internet had provided Charlotte with the means to keep her aunty on the hook.

Tilly was soon inundated with emails from Australia containing drawings of her and Charlotte in their princess dresses, handwritten letters in multi-coloured crayon telling Aunty Tilly how excited she was, plus phone calls and Skype sessions where with breathless anticipation she counted down the sleeps until they arrived.

How could one small, innocent child inflict so much guilt by merely expressing all the emotions lacking in Tilly herself? Charlotte served as a constant reminder as to why the wedding couldn't be called off and that was even before the subject of her grandmother, aunts and uncles was discussed. Tilly had to smother a groan of sheer despair at the merest hint of the disappointment and bewilderment they would feel if she cancelled now.

Her maternal grandma was making her first journey over to France or anywhere really since Tilly's granddad passed away five years earlier. Betty was a home bird who'd been knocked sideways by the death of her husband following sixty years of happy marriage. Riddled with arthritis and terrified of flying, Betty had bravely decided to make the journey from Bristol by car along with Marianne, Tilly's aunty. It would be a long and possibly painful expedition for Betty who, despite her anxieties about sailing, being taken ill whilst abroad and eating foreign food, had insisted on watching her granddaughter tie the knot.

Tilly's mum was so looking forward to spending time with Betty and fussing over her. The fact that Aunty Marianne came as part of the deal was another matter entirely and Tilly knew that at some point during their week-long stay there would be conflict between the sisters. Right now though, her aunty and mother's lack of sisterly love or tolerance for one another was the last thing on her mind.

Thankfully, Tilly's dad had no such issues with his brother Norman who was coming over with his wife Caroline, another flashing beacon alerting her to the predicament she was in. Uncle Norman was basically skint after being laid off and had been relying on Aunty Caroline's wage from her supermarket job to tide them over until they retired next year. Tilly suspected her mum and dad had either loaned them the money or had paid for their flights because normally, a holiday would be way down on their list of priorities.

Norm and Caroline would be bunking down in her parents' touring caravan, situated at the end of the garden. While her grandma and Marianne, Scott and his family, plus Tilly and her bridesmaid, Stacey, would somehow squash into the house. Luke and his best man, Darren, along with her in-laws-to-be, would be staying at the hotel where the reception was being held, which was, to Tilly's relief, as far away from her as possible. Ken and Hazel were obnoxious, loud-mouthed show-offs and Tilly had perfected the art of avoiding them at any given opportunity.

Hazel was a local councillor who ensured she was invited to as many functions as possible, making the most of hospitality and guzzling everything on offer. She had little interest in her civic duties and preferred furthering her own interests. Ken was from the same mould and accompanied his wife on her social engagements making useful contacts while he bragged about their apartment in Alicante, his golf handicap, his mid-life crisis sports car and their flourishing empire. He owned a carpet shop and, thanks to Hazel, the offices of Bristol Town Hall were covered in his very finest Axminster.

It was obvious that Hazel thought Luke could have done better for himself and wasn't remotely impressed by Tilly, her beloved career as a nurse or any of her family. Luke was their only child and in Hazel's eyes, perfect in every way. Even when Tilly found out he had cheated on her with the barmaid at their local wine bar, Hazel brushed away his guilt. Instead, his behaviour confirmed Hazel's doubts and character assessment of Tilly who she deemed extremely lacking in most areas.

When Luke proposed in the midst of desperate pleas for forgiveness and a second chance, vowing to spend the rest of his life proving how much he loved her, Tilly foolishly agreed. In doing so, she also halted Hazel's victory parade. Perversely, as much as she wanted this wedding fiasco to be a terrible nightmare, Tilly was at the same time loathed to grant Hazel her greatest wish *or* give her any opportunity to say the immortal words – 'I told you she was no good'.

How Tilly wished she had listened to Stacey's sage advice. Instead of acting like a pathetic loser who was so relieved her unfaithful, two-timing boyfriend had come home, she should have told him and his stuck-up family where to get off and kicked him right back out again. Stacey was one of a kind. A human explosion of tattooed eyebrows and body parts, brightly dyed hair in whatever colour she fancied, Stacey was refreshingly untroubled by societies obsession with weight, carrying her buxom size eighteen with pride. She was voluptuous, gregarious, outgoing and confident and fiercely protective of her best friend who she'd adopted on their first week of training.

Stacey also couldn't stand Luke or his mother and was euphoric when Tilly confided that she was having doubts about her betrothal, then immediately deflated when in the next breath, she explained that no matter what, she had to go through with it. It had all come flooding out as they lay on their twin beds in the Travelodge, just after they staggered in from Tilly's hen night.

* * *

Everyone was having a great time and far too merry to notice that the star of the show looked thoroughly fed up and on the verge of tears, all apart from Stacey. Despite meticulous planning and spending a small fortune on saucy items and bad taste lingerie at Ann Summers, Stacey sussed she was flogging a dead horse. Once the Henettes had been locked in their coops for the night, the chief bridesmaid flicked on the kettle and made her weepy friend some strong coffee, then got on with the task of interrogation.

To actually speak the words 'I don't love him' to another human being had felt so liberating yet at the same time, incredibly disloyal. Tilly's honesty and loose tongue was due, mostly, to far too many Tia Maria and Cokes and under normal, tight-lipped circumstances, she'd have kept up her ridiculous charade. Once it was out there in the open there was no stopping her. While she was on a roll and Stacey was still upright, Tilly had vented her pent-up fears, worries and deepest thoughts to her slightly astonished friend.

They talked until the morning light peaked beneath the bottom of the blackout blinds, by which time they were semi-sober and unable to agree on a sensible way forward. Stacey was adamant that it was foolish to even contemplate marrying someone you were no longer in love with, no matter how well intentioned her reasons, while Tilly was equally convinced that it was the simplest solution. That way nobody would be hurt, disappointed, out of pocket or in the case of Hazel, triumphant.

After being sworn to secrecy and made to promise that she would be there to help Tilly get through the worst day of her life, Stacey reluctantly agreed and promptly fell into a troubled, vodka-induced sleep.

Tilly had remained wide awake, going over her confession where from the outset she assured Stacey that it wasn't pre-wedding jitters, before she even said it. While Stacey snored, the sounds of the world waking up and beginning its day began to filter through the glass. Tilly listened enviously as lorries zoomed along the motorway while she entertained romantic notions of hitchhiking her way to freedom wearing her party gear, a pink frilly garter and a sash saying, 'Bride-To-Be'.

As a hot, blobby tear rolled down her cheek Tilly had managed a smile, knowing that if she did leg it onto the hard shoulder she'd have no trouble at all catching a lift. But running away wasn't an option so instead she went over and over it again. Her tired eyes began to droop while her confused brain refused to sleep, submitting to her conscience and the inevitable – her wedding.

* * *

After Freda suggested hosting the whole shebang in France, before Tilly knew it her mum was compiling a wedding dossier of suitable venues, menus, official forms and had subscribed to a glossy magazine full of dresses and handy hints. Monica from *Friends* had nothing on Freda and at first Tilly was touched by her enthusiasm so went with the flow. For a short while, she'd enjoyed perusing pages upon pages of beautiful gowns and the lengthy telephone conversations with her excited mother whose feet hadn't touched the ground since Luke proposed. Freda got the ball rolling and the date was set for the following August and things just escalated from there. It was the incident at Christmas that had set Tilly's nerves on edge and by the New Year they were well and truly jangling and the first seeds of doubt were sown.

After managing to get over Luke's infidelity, finding the courage to trust him again and then move on was one of the hardest things. Even after coming out the other side of such hurt and despair, it was inevitable that a small scar remained and Tilly was constantly on her guard. To prove that she had nothing to worry about and he was completely reformed, Luke went slightly overboard and stuck to her like glue during the whole festive period.

When Stacey commented on the fact that he was like her annoying Siamese twin and scared she'd have a revenge affair, her words hit home and rankled Tilly.

Was he guarding his property? Did he have such a low opinion of her and their relationship that he actually thought she was capable of behaving like that? Or was he judging her on his own poor morals? Perhaps he insisted on her accompanying him to his firm's Christmas dinner, not because he wanted her there, but because he couldn't trust himself to go alone. Tilly had no intention of being unfaithful and therefore didn't need a chaperone to go partying with her friends from work, which is why she dug her very high heels in and went without him. The fall-out from her actions and their difference in opinion rumbled on, right up until New Year's Eve, resulting in them sulking their way into January the 1st.

It was during a meal with a group of friends later that month that her doubts began to manifest themselves into something more disturbing, sending her mind and her heart in an unexpected direction. When Darren, Luke's best friend made what he thought was a humorous man comment, about how the new Mrs Crawford wouldn't be gallivanting without her husband, the unfunniness of his words hit home. From then on, it had been a downward spiral. For months she was aware of a gradual shifting, deep within her soul and Tilly began looking at her relationship through fresh eyes.

It began with her ID badge. Tilly loved her name. She'd had it since the day she was born and it had been an integral part of who she was. From the minute she learned how to write, in her scrawling, clumsy, five-year-old way, it had defined her and given her an identity. It was called out in assembly when she received a prize, or at secondary school when she was summoned into the headmaster's office for throwing water bombs out of the science lab window. It was written on her GCSE and A level certificates and when she gained her degree, it was there for everyone to see. Matilda Parker. Staff Nurse.

As she proudly pinned it to her uniform the following Monday morning, Darren's words rang in her ears and she realised that she wasn't quite ready to give up her maiden name, or was it more than that? Tilly had moved in with Luke when her parents sold up and moved over to France permanently. It was a shock to the system at first, making the transition from the girlfriend who stayed over a few times a week to 'partner', which was what everyone called someone they shared a house, bills and responsibilities with.

Instead of going it alone or sharing a bachelorette flat with Stacey, Tilly had taken the easy option and accepted Luke's offer. With hindsight she knew it was the wrong decision and her life wasn't quite the comfy pair of slippers it had been at the beginning. As each day and month passed by it felt like a clunking pair of steel toecap boots, weighing her down and holding her back.

It wasn't just about a name or responsibilities, it went deeper than that and Tilly found herself examining every aspect of her life and relationship on a daily basis. When Luke was away with work she enjoyed it, her mini-break, taking great pleasure from the fact that she had the place to herself for a couple of nights. She was always pleased to see Luke when he returned, but she couldn't ignore the dawning awareness that she would also manage alone.

The thought was fleeting and quickly followed by a reality check. Tilly recalled how her heart almost broke at the thought of losing Luke, not to mention the rivers of tears she'd cried as she imagined him with someone else. The recollection was sobering and temporarily tamed her independent streak. There was no way she would risk losing him again and experience the anguish of the past, so in retrospect, thanked her lucky stars when he came home at night, and silently placed her unsettling thoughts back in their box.

Most of the time they were both too busy to notice that the fault line in their relationship was opening up and huge cracks were appearing. They barely spent any quality time together, which meant they rarely argued and this lulled them into a false sense of security. If Tilly jokingly mentioned that she'd hardly seen him all week, they would roll their eyes, blame it all on work pressures and make breakable promises and vague plans to do something soon. Tilly worked shifts and weekends which fragmented their routine and made being together a work of art.

Luke put in long hours as manager for an IT company

and filled Tilly's absence wisely, enjoying the company of his friends and playing five-a-side football. Consequently, when they did find themselves at home together they were usually exhausted and content with a takeaway, a film and an early night.

When the gloom really settled on Tilly, she usually managed to fight her way through the smog and restore some order to her brain, but as her wedding day approached it was becoming increasingly clear that they wanted different things from life. They rarely agreed on which film to watch, political parties and ideals, who should win *X Factor*, how to pronounce the word scone, and the diversity of their musical preferences or taste in food sometimes rankled. Tilly found consolation in the notion that many couples were incompatible on paper yet sometimes, opposites did attract. However, once raised, the subject of attraction brought forth a whole new range of issues.

Was she still attracted to Luke? Yes, he was very good-looking with his groomed, jet-black hair and fashionably trimmed beard and he was always perfectly attired to accentuate his muscular body. Luke was a catch and Tilly was proud to be his girlfriend. But looks didn't make up for personality and once you stripped away his outer layer there wasn't a lot going on inside. They rarely had stimulating conversations unless it was about something he was interested in, like football. Even though she wasn't an authority on anything in particular, Tilly was moved by the things she saw on the news or in documentaries and did have opinions and observations she would like to share with someone.

The point was proved when she came home from work one evening, brimming with excitement and eager to discuss an idea with Luke. At the grand old age of twenty-five, while absolutely loving her job, Tilly had decided to specialise in Ophthalmology. She might as well have been talking in Latin when she discussed her aspirations with Luke. Whilst telling her to go for it, he wasn't particularly interested in hearing where her chosen career path would lead her or what it entailed. The fact that his eyes constantly strayed back to *Top Gear* while she enthused, wasn't lost on her. Tilly had hoped to make a grand plan for their future and set out some kind of route map, or at least get some indication that they were headed in the same direction. Instead she ran out of steam and gave up.

Tilly was deflated. During the journey home on the bus, she'd planned it all in her head, rehearsing exactly what she wanted to say and how.

One day, she wanted to start a family and although Luke wasn't averse to the idea, he hadn't actually embroidered on the subject either. Tilly knew that it would be wiser to get her training out of the way and climb onto the next rung of the ladder before babies came along, then, they would be set up and financially secure. Most of all, in between humdrum life, studies and childbirth, Tilly wanted to live a little and have some fun.

The world was such a wonderful place and she had always dreamed of exploring parts of it while she was still young and healthy. Top of her list was the Far East. Thailand, Malaysia and maybe even India, and then there was Australia. She had no intention of emigrating there for many reasons, the main one being her parents. Tilly was comforted by the fact she could get to France in a few hours if need be and couldn't bear the thought of not seeing them for years on end. Still, she would like to visit her brother and put a tick in that box. Next on the agenda was a skiing holiday, not to mention Iceland or whale watching in the Scottish Isles and weekend breaks to the major cities of Europe.

There was no reason why they couldn't achieve any of this if they saved up and worked hard, but Luke loved his two weeks all-inclusive in Turkey and her idea of backpacking or camping at Ayers Rock wasn't remotely up his street. As far as she was concerned, they could save family friendly hotels for when they needed the kids' club and overexcited reps to organise their holiday. They were only young once and while they had money in the bank, regular jobs and bodies that weren't falling apart, they should enjoy life. The proof of the pudding was when they booked their honeymoon, or more to the point, when Luke took it upon himself to hijack the whole thing and surprise her with something *he* would absolutely love.

Tilly suggested the Maldives. It wasn't as though she wanted him to go on the hippy trail through Marrakesh, however, she *had* set her heart on something a little more exotic than Cyprus or Portugal. In the end he splashed out on two weeks of pure luxury on the Côte d'Azur in one of the best beachside hotels that had everything a lazy, body-obsessed, sun-worshipper could wish for.

Tilly was furious. She had spent almost every single holiday since she was nine years old in France. Did he not realise she fancied a change?

Luke on the other hand thought she was extremely ungrateful and the resort he'd chosen was nothing like the beaches at Pornichet or La Baule so it would be a completely new experience. They would drive down after the wedding for a fortnight in the lap of luxury, dining in a Michelin star restaurant and being pampered like the stars, which was a damn sight better than a bowl of noodles from a street cart!

Tilly knew it was futile to argue and resigned herself to being bored to tears while Luke made the most of the gym, jacuzzi and the south facing, deluxe sunloungers.

* * *

Letting out an exasperated sigh, Tilly pushed the thoughts of her honeymoon away and checked her watch. They were almost there so she began packing away her magazine in anticipation of the announcement from the flight attendant.

The day before, she'd said goodbye to the girls at work and forced a cheery smile as the patients on the surgical ward, waved and wished her well. Tilly was truly honoured that some of her colleagues were making the trip over for her big day. The final nail that sealed her coffin was the twelve friends who would be piling into a minibus and catching a Channel ferry in order to attend the ceremony. They were all staying at a motel and then making the return journey the following day, no matter what state they were in. How could she even think of letting them down or ruining all their plans, never mind wasting their hard-earned cash on the trip and wedding outfits?

Tilly looked down the length of the plane and felt a wave of claustrophobia overtake her. She was cocooned in a metal bullet, propelling her through the sky and catapulting her towards her fate. As she rested her head on the cool plastic of the cabin walls, she closed her eyes in an attempt to shut out the images of her friends and family. To try and quell the rising panic, she breathed through lungs that were constricted by an aching heart. As the inevitable announcement came over the address system, the tears that leaked from the corners of her eyes had nothing to do with her fingers digging into the palms of her hands. By the time the plane began its descent, Tilly had managed to rein in the stampede of emotions that were trampling their way through every fibre of her body and as the wheels bounced onto the runway, some semblance of calm had settled over her.

Once the doors were opened, she purposely let all the other passengers make a dash for it rather than attract attention when she attempted to drag 'The Thing' out of the overhead compartment. Instead, she fiddled with her phone and avoided eye contact with the well-meaning lady on the adjacent aisle.

Tilly was the last one off and wearily followed the gaggle of happy holidaymakers down the steps and towards passport control, taking her place at the back of the queue. She'd barely entered the building when she spotted them both, waving and trying to attract her attention through the large glass windows of the arrivals hall. A tsunami of love and gratitude washed over her as she returned their waves and despite the turmoil in her heart and the confusion in her brain, just the sight of them made her smile. She loved them both so much and could never let them down.

They had dedicated their lives to the pursuit of making her happy, how could she scupper their plans, destroy their dreams and embarrass them in front of all their friends and family? They didn't deserve that and recently, Tilly felt she didn't deserve them either. All they were expecting was an album full of memories and a day full of joy, so that's what they would get. She would do this for her mum and dad.

When her turn came, she solemnly handed over her passport to the stern-faced official and stepped over the white line and into the future, her fate was sealed. In exactly fourteen days time, at 2pm on Saturday 22nd August, Matilda Parker was going to get married.

CHAPTER TWO

Freda wasn't in the best of moods. She was marching along a country lane like a madwoman, sweating from every pore – or perspiring as women prefer. She also looked like a fat, pink pig, much to the obvious amusement of two tractor drivers, not to mention a young lad riding a moped who gave her a 'pip pip' on his horn. Freda hated exercise; she hated being fat more but this was just torture, as was the image of the raisin and custard Danish that was hiding at the bottom of the bread bin. Today, Freda also hated low-fat food, the menopause, Lycra sweatpants that cut your bum in half, herbal tea, the arrogant control freak that emptied their bins and Luke's mother. Not particularly in that order. She knew she was obsessing over stupid things but she couldn't help it. Along with all the other minor mental health issues she'd developed over the past eighteen months, being a narky cow was right at the top of the list.

Grumpy Freda was experiencing the change and even though she hated the expression, it actually epitomised everything about her world right now, because within the space of a few months, her whole life had altered. She'd made the transition from full-time English teacher to retired ex-pat quite easily but now it was all being spoilt by

17

hot sweats and sleepless nights. Even the bloody owl that lived in the barn got more kip than her!

Following Howard's accident at work it was clear that his back would never be the same again and returning to full-time work as a fire officer was not an option. After much soul-searching they did their sums and realised that along with his compensation payment, a wisely bought insurance policy and the sale of their home in England, they were financially comfortable. Consequently, they crossed their fingers and moved over to France and into what had, until now, been their holiday home. At the time, Freda's parents were fit and reasonably well so they could manage without her being close at hand. Scott, her son, was settled in Australia and wasn't expected to return for at least five years, if ever, and Tilly was enjoying an independent working life.

They'd bought their *maison secondaire* when Tilly was eleven and over the past fifteen years they'd put down roots and made some lovely friends. Along with their French neighbours, there were lots of British families in the surrounding area.

Howard quickly settled into French village life and loved his garden, growing his own fruits and vegetables while Freda had built up a small, part-time business teaching English. It was so easy for ex-pat children to forget what they'd learned in the UK and most parents wanted their kids to maintain a good level of written and spoken English. Then there were the little ones who went straight into the French education system and benefited from a few extra lessons in English.

All in all, their move had been a blessing in disguise. Patience and tolerance were now things of the past and her mood swings weren't conducive to a classroom full of cocky teenagers, let alone the debilitating tiredness that regularly wiped her out. Freda would most likely have been sacked, or found snoring in the staffroom, or up on an assault charge, verbal or physical. No, this way of life was so much calmer and it enabled her to deal better with her conflicting personalities and varying degrees of wellness.

Freda had tried valiantly to psychoanalyse herself and put everything into perspective. On the whole she had a wonderful life and felt blessed that they had landed here, in a beautiful part of the world where they were able to live quite nicely. Therefore, she was desperate not to allow her present state of mind to ruin her every waking moment and spoil her marriage and the happiness she shared with her beloved Howard.

It was just a natural stage of transformation in a woman's life and rather than rail against it, she should embrace the miracle of the human body and enter the next phase of womanhood stronger, wiser and liberated. What a load of old bollocks that was! Freda had read this on one of the many internet sites she had visited in search of information and solutions. The menopause was crap and there were absolutely no positives that she could see. It had impacted on her daily life, ruined the quality of it, slowed her down, and worse of all she'd gained two stone of blubber.

Freda wouldn't have minded if she gorged on stodge, but up until the Big M hit, she had always been a size fourteen, ate healthy food and managed to look half decent in most things. Now, a wobbly layer of fat and cellulite had settled in nicely, right around the middle of her body and, try as she might, it wasn't shifting. Not only that, she'd never had a sweet tooth but suddenly she craved every single cake in the patisserie window and couldn't resist a chocolate biscuit. To her shame, she'd stashed a tin of Quality Street in the spare room and demolished it single-handedly over Christmas, not to mention the Ferrero Rochers at the back of her knicker draw.

And that wasn't all. The subject of all things bedroom related opened up another gaping wound and heaped more misery on her beleaguered life. For months now, any action that involved goings on below the waist were simply a non-event. Yes, it probably had a lot to do with body image and not feeling in the slightest bit sexy, but added to that, lying in a pool of your own sweat most nights with your hair stuck to your scalp wasn't a good look.

When Freda did summon the energy or inclination to have a fumble under the sheets, there wasn't a lot happening. She often wondered if the relevant parts of her body had become disconnected and there was a loose wire that needed reattaching. It was all so unfair, yet mindful that many marriages ran into trouble at this stage, Freda decided to lie back and yes, think of England – so long as it didn't take forever, required minimal interaction or acrobatics and wasn't a frequent event. Unbeknown to Howard, she was usually writing mental lists, wondering what to have for dinner the following evening, or trying to remember where she'd put her car keys.

Memory, now that was another thing that had taken flight. Sometimes, Freda seriously worried that she was going potty or, perish the thought, senile. Once upon a time she was an organised, intelligent woman who everyone thought was unflappable and invincible. Nowadays Freda's brain was actually made of mush and incapable of holding on to a smidgen of information or concentrating on one topic for any length of time. Freda was forever forgetting most of whatever Howard had told her the day before, or who said what and when. She could hear the frustration in the voices of Tilly and Scott when she forgot something vitally important from a previous conversation, and her most annoying trait was that she repeated herself about three times a day, telling poor Howard the same boring piece of trivia, over and over again.

There was something else on her mind as she trudged up the path that led to the top of the hill and it wasn't that she was only halfway through her walk, either. Freda knew she was losing her confidence and it was slipping away the closer they came to Tilly's wedding.

It was the photo of Hazel's wedding outfit that had put her in a bad mood and she'd spiralled into a pit of loathing and self-pity by the time she'd grimaced her way through her morning grapefruit.

Luke's mum was everything Freda was not. She was loud, overbearing and over-made-up, with fake boobs, fake-tanned skin the colour of streaky Bisto, as well as being opinionated and aloof and just to rub salt in the wound, a very trim size ten.

When Tilly innocently showed her mum the photo in a magazine of Hazel's wedding outfit, Freda was instantly taken over by the Incredible Hulk's twin sister, turning green with childish envy. It was exactly what Freda would have chosen for herself had she not been the shape of a marshmallow on two sticks. Hazel would be wearing a fitted silk dress embellished with sparkling jewels and sequins while the mother-of-the-bride would be covered in a tent. Freda could see herself now, floating into the *Maire's* office like an insipid, flowery, mobile greenhouse. Great, just great!

Freda's low self-esteem wasn't just about her negative body image, it was the culmination of a mish-mash of feelings that dragged her down, forcing her to examine her thoughts and behaviour in order to retain some semblance of calm in her life. Apart from teaching English lessons, where she actually felt needed and appreciated if only by the parents, Freda saw herself as being cast adrift on rocky seas, in a tatty inflatable dinghy that could pop at any second.

Howard on the other hand confidently rowed his boat along a calm river then anchored it safely on the shore of his ordered, stress-free life.

Did she talk nonsense and look like a fool who couldn't remember where she'd parked her car, frequently put the milk in the dishwasher and couldn't survive without umpteen lists? Was she boring and frumpy, could everyone in the room tell when she was having a hot sweat and felt like her head was literally going to explode in a vat of hot steam? Why did she blush at the drop of a hat or worry for days about an upcoming social event? Did the children think she was unreliable, scatty or just plain annoying? No wonder she had down days when she felt like this, forcing herself out of the gloom and squinting to see some light at the end of the tunnel.

Freda had thought that Tilly's wedding would solve all her problems in one fell swoop, but in reality she had been foolish. Focusing on someone else in order to provide an exciting distraction seemed like a solution. In the end, it had only served to compound all her insecurities and infirmities and it was getting a bit too much and she only had herself to blame, which was so bloody annoying!

Around the time Luke proposed to Tilly, Freda had just begun to feel the full force of the Big M, which had started with a touch of depression. At first she put it down to the stress of moving to France, delayed shock after losing her dad and a smattering of homesickness. When the sleepless nights decided to get in on the act, Freda took herself off to the doctor who smiled kindly as he handed down his sentence. Advising against HRT, he instead advocated a change of eating habits, drinking herbal tea (which made Freda honk) and making the pharmacist rich after spending a small fortune on vitamins and homeopathic tinctures. He also suggested finding something new to focus on.

Freda realised that Tilly's wedding could be just what she was looking for. It was a grand project to spur her on, revitalise and invigorate her and take her mind off the dark thoughts that caused mayhem in her head. It would give her something to think about while she lay in bed each night, listening to Howard's snores, the perky, loved-up owl hooting to his mate and inconsiderate foxes, screeching the night away.

What a fool she had been. Yes, it had filled up her life for the past twelve months but now the big day was fast approaching and next week, most of her family would descend and she didn't know how the hell she would cope. Freda could manage most days quite adequately because it was just her and Howard. He was adept at handling her moody moments or when she bit his head off for leaving black toasty bits in the margarine. Howard didn't mind her hoovering or taking a cool shower at 3am. They knew each other inside out and were blessed with a blissfully easy routine, spoilt only by Freda if she was 'on one'.

Just thinking about it brought on palpitations. Imagine the state of the house at the end of the day and how would nine of them negotiate the efficient use of one bathroom? When would she fit in floor mopping or take midnight showers without them thinking she was stark raving mad? Stacey and Tilly were going to be camped out on the sofas in the lounge so there would be no more early morning housework or watching *Friends* at 4am while she waited for the sun to rise. She'd never get any sleep and be a ratty cow all day, not to mention the relentless heat while cooking for her finicky, annoying sister. Freda imagined herself by the stove, melting in a frazzled pile of perspiration where they'd find a pile of soggy clothes and a spatula.

Howard had picked up on her anxiety and did his best to allay her worries, telling her that nobody expected to be waited on hand and foot, he would cook at the barbecue and devise a rota for the bathroom. He insisted that no one would notice that she hadn't mopped the floor or polished the woodwork and that for one week, it wouldn't do her any harm to ease off the housework because a bit of carpet fluff never hurt anyone. Naturally, Freda didn't believe a word of it and was even more irritated by Howard's sensible, mellow attitude. It only served to highlight the fact that she was an obsessive, house-cleaning, control freak.

Talking about freaky people, she still had the looming spectre of her sister to deal with and the thought of having to endure her for seven whole days filled Freda with dread. Marianne was twenty-two months younger – which may as well have been the equivalent of two million light years at warp factor ten. They did have moments of light in between the dark where they could actually share a joke or have a sensible conversation and act like normal siblings. These occasions were extremely rare and as a result of limiting the time they spent in each other's company, one hour was probably the upper threshold.

But it went further back. Marianne had been a drama

queen for as long as Freda could remember, craving attention, prone to jealousy and utterly competitive. Freda on the other hand was an unassuming youngster, shy and a bit boring really. She liked to read, sketch and be at home with her parents. Unlike Marianne, she didn't like birthday parties, going to youth clubs or joining in every activity known to man. Freda was quite happy plodding along and extremely happy with her lot in life.

Marianne's competitiveness was the bane of Freda's life and probably the only time when she learned to stand up for herself. There was no joy in playing Monopoly with Donald Trump's alter ego, swing ball wasn't a fun game – it was a battle to the death and even a knockabout on the school tennis courts turned into the women's final at Wimbledon. In the end, Freda grew a spine and told her to sod off and find some other mug to boss about.

In one way or another, both her parents had spent a lifetime pandering to Marianne and keeping the peace. Over the years, Freda's ability to forgive and forget *or* pander to her sister's frequent diva lapses and embarrassing scenes had waned. Nowadays it was only the distance that the Channel put between them and out of respect for their mother's feelings that had prevented a permanent severing of ties. The worst time of all came shortly after they'd moved to France – just five weeks later to be precise.

* * *

Freda's father was a sprightly seventy-eight-year-old who was more than capable of looking after Betty and himself and, despite his age, was rarely ill and had no serious ailments. They had assured Freda and Howard that they would be just fine in England with Marianne and Tilly on hand and would pop over to see them throughout the year. In return, Freda promised to fly over every couple of months or whenever she was needed.

On the day she took the devastating call from her sister, announcing that her dad had suffered a heart attack and died, Freda was consumed by grief, anger and despair, but most of all, guilt for not being there at the end. Whilst making arrangements, and during the actual service and wake itself, everyone, especially the two sisters, managed to get along. It was only shortly afterwards that Freda picked up on an undercurrent of something unsaid and soon realised that Marianne was gearing up for one of her performances. It was during tea and biscuits at her mother's, just before Howard and Freda were preparing to make their sad journey home, that the root of the problem was unearthed.

Marianne was perturbed by the injustice of the situation she now found herself in and made it known to one and all that she was not one bit happy about shouldering the burden of responsibility for their mother. Not only that, she accused Freda of being selfish in the first place for leaving their parents and that if she was any kind of daughter, would return and take on some of the duties herself.

The mother of all rows erupted as Freda pointed out that she had gone to France with her father's blessing and that it was impractical and unnecessary for them to return. Tilly was only a short drive away and quite willing to help in any way she could.

Marianne wasn't having any of it and wanted to know how she was expected to cope with her very high-pressured job in the prison service *and* have a life while being the primary carer for Betty.

When Freda pointed out that she sat at a desk for eight hours a day and only had herself to look after, Marianne flipped. In her opinion Freda didn't know what hard work was because she didn't even have a proper job and spent all day slobbing about in France. Not only that, abandoning their father in his final years had probably caused him hidden distress and finally killed him!

Freda cried throughout the five-hour crossing home and stayed locked in the cabin for the duration. It had taken almost four years to heal the wounds, and after awkward

Christmas visits to the UK the sisters were now on semi-friendly, speaking terms.

* * *

This was why navigating her way through the upcoming visit was going to severely test Freda on so many levels. But while she had breath in her body, no matter how much Marianne irritated or upset her, Freda would not let her sister, or anything else, ruin this wedding.

It would be a day full of wonderful memories, captured by photographs of happy guests that would be placed in an album and treasured forever. The special day in their family history would never be forgotten and as they pored over the images, they would smile and remember being together. Having fun and sharing the moment that two young people sealed their love for each other and took the next step on their journey, as man and wife.

Freda had read those sentiments in a bridal magazine and got all teary just thinking about it. Tilly's wedding day would make all her hard work and worries worthwhile. Until then, she had to face facts and struggle on as best she could.

Turning into the lane she could see Tilly in the garden and hoped she was in a more cheerful mood. Over dinner last night and again this morning, Freda detected a hint of something she couldn't quite put her finger on. Tilly wasn't exactly short-tempered, more irritated and a bit quiet or distracted. Maybe she was just tired from her journey and needed a couple of days to settle into the swing of things. Freda doubted it was pre-wedding nerves, it was a bit early for that, then again, Tilly was a little on the shy side so maybe she was feeling daunted by the whole occasion.

Well, they could have a nice relaxing Sunday together and lunch in the garden. Freda was already concocting a salad of humongous proportions in her head, followed by lemon meringue and a glass of white wine. She deserved a treat after a week of starvation and surely she'd burned enough calories for at least a small slice of dessert.

Sod it, Freda thought rebelliously as she sped up for her home run, she was allowed to celebrate the arrival of her daughter and would make one last almighty effort next week. With a bit of luck, the combination of nervous energy and stress might transform her back into a size fourteen, just in time for the wedding. Freda released a snort of sarcastic laughter at her own delusional state of mind before opening the gate and going inside to have a shower, and a sneaky bite of that Danish pastry.

CHAPTER THREE

It may have been some comfort to Freda had she known that a few miles away, in the village of Le Pin, there was someone else in a similar mood to hers who had spent most of the morning fuming and cursing and banging pans about in the kitchen.

Pippa, Anna's faithful bulldog wasn't going to let her mistress's mini-tantrum get in the way of a few extra moments in bed and contentedly snored through the drama, while keeping one eye slightly open and on the mountain of bacon by the cooker. Anna was still fizzing from the previous night's mini-drama, caused as usual by Louise, Daniel's darling daughter and right royal pain in the neck. Anna loved Daniel with all her heart and during the four blissful years since they had met, they rarely had a cross word or serious disagreement and only one full-blown row. Lately, though, whenever Lady Louise of Limousin was brought into the mix, feathers became decidedly ruffled.

* * *

It all started in earnest at Christmas, however, the signs were there from the start but Anna had been far too eager to please and impress Daniel's family to notice. Louise was all sweetness and light on their first visit to Corrèze, giving Anna no cause for concern or suspicion. In reality, Louise was probably just checking her out and sizing up the opposition before battle commenced and the mind games began.

Daniel always visited his daughter and seven-year-old grandson, Jules, during the school holidays, alternating with his ex-wife and her new partner to avoid unnecessary aggro. At first, they had combined short breaks at Anna's holiday home where he would drop her off and continue south to Corrèze and visit Louise by himself. It wasn't an issue and had worked well, however, on the last two trips Anna had accompanied Daniel where she noticed a swing in Louise's attitude and the atmosphere was distinctly chilled.

Louise was clever with it and never let her guard down in front of Daniel. On the surface she was perfectly pleasant and accommodating but thoroughly sly, bitchy and slightly childish when she was alone with Anna. Even when she pushed the boundaries in front of her father it was only just perceivable and could be argued in favour of either the prosecution or the defence, that's how crafty she was.

It started with the strolls down memory lane, usually during dinner. Anna suspected Louise chose this time as it pinned her victim down to one spot with no other option than to endure the tales of happy family days gone by. Jolly reminiscences of 'the best holidays ever' and some 'really funny' anecdotes and references to 'Wright family Christmases' was like watching a soft focus Doris Day film and Anna had to control the urge not to stand up and leave the table. Common sense somehow prevailed, knowing it was exactly what the storyteller wanted and would make her look extremely childish to boot.

Then there was Louise's fabulous, witty, stunningly beautiful mother who sounded so bloody wonderful that Anna was beginning to wonder why Daniel actually divorced her in the first place, because according to Louise, they were the perfect family. Carys could do no wrong and ironically, neither could her partner Ed who had been accepted and given the stamp of approval by Louise. She seemed never to tire of talking loudly on the phone when Mother Superior rang every five minutes to update her on her cruise, the generous gifts Ed had splashed out on or dinner at the Captain's table. Next, they had to endure the toe-curling sending of big kisses and honey hugs. Anna just wanted to chuck up, especially when Louise shouted to Daniel, 'Mum says hi and hopes you're taking it easy and not working too hard.'

You could have cut the air with a knife as Louise smirked and scored herself three bonus points, while Anna seethed and watched Daniel cringe and mutter a quick reply. Going off what Mr Spineless had told her, Carys didn't seem to mind him working all the hours God sent to keep up with her endless needs. Then, when she finally tired of him *and* their marriage, she grasped the opportunity to flee, conveniently just as Louise left university and secured her first job. Then Carys took him for half of everything.

Rather than take on a huge debt to pay Carys off, Daniel sold his business and their family home and divided everything in half, then set up his consultancy firm and got on with his life. Carys didn't let the grass grow under her feet, gleefully embracing her freedom, totally committed to living the dream and being loved by more than one willing chap whenever the opportunity arose. It was quite obvious that Louise was completely comfortable with her mother having significant others as long as she regularly paid homage and indulged both her and Jules. However, for some reason these rules didn't apply to Daniel, and Daddy's Little Princess assumed she had sole rights, leaving Anna with the opinion that she was a jealous, selfish, two-faced attention-seeker.

When she tactfully brought up with Daniel that sometimes Louise made her feel uncomfortable by going on and on about the past, Anna was met with reluctance to admit the truth or accept his daughter was being slightly insensitive. Daniel brushed off the comments, assuring her it wasn't Louise's intention to make Anna feel that way and maybe she was just filling in the gaps or talking about a part of her childhood that she enjoyed. It wasn't a crime. They did manage to agree on the subject of Carys, because he didn't really want to hear about where she was spending her holidays and what a great tan she had, so he offered to have a subtle word with Louise where her mother was concerned.

Anna was at first relieved and then triumphant that she'd made a valid point, then went into a paranoid panic when she realised that both parties would see it as a form of jealousy and one would take pleasure from the fact it bothered her. When she told Daniel to leave it, his rolling of the eyes and irritated tut added further to Anna's discomfort and niggling unease. He also sounded mildly annoyed when he asked why she'd made a fuss in the first place. Anna's response to this was hurt feelings, a huge sulk and a thorough re-examination of her strategy.

Naturally, this conversation marked the beginning of a battle of the wills, constant game-playing, childish point-scoring, second-guessing and a great deal of patience and tongue biting on Anna's part. Louise scrutinised every aspect of Anna's life and she endured deep, probing questions about the family business, probably in order to assess her current financial status. Next, Louise enquired over Anna's three children, obviously trying to ascertain if she was of superior intellect or wealth. And as for living in an apartment, anyone would've thought Anna lived in a halfway house or a brothel, not the penthouse suite of a luxury building. Although, after producing some photos on her phone, Louise turned a delightful shade of green. No matter what Daniel thought, Anna knew it wasn't out of polite interest or a desire to get to know her better; she was just a nosey cow who was gathering information to relay back to Mommy Dearest at Bitch Central.

The whole thing was draining and tiresome, especially when Anna presumed she had somehow been unwittingly entered into a game show where she was required to prove how much she knew about Daniel's likes and dislikes on a daily basis. Did Anna know how much Dad loves anchovies on his pizzas and his eggs sunny side up? What about music? Had they been to any concerts together? Dad loves musicals – I bet you can't guess his favourite? And so it went on and on, even down to the mind-numbing fact that he hated eating from cold plates, loathed jellied eels and the smell of cinnamon. Everything was cleverly mentioned in the context of an innocent little anecdote or slipped artfully into a conversation, spoken so sweetly and with sickeningly false, well-meant intention that it flew right over Daniel's head.

During their stay over Christmas, Louise's behaviour bordered on the obnoxious and downright rude which in the end, resulted in Anna and Daniel having their first major row. Anna was irked that it had become necessary to proceed with caution on all levels, resulting in a permanent, tension-related headache due to a real-life pain in the neck. Everything she did or said was like tiptoeing through a minefield and had to be carefully thought out, just in case it gave Louise a chance to have a pop. What riled Anna the most was the two-faced hypocrisy where Carys was concerned. It was acceptable for her mother to have Ed but Louise obviously preferred her father to be a single, lonely bachelor for the rest of his life. And if he didn't pull his socks up soon, that's exactly how he would end up.

Anna hadn't really wanted to go to Limousin for Christmas but felt obliged to make the effort as Daniel had spent the last two with her family in Portsmouth. As luck would have it, she wasn't forced to abandon any of them because Sam would be away in Afghanistan on, what Anna hoped, would be his last ever tour of duty there and Joe had been press-ganged into spending Christmas with his girl-friend's family. Melanie was already working in France at Nantes Metropole and therefore quite happy to spread herself between her boyfriend's home and Anna's small circle of French friends. Anna's mother, Enid, had already booked to go to Llandudno on an all-inclusive knees-up with her partner in crime, Gladys, leaving her free to spend the festivities within the bosom of Daniel's family.

Before she even got into the car with Daniel, Anna already secretly dreaded the three day stay with Louise. However, putting her best foot forward, she ensured the gifts she bought were tasteful, thoughtful and beautifully gift-wrapped and had included some special English treats for them all to share. Anna had asked Louise what she should get for Jules and, along with the games for his Xbox, had enjoyed buying him a Batman onesie, slippers and a traditional stocking stuffed with fun bits and bobs. By the time they arrived, Anna had mustered some festive spirit, purely for the sake of Daniel who was looking forward to seeing his grandson and for some unknown reason, Louise.

Sadly, despite her best efforts and earning herself a degree in diplomacy and self-control, Anna had a thoroughly miserable time and couldn't wait to leave and head north. Nothing she could do or say was right where Louise was concerned. If Anna offered to help in the kitchen she was turned down flat and it was blatantly obvious that any interaction with Jules irritated the hell out of his mother. For the whole time they were there, Louise pandered to her father and virtually ignored the existence of Anna.

Louise's husband, Tomas, was a lovely man and Anna wondered how he put up with his wife. Despite her outward, sugar-sweet and fresh appearance, when you got down to the nitty-gritty, on the inside, Louise was rotten.

Maybe escaping to work for eight hours a day enabled Tomas to survive. He thoroughly enjoyed his job as a research scientist at a leading pharmaceutical company where no doubt he could have a laugh with smiley, friendly people.

On each of her visits, Anna had observed him surreptitiously and concluded that even though he appeared to love his wife, his son was the true apple of his eye. While Louise seemed content with reaping the rewards of his well-paid job, Tomas lived in comfort while stealthily avoiding her wrath. For the most part, Tomas appeared to ignore her negative traits and let his wife's crassness go unchecked, just like her father, and it made Anna's blood boil.

Since her husband's death, Anna had toughened up and wasn't prone to self-pity or letting insecurities rule her life. But, gradually, any confidence she had in her relationship with Daniel was being eroded, not directly by Louise, more by his reaction to her behaviour.

Previously, Anna admired so much of Daniel's character and really, there wasn't anything she could pick at or complain about. He was honest, loyal, sensible, kind and understanding and everyone in her family adored him. He had never given her any reason to doubt him or feel insecure, in fact, he had gone out of his way to make her feel the opposite, she felt cherished and loved. Somehow, though, the minute they walked through Louise's door the strong, principled, reliable man Anna loved simply evaporated and she was left with a partially sighted, hearing-impaired, fence-sitter.

On Christmas morning, Anna tried to banish thoughts of her children from her mind and focus on the fact that they were adults now and she needed to get used to the idea that things change and they couldn't always be together.

It was all going quite well as they took turns opening their gifts. Anna was momentarily taken aback by the suede Longchamp handbag, a gift which came with a tag saying 'love, Louise'. Until she reminded herself that the generosity was merely for show and there was not a scrap of feeling attached to the gesture. The tide began to turn when Louise opened her presents.

She did an appalling job of feigning pleasure at Anna's choice of cashmere sweater, commenting that it wasn't really her colour as she flicked over the label to check out its origin and worth. And as for the lovely nightwear, Louise didn't even bother to take it out of the paper, instead she flung the parcel aside whilst commenting coyly that Frenchmen prefer something less practical in the bedroom.

Daniel for once seemed to notice her rudeness but

instead of speaking out, attempted to diffuse the atmosphere by suggesting that Jules should open his gifts. When the seven-year-old boy excitedly tore open the paper to reveal what was quite obviously new games for his console, his face dissolved and was awash with disappointment.

It seemed that these weren't the ones he'd asked for and Anna had bought the wrong thing, which was a bit odd, as they were exactly what Louise told her during a very brief chat. It also struck Anna that instead of emailing her his list as requested, Louise had made a rare phone call that now, couldn't be used as evidence.

While Daniel assured Jules that it was just a mistake and they could have them exchanged and posted over as soon as they got to England, Louise was furious and wouldn't let it go.

Not only had Jules been disappointed, he'd been so looking forward to his new games and now he would have to wait ages for them to be sent over. Louise made such a song and dance about it that Daniel offered to take him into town the very next day and buy some more, but in the meantime, nervously averted a major row by continuing with present opening.

Anna had felt awful, embarrassed and unfairly treated, yet couldn't prove that Louise had pulled a fast one and it would make matters worse if she even tried to defend herself. As Jules opened his pyjamas, slippers, jumbo selection box and gifts from his red stocking, Anna heard Louise mutter 'load of old tat' under her breath. It was the final insult and Anna could take no more. The tears of frustration and hurt she'd held back all morning welled in her eyes, before they burst their banks, she excused herself from the room and fled outside.

In the privacy of the frosty garden, Anna gave in to missing her family, and feeling foolish and unsure, all rolled into one. When Daniel came outside to find her, he at least had the grace to apologise on behalf of his daughter whilst assuring Anna it was a genuine mistake that could be easily rectified. Through sobs, Anna told Daniel that it wasn't her fault and she'd been set up by Louise and that she was rude, bad-mannered and ungrateful.

Daniel, taken aback and lost for words, was more inclined to believe that Anna had misunderstood, unable to believe that Louise would purposely ruin her son's day by asking for the wrong thing. Louise had thanked Anna for her gifts but if she didn't suit a colour or like wearing fleece pyjamas, well, there was nothing he could do about that, was there? Daniel gave her a hug and suggested she was overreacting and not to be so sensitive. He knew she was missing the kids, Sam especially, so he would just tell everyone indoors that she needed a minute and would come inside soon. Kissing her on the head, he reminded her that Jules was waiting and it wasn't fair to spoil his morning so they should put the incident behind them and get on with the day.

As Anna watched him walk away, she wondered what happened to the Daniel that she loved. Right then she wanted to be anywhere else other than Corrèze and, if she was completely honest, she didn't want to be with Daniel either. He had let her down where his precious daughter was concerned, and Anna knew that it would be hard to forget Louise's deceit and sarcasm, or summon enough grace to move on.

Breathing in the cold, crisp air she had tried to assimilate her thoughts and gave herself a good talking to. She would've hated anyone or anything to spoil Christmas Day for her three children and, after all, Tomas and Jules had done no wrong. They all thought she was upset over her own children so she would play on that and milk it for all it was worth. As for Daniel, she would deal with him as soon as they were out of sight and earshot of the devil-child. Anna wasn't going to give her a moment's pleasure from seeing them argue. If Louise thought herself as master of the game, well, Anna would give her a run for her money. She'd crossed the line and prodded the beast so during the next forty-eight hours, if Madame wanted a war, then Anna would give her one.

Back inside, Anna threw herself into being the best step-grandma Jules could wish for. She promised him a trip into town the following day and a special lunch at a place of his choosing, and to make up for his disappointment he could have an extra game for his Xbox.

Jules was thrilled and couldn't wait. After he had given Anna a huge hug they set about playing with every single one of his toys whilst she triumphantly told him all about Christmas Day in England *and* how much Granddad enjoys cooking the lunch and carving the turkey for her family.

Anna could feel the death ray stare, burning holes into the back of her head as she played Operation, smirking as she imagined removing each of Louise's vital organs, one by one, minus anaesthetic.

When she looked a bit teary after phone calls from Melanie and Joe, Tomas brought her a glass of champagne and some canapés, insisting she relax, much to the irritation of Louise who was looking flustered and sweaty as she slaved over a hot stove. After a grand feast that Anna picked at and didn't enjoy one bit, nothing could beat a good old, traditional Christmas dinner, she remained firmly planted in her seat drinking coffee while everyone else cleared away the dishes. What was the point of offering to help when, in the past, she was always shooed out of the kitchen by Mary Berry's despot twin? Instead, Anna sat back and was waited on hand and foot while she cuddled up under a blanket by the fire and watched a video with darling Jules.

When Sam eventually phoned from Afghanistan to wish his mum and Daniel Merry Christmas, the tears she shed were genuine, because she missed him so much and was desperate for him to be away from that godforsaken country. Nevertheless, in an attempt to cheer her up, Tomas looked through all her photos of Sam, ever since the day he joined the army while listening patiently to proud tales of her soldier son. Anna thoroughly monopolised Tomas and Jules, and just to demonstrate to her adversary that there was an art to being hard-faced, she didn't utter a word to Louise or acknowledge her existence.

By the time they'd said their goodbyes, setting off in the midst of terrible driving conditions – blizzards and snow drifts were not going to prevent her escape – Anna thought she'd won hands down where getting on Louise's tits was concerned.

Jules was going to write to *Mémère* Anna and wanted to visit her in England and stay at her house by the sea. Tomas was equally looking forward to receiving a bottle or two of the scrumpy he'd heard so much about. When it was time to go, Anna hugged Jules and Tomas while Louise was bidding a fond farewell to Daddykins. Having no intention of hugging Lady Lou, Anna trundled her case down the path and chucked it in the boot from where she wished everyone a happy New Year and then plonked herself in the passenger seat.

They managed to get onto the main road and endured five excruciating minutes in total silence before Anna vented her frustration. The mother of all rows ensued where they went round the houses for five long hours during the journey to Anna's cottage. As they battled with atrocious driving conditions on the outside, there was a silent, almost blue and extremely frosty atmosphere on the inside.

Once they had calmed down, Daniel finally admitted that looking back, even though he hadn't realised it at the time, some of Louise's behaviour was unacceptable. He then promised he would speak to her about it, assuring an unconvinced and slightly cynical Anna that he wouldn't let Louise undermine or insult her in the future.

In return, Anna assured Daniel that while she had breath in her body she had no intention whatsoever of setting foot inside that house again. Louise was thirty-three and her parents had been divorced for almost twelve years, yet she was behaving like a moody, immature, precocious teenager, which was laughable. Louise was so self-absorbed and selfish that she couldn't find it in her heart to be as happy for her father as she was for her mutton-dressed-as-lamb mother. Therefore, if it upset Louise to have to share, then she could have Daniel all to herself.

Since then, Daniel had made solo trips to visit Louise, once at Easter and then another at half-term. He was disappointed, but Anna was resolute that he and Louise had to learn the hard way. This was a result of his daughter's behaviour, not hers. Who knew whether Louise would have a personality transplant in the near future? So just in case she did, Anna remained distant and detached, but not completely invisible.

* * *

Anna dragged herself into the present and concentrated on opening packets of bacon for breakfast. She knew full well she was making things worse by dredging up the past, or obsessing about Louise and sometimes worried that she was losing the plot. Anna could spend a whole day festering about an impending visit to Louise's or if she'd heard Daniel laughing and chatting to her on the phone. Were they talking about her? Would Louise manage to fill Daniel's head with nonsense while he was away? Anna admitted that her feelings were bordering on paranoia and slightly hypocritical because now she was the jealous one, consumed with childish, irrational thoughts.

Take for example, the photograph in the lounge at home in Portsmouth. It was taken in France during a wintry walk along the riverbank and told a false tale of a happy family day out. They'd asked a passer-by to capture the moment as they gathered together and smiled for posterity. Anna couldn't bear to look at it because on the day, she could've happily punched Louise in the face after a round of sniping and one-upmanship.

No doubt whenever Daniel looked at the photo that was proudly displayed amongst the homages to her own children, he remembered a lovely day and looked fondly on the face of his daughter. However, to Anna, it was like staring into the eyes of a peevish tormenter and only brought back unhappy memories. She had been so tempted to chuck it over the balcony and watch it smash into tiny pieces.

Hearing heavy footsteps above alerted Anna, one or both of her sons were about to make an appearance so she pulled herself together and painted a smile on her face. She couldn't let last night's performance by Louise spoil their first day in France and even if it killed her, she wouldn't row with Daniel and let that monster win.

* * *

They had just flopped into bed after spending a lovely evening outside, eating on the terrace with Joe and Sam as they discussed plans for their three week, boys-only road trip. After spending seven days with her they'd be heading down to the Vendée for a fortnight of surfing and hopefully, attracting the opposite sex. Anna's daughter Melanie worked in Nantes and lived at the cottage full-time, and was looking forward to hanging out with everyone in the evening. Anna's brother, Phil, and her best friend Jeannie had recently married and would be arriving later that day with his two children, Summer and Ross, and she was looking forward to having her family together for a while.

Anna had been planning and preparing for ages and had day trips, barbecues and picnics all arranged in her head. Then, in one phone call, Louise had threatened to jeopardise everything. When Daniel picked up his mobile, Anna could tell instantly from his body language and tone of voice that something was wrong, however, after ear-wigging she realised that it wasn't anything serious, just Louise having a strop. Piecing together the snippets of a one-sided conversation, it was clear that after a huge row, Tomas had stormed out, taking an overnight bag and Louise presumed he'd left her. Daniel did a great job of doling out soothing advice and playing devil's advocate but nothing seemed to be working. When he began making excuses as to why he couldn't drive down in the morning whilst desperately trying to assure Louise that Tomas would probably be back in time for dinner, Anna saw red and shrill alarm bells started ringing in her head.

How dare Louise try to drag Daniel away when she knew damn well that almost all of her family would be arriving for their summer holiday? She had heard Daniel tell her as much a few days earlier, so she was probably making everything up, just to spoil things and score some points. Anna lay in the dark, tense, almost hyperventilating and desperately trying to control her anger and prevent her lips from releasing an outburst of epic proportions. In the end, Daniel had gone downstairs to talk things through with Louise rather than disturb Anna. Sleep was impossible though because she was wound up like a bobbin so instead, she sat at the top of the stairs listening in to their conversation.

When she heard Daniel say goodnight after promising to call her first thing in the morning, Anna leapt up from her spying position and pounced into bed. He had been down there for over an hour, cajoling and reasoning with the vile attention-seeker, so when he crept into the bedroom and slid under the sheets Anna feigned sleep.

As he drifted off into his peaceful, no doubt venom-free dreams, Anna lay there wide awake, making contingency plans, preparing her speech for the morning if he even dared to suggest running to Louise's aid and how she would exact her revenge if he was stupid enough to actually go.

* * *

Clomping feet on the stairs prompted Anna to throw bacon in the pan and flick on the kettle. Hearing her sons' voices rejoicing in the smell of breakfast cooking instantly wiped away her negative vibes and lifted her tense and troubled heart. Nope, nothing was going to ruin the coming week. By the time Daniel appeared for his breakfast and made his call to Louise, she would be calm, collected and prepared for a grand battle of the wills.

. . .

Well, we all know the saying about Mohammed and the mountain. Unfortunately, for poor, delusional Anna, she may have won the battle but she certainly hadn't won the war because within twenty-four hours, the mountain would be coming north, directly to her.

CHAPTER FOUR

D*ear Diary,*

Mum is driving me mad and I swear I am going to kill her if she asks one more time 'are you okay?' or 'is there anything wrong?' I know she means well and I'm being a snappy cow but I cringe every time she mentions the wedding. I'm finding it hard to act like I'm happy or excited, and it's only Monday morning for God's sake! How am I going to keep this up for two weeks? I wish Stacey were here so we could escape and I'd have someone apart from you to rant to. Yes, I know it's my own fault and I've brought it on myself, but I really didn't think it would be this difficult. Even poor Dad is keeping out of her way and has been in the garden all morning after she bit his head off about toast crumbs in the butter. I suppose it's not Mum's fault she's in a foul mood, she's had her head down the loo since she got up and thinks she's got a virus. I've been banished from the house so I don't catch it. Luke rang last night to check that I was okay and then irritated the hell out of me by yawning through his mind-numbingly boring attempt at conversation. I made an excuse that my bath water was getting cold, then after he hung up, I realised there's no bath here, just a shower. I don't care, he probably won't even remember. Anyway, I've been sent on an errand to the village for bread (thank the Lord) so now I can get some fresh air and a bit of peace and quiet. I might just keep on pedalling and head for the hills and never come back but I'll get the baguette first so I don't starve. Okay, that's enough, you'll be glad to hear that's my morning moan over with. I'll go and have a conversation with Mum through the bedroom door and see if she wants anything from the pharmacie then I'm off for a ride. At least I can indulge myself in something I love to do for a change. If I don't come back you will have to find a way of self-destructing like the messages in Mission Impossible so my secrets are never revealed. I can't have my darkest thoughts exposed because, for some reason, everyone thinks I'm a nice person – the crazy fools! Catch up with you later, bye, Diary.

Tilly loved cycling in France. It was a completely different experience from Bristol, where you took your life in your hands if you so much as dared venture into the city on a bike. She'd given it a try last summer in an attempt to get fit and save money by pedalling to and from work, but it was just too stressful and downright dangerous. Here, you could go for miles and miles and not be bothered by a raging white-van-man or a stressed out school-run-mum.

The morning sun gently warmed her face while the soft breeze cooled her body as she made the journey to the shops. Tilly was taking the long way round and circumnavigating the village in order to prolong her expedition, free from germs and her mum's incessant questions. It was hard to ignore the beauty of the surrounding countryside as she freewheeled down the hills and inhaled the scent of the wild flowers that bordered the fields. Every now and then, a less-pleasant whiff of whatever the farmer was spraying on his crops invaded her nostrils and stung her eyes, but still, Tilly loved it here and felt at home amongst all the villagers and neighbours she'd known since she was a child.

When her parents bought the ramshackle farmhouse all those years ago, the whole family got stuck in and helped them painstakingly restore it to its former glory. As time went by, it was transformed from a damp, neglected eyesore into a cosy, family home. She remembered with affection, hot summer days and Easter breaks when she and Scott donned overalls and helped their parents scrape walls and mix plaster, or drag tree branches into the centre of the garden ready to be burnt once autumn arrived. At first, they didn't have a proper cooker so they used an electric hob placed on the stone floor and ate at a plastic table and chairs. Tilly and her mum would wash the dishes in the downstairs bathroom and scrub their clothes in the same sink. They didn't have a telly so in the evenings they'd all play cards and listen to the radio, or sit in the garden and watch the stars. They still laughed at the time when Freda made hot dogs and beans then served them up on white rolls, which were actually brioche and sweet, a faux pas they managed to disguise with ketchup and ignore because they were starving. Slowly but surely it all came together. One by one each room in the house was made habitable and their working holidays became more fun and relaxed. They forged a friendship with their neighbours who introduced them to a wider group of locals and ex-pats and soon, going to France also seemed like going home, albeit temporary and for the duration of the school holidays.

Even in winter, Tilly found their French house inviting and tranquil. They'd spend New Year there, never Christmas as her mum insisted it was the only day out of 365 they were all together, even if it included Aunty Marianne, and February half-term break was always a shocker as it was so cold.

In their teens, Tilly and Scott were able to spread their wings and spent days splashing in the open-air swimming pool in Saint Mars or jumping onto haystacks and cycling for miles with their friends. Evenings were long and lazy, enjoying al fresco meals that lasted forever, surrounded by neighbours and visiting relatives. They were allowed to stay up as late as they wanted and warm themselves on the garden heater, talking rubbish and giggling with their *amis français*, huddled under blankets on the sunloungers. They scared themselves to death by daring each other to walk up the lane in the pitch black without a torch, and after watching the film *Signs*, were too terrified to look out of their bedroom windows in case there was an alien in the corn field.

Tilly got over her fear of snakes when she found one in the barn and bravely picked it up with a rake and chucked its wiggling body into the field. There was no way she was telling Didier, their neighbour, because he would've killed it and she couldn't bear the guilt so she lobbed it into the swaying corn and wished it the best of luck. Once they left school, Scott and Tilly spent less time in France and concentrated on their studies, boyfriends and girlfriends, and other teenage activities but, at least once a year, they joined their parents for an infusion of countryside living and topped up their bank of memories.

As she cycled towards the shops in Vritz, Tilly decided she would take a further detour past the windmills and through their neighbouring village of Le Pin. She was relishing the feel of the sun browning her arms and legs, so turned left and headed up the steep hill towards the swooshing turbines. Once she reached the top she would be able to see St Pierre on the other side of the green valley and then enjoy the thrill of the ride down the winding road into Le Pin. When she was here, Tilly hadn't a care in the world and could almost extinguish the subject that had plagued her every waking moment and restless dreams.

She pedalled hard and forced the wheels of her bicycle round and round as they propelled her slowly to the summit. With each push, Tilly imagined she was pounding away her worries and fears, expelling them from her life and banishing the thoughts that poisoned her mind. Finally, she reached the top and as the road levelled out she rested and sucked in a deep lungful of air, taking in the beautiful scenery. She hadn't visited many foreign lands and if one day she finally got the opportunity to do so, Tilly knew without a doubt that France would still hold a special place in her heart.

It really bothered her that the genuine love she had for her second home and all the memories she'd made were going to be tarnished by the upcoming event. Without warning, tears began to blur her vision of the lush green, rolling hills and the tiny homesteads that dotted the landscape and as her pumping heart slowed, it also became heavy with the burden of its secret. Shaking away the images and doubts that inhabited her brain, Tilly jumped back on the saddle, wiped her eyes and prepared to set off down the sloping road. Maybe by the time she reached the bottom the wind would have blown her troubles away. Or there'd be a miracle and the answer to all her problems might be waiting at the bottom of the hill to save her from herself. Tilly didn't think she was that lucky and if she was honest, didn't believe in miracles either but what had she to lose? Taking one last glimpse of the view, she pushed away and pedalled for all she was worth, freewheeling straight into her destiny.

* * *

Joe was on his way back from doing the 'bread run' for his mum who, for some reason, thought they'd need six giant baguettes and three boules. Maybe there was going to be a wheat shortage or some kind of war rationing that he hadn't heard about. Still, it was best not ask questions and do her bidding, so while Sam filled up the swimming pool, he'd volunteered to nip to the *boulangerie* in the village. Joe also loved driving his brother's classic VW campervan.

The VW was a birthday gift to Sam from their mum and after months of trawling the internet on her behalf, Joe had found a wreck that needed restoring and had it delivered to the garages of their haulage company. It was a pipe dream of Sam's to buy and do up a campervan, then spend his summers surfing and chugging back and forwards from his army base. Now it had become a reality. Joe remembered them all being gathered inside the maintenance sheds one cold, March morning. His mum proudly pulled off the cover to reveal the beaten-up restoration project, and the look on Sam's face told them he was genuinely over the moon. To his credit he'd worked hard for the past year, spending most weekends, and any leave he had, at Harrison's Haulage, where he painstakingly stripped it down and lovingly put it back together. Joe had to admit that Sam had done a fantastic job because his pale blue and cream, split screen camper was now gleaming like new and probably worth a small fortune.

Joe also enjoyed having Sam spend time at the yard where, from his office window, he could see into the garages below and from this vantage point he'd watched the step by step transformation with pride. The lads in the garage didn't mind a bit that Sam had commandeered a section of the workshop, but then his mother owned the company and his brother was the managing director so they didn't really have much say in the matter. Their father had wanted Sam to take over the running of the garages when he eventually left the army and hopefully, one day, his wish would come true. For now, Joe would make the most of having his brother around when he was on leave and keep his fingers crossed for the future.

Since Joe returned from New Zealand, he and Sam had become much closer. He still wasn't into the 'my body is a temple' fitness regime like Sam, but they did enjoy the odd workout, runs along the beach and going to football matches together. Sam had also been the one who dragged Joe out of the doldrums just after Christmas when he split with Hannah, his girlfriend of *almost* six months. Sam was adamant that she was a bit of a user and had a reputation for being on the lookout for a fatter wallet, that's why she hung about until she got her Christmas present and then dumped Joe for the boss of a recruitment firm.

When Sam suggested they went on holiday together, along the west coast of France and try their hand at surfing, Joe jumped at the idea. He'd worked non-stop since he took over from Dennis, his dad's partner who was now semi-retired and everyone, especially his mother, thought he deserved a rest. After researching the best places to surf, spending a fortune on boards, jazzy shorts, surfer T-shirts and sleeping bags, Sam and Joe put in three weeks leave, packed their rucksacks, filled the camper with food and fuel and set off for France on their Boy's Only Road Trip.

Their mum absolutely loved having everyone over for the summer and fussed about like it was her mission in life to serve three meals a day while organising a full programme of events and excursions to keep the whole family occupied and entertained. Presumably, that was why she needed all this bread. In a few hours, his uncle and two cousins would all be arriving so they'd all be spending the afternoon in the garden, eating and messing about in the huge inflatable pool. Joe still couldn't get his head around calling Jeannie 'Aunty' since she'd married Phil, mainly because she was slightly bonkers and even when they were little kids, never acted like an aunty... more like a crazy, grown-up friend. Despite the house being full to the rafters and his mum behaving like a tour guide on speed, Joe knew it would be a laugh spending time with family before heading off to the coast.

As he approached the steep hill that led up to the wind turbines, Joe could make out the figure of a lone cyclist, zooming down the road towards him. As they got closer, he smiled when he realised it was a girl and she looked like she was having fun, freewheeling down the hill with her legs stuck out at angles, allowing the bike to fly along the road. She was approaching quickly as the bike gathered momentum and he could just about make out that she had long dark hair, which was streaming behind in the wind. The lone rider was well within sight when suddenly, a flash of something dark and fast moving appeared in the corner of Joe's eye. It all happened so quickly, like the clicking shutter of a camera, capturing the awful moment when a lone, disorientated deer shot through the gap in the hedgerows and darted across the road and into the field opposite.

Joe slammed on his brakes, involuntarily scrunching his eyes and wincing as he waited for impact. The van skidded as rubber burned and tyres screeched, while his terrified eyes were transfixed by the girl on the bike. She had been travelling far too fast to stop and the shock of seeing the frightened beast as it pounced in front of her resulted in an instinctive reaction – she pulled hard on her brakes. Joe saw her skid and the rear of the bike flip up, jettisoning her body over the handlebars as she glided in, what seemed like, slow motion through the air and into the deep verge at the side of the road. For a fraction of a second time stood still as Joe tried to catch his breath and get his head together. There had been an awful moment as the van slid sideways that he thought he was going to slam into her, but somehow he had stopped in time and now she was lying in the ditch up ahead.

A wave of panic flooded through Joe as his shaking hands fumbled with the old-fashioned seat belt as he tried to unfasten himself and get out of the van. He jumped down and into the road, then sprinted to where he'd seen her fall, all the time preparing himself for broken bones and blood-spattered clothes. When he looked into the deep gap between the road and the farmer's field his breath caught in his chest. Her body was sprawled motionless and partially obscured by tangled brambles and deep grass. Gathering courage, he jumped down and knelt beside her and with a very shaky voice, tried to rouse her, praying she would reply.

'Are you okay, can you hear me?' Then Joe realised she might not understand so tried some schoolboy French instead. 'Ça va, mademoiselle?' It was the best he could do under the circumstances.

For a moment there was silence and then she moved her arm and tried to lift her head.

'Look, don't move, whatever you do, stay still in case you've broken something. I need to phone for help, don't worry, just keep calm. You're going to be okay.' Joe placed his hand gently on the girl's arm to reassure her and himself, that she really was going to be alright.

· · ·

Tilly felt like she'd been punched in the head and the wind had been knocked out of her. Her arms and legs stung like hell but there was someone close and their voice was kind, telling her she was going to be okay. How the hell did she end up down here? Then she remembered the deer; her body flying through the air and her heart contracting with fear just before she felt the thud. As her thought process became more orderly, Tilly knew she had to get up and away from this awful stinging so mustering any strength left in her bones, she tried to move.

'Can you help me up, something's prickling me?' Tilly held out her arm and turned her head towards her rescuer. She couldn't see his face clearly as it was partially shadowed by the morning sun that was glaring behind him.

Joe was relieved to hear her speak and see her limbs move. The face speaking the words was obscured by a mass of black, tangled hair, which was embellished with bits of grass and stray ears of wheat. As he reached out and his hand connected with hers, she turned to face him. His stomach flipped over and his heart literally missed a beat the second their eyes connected. He recognised in an instant a face from the past and remembered a fleeting moment of something special, filed away in his memory. Gathering his wits, Joe dragged his gaze from the pale grey eyes and the flawless complexion of someone who was beyond his reach and up till now, best forgotten.

* * *

It had been a balmy summer's evening when they first met, last June at the Fête de la Musique which was held each year in Le Pin village square. The festival was celebrated all over France, an event where everyone and anyone could join in and showcase their musical talents. Most towns and villages put on some kind of entertainment that usually included eating and drinking the night away. Joe had been in France for his mum's birthday, so they walked into the village to join in the fun where everyone had brought their own food and drinks and set up camp outside the *Mairie*.

Joe and his family found themselves sitting next to another group of Brits, who, as the night wore on, relaxed and introduced themselves. Freda and Howard were accompanied by their daughter and her boyfriend, who seemed a right misery guts. Before long everyone merged together, French and English, farmers and villagers, committee members and Monsieur le Curé – the village priest. As was the custom, they shared their feast amongst one another, chatting and laughing in between the acts that performed on the bunting-festooned, makeshift stage.

They were also entertained by possibly the worst DJ in the whole of France who played the most abysmal, obscure pop music in history. Nobody seemed to mind though, especially after a few boxes of cheap supermarket wine and once the karaoke started there was no stopping the merry audience. Some of the participants took their performances extremely seriously. If you think that Elvis died in Grace-land, Tennessee, well you're wrong, because four of his greatest hits were murdered on stage by Monsieur le Maire who gave it his best shot, all dressed up in his blue suede shoes. Then there was Lucille, the post mistress who sang Édith Piaf's famous lament, 'Je Ne Regrette Rien', complete with red lipstick, tears and a bit too much thigh on show for the likes of Monsieur le Curé. After wild applause and encouragement from the contingent of randy bachelor farmers, she jazzed things up a bit with 'La Vie en Rose', which, despite the dreadful sound system was rather good.

As the night wore on, Joe, Melanie and her boyfriend, Pascal, became increasingly giggly each time a new act took to the stage, so when DJ Blocoques introduced himself – yes, that really was his name, they were all helpless. Even though her boyfriend didn't see the funny side of anything, Tilly was having a ball and had moved her plastic chair closer to Joe's table, leaving Luke to play games on his phone. After a while nobody seemed to notice the dreadful music so took to the cobbled streets and danced the night away.

During the dancing, now and then, he made contact with Tilly when their hot bodies touched briefly, or her hand would brush against his. Despite being under the watchful gaze of Luke, he felt an almost uncontrollable, erratic urge to wrap his fingers around hers and pull her closer. While they danced, her eyes held his and as she smiled and laughed in his direction, the rest of the crowd melted away. In his wine-fuzzed head Joe imagined it was just the two of them, alone in the square.

It must have been around 3am by the time the party came to an end. The final part of the evening was more subdued and involved finishing off the bread and cheese and chatting in small groups. Luke still hadn't cheered up and Joe could tell he was peeved that Tilly was having fun, and throwing the odd, dark glance her way whenever she laughed at something anyone said. Joe couldn't help thinking that, apart from both being very good-looking, Tilly and Luke didn't seem well matched or to have much in common. He'd based this wild, slightly biased assumption on the snippets of information he'd stored away during his tentative enquiries into Tilly's job and interests.

When the time came to go, Joe felt something akin to sadness wash over him. He really didn't want to say goodbye to Tilly and felt himself drinking in everything about her, storing it in his memory. Had he not been going home the following day he would've suggested they all come to his mum's for something to eat. As they packed up their picnic box, Joe was quite forlorn. Everyone began to say goodbye and shook hands or hugged, so when Tilly wrapped her arms around his waist and held him just a little too tightly, for a second too long, a thrill of something exhilarating shot through Joe and his heart missed a beat. The feel of her soft hair against his cheek, her delicate body under his hands and the way she fitted perfectly between his arms, took his breath away. Tilly pulled away and looked Joe in the eye, saying she hoped they'd meet again, then held his stare for a fleeting moment as though trying to convey a secret message before turning and walking away.

The groups bade each other farewell and went their separate ways and Joe presumed he'd never see Tilly again, or if he did, it would be a miraculous coincidence. They hadn't swapped numbers and he didn't even know her last name so he couldn't look her up on Facebook. He could've got Pascal on the case as he knew everyone for miles around, but deep down, Joe knew it would be wrong to pursue someone who was attached.

He'd not returned to France since that day, but Joe always hoped his mum would bump into Tilly and give him some clue as to how she was. Deep down, he wanted to hear she was single and Luke was no more, and then he would pluck up the courage to get Pascal to track her down. When common sense kicked in, shortly after his imagination had run riot, he would remind himself that they had been together for only a few hours, drank a lot of wine and he'd probably imagined the whole thing and misread her signals.

* * *

Tilly was still a little shaken and very wobbly on her legs but her nursing instinct took over which she applied to her own body. There was definitely nothing broken and apart from mild scratches the only concern was the big lump on her head. As she brushed the stray bits of grass from her bare legs she winced at the angry blotches where she had been prickled by the thistles and briars in the ditch. Apart from the miracle of surviving a near collision with a large deer or being squashed by a blue campervan, there was something else zapping through her mind. While she checked her body over, Tilly was desperately trying to regain her composure and a smidgen of dignity after being found sprawled in a ditch by the gorgeous man she'd met last year. She also prayed she wasn't flashing her knickers when he found her.

Perhaps he wouldn't remember her, but she hoped he did. Even though they'd only spent one long summer evening together, Tilly had thought of him often, especially when she drove through Le Pin. As she straightened, Tilly hoped Joe would remember her.

'Well, I don't think I've broken anything which is a shame. Thanks for helping me out by the way. Are you okay? I bet that skid shook you up as much as my amazing stunt-fall. Do you want me to check you out? I'm a nurse so you're in safe hands.' Tilly looked into her rescuers face, waiting for a glimmer of recognition.

'I'm fine thanks and I know you're a nurse. We met last summer at the music festival, you might not remember but our families sat next to each other. I bet you've forgotten, well I sort of hope you have because my dancing was *not* cool.' Joe was rambling as nerves, perhaps a bit of delayed shock started to get the better of him.

Tilly began to laugh, more out of relief and happiness that he had actually remembered than the cringeworthy image of them dancing to 'Grease'.

'Of course I remember. It's Joe isn't it? I'm Matilda, just in case it's slipped your mind, but most people call me Tilly.' Despite the strangely giddy feeling inside she really needed a drink of water and to get something for her grazes and stings.

Joe could not believe his luck. The girl he'd thought about so often was here, right in front of him. As he carefully lifted Tilly out of the ditch, fussing and gently brushing away bits of foliage, he tried to quell his joyous heart and tell his overexcited head not to get its hopes up.

Sensing she was in pain and possibly had a touch of shock too – her comment about broken bones was a bit odd – Joe suggested that Tilly rest inside the camper while he retrieved her bike which looked a bit knackered.

'Come on, you sit in here while I sort your bike out, then we can get your injuries looked at. My mum lives just round the next bend but if you prefer to go home I'll run you there instead, it's no bother.' Joe guided Tilly towards the van and settled her inside before retrieving her bike.

As he scurried across the road to where it lay, Joe tried to calm himself. His giddy state had nothing to do with the near miss, and everything to do with Tilly. Picking up her bike, he carried it to the camper and placed it in the back. The front wheel was buckled and the tyre had popped so there was no way she'd be riding it home, a thought which made him feel childishly happy.

'Right, I think your bike is going to need a new front wheel but my brother is a dab hand with stuff like that and I reckon he'll be able to fix it, so now we just need to get you sorted out. Are you feeling alright?' Joe looked over at Tilly who smiled and nodded.

Knowing that her mum was sick and her dad would insist she went to the hospital, while she watched Joe collect her crumpled bike, Tilly had decided to accept his offer, besides it would prolong her time with him.

'Thanks, Joe, I'm fine, but I could do with some water and a couple of painkillers for this headache. If you're sure your mum won't mind, do you think we could go there, my parents have got a bug and they'll just flap if I go home like this.' Tilly smiled at Joe and for the first time in ages, her heart felt ridiculously happy.

She knew under the circumstances it was bizarre, because let's face it, she'd just had a near-death experience and felt like she'd gone ten rounds with Mike Tyson. Pushing the unavoidable fact that she was about to get married to the back of her mind, Tilly decided to take a break from worrying and stress and enjoy being with Joe again. What harm could that possibly do?

CHAPTER FIVE

Despite her slowly receding headache and sore arms and legs, Tilly was having a lovely afternoon being pampered by the Harrison family. Just as he'd assured her, Joe's mum didn't mind one bit that she had gatecrashed their family barbecue. After rushing about bringing cold water and a fully equipped first aid kit, Anna had gently tended Tilly's injuries before ordering her to lie on a shaded sunlounger and wait for the pills to take effect.

They all seemed like a friendly lot, even the cute dog that jumped onto a deckchair the second it was vacated and was now sleeping beside her, snoring gently. Tilly remembered Daniel and Melanie from the festival and had learned that Pascal was away in Martinique, on some kind of university cultural exchange. He was taking his Masters in Agricultural Science and it was obvious that Mel was very proud of her boyfriend and missing him too. As she listened, Tilly experienced a pang of envy for the type of relationship where you pined for and admired someone.

Shaking the thought away, Tilly focused on the scene around her. The brother's got their money's worth where teasing their sister was concerned and it was a foregone conclusion that at some point Mel was going to end up being chucked into the pool. Summer and Ross were squealing in delight as Sam squirted them with the hosepipe, and was then promptly told off for wasting water by his mother. Anna was hovering, waiting for Phil and Daniel to light the barbeque, obviously eager to start cooking. She had asked Tilly to stay for something to eat and suggested she ring her parents and invite them too, as well as letting them know what had happened.

After making the call then excusing her parents who were conveniently indisposed, Tilly said she would love to stay. She did feel sorry that her mum and dad were suffering while she was enjoying herself but just as her dad had said, there was absolutely nothing she could do and they'd worry more if she caught it too. Utterly absolved of guilt and grateful to be set free, Tilly settled in for an afternoon of germ-free air and fun company.

Joe was having a great time up until the point when Melanie ruined everything. She didn't have any idea of the impact the question or answer had on him, when she innocently enquired after Tilly's boyfriend. Joe didn't want to hear that he was fine but far too busy at work to join her for all of her holidays. Neither was Joe pleased to hear that he would be arriving at the end of the following week. He did notice that Tilly looked hesitant and slightly embarrassed at the mention of Luke so he took this to be a sign. Perhaps all wasn't well in their relationship and let's face it, if she was his girlfriend, nothing would keep them apart.

The second he had the thought, Joe recognised the crassness of it and reminded his conscience that two-timing or unfaithfulness went against everything he believed in. Yet despite his set-in-stone code of conduct, Joe couldn't banish the idea. Maybe, if their relationship was in trouble already, showing Tilly what she was missing wasn't quite the same thing. What if she was ready to give Luke up? Once he'd salved his inner conscience, Joe put his best foot forward and threw himself into having a good time and making the most of the unexpected turn of events. He'd quiz Tilly later on the subject of her absent boyfriend and the state of play.

Tilly had wanted the ground to open up and swallow her *and* the sunlounger when Mel asked about Luke. It was stupid and naïve to think that she'd get away with not mentioning him. She was just hoping that it would be later rather than sooner. It had been the perfect opportunity to say 'well actually, I'm getting married next week' but the words that came out were a slight deviation from the truth and not exactly a lie.

Knowing that it was unfair and stupid not to come clean, Tilly resolved to tell Joe later when he drove her home. That way, she could save ruining the evening right up until the last possible moment. For now, she was going to eat some of the splendid food and have a chat with Jeannie, Anna's best friend who was quite a character and in full flow after sampling a bottle of Chablis – all by herself.

Anna was having a wonderful time. Finding herself banished from the barbecue area she was now listening to Jeannie tell rude stories, much to the delight of her audience who said they had no idea that cabin crew had so much fun at the expense of their passengers. After all her worrying about Louise, the day had turned out just as she had envisaged and her meticulous preparations hadn't gone to waste. That said, she was still wary and had been on pins every time Daniel's phone rang or she heard the ping of a message coming through.

As far as she was aware, Louise had cooled down and the crisis seemed to have been averted, so she had no intention of bringing the subject up again. Anna had overheard Daniel telling Philip that he felt between a rock and a hard place where his daughter and the love of his life were concerned. Yes, they were making a joke and she was glad that Daniel felt he could confide in her brother, but deep down, Anna wished he would talk to her about it instead. The arrival of their friends, Dominique and Zofia, halted Jeannie mid-tale and Anna was forced from her ruminating. The newcomers' appearance instigated much hugging and kissing before they all settled in for a long night around the garden heater as the summer air cooled slightly and the sky turned a moody pink.

Summer and Ross were now in the lounge watching videos, making the most of holiday rules which say you can stay up late as long as you wake up the next morning in a good mood. Sam was telling desert stories to his enthralled audience, whilst Jeannie was asleep under a blanket after eating and drinking far too much of everything. Anna was seated by Daniel who had fulfilled his chef duties so joined the group around the table. She hated that there was an invisible wedge between them that just wouldn't budge, both knowing full well that to discuss the subject of Louise would only create a further divide and an uncomfortable atmosphere. Just admitting that his daughter was the cause of their discord seriously irritated Anna and she had to caution herself in order to remain calm. Putting her ministrations to good use, Anna reached out and wrapped her hand around Daniel's. When he responded by closing his fingers around hers she relaxed and forgave him for having a wicked troll for a child.

Anna's gaze then fell on Joe and his new friend, Tilly. She was such a delicate, pretty girl and, on the face of it, seemed like a lovely person. On the down side, from the way she was looking at Joe and he her, they both had what might be described as a developing crush. Anna hoped that's all it was because Tilly was spoken for and the last thing she wanted was for Joe to fall for someone out of reach. It had taken him a while to get over his last girlfriend who wasn't exactly Anna's cup of tea but she'd put up with her for Joe's sake. Her heart always went out to her eldest son. He was the quieter of her two boys, deep and less outgoing than his confident younger brother. Anna sometimes felt that Joe took life a little too seriously.

Joe fell into the workaholic category and everyone, in the family and company, was impressed by the way Joe had conducted himself since he came back from his travels. He'd brought in some lucrative contracts and made influential new contacts since he took over his father's role. Thinking about Matthew always made Anna's heart contract just for a second, still, she remained convinced that her husband was looking down from heaven and was just as proud of their son and his achievements as she was.

Anna tactfully observed Tilly while listening to the conversation around the table. Yes, they would make a lovely looking couple and it was a shame she had a boyfriend. The thought that Tilly was here alone struck Anna as odd. Most couples take their leave at the same time and it's not like you had to book in advance to stay at your parents' house, so why wasn't she here with Luke? Anna's mind began ticking over and unsettling thoughts raced through her head.

'Mmm... she's too friendly, not flirty but perhaps slightly eager. Is she a cheater – does she fancy a holiday fling while her other half toils away in England – what would her parents think if they saw her laughing and yes, enjoying Joe's company a bit too much?' Anna decided she would keep an eye on Miss Tilly, and ask Jeannie and Mel what they thought of her, and maybe Zofia knew her family. It wouldn't hurt to make a few enquiries, would it?

Just to arouse her suspicious, overactive imagination further, she saw Joe hold out his hand and help Tilly up from her chair and then watched them as they made their way inside. Should she follow? No – he was an adult and she had to let him make his own mistakes and anyway, he wasn't that sort of boy, was he? Anna decided she'd give them five minutes then nip inside to get the pudding out of the fridge, there was nothing wrong with being cautious and besides, everyone needed cake.

· · ·

Joe sprinted upstairs to the bunk room to get Tilly one of his sweatshirts. As always, after a sweltering day, the evenings could turn chilly and he'd noticed her shivering so he offered to fetch her something warm. He also wanted time to talk to her away from the others so suggested he make some coffee that they could drink on the patio, somewhere a bit more private. He really wanted to spend time alone with Tilly before he drove her home. Not only that, he'd been aware of his mother's beady eyes on them so it was time for a change of venue. Not that he planned or expected any hanky-panky – as his gran would put it – he just fancied a one-to-one chat without Sam butting in or Melanie asking another awkward question.

When he came back downstairs, Tilly was sitting on the sofa with Summer who was watching *Earth to Echo* and explaining the story so far in great detail. While they were occupied, he nipped into the kitchen and made two mugs of coffee. When he popped his head back inside the lounge to ask if she took sugar, Tilly was in the process of covering Ross with a blanket, signalling with her fingers against her lips that he should be quiet. Waving bye to Summer, Tilly made her way into the kitchen to collect her coffee then followed Joe through the back door towards the patio that was tucked under the sturdy oak legs of the bunk room, and well out of sight of his mother.

Joe lit the chimenea and once they were settled on the wicker furniture, he decided to delve a little further into the 'Luke situation'.

'Are you okay sitting out here? I've heard Sam's war stories before and I can guarantee they will be getting Uncle Phil's CD collection out soon, and trust me, you don't want to listen to that.' Joe took a sip of his coffee and spread his legs out towards the fire, his feet were getting cold and he wished he'd changed out of his flip-flops.

'No, I'm fine, honestly. As long as your mum doesn't think we're being ignorant, she's been so lovely to me today and I'd hate to offend her.'

Joe shook his head before setting her mind at rest. 'Nah,

don't worry about Mum, she's quite happy force-feeding everyone, she won't even notice we're missing.'

'Oh good. So, what plans have you made for the rest of your holiday?'

'Mum's arranged a few days out, and then next week me and Sam are heading south. We're going to try our hand at camping out and I'm going to teach action man to surf. I loved it when I was in New Zealand and can't wait to have another go. Have you done any surfing?'

Joe felt slightly odd when he told Tilly he'd be leaving. A sort of sinking sensation had taken hold of his heart at the thought of leaving her but there was no way he'd bail on his brother. For a start, he'd never live it down and anyway, he was getting ahead of himself again.

He remained lost in thought and watched as Tilly flicked off her shoes and curled her legs onto the sofa as he waited for her to reply.

'Chance would be a fine thing. I'd love to go on a more adventurous holiday and I am *so* jealous that you have been to New Zealand, but Luke won't even contemplate going anywhere other than Europe, no matter how much I drop the hint or bring home brochures for the Far East and Asia. He's a bit boring when it comes to travel so I don't think I'll be surfing anytime soon.'

'That's a shame, so where would you like to visit? I've always fancied doing the whole Thailand, backpacker trail but I pushed my luck being away for two years and I reckon Mum and work would have something to say if I disappeared again. Maybe in the future I'd get away with taking a month off, there has to be some perks of being the boss's son.' Joe's legs were burning now so he moved them away from the fire, totally ignoring the mention of Luke but registering the comment about him being boring.

Tilly was glad that Joe asked her about travelling especially as it diverted and delayed the impending moment of truth. She hadn't wanted to mention Luke though, he was like the elephant in the room and she wished someone would just lead him off to the circus, or the zoo, anywhere remote and far away from her, would do. But he was a fact of life and she might as well get used to it.

'That's exactly where I would go and I quite fancy exploring places closer to home as well, you know, like the cultural cities of Europe and I wouldn't mind going to Iceland sometime. It seems daft not to take advantage of so many cheap airlines flying all over the place. All I do is sit at home most weekends watching telly while he plays football. I've always wanted to drive up to the Scottish Isles and see the Northern lights… and go whale watching, how fab would that be? There are just so many things I want to see but it's no fun on your own, is it?' Tilly placed her coffee on the table then laughed before continuing.

'Listen to me, moaning. Ignore all that and tell me about what you got up to in New Zealand, I bet it was awesome.' Tilly could feel a dose of gloom creeping up on her, not only because she'd mentioned Luke and how incompatible they were – and that was just on the travel front – but also because Joe was going away, one week from today, and it made her feel sad.

'That's so weird! All of those places are on my bucket list too. What about Canada? I've had my eye on going there skiing and then sightseeing. Hang on. I've got some photos on my phone of my trip. I'll go and get it, won't be a minute.' Joe jumped up from his chair and shot inside the house.

All he could think of in the minutes it took to grab his phone from the kitchen and plonk himself beside Tilly on the sofa was that life was *so* unfair. The girl he thought he'd never see again had landed quite literally at his feet and not only that, the more he got to know her, the more they seemed to have in common. As he flicked through his album, explaining each photo and answering all her questions, Joe tried to ignore the thrill he felt at being in such close proximity. He really had to concentrate to sound interesting and intelligent while doing his best not to let her catch him staring.

. . .

Tilly was experiencing something of the same.

She was cursing Cupid and any other supposed 'guardians of love', they had seriously let her down and seemed to be taking great pleasure in rubbing her nose in it. When she was at her wits' end and trying desperately to steel herself for the dreaded day, the wise gods had chosen this precise moment to present her with a fine specimen of everything she had ever hoped for. To say they had rubbish timing and a warped sense of humour was an under-statement.

Regardless of their joint frustration, for the next hour they warmed themselves by the fire, laughing at Joe's photos and travel stories, and despite being interrupted by the sounds of the Carpenters and Anna popping her head outside to ask if they wanted cake, were immersed in a world of their own. With each tick of the clock and beat of their heart, Joe and Tilly drew closer together, if only in mind and spirit, separately acknowledging that if there was to be anything more, the people they would betray the most was themselves.

Anna had given up on spying after she interrupted Joe and Tilly looking at photos of turtles. They didn't want any cake, so she left her son to wander down memory lane and went back to her family gathering. They had invited Rosie and Michel over but both were far too busy at this time of year and she'd barely seen them in the past week or so. Anna knew they were rushed off their feet with a string of events during the summer, including a couple of weddings, then a christening and numerous birthday parties. Some-times, she would pop into the hotel just before lunch to catch Rosie at a quieter period but as it was the school holi-days, she'd have her two little girls to keep an eye on plus her niece and nephew, meaning her friend really had her hands full.

Anna told herself that it was all well and good worrying about other people but she should concentrate on her issues with Daniel and stop pussyfooting around the issue of Louise. He was on the phone *again*, listening to her woes and trying to placate her. No matter how curious or concerned she was that he might be tempted away, Anna still couldn't bring herself to support Daniel or show interest in Louise or her domestic crisis.

Jeannie had woken from her slumbers and after a cup of tea and a wedge of cake, was giving Anna the beady eye from across the table. Even though Daniel knew her well, the person that knew her best was sitting opposite and Bossy Boots Brown was about to impart some words of wisdom, she could tell. Anna smiled. Her Jeannie never changed, apart from her name and would always be the same Jean Brown that took a shy six-year-old under her wing, all those years ago in the schoolyard.

'I think you're being a bit mean to Daniel, you know? It's not his fault that Miss Fancy Pants has kicked off and sent you into one of your meltdowns. You should've had a bit more faith in him than to expect he'd abandon you and go trotting off to be with her. He's got the weight of the world on his shoulders yet he was happy to be your slave and managed to fry ten thousand sausages. *Why* did you buy so many by the way, were they on special offer or something?' Jeannie loved to tease Anna at every given opportunity, however, on this occasion, she was being serious and seemed a little bit ticked off with her friend's lack of compassion towards Daniel.

'Stop exaggerating, there weren't that many and yes, they were on offer at the butchers but I think he misunderstood me and started wrapping up the whole tray. I was too embarrassed to tell him to stop because the shop was packed. Something must've got lost in translation so I just paid for the lot. I'm obviously not as good as Roland from night school says I am. Thank God I didn't point to anything else otherwise I'd have ended up with half a cow in the back of the car. Sometimes, going shopping here is really stressful, you know! Anyway, we can have the leftovers for lunch tomorrow and I've put the rest in the freezer.' Anna took a sip of her wine and blatantly ignored Jeannie's reference to Daniel.

'Okay, so after the fascinating insight into the fact that you're crap at French and have a secret sausage fetish, why aren't you being nice to Daniel? He's always been so supportive where you and the kids are concerned, so don't you think you should return the compliment? If you're not careful, Louise will score a point because you've been peevish and uncaring in her hour of need. Daniel's got nobody to talk things through with, except for Phil and he's rubbish at giving advice.'

Jeannie was being deadly serious and allowed her words to sink in before Anna sighed and turned to face her friend.

'Don't you think I know all that? Smart arse. But every time the subject of Louise comes up he goes all moody and clams up, or we end up having a row, so it's best just to leave it. But if you think I'm so out of order, feel free to stick your oar in and do a bit of counselling. Maybe he'll take notice of you.' Anna was a bit put out that Jeannie hadn't taken her side, then again, that's why she was such a good friend because she always told her the truth, however brutal.

'Not a chance! I have absolutely no intention of wading into this one. It's between the two of you, so get yourself inside and see if he's okay. You don't have to sympathise with Louise, just let him share the problem and if it's not too much trouble, ask him if there's anything you can do. Go on, don't sit there with that stubborn look on your face, he needs you, so play nice.' Jeannie gave Anna a gentle push.

She responded by shaking her head and laughing, just before rising from her deckchair, indicating to Jeannie that she'd won. Collecting a few empty glasses on the way, Anna wandered back towards the house in search of Daniel knowing Jeannie was spot on with her analysis. If Joe, Sam or Mel had a problem of any kind, Daniel would be there in an instant and someone she could turn to for help and advice. They were partners, a team and she loved him beyond compare. As she tentatively turned the door handle, Anna took a deep breath, prayed for patience and inspiration, and then went inside.

CHAPTER SIX

When Anna found Daniel in the kitchen he was midway through filling the kettle. After dumping the bottles in the recycling bin she walked over to where he was standing and slipped her arms around his waist and placed her head against his strong shoulders. There was silence for a while as Anna took a moment to savour the comforting embrace and gather her thoughts. Anna spoke first.

'I've just been told off by Jeannie. She says I've let you down by not supporting you over Louise. I know she's right and I'm sorry. I'm just so scared of starting a row or you leaving me and going down there, so I thought it'd be best to keep out of it. But I realise now that I'm being selfish and I should have more faith in you. No matter what's gone on in the past, I'm always here for you and will do anything to help. I hate not feeling close to you or sharing things. Please can we start again and most of all, do you forgive me?' Anna felt dreadful.

She truly meant each and every word and desperately needed to be absolved because thanks to Louise, her life had been reduced to a trivial, point-scoring, board game.

Daniel turned to face Anna and enveloped her in a warm bear hug. He kissed the top of her head before replying.

'There's nothing to forgive, Anna. I know why you kept your distance and I don't blame you. Louise can be hard work sometimes and she's hurt your feelings in the past so I don't expect you to be false and offer her sympathy, when from the sounds of it she's brought all this on herself. And just for the record, I would never abandon you, especially when we've made so many plans for the next fortnight. I've been looking forward to seeing everyone too and have no intention of driving all the way down there just because Louise is being a prima donna. So, are we friends now?'

Daniel pulled away from Anna and looked down onto her extremely relieved face.

'Of course, and I am sorry, even if you think I don't need to be... so dare I ask what's going on?' Anna was more curious than anything but at least she was making the effort.

'If I'm honest, I have no idea. One minute I think I've calmed her down and she's seen sense, then she flies off the handle and we're back to square one. Perhaps you might be able to tell me where I'm going wrong because I'm buggered if I know.'

Daniel proceeded to take cups from the shelf and arrange them on a tray while Anna brought milk from the fridge.

By the time they'd filled the cups with coffee and placed the cheese and biscuits on a plate, Anna had got the gist of the story so far and was now totally convinced that Louise was a malfunctioning, Stepford Wife who needed reprogramming. Or failing that, her circuit board removing for good. Despite having a gorgeous husband who provided her with much more than she deserved, it simply wasn't good enough so she'd spat her dummy out and had a tantrum of epic proportions, the result of which was that Tomas had left her.

* * *

The cause of the discord was simple. He had received a huge

promotion at work and the bigwigs wanted Tomas to relocate to their research institute in Geneva. Naturally, he was thrilled, not only with the promotion but the opportunity to live in one of the most beautiful cities in the world, all paid for by his company. Tomas had been given the chance of a lifetime, doing ground-breaking, exciting work and soon, they'd be living in a luxurious home surrounded by breathtaking scenery and Jules would attend one of the most prestigious schools in the area. When he told Louise, she flipped.

Apparently he hadn't taken her into consideration or even had the decency to ask her and Jules if they wanted to relocate. Instead he just marched in and told them how it was going to be. He had no respect for her feelings, or Jules's and he expected them just to leave their friends and start all over again, just because he had been promoted. Tomas was flabbergasted at first, and then gathered his wits and apologised for not asking first, he wasn't thinking straight because he was so excited and simply assumed that she would be too. He tried to bring her round by tempting her with photographs of beautiful homes and listing the wonderful culture and history of Geneva and in desperation, his whopping new salary that she could spend on anything she wanted, if only she would agree.

Unfortunately, Louise had sworn over many dead bodies that she was going nowhere and the stubborn, pig-headed streak that ran through her marrow refused to back down. Tomas was stunned and as the cold water she had poured over his dreams dried up, a fire ignited in his belly, enraging his normally gentle soul, encouraging him to voice a few niggles of his own.

Louise didn't like or appreciate being told that she was a spoilt, ungrateful, selfish woman who did nothing for others unless it directly benefited herself. She was shallow, self-obsessed, manipulative and unkind.

Once the words were said there was no taking them back, and knowing full well that he was probably going to get kicked out anyway, Tomas packed a bag and left, leaving

Louise in tears and catatonic with rage. Ever the tactician, and just in case Tomas got on the phone to ask her dad for advice or give his version of the story, Louise decided to get in there first.

* * *

Daniel was exhausted from retelling Louise's tale but at least now, Anna was in the loop. He was under no illusions regarding his daughter's numerous shortcomings, however, he still remembered the lovely child she once was and hoped one day she might morph back into 'their' Louise. Daniel was adamant that her behaviour wouldn't ruin his relationship with Anna so while he tried desperately to work out how to accomplish this, and stay friends with his daughter, he now had to sort out the problems within her marriage.

He began by playing devil's advocate and tried to make her see sense. Perhaps Tomas should have approached the idea of upping sticks in a slightly more sensitive way. That said, surely Louise could understand how exuberant he must have felt as he drove home, eager to share the wonderful news with his wife – and what about Jules? It was a marvellous opportunity for him and he would sail through moving schools, he was a clever, confident likeable boy. Geneva was French speaking so there would be no language barriers, and imagine the beautiful home she would have.

He may as well have been talking to Pippa the bulldog for all the notice Louise took of his words. Daniel wished his ex-wife wasn't trekking through the Andes and incommunicado because he was at his wits' end. One thing he did draw the line at was driving down there to be with Louise, knowing full well how much it would hurt and disappoint Anna.

As Anna picked up the tray and made her way into the

garden, she was in two minds on the subject of Louise. Daniel had done everything he could to help, but perhaps – and she couldn't quite believe she was saying it – they were being a bit harsh on Louise. Anna tried to put herself in another's shoes, because it was usually the best way to fathom how they were feeling.

'I think we should look at it from another angle because maybe, once they were married, Tomas just flung himself into his research work while Louise had to learn French, make new friends and forge a life for herself in France. It can't have been easy for her and now, Tomas is expecting her to do it all over again.' Anna let her words sink in and when he replied, it sounded like Daniel understood.

'I suppose you're right, I didn't think of it like that. Hopefully Jules would be fine at school, children can be surprisingly resilient and Tomas will make new acquaintances through work, whereas Louise would be left alone all day to flounder.'

Anna nodded and then thought of something else. 'I know from experience that as you get older, your confidence can gradually slip away and making friends and being the outsider isn't that easy to deal with anymore. Your doubts and insecurities aren't simply brushed away. Instead, they drag you down. Louise is an intelligent young woman and will be aware of the benefits of living in Switzerland, but it's a daunting prospect and Tomas should give her time to come to terms with it.'

When Anna's words finally hit home, Daniel's face became awash with gratitude. After kissing her rather passionately he then thanked her for being the most understanding, wonderful woman on the earth. He was going to ring Tomas straight away and suggest he back off and give Louise some space, then suggest to his daughter a period of calm contemplation would help make up her mind.

While he searched for his phone, Anna trotted back into the garden with a smug look on her face, much to the amusement of Jeannie.

'I take it you're friends again? You've been gone ages. I

thought you might have blown it and had a rant, but Madame looks a *little* bit pleased so I reckon you've kissed and made up, am I right?' Jeannie began helping herself to some cheese as she waited for a response from Anna.

'Yes, we're all friends again. And you were right as usual, he did want to talk it through and get my take on the whole Louise thing. He's on the phone now. He'll be out in a minute, once he's passed on the oracle's words of wisdom. I really do amaze myself sometimes. I think I should be an agony aunty or a psycho-whatsit, you know what I mean, someone who sorts your head out.'

When Jeannie started to cough, Anna whacked her on the back, presuming she was choking on a cracker. Once recovered, Jeannie managed to speak to her bemused friend.

'Are you mad? The only psycho you'll ever be ends in path. And the reason you'd want to be a psycho-whatsit is because you're a nosey cow and could sit there listening to someone else's problems all day, then you'd come home depressed and feeling sorry for them. You start crying at *Surprise Surprise* so there's no way you could listen to the ins and outs of some poor sod's life. Just stick to being who you are, you're very good at that, trust me, because *I'm* the one who's always right.'

Anna was about to protest when she saw Daniel making his way over so instead, she took the plate away from Jeannie and passed it to Phil and Sam, leaving her cracker-less friend holding a huge lump of cheese.

Everything would be alright now she had shown Daniel that she did care and perhaps it could be a new start once Louise found out that Anna had batted for her team. As the sky overhead turned bluey-black and the stars twinkled, Anna put her troubles to one side and relaxed properly for the first time that evening, and in the spirit of peace and reconciliation, passed Jeannie the cream crackers.

* * *

Tilly looked up into the clear, ebony sky and traced the

constellations, which she knew off by heart. She had spent many nights in France doing the same thing in the company of her family. Thinking of them reminded her that it was about time she headed home. It was all well and good being in quarantine, but her parents might be lying in a pool of poo and vomit for all she knew. There wasn't much Tilly could do to help them, they just needed to stay warm and hydrated, you didn't have to be a nurse to know that, but she would look heartless if she didn't go home soon. Tilly wished she could've strung the night on forever and still had to tell Joe about Luke so the sooner they set off, the sooner she could get it over with and put an end to whatever she was feeling right now.

Once she'd said goodbye to everyone and fended off Anna's attempts to send her home with cake and sausages, she climbed into the campervan and waited for Joe to start the engine. As they drove down the lane, the glow from the barbecue and the gas heater faded into the distance and Tilly's heart was weighed down with leaden guilt and a myriad of emotions, none of them good. They were such a nice bunch of people, a family that she would love to be part of; they were nothing like Hazel and Ken.

As they turned onto the main road and Anna's house disappeared out of sight, Tilly had to face up to the fact that she would never see them again. Once she told Joe she was getting married, they would all think she was a complete fake and probably a bit of a weirdo into the bargain. Looking down at Joe's grey sweatshirt, she touched the soft fabric with her fingers. It would smell of him, or at least the fabric conditioner that his mum used. Tilly wondered if she'd get away with keeping it, a token of their few hours together, a talisman of what could have been. She looked heavenwards, consumed by the desire to just drift away, float around in space without a care in the world. Recognising the onset of tears she quickly turned her head towards the small side window and casually brushed them away. The rumbling sound of the engine was the only sound Tilly could hear while the motion of the old camper was strangely comforting. She wished they could just keep driving and never stop. The silence was eventually broken by Joe, his voice snapping her out of a trance.

'Have you got anything planned for tomorrow? Do you think your mum and dad will be better, only if you fancy a ride into town we could go and get a new wheel for your bike and have some lunch? Dominique said there's a cycle shop in Chateaubriant and Sam will let me borrow the van, it's no trouble.'

Joe looked across at Tilly and on seeing his hopeful eyes, her mind went into overdrive.

He had thrown her a lifeline, right across the double seat and it was for her to decide whether she grabbed on or let him down, not gently either, but with one huge, resounding thump. All she had to say was that she'd wait for her dad to get better so he could fix it, or that they had spare bikes in the garage. Then she could add that her parents wouldn't be too pleased if she went for lunch with a gorgeous, single, lovely man because next week, she was getting married. BAM! Job done. But then again, would one more day hurt? Just an extra twenty-four hours of let's pretend, and then she would do the right thing – honest. As Tilly looked into Joe's earnest eyes and drank in his serious, freckle-dusted face, she knew without a doubt that her heart was winning the battle with her head.

These were her last days of freedom and if she had to go through with the wedding from hell then she deserved a few moments in heaven. It was a totally innocent friendship and they were doing nothing wrong. They could go for lunch, he would make her laugh and she could pretend he was her boyfriend – nobody but her would know and for one day she could exist in a fantasy world and live someone else's life. She wouldn't lead him on or do anything improper and he wouldn't cross the line. Joe wasn't like that, she could tell, which meant she was perfectly safe. Time was running out and the virus that had gripped her parents would soon release them. Just the thought of being with Joe made Tilly happier than she'd been in a long while.

Her heart felt light and liberated, over-ruled her head and took an independent, bold step.

'Okay, if you're sure it's no trouble. My parents don't need round the clock nursing so I won't feel *too* guilty abandoning them. I'll give you my number then you can text me in the morning, just in case I'm up to my eyes in all sorts of bodily fluids. I've not been into town for ages so it will make a nice change and we could do a bit of shopping, or would you hate that?' Tilly was getting carried away but determined to cram as much as she could into her fantasy-bubble.

'No, I don't mind. So long as it won't involve me telling you your bum doesn't look big, or sitting on a stool on the other side of a curtain praying for it to end, then I think we can hit the shops.' Joe was only teasing and in truth, was so glad that she'd agreed he would've happily sat on every stool in every shop in Chateaubriant.

Tilly laughed and gave him a slap before pointing to the turning on the main road that led to her house. It was imperative that she got out quickly, just in case one of her parents spotted her through the window. The less they knew, the better. She could easily fob them off for one more day, providing they didn't ask questions and she didn't have to tell whopping big fibs, only tiny white lies. While they trundled up the dark road, Tilly typed her name and number into Joe's contact list.

The gates to the driveway were closed, which required a three-point turn and once they came to a halt, Tilly prepared to make her getaway.

'Right, I'd best let you get back to your mum's. Thanks again for looking after me today and coming to my rescue. Text me when you get in so I've got your number too, okay? And take care on the way, just in case Bambi is having a wander.' Tilly had opened the door and disembarked, slightly edgy and eager to get off.

'Okay, I'll watch you go inside then get on my way. I'll text you later. And today's been a laugh, even though it started off a bit weird. See you tomorrow.'

And before he had chance to add anything else, Tilly said goodbye, shut the door and scooted inside.

It did occur to Joe that she seemed a bit nervy and tense when they pulled up, and then the light dawned. Maybe she thought he'd make a pass. There was no way he'd try anything, Tilly wasn't that kind of girl and he would be stupid to spoil things. But right now, Joe didn't care. He'd be seeing her again tomorrow and apart from crazy, road-rage deer lurking in the hedgerows, the only other thing he was concerned about was if they'd saved him some cake, and hoping that Phil's Carpenters CD had finished before he got back.

As Tilly gave him a quick wave and a thumbs up from the door, Joe put the van into gear and set off for home, a big slice of cake and no doubt, a deep and thorough interrogation by his mother.

* * *

Joe was eating his toast and trying to contain his eagerness to get over to Tilly's at the same time as not making eye contact with his mother, or being drawn into conversation about his plans. He could tell she was gearing up to the Spanish Inquisition and there was only so long he could keep her at bay. He had managed to avoid any probing questions the previous evening, mainly because she was being entertained by Sam or deep in conversation with Jeannie.

Joe knew what his mum was going to say before she even opened her mouth and he was beginning to think that she had a vendetta against any member of the female race he became involved with. His mum couldn't stand Hannah (although she did have a point where she was concerned) and none of the offerings he brought home from college or university seem to reach the mark either.

The night before, Joe had casually mentioned his 'date' to Sam who was totally cool about the fact that Tilly had a long-term boyfriend and they were just mates and nothing was going to happen. He had girl-mates all over the place so it was no big deal. That said, Sam's idea of platonic or casual may have involved a bit more than a shopping trip and lunch in town, but while he had an ally, Joe wasn't going to complain.

He knew his mum was worried that he was going to get hurt, so Joe was armed and ready with his defence should she manage to corner him. He would solemnly assure her that he wouldn't break the code, but as for the falling for Tilly, he was halfway to being besotted already.

There was just something about her that made him feel... well, happy really. She was extremely pretty in a natural, comfortable-in-her-own-skin sort of way and had a wicked sense of humour. She was clever, focused on her career and her chosen profession, caring for other people, appealed to Joe's philanthropic nature. They had talked about everything last night, from travel to charity fun-runs, the type of food they liked and the stuff they hated. Even where differences occurred, instead of it flagging up incompatibility, it sort of made Tilly more interesting and diverse, and definitely not the type to agree just for the sake of it.

They both fancied camping at a festival and liked the same music, apart from country and western. Tilly had confessed to this being one of her guilty pleasures. She said that the words of most songs were poignant and sometimes made her cry, and she didn't seem to mind when Joe teased her about it. Both had similar political views that erred to the left, working-class values and strong environmental concerns, although neither would go so far as to live in trees or join the Communist Party.

Joe hadn't wanted the night to end and, in an attempt to string their connection out for longer, sent her a text as soon as he pulled up at his mum's house. When his phone bleeped and he saw her name pop up, he experienced a flood of teenage-like excitement and as a result, they spent the next few hours texting back and forth, talking about nothing in particular. By the time his head hit the pillow and his tired eyes began to close, Joe's only thoughts were of the raven-haired beauty that he'd almost squashed, then rescued and, in the space of twelve hours, had turned his world upside down.

* * *

Tilly had changed three times and couldn't decide on going make-up free or adding just a touch of something here and there. With each question she asked and every decision she made, she forcibly squashed the messages that were being relayed from the, very annoying, Conscience Department of her brain. They insisted on asking questions that poured ice-cold water on any fun she was having and if she wasn't totally committed to meeting Joe, a weaker willed person may have chickened out.

Her parents were still suffering and she'd heard them trotting (literally) back and forth from the toilet all night. The walls of the house were made of sturdy stone yet not quite soundproof and it was abundantly clear that the virus still had work to do. Tilly knew from experience that it would likely last for forty-eight hours, followed by a couple more days of feeling rather delicate and prone to minor relapses if they didn't watch what they ate. Therefore, Tilly knew that for now, her parents would probably be best left alone. However, tomorrow really was another day and if they improved (which she hoped they would) it would mean being confined to barracks and doing what she was trained at – caring for the sick. That was why it was imperative she stood fast, ignored the agitators in her brain and allowed her weary heart a little bit of light relief.

* * *

The night before, once she'd crept in, Tilly had a bizarre conversation with her parents from between a gap in the bedroom door, totally forbidden to step over the invisible barrier. They both looked dreadful and were surviving on sips of water and whatever scraps of sleep they could manage in between visits to the loo. At their insistence, Tilly then explained the whole deer/bike/campervan episode, and her relief at being rescued. Whilst they were concerned and relieved that she had escaped virtually unscathed and been well cared for elsewhere, their own ailments left them preoccupied and less than chatty.

Tilly told then all about Anna and her lovely family and that she had been invited out for lunch and a bit of shopping in town, conveniently leaving out the name of the one and only person she would be going with. They appeared unperturbed by the fact that she would be out again for a few hours and innocently encouraged her to have some fun in a more sterile environment. Their only proviso was that she kept in touch, took care and had a lovely time.

As Tilly gently closed the door, she did have the grace to feel guilty and acknowledge the fact that she had told a white lie to her parents, but then, her whole life for the past seven months had been a big fat fib, so what would one more matter? By the time Tilly was ready for bed and had received her first text from Joe, she'd absolved herself of sin and her lie had been downgraded to a half truth.

The fact she had two missed calls from Luke didn't unduly trouble her because if he was that bothered, he would've sent a text, kept ringing or tried the house phone and left messages on both. As neither had occurred, Tilly left him a voicemail where she described the house as a germ-infested zone and casually mentioned she'd had a minor altercation with a deer. After apologising for missing his call, Tilly said she ring him in the morning, then concentrated on replying to Joe's text.

It must have been 1am by the time she finally called time on the conversation with Joe, and drifted off into an exhausted, yet strangely contented sleep for the first time in a long, long while. Instead of lying awake, looking at the ceiling and turning her mind inside out, Tilly, for once, floated happily into the land of peaceful, untroubled dreams.

* * *

Realising that Joe would be on his way Tilly checked the bedside clock and abandoned any ideas about make-up and made do with a squirt of her favourite perfume and a coat of lip gloss. She scrutinised her appearance in the mirror, giving her floral, knee-length, flouncy sundress the seal of approval before putting her phone on silent and closing the bedroom door. There was no way she wanted to be inter-rupted by a call or text from Luke, however, she resolved to check her phone regularly in case her parents needed her. When she reached their door, Tilly opened it slowly and peeped through the crack. They were fast asleep and for now, symptom free, so she left them to their slumbers. There was just enough time for a final glance in the hall mirror before she let herself out and into the bright morning sun.

It was a real towny thing to do, inhaling the clean coun-tryside air and imbibing a lungful of something fresh and healthy. On this occasion it left Tilly wishing she hadn't bothered after being treated to a pungent whiff of whatever Didier had stacked up on his trailer. Deciding it would be best to get upwind of the steaming dung pile, Tilly set off with burning nostrils and a giddy heart. Even before she reached the end of the lane, she heard the chug, chug, chug of Sam's van as it made its way along the winding road and within minutes, Joe was there, waving at her.

Tilly opened the door and climbed eagerly inside, escaping the wafts of dung and savouring the unmistakable scent of a classic vehicle interior, mingling with a hint of Joe's aftershave. No matter how much she tried, there was no escaping the giddy feeling she experienced as she looked into the happy blue eyes of her chauffeur. As she fastened her seat belt and they set off towards town, Tilly had only one thought on her mind. How could something so very wrong, feel so completely right?

CHAPTER SEVEN

Freda checked the clock and groaned. It was late afternoon and another day had been lain to waste. She had never, ever felt so ill in all her life. The past forty-eight hours were a hideous mélange of emergency trips to the bathroom, numb feet on cold tiles as you prayed that your bowels didn't actually explode and disappear down the loo, followed by cramp after kneeling on the floor, hugging the toilet bowl. It would've been so much easier to sleep next to the bath. Freda wasn't actually sure what day it was and if she was honest, didn't really care. The worst seemed to be over and now, all she wanted to do was sleep.

Thank goodness Tilly had found some new friends and wasn't stuck in this germ-infested house. The minute she was up to it, Freda was going to get the mop bucket out and bleach every inch of her home and eradicate any trace of this bug. She also felt dreadful about passing it on to poor Howard, who was now snoring quietly by her side. All Freda could think of as she'd purged her body, was that she must prevent Tilly getting sick at all costs. Images of a stricken bride and the kitchen bowl flashed into Freda's head. She would Google summer sickness bugs and check out the incubation period. Hopefully, Tilly would be in the clear especially if she stayed out of their way.

Freda had started to believe it was a warped premonition and knew she was obsessing about something she had no control over. If Tilly did get sick, there was sod all anyone could do about it, just like the awful incident with a frightened deer and a campervan. Freda's overactive imagination went into warp speed as she imagined Tilly in hospital, covered from head to toe in plaster casts with her leg held up by one of those pulley things, while the wedding ceremony took place around her bed. Freda shook the images away. Nothing and nobody was going to stop this wedding and ruin her daughter's day, or lay waste to a year's worth of meticulous preparation either.

Tired eyes began to droop as Freda's thoughts strayed to Tilly and what a good girl she was, vowing to make it up to her next week. They'd be busy as bees getting ready for the arrival of the wedding guests but somehow, Freda would squeeze in some special time for the two of them. For now, she needed to sleep and get herself well. Tilly was fine and spending the day with that nice Anna from the next village. Howard was well away in the land of nod so for a few hours, Freda could switch off and forget about weddings and by the time she woke up, everything in the world would be just fine.

* * *

A few miles away, Anna was in an extremely buoyant mood. Everyone had thoroughly enjoyed their day out which had been topped off (by special request of Summer and Ross) with a visit to a French McDonald's. Despite everyone trying to explain that it was more or less the same as at home, they were adamant and unconvinced, eventually wearing the adults down and beating them into surrender.

Thankfully, owing to full tummies and a hard day bouncing about and riding on mechanical elephants, they conked out in the back of the car and gave everyone a bit of peace. The journey home in Phil's rented people carrier was restful, interspersed with scenery related observations and thoughts of a relaxing evening in the garden.

Anna's mind had wandered to her kids and what they'd been up to all day. She knew Sam would be fine and more than likely amply fed and watered by Zofia and Dominique. It was Joe she was more concerned about because he'd been avoiding her that morning and couldn't wait to get out of the house and over to Tilly's. Still, he wouldn't get away with it forever and before the evening was out she was going to make sure they had a little heart to heart. She couldn't quite put her finger on it but there was something that didn't sit right about Tilly, call it a mother's intuition, but Anna got the distinct impression that she wasn't quite as perfect as she made out. She'd run her thoughts by Jeannie earlier, who comfortingly, was of the same opinion.

Jeannie had agreed that there was a fine line to tread where 'just being friends' was concerned, then again, maybe they were turning into a pair of old farts who didn't understand how young people did things these days. Having said that, if the shoe was on the other foot, Joe wouldn't be too pleased if he found out his girlfriend had been gadding about and going for lunch with a good-looking bloke, so in her opinion, he was treading on thin ice. To make matters worse, Jeannie was very protective of all her god-children and knowing that Joe in particular had a fragile heart, always felt he required extra surveillance and would now benefit from her undivided, special attention.

On hearing this, Anna sort of wished she'd kept her mouth shut, knowing full well that Jeannie had a tendency for being a bit too outspoken and in some cases, eye-wateringly honest.

Daniel and Phil on the other hand, had been ear-wigging and had an entirely different take on the matter. They thought Anna and Jeannie should leave Joe to make his own mistakes and not go interfering and spoiling his harmless fun.

True to form, both Anna and Jeannie decided to

completely disregard their advice, which meant keeping close tabs on Joe and their increasingly mistrustful eyes on dear sweet Tilly.

When they pulled into the drive, Anna spotted Sam's van and scanned the garden for signs of life. Pippa was already at the door and overjoyed to see them all, wagging and wiggling for England as they all fussed over the stay-at-home, sleepy-eyed dog. Anna knew full well Pippa would have snored her way through the day, conserving her energy and making the most of the peace and quiet, but would now demand attention and compensation for having to remain behind. Placing the picnic box on the kitchen worktop, Anna rummaged inside and found some chunks of ham wrapped in tinfoil which she fed to her expectant dog. Once the little diva was placated, Anna went in search of the rest of her elusive brood.

She found them on the patio listening to music. The second she spotted Tilly, Anna became irritated, so much so that she had to forcibly paint a smile on her face, which probably looked as false as it felt. Unkind, unwelcoming thoughts zapped through her brain, like 'have you not got a home to go to, or a boyfriend to call?' The second she acknowledged them, Anna felt spiteful and slightly silly.

They weren't doing any harm, Sam was there as a chaperone and Tilly wasn't exactly cuddling up to Joe, just sitting quite close, too close if she was honest. The whole scene rankled with Anna who, nevertheless, attempted to be a good hostess and force out some kind, nice-person words.

'Hiya, sorry we're late getting back. Have you eaten yet because we've all been to McDonald's? I could rustle a snack up if anyone's hungry?'

'We're fine thanks, Mum, we had lunch in Chateaubriant... did you have a good time in Nantes?' Joe spoke on Tilly's behalf.

'Oh good, and yes it was brilliant, the kids absolutely loved it, I'm exhausted though.' Anna flopped into the chair next to Sam, determined to be a gooseberry. 'And what about you, Sam, what have you been up to, are you hungry, there's some bits and bobs in the picnic box you could have?'

'I'm fine, Mum. I had a huge lunch at Zofia's and brought some back for Pippa as well, so don't give her anything otherwise she'll pop. I'll get a sarnie later on if I'm hungry. I totally whipped Dominique at tennis but I still can't beat him at *pétanque*, he's too good. I'm glad the kids liked it in Nantes. I'll just finish this and see if they want a game of football or are they too tired?' Sam took a sip of his beer, oblivious to his mum's mood and continued fiddling with his iPod.

Smiling at Sam's tennis victory and relieved that for once he was full up, Anna ignored the fact that she'd just given Pippa half a pig and turned her attention to Joe and Tilly.

'So, how did you two get on, did you buy anything nice? There are some lovely shops in town but I think the boutiques are a bit pricey.' Anna didn't really want to know but was stuck for anything else to say.

Tilly spoke first. 'Joe took me to a lovely bistro in the main square and we spent ages people watching. It's one of my favourite things. We had a huge bowl of moules marinière and the biggest serving of frites I've ever seen. I don't think I'll eat for a week.' Tilly looked to Joe for confirmation then continued enthusiastically. 'Then it felt as though we wandered along every single street in Chateaubriant. Your son is very patient, Anna, he put up with me staring at shop windows, and you're right, those boutiques are a bit too pricey for a nurse's wage.' Tilly put her glass down and began rummaging in fancy paper bag.

As Tilly faffed, sarcastic thoughts raged through Anna's head.

'Oh, I bet you enjoyed having Joe follow you round like an obedient puppy and then pay for your lunch. If I find out he's bought you something from one of those boutiques I will hit the roof. Get your own boyfriend to buy you clothes, not my foolish, lovesick son!' Anna had been watching Joe intently and it was

as clear as the nose on his adoring face that he was smitten by Tilly.

Boy, was he going to get a dose of home truths once Little Miss Perfect over there went home, and the sooner the better as far as she was concerned. Anna knew that Daniel would say she was overreacting and getting ahead of herself, especially as the poor girl hadn't committed any cardinal sins – yet! However, experience and common sense told her that whatever was going on, wasn't going to end well and if it was one-sided, Joe was heading for a fall.

Anna was just about to direct a question to Mr Puppy-dog Eyes, when Tilly found what she was looking for and retrieved it from her bag.

'Here, this is for you, Anna, just to say thank you for taking care of me yesterday and making me feel so welcome. I hope you like macaroons.'

Tilly produced an elegant, pastel green box tied with a white ribbon and the prettiness of it told Anna instantly that it was from one of the artisan patisseries in town.

Now, she was torn in two. Whoever was sitting on her right shoulder whispered that she was a suspicious old bag and should be ashamed of her ungracious thoughts. While on her left, someone hissed that Tilly was just a crafty, suck up and her sugary gift was purely a smokescreen. Either way, with all eyes on her, Anna had to ignore both and accept the box with good grace and a rather embarrassed smile.

'Oh, thank you, Tilly but there really was no need, what a lovely box, and yes I do like macaroons, how did you guess? And you're more than welcome here anytime, we love having visitors, don't we, lads?' Anna was rambling now and could not believe she had just said that!

Knowing when it was time to quit, she rose to her feet and taking her present with her, set off for the kitchen before she asked Tilly to move in, or something as equally stupid and two-faced.

'Right, I'm going to make a pot of tea, would anybody like some, we can share the macaroons?' Seeing all three shake their heads and decline, Anna slunk into the safety of the house, shoved the box inside the cupboard, slammed the door and then went in search of Jeannie. She'd be on her side and would tell her how to get rid of the limpet.

Luckily, Jeannie completely agreed and said that Tilly was obviously applying the tried and trusted method of getting 'mum' on side, commonly known in the trade as 'creeping'. She did, however, point out to Anna that if it was anybody else, they'd both be commenting on what a polite, well-brought-up girl Joe had met and that it was nice to see him with someone normal and friendly. Not stuck-up and spoilt like his ex.

This only threw Anna's brain into disarray and they spent the duration of one pot of tea trying to decide if they were being a bit mean to a pleasant young woman who was feeling lonely because her folks were sick. Or they had in fact identified a heart-breaking, two-timing leech.

When Melanie came home from work, she was immediately filled in on the situation and after listening to all their evidence, told them both they were completely bonkers and needed to get out more! Apparently, in the twenty-first century, young people were allowed to have friends of the opposite sex without being burnt at the stake or cast out from society. They should also give Joe a bit of credit for not being so naïve as to fall in love with the first girl that came along, especially one with a boyfriend. And while they were at it, try to remember that he wasn't fifteen either! Giving them both a warning stare and a disbelieving shake of the head, Melanie left them to their cackling and went upstairs to take a shower.

Anna couldn't believe that lately, it seemed as though she was always the one at the end of withering looks and exasperated sighs, and that was just from her kids. Daniel had his own way of dealing with her ramblings and way-off-the-mark observations. He just tuned out or shook his head at the village nutter!

After taking Mel's 'helpful' comments into account, both witches agreed to give Tilly the benefit of the doubt but thought it wise for Anna to have a gentle word in Joe's ear, just to set their minds at rest. With the world almost put to rights, Anna and Jeannie decided to head outside and make the most of the last few hours of sunlight and enjoy the peace and quiet of the countryside, and a bottle of rosé.

Little did Anna know that within the space of a few short minutes, whatever peace and harmony resided within her soul would be fleeting, and that Tilly, the creeping limpet, would be the very least of her problems.

It had been such a lovely day. The sun was moving around the earth, signalling the passing of daytime hours and the approach of sunset. Tilly held in a sigh, and was loath to look at her watch because each time she did, it told her that her sojourn into Happy Land would soon come to an end. Not only that, the inevitable truth loomed and no matter how hard she tried to come up with a solution or a good enough reason to prevaricate further, Tilly knew she owed it to Joe to come clean. There it was again, that sinking feeling that came every time her brain reminded her of the truth.

During the day, Tilly had compiled a list of things she liked about Joe, just to torment herself further. He didn't think he was funny, but he was. He probably didn't see himself as good-looking, charming, kind and thoughtful either, or notice that she valued his observations on every single subject they discussed and shared most of his opinions. They had come across topics where they differed yet instead of seeing it as a sign they were incompatible, Tilly admired his strength of character and that he was honest enough to disagree. The truly sad part about all of it was that despite her positive analysis of Joe's personality, he may as well have been a flesh-eating alien from a far-off solar system for all the good it would do her. They were never meant to be and that was that, so the sooner she confessed the better.

On the up side, there was a microscopic possibility that he might be cool about the whole marriage thing and wish her well. Hey, he could even come along to the service and drink a toast to the happy couple. What made her think he even liked her anyway? He might just shrug it off because in contrast to her, Joe really did see their friendship as just that, full stop. *'Watch your big head, Tilly Parker, just because you feel like a lovesick schoolgirl each time he smiles at you, he's probably on the level and just helping to get your bike fixed.'*

To add insult to her impending injury, she got the distinct impression that Anna didn't like her and she knew why of course, it was because of Luke. Tilly didn't blame Anna for being suspicious and mistrustful because let's face it, any mother would want to protect their son from a woman who had an absent boyfriend that she neither talked about, nor displayed any interest in.

Maybe it was her guilty conscience talking, however, Tilly *had* caught Anna out a few times, surreptitiously watching and weighing her up. Even though Sam and Joe failed to spot it, the momentary flash of irritation that crossed Anna's face when she spotted her was accompanied by a slight narrowing of her eyes and the almost imperceptible twitch in Anna's jaw whenever she directed conversation Tilly's way.

Still, Tilly was glad she had bought Anna a gift and had hoped her hostess would accept it in the spirit it was intended, yet it was clear Anna was nobody's fool and took the offering for no other reason than because she had to.

It seemed to put her on the back foot for a moment, probably owing to the fact Sam and Joe looked rather chuffed that their mum had been given a present, which then resulted in what Tilly suspected were a flurry of false platitudes and half meant invitations.

If only Anna could see it from her point of view, then she might understand why Tilly held every second in Joe's company dear. Regardless of the inevitability of her plight and no matter what happened when Joe drove her home, Tilly would always have today. Whether it was a good thing or bad, a tortuous reminder of what you couldn't have, or a secret memory to get you through the gloom, she would cling on to it always.

* * *

They had started the day at the bike shop where Tilly had a chance to shine, speaking not bad French to the guy over the counter, and then basking in the glow of Joe's admiration afterwards. They headed off into town and did a spot of shopping where, despite his teasing the day before, it was Joe who turned into the shopaholic, not her.

After splashing out on some very cool T-shirts and beach shorts, Joe had turned his attention to Tilly and persuaded her to buy the tie-dye sundress she was admiring in a boutique window. Joe was obviously far more solvent than she, and to him the exorbitant price tags not too much of a stretch. Whereas her nurse's wage didn't quite run to extravagances on a regular basis, so Tilly restrained herself.

Not that Joe was a show off or flashed his cash. He even offered to buy her the floppy, straw cowboy hat that the mannequin wore so well with the dress but Tilly declined.

Next stop was lunch and after finding a street-front bistro where they bagged a table close to the passing crowd, they watched the inhabitants of the town flow past while they talked non-stop, ate their moules frites and shared a bottle of crisp white wine. After stashing their shopping inside the van they explored the château, strolling around the castle courtyard and grounds in the bright, afternoon sunshine.

The wine had gone to Tilly's head so she had to constantly remind herself not to do or say anything stupid, or let her imagination get carried away. It was so easy to pretend that Joe was her boyfriend and knew that's how the other tourists would perceive them. Just the thought of it made Tilly feel euphoric, then melancholic and on the verge of tears. Thankfully Joe didn't seem to notice and was too busy reading the tour guide to be aware of her fluctuating mood and thankfully, her sinful, innermost thoughts.

They spent a sobering time inside the Musée de la Résistance. As they read the story of the massacre of twenty-seven young resistance fighters by the Nazis and the heartbreaking, last letter of seventeen-year-old Guy Môquet, both were moved to tears by his words of love for his family.

When Joe had regained his composure, he remarked to Tilly that he would bring Summer and Ross here when they were a bit older, but for now, he thought it was somewhere that Sam would like to see.

Emerging into the sunlight, Tilly shook off her gloom and reminded herself that she was alive and had plenty to be grateful for, unlike the poor souls who were remembered inside.

As they made their way back to the van, Joe also recovered his form and suggested they went back to his mum's house where they could relax in the garden before everyone came home and bedlam resumed.

Tilly had agreed in a heartbeat and resolved not to drink one more drop of alcohol, otherwise she might just lose it. At the same time as being sensible, she was going to make the most of every last second she had with Joe because the clock was ticking and her bomb was about to explode.

* * *

Joe had also been thinking about their afternoon together, regarding their trip as a huge success and awarding it five stars. At the same time, and despite his best attempts, it was becoming quite hard to keep his feelings in check and behave like a true gentleman. Had Tilly been single, he knew without a fraction of doubt that he would have made some kind of subtle move just to test the water because he was picking up vibes and all of them were good. Yes, he knew he was being a complete idiot and could get his fingers burned, but there had to be some way of finding out exactly how things were between Tilly and Luke without coming right out with it. He could try, *'Look, I really fancy you so is there any chance you might be sick of your boyfriend, or even better, could you just give him a call and dump him?'*

Joe couldn't quite believe that he was thinking that way, but he was, and he didn't care either. He knew from the first time he met her, over a year before, that there was a spark. In the short space of forty-eight hours, that spark was now a military grade rocket launcher! But until he knew the score, he'd decided to spend as much time as possible with Tilly – he even hoped that her parents would have a relapse and be confined to their beds for another three days, how bad was that?

Luckily, Joe didn't have to try too hard or come up with a reason to invite her over because Sam was about to do the hard work for him.

'Mum said she wants to chill out here tomorrow and then go to the beach on Thursday. It looks like it's going to be a scorcher. Do you fancy tagging along Tilly? There's plenty of room in the camper.' Sam was checking his Facebook and missed the look that passed between his companions.

Joe could've hugged his brother there and then and knew when his eyes met Tilly's that hers were saying, *'Yes, if that's okay with you'* while his implored, *'Just say yes, it's cool.'*

Tilly took the hint. 'Oh, yes please, I'd love to come, but I need to make sure my mum and dad are okay with it first. I've hardly seen them since I got here and I don't want them to get the hump with me. Come to think of it, Mum teaches on Thursdays and Dad plays *pétanque* in the village so I might not be missed. Can I let you know for sure tomorrow?'

Inside her chest, Tilly's heart was doing a happy dance at the idea of spending a whole day with Joe, and Sam of course, until it thudded then hurtled downwards and landed in a soggy pit when she remembered that tonight was supposed to be truth night.

Sam's voice brought her further back to reality. 'That's fine, just let us know and we'll pick you up on the way. I think Melanie will be coming along as well so it should be a laugh. Right, I'm going to make a sandwich, does anyone want one?'

As Sam got up to go to the kitchen, they heard the sound of a car approaching slowly along the gravel drive, diverting him from his task, then popping his head round the gable end of the house to see who their visitor was. When he sprang back with wide eyes and a mischievous look on his face, he chuckled before telling Joe and Tilly who it was.

'Oh-oh, there's going to be trouble now! Guess who's just turned up?' Sam had his back to them while he peeped around the corner again, and spied on the new arrival.

Joe was curious as to who could bring trouble to their door, then for an instant, he thought of Luke.

'Sam, who is it? Don't just stand there peering, dish the dirt, what's happening?'

'It's Louise and Jules! I can't see Mum, just Daniel giving her a hug and it looks like she's crying. Here comes Mum now, this is going to be good. She can't stand her, oops, think Mum's spotted me.' Sam ducked out of sight and turned to face the others.

'Probably best if we stay here till things calm down, I was looking forward to that sarnie too. Joe, run in and grab the biscuit tin while I keep watch, hurry up, they're still in the garden.'

Joe did as he was told and left Sam to be the lookout.

When he ran back outside, Joe was loaded up with crisps, chocolate, the biscuit tin and a bottle of Coke. While the drama unfolded in the garden, Sam, Joe and Tilly tucked into their feast, listened to music and made plans for beach day.

Just a few feet away, out of sight and mind, a drama was

unfolding and at its centre was Anna and her arch enemy, Louise.

Anna could not believe what she was seeing. As she and Jeannie had made their way towards the front garden carrying wine and glasses, they heard the crunching of gravel and the engine of a car as it rolled towards them. Anna didn't recognise it at first but when she spotted the figure in the driving seat, all blonde hair and Audrey Hepburn shades, she knew who it was. Her heart froze and her whole body stiffened. Anna watched motionless from just inside the house as the car came to a stop and the driver got out.

Over Anna's shoulder, Jeannie asked the obvious question.

'Is that who I think it is?'

'Yep… it's Louise. She's got a bloody nerve coming here, what the hell am I going to do now? You said she'd have kissed and made up by morning, well that was a load of bollocks! I thought you were always right?'

Anna was watching the scene unfold as she hissed at a dumbfounded Jeannie.

'I can't be right all the time, you know! But you'd better get out there and make her feel welcome. You know what a drama queen she is and she'll love it if you give her a bit of attention. She's probably expecting Nasty Anna so do your best to be nice and then you'll wrong-foot her. Whatever you do, don't give her a reason to cause trouble between you and Daniel. She's had hours to plan this on the drive up and she'll think she's caught you off guard, the crafty cow. Go on, play nicely, I'll back you up.'

Anna was livid but knowing she'd have to face Louise sooner or later, went outside to welcome her very unwelcome guest. Stepping into the sunshine, Anna surveyed the unfolding scene.

Daniel was hugging a tearful Louise while Jules sat patiently in the back of the car, looking tired and sweaty and slightly nervous too. Anna felt instantly sorry for the little boy who had been dragged away from his papa and was most likely traumatised by the whole turn of events. Weeping Girl wasn't helping, or thinking about her son's feelings while she lapped up Daddy's attention.

Putting her best foot forward and with her trusty friend two steps behind, Anna slipped on a 'concerned' expression and approached the car. She would do this for Daniel and Jules, no matter how much it made her cringe.

'Oh no, Louise, what's wrong? Come on, don't cry, let's get you inside.' Dipping her head so she could see inside the car, Anna smiled at Jules. 'Hello cheeky, what a lovely surprise to see you. Will you help Granddad bring your things and then we can all have a nice, cool drink?'

After seeing Jules nod and undo his seat belt, Anna placed a caring arm around Louise's shoulders as she guided the sniveller towards the house. Taking control of the situation gave her a sense of power and allowed Daniel to focus on Jules, who was scrambling out of the car.

Once inside the house, Anna seated Louise at the table where she was joined by Jeannie who seemed to be loving every minute, intently weighing up the newcomer as coffee was prepared and various orders given to Daniel who was wheeling a worryingly large suitcase into the room.

After parking it at the bottom of the stairs Daniel turned to his shy grandson and spoke.

'I know, why don't we ask Summer and Ross if they fancy a swim in the pool, would you like that? They're upstairs tidying their room, why don't we surprise them.' Seeing Jules nod enthusiastically, Daniel led him up the stairs in search of younger, more cheerful allies.

Once the women were alone, Anna placed three mugs of coffee onto the table and got straight down to business. Louise had composed herself and began sipping her drink, seeming quite comfortable in her role of interloper and uninvited guest. She did at least have the grace to apologise for turning up unannounced.

'I'm so sorry to tip up like this, Anna, but I just didn't

know who else to turn to. I can't get hold of Mum and most of my friends are away on their two-week holiday. I just felt so isolated and no matter how hard I've tried to sort things out with Tomas, we just argue and he refuses to come home. In the end I just panicked.' With that, Louise's bottom lip began to tremble and the water works started up again.

'Come on, Louise, you've got to be brave for Jules's sake. You mustn't let him see you like this. Does he understand what's going on?' Anna patted Louise's hand kindly and was surprised to hear genuine concern in her own voice. It was horrible seeing anyone cry.

'Yes, I've explained it all to him and Tomas put his sixpence worth in, too. He's told Jules that *I'm* being unreasonable and *he* would never do anything to make him unhappy… oh, and that Geneva is the best thing since sliced bread. I explained to Jules that Daddy should have asked us first and let us choose together, instead of deciding for us. He's hardly spoken all the way here and I can tell he's confused. I feel so bad about everything. I just needed to be with my dad and have some support.'

With that, the tears and sobs came for real and in abundance, leaving Anna with no choice other than to stand up and give Louise a hug while they all waited for the tears to subside.

Jeannie watched Anna, mild amusement written across her face, then piped up with a question of her own.

'Have you actually asked Jules whether he would like to go to Geneva or are you speaking on his behalf? Just because *you* think he won't want to leave his friends behind doesn't necessarily mean that's the case. He might see it as a huge adventure but feel too scared to admit it in case he upsets you. Kids don't like to take sides and he's probably wary of saying how he really feels, especially if this is how you are at home.'

Anna winced and gave Jeannie the daggers. Sometimes Ms Brown could be a bit too 'in your face'.

Louise blew her nose on the kitchen roll Anna had handed to her, before speaking.

'Yes, I have asked him and he just repeats that he wants to be where Mummy and Daddy are, as long as we're together. He clams up when I press him about leaving school and all that, so I have no idea what he really wants. I'm hoping Dad can get it out of him, or maybe you, Anna.' Louise smiled and flicked a stray tear away.

Jeannie rolled her eyes, not remotely taken in by the 'New Louise' whereas Anna felt flattered that she had been considered, but before she could get a word in, her friend had further wisdom to impart.

'Well, he's never going to say he wants to go when he knows you're against it, and he's not likely to tell his dad to shove it and risk upsetting him either, so no wonder the poor kid clams up. Still, I think you've done the right thing coming here, it will put the wind up Tomas when he realises you've cleared off. It might bring him to his senses. When he panics, you can try to have a grown-up conversation and sort it out. In the meantime, both of you need to remember that the most important person in all of this is Jules. He just wants his mum and dad in one place, in any country. It's not exactly rocket science! Right, I'm going to open some wine, I've had enough soft drinks for the day!'

And with that, Bossy Boots Brown marched off, leaving Anna and Louise alone.

Taking the lead Anna spoke first. 'I think the best thing is to get you and Jules settled in and then tomorrow, we can put our heads together and see if we can sort this mess out. As Jeannie said, a change of scenery and a few days apart might be just what you both need, and Jules can enjoy some time with us and the kids. I'm sure they'll get on great. Now, do you fancy a nice warm shower while me and Jeannie watch them play in the pool? I'll make us all something to eat later.'

Anna smiled kindly at Louise who seemed to have bucked up a little.

'That would be lovely, Anna, thanks. And your friend's right, we have to put Jules first and if it means me giving in and going to Geneva, I will, for his sake. But I'm still so mad with Tomas for walking out and the awful things he said to me, not to mention just presuming I'd trot off after him like an obedient wife. The whole thing makes my blood boil.'

Louise was back on form so before they were subjected to another rant, Anna decided to show her upstairs and point her in the direction of the bathroom.

Once Louise was settled and Jules was having a splash in the pool with Summer and Ross who were thrilled at having a new playmate, Anna went outside to sit with Jeannie, and Phil who had been enjoying a sneaky nap until the visitors arrived.

Daniel spotted her and before she reached the others, took her in his arms and hugged her tight.

'Thank you for looking after Louise. I know she's been a pain in the past, so I do appreciate you letting it go and taking her in. And just so you know, I won't stand for any funny business from her, okay? Any nonsense and I will put her in her place, I promise.' Daniel's eyes were sincere and held Anna's as he waited for her response.

'It's fine, Daniel. Let's have a fresh start and see if we can help her sort it out. Everyone has ups and downs in their relationships, we're no different and it's an awful time when you row, especially for the kids. Hopefully it will all turn out for the best and in the meantime we get to spend time with Jules.' Looking across the garden, they smiled at the three children who were squirting each other with water pistols and squealing with delight.

'Well, you go and put your feet up for a while and I'll see what I can rustle up. Those three will want feeding before bed and I'm a bit peckish. Go on, sit down and relax.' Kissing Anna's forehead, Daniel shooed her in the direction of the deck chairs and made his way inside.

Sitting down between Jeannie and Phil, Anna commented that he seemed to take more naps than Pippa and that her big brother must be finally getting old, either that or he was bored.

'Are you kidding? Nobody could get bored *or* get any kip around here! There's crazed animals who attack innocent cyclists, kids with hundred decibel screams and never seem to sleep, a sex maniac in bed with me at night, a sister who thinks she's a tour guide on speed and then the daughter from hell turns up. There's only Daniel who's normal! Do you think I could swap beds and sleep next to him, at least then I might get some peace and quiet?'

Phil then got a thump on each arm for his comments and a promise that if he wasn't careful, he'd be kipping in the campervan for the foreseeable future.

Then, just as Anna knew she would, Jeannie brought up the scene in the kitchen.

'I must say that I was most impressed by your touching show of compassion for darling Louise, have you been taking acting lessons too?'

Anna rolled her eyes and allowed Jeannie to continue.

'Don't be taken in though. I wouldn't put my trust in her just yet but I hope for Lady Louise's sake she's being genuine, otherwise I'll just have to kick her arse for you.' Jeannie winked at Anna who smiled back and nodded in agreement.

'I know exactly where you're coming from. If she's already resigned herself to following Tomas to Geneva, why is she here? I don't buy the part about needing support, either. I've got a feeling this is all a well thought out hissy fit designed to extract the maximum level of compensation and enjoy a bucketful of attention in the meantime. Let's keep our fingers crossed that Tomas plays ball and comes running... the sooner the bloody better.'

Jeannie leant over and poured Anna a glass of wine and passed it to her beleaguered friend.

'Here, drink this. I think you're going to need it. We've still got love's young dream to sort out and now, darling Louise needs a shoulder to cry on. Cheers big ears!'

Out of earshot, Joe sat with Tilly, oblivious to the fact that he was the subject of conversation and also unaware that his foolish heart was eventually going to be broken, and his mother was gearing up to give him one of her talks.

Upstairs, Louise languished in a hot shower and let her troubles trickle away. She was going to have a nice few days with her father and was also extremely content in the knowledge that around about now, Tomas would be arriving to collect Jules and find an empty house and his family gone.

Anna on the other hand quietly sipped her wine, processing the myriad of information gathering in her head before storing away Jeannie's sage advice. As she prepared for the following day, making a list in her head of things to do, cook and see, Anna sighed and resigned herself to the inevitable – waiting for the 'Louise Show' to begin.

CHAPTER EIGHT

Dear Diary,

What have I done? I've made things worse, I know I have, but I just couldn't help it. I'm glad you can't answer me back because you would give me a proper ear bashing, which I deserve. I'm just yellow through and through and instead of growing a spine and doing the right thing, I leap from one mistake to another. I swear I was on the verge of telling Joe, I really was, until he told me all about his mum, and worse, how he felt about cheaters, and then I just bottled it. Not only that, I know for a fact that if I'd told him about the wedding he'd have ended it, whatever 'it' is, right there and then. I just I want one more day with him. I know I've said that before but please, let me have the beach day, and then I swear I'll come clean. As long as I don't do anything that is classed as unfaithful or lead him on in any way, I think I can hold my head up and look people in the eye and say I've done nothing wrong. We are just friends. Full stop!

I've got enough going on in my head with Mum asking questions every two minutes and Luke boring the crap out of me each time he rings. Yes, I know... it's my own fault and if I wasn't a BIG FAT CHICKEN then I wouldn't be in this situation. But I am, and if meeting Joe has proved one thing, it's that Luke and I should not be together and if I was a decent human being, I'd set *him free. Well I'm not and I haven't got the guts to tell everyone it's off so I'm sticking to plan A. Once we're married, who knows what could happen? He might change or perhaps someone will give us a voucher for a personality transplant as a wedding gift, but then again, which of us should cash it in, me or Luke? Maybe, if I'm the worst wife in the history of the entire world, Luke will have no other option than to divorce me. I wonder how long it would take for me to drive him mad before he calls his lawyer?*

Does that make me sound callous? Anyway, what's done is done. Mum seems cured and Dad has got a spring in his step so I'm staying here today to help her disinfect the house (for some reason she thinks it will make her feel better) and spend a bit of time with them both. I just hope I can steer her away from the subject of the wedding, although I doubt it. They're both happy for me to go to the beach on Thursday as they'll be busy elsewhere and I don't fancy watching Dad play pétanque or helping eight-year-olds with their spelling.

Poor Stacey hasn't got a clue about any of this so I'm also guilty of stringing her along every time I reply to her messages. I've got to ring Luke now as I missed his call yesterday, okay, I ignored it, but I had nothing to say to him anyway. His text just went on about winning 5–0 at five-a-side and, hold the front page, Jacko has had another tattoo. Absolutely fascinating! And you know what else is weird and annoying, or both, is that I don't think he's really that bothered when he can't get hold of me. He's not suspicious or pining either... how sad is that? Well, that's it for today. I will update you on my freak show life later on tonight. Wish me luck with Luke and the bleach-monster because I'm going to need it.

Fill you in later, Diary x

Tilly threw herself onto her back and stared at the ceiling. Her conversation with Luke had been, scintillating (not), however, she somehow managed to make her day sound interesting, innocent and completely Joe free. Luke on the other hand seemed forced and slightly irritable, which was nothing fresh and probably her fault for ringing him at work. He was always tetchy and lacked concentration when she spoke to him in the office, not that she really cared.

It was so tempting to ring Stacey and tell her all about Joe, then she thought better of it. She might come across as a lovesick teenager and put her friend in a predicament. Not only that, it might set Stacey off on the 'end it' mono-logue and Tilly knew her comments wouldn't be aimed at Joe, it was Luke she wanted out on his ear!

Closing her eyes, Tilly could picture Joe's lovely face the night before. It caused her heart to flip.

* * *

They'd parked at the end of her lane and talked under the moonlight in the camper. Tilly had told him to stop there, just in case the sound of the engine woke Didier's three dogs and they started to bark, because once they were off there was no stopping them. The last thing she wanted was one of her parents coming outside to say hi or getting into a conversation, God only knew what they'd mention.

Joe had been talking about their upcoming day at the beach and what time they would be setting off, when Tilly asked a question which was supposed to lead to her confession. It didn't go quite how she had planned.

'Are you sure your mum doesn't mind me coming along? She looked a bit put out when you told her earlier and I've got a feeling that she's not too keen on me. I think I know why and I'm not surprised really, it's because I've got a boyfriend.' Once she'd brought him up, all Tilly had to do was say the next bit, the part she'd rehearsed where she would say 'well she's really going to hate me when I tell you this'.

Then Joe butted in and the moment was lost.

'She does like you, why wouldn't she? But you might be right about the boyfriend part. Mum's probably a bit wary because of Luke but I swear she's not being mean or judgemental, she's just cautious after what happened to her.' Joe paused for a second. It was as though he was scrabbling for the right words.

'Why, what happened to your mum?' Tilly was concerned and also inquisitive.

Joe looked over to Tilly, he was wide-eyed and sincere. 'Right, if I tell you, you've got to promise this stays just between you and me. It's not common knowledge or something she ever talks about, okay?' When he heard Tilly promise, Joe turned towards the windscreen and in a hushed tone, carried on.

'About four years ago, my dad was killed in a car crash. We were all devastated but just before it happened, Mum found out he was having an affair. She kept it a secret for ages and the whole thing tore her apart. When I found out, at first I couldn't believe it and then when I got my head round it all, well, let's say it left me with a less than perfect image of my dad and a dislike for anyone who cheats. My mum obviously feels the same way, not that anyone is accusing you of that, but the fact you're with someone *will* play on her mind. I swore on the day I found out that I would never, ever be unfaithful and in her own way Mum's just trying to protect me from going through what she did.'

Joe swallowed and turned to face Tilly who was lost for words.

'Look, I know that you are with Luke and some people might say that we shouldn't be spending all this time together, especially alone, but as far as I can see we're doing nothing wrong. I really like being with you and as long as you're okay with it, I don't feel like I'm being a big hypocrite and my mum hasn't got anything to worry about.'

Joe was obviously looking for confirmation, agreement or just something positive from Tilly who had thankfully found her voice.

'God, Joe, that's awful! Your poor mum. I can't imagine how she got through all that. She must be an incredibly strong person. And I totally respect you for your views and having morals. But nobody can throw stones our way because we are just friends who enjoy each other's company, and if I'm honest, I don't want to stop hanging out with you just because of what other people might think. Will you tell your mum that we are on the same page and I wouldn't do anything at all to offend her?' Tilly smiled hopefully at Joe who looked slightly drained from telling his story.

'Course I will. And we'll have a fab day at the beach on Thursday. I'm looking forward to it.'

'Right, that's settled then. I'm sure Mum and Dad will be fine about me tagging along with you, so I'll say goodnight and ring you tomorrow, just to confirm times and stuff.' Tilly felt deflated and needed to get inside and unscramble her head.

Closing the van door quietly, Tilly gave Joe a quick wave and then ran up the dark lane.

After letting herself into the silent house, Tilly crept towards her bedroom and nearly died of fright when a voice said, 'Boo!' It was her dad, obviously amused, chuckling away in his armchair where he was having a quiet cup of tea. The only light came from the silver moon that bathed the lounge in an eerie glow and cast creepy shadows into corners of the room.

'Are you okay, love? Sorry I scared you but I couldn't resist. What have you been up to, sneaking in like that? I hope you've been behaving yourself.'

Howard was only teasing but Tilly went on the defence, just in case.

'Bloody hell, Dad! You've just taken ten years off my life and for your information I haven't been up to anything. I just didn't want to wake you or get Didier's hounds barking. Honestly, you are such a drama queen. Anyway, where's Mum, is she asleep?'

'Yes, she's well away and keep your hair on, I was only teasing. Come on, let's call it a night. You can tell me all about what mischief you've been making tomorrow. I know that look Tilly Parker, it's the same as when I caught you climbing through the kitchen window, remember, when you sneaked out of your room to meet that lad from off the estate? You can't kid your old dad.'

Howard ruffled her hair and laughed, and still not sure if he was onto her or not, Tilly quickly kissed him goodnight and fled to the sanctuary of her bedroom.

The stillness of the four stone walls provided her with a safe haven and some welcome peace, from where she could dissect Joe's surprise revelation. First off, Anna was a victim of unfaithfulness and, as a direct result, the whole family hated cheaters. She'd actually felt her blood run cold as he said the words, knowing that her courage was abandoning her by the second and, after such an honest and personal conversation, there was no way she could hit him with her own horrible truth. If Tilly knew one thing, the moment she mentioned the word wedding, whatever dynamic there was between her and Joe, any hope of a happy ever after, would shrivel and die.

Then it occurred to Tilly that Anna had kept secrets too, from her children of all people and she must have felt justified in doing so. Tilly also had secrets. She wasn't in love with her fiancé, she didn't want to get married and there was a damn good chance she was actually falling for Joe. Her reasons for secrecy were equally noble and for the good of everyone.

Her only hope now was to impress Joe to the max with her personality, then, when she was forced to tell him the truth, she might be able to make him understand why she had behaved this way and persuade him to wait for her. It was a crazy, risky long shot but still worth a try.

What a mess! What a truly awful mess.

Tilly lay awake for most of the night concocting 'what if' scenarios in her head, imagining things she shouldn't, wondering what it would be like to be with Joe in every sense possible and when her heart couldn't take the pain of not knowing any longer, she gave in to tears and cried herself to sleep.

* * *

When she was roused from her slumbers the following morning by Freda and her mop bucket, humming something tuneless and slip slopping along the hall outside her bedroom, Tilly was exhausted and none the wiser. She dragged herself out of bed to face the music and the smell of bleach and decided to put her best foot forward and face the day head-on, no matter how much it dragged. Tilly knew she would spend it watching the kitchen clock tick slowly by as she counted down the hours until she could see Joe again.

Freda sloshed the mop along the hall, hoping that Tilly would wake up soon. She felt so much better and a lot lighter, which was the only silver lining in the dark cloud of the sickness bug. Yes, she may have paid a hard price for a looser waistband and wouldn't recommend it as the most pleasant way of shedding a few pounds, but she was on the mend and even if it was slightly perverse, quite chuffed with her new figure.

Today, the house would be sterilised and rendered germ-free. Tilly had offered to help and Freda was happy to be spending some time with her daughter who had been such an angel while they were sick, and hadn't complained a bit about being left to fend for herself.

Freda acknowledged that a) Tilly was a nurse and used to illness, b) She was a big girl and quite able to look after herself for a few days, and c) She hadn't exactly been on her own thanks to that nice Anna and her family. Nevertheless, she was supposed to be on holiday and the first few days had been ruined by their bug. Well, today they could catch-up and once the cleaning was done they were going to pop into town and get some fresh, healthy supplies then sit out in the garden and relax. Perfect.

On the other side of the valley, Anna's day had started surprisingly well, owing mainly to having Jeannie around, which made her feel bolder than usual, now that Louise was on unfamiliar territory and the shoe was firmly on the other foot.

The previous evening, when the new sleeping arrangements were discussed, Joe and Sam both offered to give up their bunks and sleep outside in the camper. Before anyone could accept, Anna put her foot down and suggested that Jules either slept in the bunk room on a spare camp bed or topped and tailed with Ross. Louise could share with Mel as there were two single beds in her room – it was either that or the sofa. If Jules wasn't keen on either option, he could snuggle up with his mummy because there was no way Melanie was giving up her bedroom *or* the boys being turfed outside on account of Louise. That was for damn sure!

Luckily, both Ross and Jules were getting along famously and seemed thrilled at the opportunity to share a room and prolong their evening. Mel had caught them shining torches and pulling scary faces in the dark and going by the sticky remnants of sweets that were now welded to the duvet, they'd somehow managed to smuggle a secret feast to their room.

Melanie said she was happy to share with Louise, despite hearing horror stories from her mother about how mean she had been, and decided to give her the benefit of the doubt and a second chance. Having said that, if at any time her new roomy got out of line, she'd soon put her in her place because Mel wasn't a soft touch, not like her mum.

Breakfast had gone well, the kids wolfed down their food and then ran off to explore and play. Sam was currently helping them make a den at the back of the small barn from plastic sheeting and odd bits of wood. As planned, today was going to be spent relaxing by the pool and sunbathing in the garden. Daniel and Phil had offered to cook so all the ladies had to do was provide the ingredients, which required a quick whizz down to the supermarket.

Fortuitously, while everyone was either taking a shower, reading the paper or searching for useful bits of wood in the garden, Anna got the opportunity to speak to Joe. He had let his guard down and found himself alone and unprotected in the kitchen.

'No Tilly today, I take it her parents have recovered now?' Anna dried the dishes and kept an eye on her son as she waited for his answer.

'Good spot, Sherlock! Tilly's spending the day with her mum, she's a lot better so they're doing a bit of cleaning or something, but she's coming to the beach tomorrow. You don't mind her tagging along do you?' Joe continued drinking his tea, waiting for the inevitable.

'No, not really, but what do you think her boyfriend would say if he knew she was spending so much time with you? And don't say that she's hanging out with Sam as well because that's not true and you know it.' Anna was on a roll now and felt quite justified in her line of questioning, even though Joe was almost twenty-eight and big enough to make his own mistakes.

'Mum... I know where this is going so just to set your mind at rest, we've both made it quite clear to each other that we are just friends. I respect the fact that she's got a boyfriend and she respects him. End of story, okay!' Joe got up and washed his mug in the sink and waited to use the tea towel that his mum was holding.

'That's all well and good, Joe, very honourable and exactly what everyone wants to hear, apart from the tiny flaw in your argument which is the way you look at her and vice versa. And she's not exactly loved-up where her boyfriend is concerned, is she? She hardly ever mentions him and if anyone else does, she soon changes the subject. Now compare Tilly to Melanie who never shuts up about

Pascal and maybe then, you might see my point.' Anna had surpassed herself with the case for the prosecution so she waited patiently to hear what the moody looking defence had to say.

'Well, maybe she's a private type of person who doesn't feel the need to tell everyone the ins and outs of her relationship, or perhaps she's just enjoying having a bit of time apart from him, it happens, who knows? And to be honest, Mum, I don't care. She's a nice girl who I get on with and so does Sam and Mel, so I really don't see the problem. It's not like we've been at it like rabbits while you've been out, so can you just drop it? There really isn't an issue apart from the one you're inventing and making a song and dance out of it, as usual!' Joe looked a bit narked as he held out his hand.

Anna could tell he was eager to get away so passed him the tea towel which he just about managed not to snatch from her grasp, dried his mug and placed it back on the shelf. The thing was she had come this far and couldn't give up now.

'Joe, there's no need to speak to me like that! I am not making trouble. I just want you to be careful that's all.'

'Mum, I get it, just leave it okay.'

'No, Joe, I don't think you do. How would you feel if she was your girlfriend? Would you be happy for her to be taken out for lunch, spend a day at the seaside and hang out at another man's house?'

'Yes, if they were just friends, and if you didn't notice, that's exactly how we behaved so what is your problem?'

'I'll tell you what my problem is… just remember that if she behaves like that with you, she could do the same with anyone… she makes me uneasy that's all. We don't know anything about her apart from what she tells you, so if you do have any romantic notions about her, which I know for a *fact* you won't admit to, you're treading on thin ice.' Anna heard the dramatic sigh and saw the bored roll of Joe's eyes and knew she was pushing her luck so decided to back off.

'That said, I've got to let you make your own mistakes so

now I've said my piece, I'll stay out of it.' Anna felt slightly flushed and could sense that what started off as a casual conversation was on the verge of turning into a heated debate. And she certainly didn't appreciate his condescending tone, either.

'Right, Mum, I get the message, but you've no need to worry because I won't see her after Sunday and then the problem, as you see it, will be solved. Can you just let it go and leave me to look after myself? I'm sure I can manage.'

Joe looked a little bit taken aback by the veracity of her argument. Maybe he didn't like Tilly being cast as some kind of scarlet woman, but Anna hoped that something in the recesses of his mind told him she could be right, and that mere fact pained her the most.

'Okay, Joe, I won't say another word, apart from I don't trust her and I can sense that she's not on the level, call it a mum's intuition if you like. But if she makes you happy then she's welcome here. The last thing I want is to fall out with you so I promise I will back off, Guide's honour.' Anna smiled, knowing when to give in and hoped that they could leave it there and be friends.

Joe didn't smile back, instead he just passed her the tea towel, totally ignoring her final comment and made towards the door.

'I'm going to find Sam and the kids, oh and by the way, Pippa's sitting on Louise's posh bag. You'd best move it before she comes down and sees her.' And with that he was gone.

Anna sighed and went into the lounge to shoo the dog off the settee and brush the hairs and dribble off a very nice Louis Vuitton. As she hastily removed the evidence, she didn't know who she was more annoyed with, Pippa, Joe, Tilly or herself.

Tilly was sure that she smelled of bleach and her hair had a whiff of furniture polish about it too. Once Freda was satisfied that her house was a germ-free zone, they set off for the supermarket to buy fresh provisions. Tilly insisted on driving after informing her mum that she shouldn't do too much, all at once, and needed to give her body chance to recover, otherwise she would end up back in bed. Taking heed of her daughter, Freda allowed Tilly to take control and supervise the purchases and left the store without anything remotely stodgy or laden with calories. For the next few days, Tilly was insisting on light meals and plenty of fluids (preferably alcohol-free) so their bodies could rehydrate and recover gently.

They had just finished loading the shopping and were fastening their seat belts when Tilly spotted a familiar car bearing English number plates entering the car park, and nearly threw up all over the steering wheel. There were umpteen empty bays available but no, they had to choose the space right opposite and yes, just as she suspected, Anna and Jeannie got out. To make matters a million times worse, her eagle-eyed mother clocked them instantly and began waving to attract their attention.

'Oh look, Tilly, there's that nice Anna who you've been visiting, wind your window down so I can say hello, bother, she's not seen us, honk your horn to attract her attention.' Freda was leaning across the driver's seat and waving like a lunatic as Anna went into the plastic hut and pulled out a trolley.

Tilly was having none of it, completely ignoring her mother and instead put the car into gear and pulled out, driving straight past Anna who spotted Freda's frantic waving, just as the car sped by.

'Tilly, what on earth are you doing? I wanted to say hello, what is the matter with you, have you fallen out with her or something? Now she'll think we're rude!' Freda sounded really ticked off with Tilly whose cheeks felt like fire.

Completely flustered, she was desperately trying to think of an excuse for her behaviour and mortified that she'd had to drive past Anna, who it had to be said, looked rather bemused as they zoomed by.

'Sorry, Mum, I really need the loo, I feel a bit odd. I think it's best we get home quickly, just in case. I don't want to get caught short or be sick in the car. Anna will understand, I'll explain when I see her, so no harm done.' Tilly kept her eyes on the road and avoided eye contact with Freda and for added effect, gave a little grimace and rubbed her stomach as she drove.

'Oh no, I bet you're coming down with our bug. You do look a bit flushed come to think of it. I flipping knew this would happen. I suppose it's better now than next week.' Freda put her hand on Tilly's forehead and tutted as if to confirm a high temperature and the onset of the dreaded virus.

'Mum, stop fussing. I'll be fine. It might just be something I ate. Let's go home and see how I am, there's no need to panic.' But Tilly did feel a bit sick and she wasn't sure whether it was the close encounter or talk of her guests arriving that unsettled her stomach. One thing was for sure, she wasn't cut out for a life on the edge, or subterfuge, because her jangling nerves just couldn't take it.

Anna was perturbed about two things. The first worrying occurrence was to do with Tilly who had just blanked her in the car park of the supermarket, and the other was that once again, in less than twenty-four hours, Louise was beginning to irritate her. Jeannie was too busy looking for her purse to witness Tilly's snub, which really was pecking Anna's head.

'Found it! It was under the front seat, I thought I'd lost it. Right, let's get going before we miss all the sun. I want to do my back today. What's wrong, why are you standing there?' Jeannie was proudly holding up her missing purse and eager to get on.

'Did you see that? Tilly just drove straight past and totally ignored me! Her mum was waving but she just looked straight ahead and shot off out of the car park.

What's got into her?' Anna was standing by her shopping trolley, perplexed.

'Really! Maybe Joe's text her and told her what you said about her being a bit of a slapper. You're lucky she didn't run you over.' Jeannie was laughing but Anna didn't find it at all amusing.

'Oh God, I bet that's it. Do you really think he'd be that stupid to repeat our conversation? Surely he would've kept it to himself, but he did look really annoyed with me so perhaps he has blabbed. The bloody idiot! And just for the record, I did not call her a slapper, stop exaggerating.' Anna really had enough on her mind without Tilly adding to her woes.

As they trundled inside with their wonky-wheeled trolley, Anna's brain was consumed by thoughts of two annoying women, Tilly *and* Louise. For now, Anna resolved to concentrate on the latter, more determined than ever to ignore her petty comments and wouldn't rise to it or, fall out with Daniel because of his daughter.

There had been three minor incidents that she had dealt with swiftly and with minimal fuss, yet Anna was convinced that it was a taste of things to come and that Louise was gearing up for a repeat performance of Christmas, now that she had her feet under the table. Funnily enough, it was a comment about the same piece of furniture that started it off.

* * *

They had eaten breakfast outside that morning, mainly because the table in the garden was bigger and the weather not as chilly as previous days. Everyone was happily eating Anna's version of a luxury continental breakfast or drinking coffee, when Louise made the first of her disparaging statements.

'Why is your garden furniture at the front of the house? I've noticed that a lot of country houses have their plastic bits and bobs on show for everyone to see. I can't understand why rural families feel the urge to eat in full view of passing cars and their neighbours. Everyone I know has their furniture in the back garden where it's more private.' Louise flicked away a crumb and waited.

Anna was trying to think of an answer, and it didn't go unnoticed that Louise had winced theatrically as she tasted the Nescafé Gold Blend.

'I've noticed that too, but in our case it's because we get a lot of sun on the front all through the day and there's just enough room for my vegetable patch and the washing line in the back. Anyway, nobody can see us from the road so we are still quite private and there's loads of space here as well.' Anna thought she'd laid that criticism to rest quite well.

Next, Anna's culinary skills came under scrutiny. Sam had asked if anybody wanted the remainder of the fruit salad that she'd made fresh and presented in her favourite rustic platter. It looked extremely wholesome and everyone had tucked in. Once he got the green light to finish it off, Sam scraped the fruit and juice into his bowl and continued to eat in silence until once again, Louise had something to share with the group.

'I do enjoy fruit salad but find it can be a bit bland. I always add a dash of fresh mint and chopped nuts, Dad loves mint, don't you, Dad? Have you ever thought of adding some cheese made from sheep's milk, Anna, it's delicious?' Louise glanced down at her half-eaten bowl of salad, just to push home the point.

'I can't add nuts as Summer's allergic to them and none of us like that type of cheese. Your dad's a big boy and knows where to get mint from if he's desperate, there's a giant bush of it in the back garden.'

Anna couldn't hide the irritation in her voice which caused Daniel to turn away from talking to Phil and give Louise a hard stare.

There was an uncomfortable silence around the table for a few seconds until Jeannie diverted the conversation onto something she'd seen on Sky News, which continued amiably for a while until Sam asked Anna to pick up some sun cream for the beach the next day.

'Who's going to the beach? Oh God, that's my idea of complete torture at this time of year. It will be jam-packed with families and annoying kids kicking balls about, and there's never any shade. I avoid taking Jules to the sea unless it's a mild day and tomorrow will be boiling. You must be mad! Why don't we go into Nantes and do some shopping and have lunch? It will be lovely and cool in the malls and I could do with picking up a few things, who fancies that?'

There wasn't exactly a show of excited, eager hands, just a sea of blank, unenthusiastic faces accompanied by a chill in the atmosphere. Anna was just about to open her mouth when Daniel got in before her.

'Stop complaining, Louise. We've got parasols and a sun tent for the kids so you can hide in there if you get too hot and just so you can't say we didn't warn you, we'll be one of those annoying families with kids who kick balls about. If you don't want to come, we'll take Jules and you can have a day on your own shopping in Nantes. He'll be fine with us.' Daniel let his words settle on his mildly stunned daughter then carried on his conversation with Phil.

Anna decided to take some plates into the kitchen in an attempt to hide the huge grin of satisfaction that spread across her face, thanks mainly to Daniel doing *and* saying the right thing, for once!

By the time the dishes were done and she'd finished offending Joe and shouting at the dog, Jeannie was finally ready and they headed off towards the car. Out of politeness, Anna invited Louise along, thinking that a jaunt around the supermarket might satisfy her urge for retail therapy. The reply only served to wind her up even more.

'No thanks, Anna, I hate food shopping, it's *so* tedious. I do all mine online which is almost as dreary as actually trudging around the supermarket. I'll stay here and spend some time with Dad. We need some quality time together to catch-up, don't we?'

Louise slipped her arm through her father's, who at least

had the grace to look embarrassed and annoyed at his daughter's crass comments.

By this time, Anna was thoroughly sick of Louise's grating voice and was glad she wasn't coming, so she turned and followed Jeannie to the car without passing comment, it was too risky. Once inside, the air turned blue as they indulged each other in giving Louise a royal slagging off, all the way to the shops.

* * *

When they pulled into the drive later, everyone was playing cricket on the lawn, minus Louise who it seemed had gone for a lie down after a screaming match via telephone with Tomas. He was none too pleased that she had taken Jules without telling him. It also hadn't gone down too well when she got a good ticking off from her dad, the second Anna was out of sight. This snippet of information came via Philip who had a juicy bit of gossip, which he'd passed straight on to Jeannie as soon as the coast was clear.

It seemed that Louise hadn't exactly been telling the whole truth where Tomas was concerned and the only reason she was found out, was because Daniel answered her phone while she was in the loo. Tomas told his astounded father-in-law just how livid he was that Louise had upped sticks with his son, thus depriving him of time together before he left for a business trip. Whilst Tomas admitted it was bad timing, he had a long-standing commitment to give a series of lectures and his reputation would be damaged if he pulled out at the last minute. Louise, it seemed, was fully aware of his plans and desire to see Jules, and had purposely prevented Tomas saying au revoir.

Anna was furious. Poor distressed Louise must've thought she was so clever. Punishing Tomas via his son while conning everyone into thinking she had fled north to seek comfort when in fact, she probably just fancied a bit of a break and a bucketful of attention.

Jeannie wholeheartedly agreed then pointed out that she

would be feeling rather stupid now, knowing that Daniel would tell Anna the truth. From all accounts, she went ballistic on the phone, screaming so loudly that everyone was now privy to the finer points of her marriage and, in particular, her husband's growing list of failings, which Philip said were a bit on the rude side.

Daniel was furious with his daughter for preventing a father from saying goodbye to his son. As for the fact that she had been rather sparing with the truth, he warned her that not only would he not tolerate lies, he wouldn't take her side either. Just to make sure she got the message, Daniel advised her to pull herself together and sort her marriage out because running away certainly wasn't the answer.

Louise was absolutely furious with Tomas and utterly shocked by her father's treacherous reaction, not being used to a telling off, she stomped upstairs to bed.

Knowing that Billy Fibber was out of the way for a while and that Daniel had grown some previously mislaid parts of his anatomy, Anna settled herself in for an afternoon of being waited on hand and foot and basking in the glory of being top of the leader board where scoring points was concerned. Hopefully, once sleeping beauty rose from her slumbers, she would be in a more good-natured mood, but until then, Anna was going to put her *and* the curious event with Tilly out of her mind. Instead she would take pleasure in the beauty of her front garden with its plastic bits and bobs, admire the sun-baked, pastoral surroundings and enjoy a nice bottle of the local Sancerre.

Tomorrow was beach day, and everyone was looking forward to visiting Anna's favourite seaside location, which would be followed by their traditional pizza dinner at a nearby Italian restaurant. She had Jeannie for backup, her family all around her and if she was really lucky, the two interlopers, Tilly and Louise, might just cry off and stay behind.

. . .

But as we all know, whilst ever the hopeful, Anna is never that lucky. Where Daddy Daniel and Lovesick Joe were concerned, her female adversaries were going nowhere fast, and despite her wishful thinking, both would stick like the proverbial superglue to their blankets!

CHAPTER NINE

Dear Diary,
    I can't stay for long as I'm waiting for Joe to pick
    me up. I was too tired and grumpy to talk to you last
night, thanks to Luke! He got a bit arsey with me because I kept
yawning throughout the conversation and then he had the cheek
to tell me that I was being uncommunicative and purposely vague.
I suppose if I'm honest, I wasn't exactly Little Miss Chatty but
really... what could I actually tell him that was remotely interesting or God forbid – the truth? I didn't think he'd want to know
the ins and outs of my day which entailed a cleaning routine that
would put Mr Sheen to shame, then a wander around a supermarket that I've been to ten trillion times. This whacky adventure
was followed by an afternoon and evening in the garden with
Mum and Dad, reading the same line of my book over and over
and trying to steer them off the dreaded subject. I'm sure he
would've been thrilled to know that the real highlights of my day
were one phone call and about twenty texts from Joe, oh and let's
not forget my getaway routine in the car park when I saw Anna.
Due to the fact that I had to ad lib about feeling poorly, Mum
forbade me anything remotely alcoholic and insisted I drink warm
water or herbal tea. Yuck! I could've murdered a glass or two of
wine, or a whole bottle, at least it would've numbed my brain and
given me a good night's sleep. I even managed to tell another fib to

Joe when he asked me about driving past his mum at the super-market. I had no alternative but to repeat the story I'd told Mum, but this time, I said it was her who needed the loo, not me, and I had to get her home quickly to avoid pebble-dashing the car. He seemed to fall for it so hopefully I'm out of the woods and haven't done anything else to annoy Anna or deserve the evil eye. In the end, Luke apologised for being tetchy and blamed it on working overtime and forgetting to pick up his suit from the cleaners, he needed it for his seminar, or should I say all expenses paid, two day shirk. I said sorry too for being the dullest fiancée in the world (I felt I owed him that at least) and I could've added plenty of other adjectives to my description but it might have given the game away, so I left it at that. It would've been nice if he'd disagreed about my failings but instead he just sort of laughed and said he was knackered and going to bed. Charming! I need to get ready now and get my peace offerings out of the fridge. Joe said I didn't need to bring anything but I feel that I should take some-thing for the picnic so I bought a huge box of strawberries and a lovely bottle of crémant and I'll get the kids an ice cream while I'm there. There's only you who I can really confide in and under-stands why I can't see Joe again after today. I could literally weep knowing that this will really have to be my last few hours with him. Mum reminded me that we've got to go over to Rosie's on Sunday and go through the menu with Michel. It's also Joe's last day here, so on either Friday or Saturday, I'm going to have to do the deed, and I'm dreading it. Even if he doesn't feel the same way about me, I know how I feel about him, and it gives me a pain in my chest just facing up to never seeing him again. Maybe he will forgive me and we can stay friends but that would be a torment so it's better that I just end it. Mum and Dad have been so lovely to me, even when they were ill they just wanted me to be happy, like they always have. I've got to let them have this one day, haven't I? Don't answer that, I know what you are going to say, I've heard it all from Stacey. Bless her, she's trying to lose a few pounds because her dress is a bit too tight and she wants to make room for the wedding feast. I sent her the menu which she stuck on the fridge and has been salivating over ever since. I ask you, how can I deny my best friend her five-star lunch? She'd never forgive me! I'll fill you in on my day when I come home. I want to write everything down so that I never forget one single detail. If I put it into words, then I can read them again and again if the memories start to fade. I'm going to get some photos of Joe today, then I'll be able to look at his face whenever I want to, even if he can't be mine for real.

Got to go now, he'll be here any minute. Thank goodness Mum's teaching and Dad's at the end of the garden digging up beans, so I should be able to sneak out. Bye, Diary, wish me luck!

* * *

Joe had been up for ages and had hardly slept a wink. His mind was full of lustful, tormented thoughts and he knew he was behaving like a lovesick teenager. He'd felt like this since they'd parted company at the end of her lane, Tilly's face and name never far from his thoughts.

After he'd watched her step through the gate, Joe started the engine and drove off. The road ahead had been pitch black, a bit like his mood. He hadn't managed to say what he intended or ask the questions that might give him a clue as to how she felt.

Instead, after exposing his dad's imperfections, Joe had then confirmed he was the complete opposite and a perfect gentleman. To make everything a million times worse, Tilly then went on to pour cold water on any hopes he had about her ditching Luke. Her impassioned affirmation of their 'just friends' status merely confirmed this. Or had their family history and his mother's evil eye, scared Tilly off?

Joe had decided there was only one thing for it, he'd ask Sam and then, act on whatever advice his brother gave. One thing he knew for sure, he wasn't going to give up and before they headed south on Monday, he'd know if there was any shred of hope with Tilly, and if there was, he'd cling on to that. In the meantime, he'd do his very best to impress the life out of her, that bit he thought, was easy.

Unfortunately, his talk with Sam had done nothing to soothe his troubled soul and in fact, had only served to

124

encourage his fanciful notions of somehow having a relationship with Tilly. As the sun set in the west, Sam, Joe and Pippa took a walk down the lane and while the diva sniffed out rabbits, or whatever else lurked in the undergrowth, the two brothers managed to get some time away from their screeching cousins and watchful mother and had a heart to heart.

Joe was half listening to Sam going through a list of essential items they needed to buy for their upcoming trip, but he wasn't really concentrating, his mind was elsewhere. Whilst he pondered on the best way to broach the subject of Tilly, Sam finally put him out of his misery.

'Are you listening to what I'm saying or is your mind on a certain nurse who lives not a million miles from here? Mate, you really have got it bad haven't you? I've never seen you like this, apart from when you had a crush on that girl who worked at the chippy... what was her name? Can't think of it now but you spent a fortune in there. No wonder you had spots and greasy hair. I bet that's why she never fancied you!'

Sam was clearly tickled by his own observations, however, his anecdotes didn't amuse Joe or raise even a faint smile to his lips.

'She was called Lacy and actually, she did fancy me. It's just that her dad had a chain round her ankle so she couldn't leave the shop, otherwise we'd be married now with six kids, all with greasy hair and zits.' Joe forced a grin and shouted for Pippa who had squeezed through the hedge and was now trotting about the farmer's field.

Before Sam could wind him up any further, he continued. 'If you must know, I am thinking about Tilly and if you can manage not to take the mick, I need a bit of advice, though with your track record I'm not sure if it's the greatest idea I've ever had. My only other options are Daniel and Phil, so it looks like you're it.' Joe glanced quickly sideways to gauge his brother's reaction.

'Go on then, fire away, what's up? I can tell you like her

and before you start, from what I've seen, I'm sure she likes you too. So what's the problem, is it the boyfriend?'

Sam had hit the nail right on the head.

'Yep, you've got it in one. It's like it's fate. I remember when I met her last year and I thought she was pretty special then, like when you click with someone straight away. I didn't think I'd ever see her again but now it feels like it's meant to be. We got on really well at the music festival, even though it was just for a few hours and, if she'd been single then, I'd have made the effort to get her number and all that. In the end, we just said goodbye and she went off with him, the miserable boyfriend. I did think about her for a bit and always wondered if Mum would bump into them and mention her but it never happened, and then boom, I nearly ran her over. That's got to mean something, hasn't it, do you think it's fate or are you still a non-believer?' Joe was bursting to unburden his innermost thoughts but before he did, thought it prudent to check if Sam thought he was being a complete moron.

'Nah, you know I don't have any time for anything mumbo jumbo, but I do believe that you know when you meet someone special. The way I look at it, you let her walk away once and regretted it so just don't make the same mistake twice.' Sam was whacking the bushes on the side of the road with a stick he'd picked up along the way.

As he watched, it occurred to Joe that, despite his travels into war zones and the grown-up world in which Sam lived, there was always something of the carefree teenager left in his younger brother. Joe loved Sam's ability to see things simply, in an uncluttered, less complicated way, yet still embrace life and run headfirst into danger and situations that most would shy away from. Nothing seemed to faze Sam, and Joe envied and loved him for it in equal measure.

'The thing is I don't know what to do next. There's no way I would make a move while she's got a boyfriend but at the same time, I want her to know how I feel and see if she feels the same way. I'm going to look like a fool if she's just biding her time till Luke arrives next week and using me as entertainment. But when I think about it, she hardly ever mentions him and does her best to avoid getting into conversation about their relationship. That can only be a positive sign, can't it? Or is it just wishful thinking on my part?' Joe's head was buzzing with questions he desperately wanted only positive answers for.

'Well, I do think it's a bit weird that I've never seen her text him, or anyone really and I know for certain that he rang her the other day and she switched her phone off. I saw her do it while you went inside to get some drinks. She thought I hadn't noticed but I *am* a trained spy and never miss a trick. Maybe he's the jealous type who'd go apeshit about her hanging out with two top-class specimens, but something tells me she hasn't got much time for him. Perhaps Tilly's come here to escape and work out how she feels *or maybe*, they had a huge row and she stomped off to her mum's to teach him a lesson... like Louise. Honestly, mate, the best thing you can do is ask her. Don't say anything about how you feel until she's told you the score. Then if it's good news and she hates him, you can drop the hint that you're interested and see how she reacts.'

Sam made it all sound so easy.

'But don't you think that's really sly, telling somebody else's girlfriend you like them? Mum's already made it clear that she's not happy about Tilly hanging around and is suspicious of her motives. She thinks I'm going to get hurt by a black widow or something just as flaming dramatic. You know why she's like that, but Tilly is really nice and I can't see her being a two-timer or the type to use someone either.'

Joe waited for a response but Sam was engrossed elsewhere, prodding a snake hole with his stick.

'And what if she still runs a mile when I tell her I like her, how embarrassing would that be? It's easy for you. You're loads more confident than me and never seem to have any trouble with women, whereas I always pick the wrong one.'

Joe was talking himself out of things and going by Sam's raised eyebrows and withering look, he knew it.

'No way is it sly, just human nature, that's all. Loads of blokes chat girls up and flirt even when they're attached, most of the time it's harmless fun and anyway, it's not like she acts all loved-up. Let's face it, she probably suspects you like her and is more than likely wondering the same thing. You only live once so just suss her out, see how the land lies. Say it in a jokey way, as long she gets the message loud and clear.'

Sam hoped that he'd got through, but he was wrong.

'Okay, just so we're on the same page here, what message *am* I trying to give her?'

Joe could sometimes take caution to another level.

'Bloody hell, Joe! Just tell her that if she's sick of her boring, miserable boyfriend and has any intention of dumping him now or in the future, you will be there, ready, willing and able but until that time you think she's a great girl and you are happy to be friends and stay in touch. Have you got it now?' Sam stopped in the lane and waited for a response.

When Joe's face lit up it was clear that he'd received the message, over and out!

'Sam, you are brilliant. You make it all seem so clear and logical. That's exactly what I'm going to say, I just need to remember it. I'll practice. Either way I can't lose, can I? We can still be mates while I wait for her to make up her mind no matter how long it takes, because I'm sure she's sick of him. I can just tell. Anyway, we'd best get back, Mum was making crêpes and they might eat them all. Shit! Where's Pippa?'

Joe and Sam looked warily around them and scanned the lane but she was nowhere to be seen.

Sam ran over to the wire separating the field from the lane and called out to Joe.

'You've got to be kidding me! I bet she's gone into the corn. That flipping dog drives me mad. Come on, we'd best go in and look for her, she'll be sorry if the farmer comes with his gun, or his tractor.'

Sam ducked under the wire, however, Joe wasn't too keen on the idea.

'No way am I going in there, Daniel says there's snakes in the corn and we've only got flip-flops on, what if we get bitten?' Joe remained firmly on the other side of the wire.

'Stop being soft and get in, if there are any snakes they'll be more scared of us, or Fatty, come on, man up. If I see one I'll whack it with this stick. And best not tell Mum, it'll all be our fault, not the princess's.'

With that, Tilly was forgotten as Joe ducked under the wire and gingerly entered the field where they spent the next half hour chasing a giddy bulldog through the rows and rows and rows of corn.

Pippa loved every minute and thought it was a great game and only gave up when she ran out of puff and needed a drink. The farmer on the other hand had a right old tale to tell everyone in the village bar the next morning. He was convinced that aliens had landed in his field overnight as there were strange imprints in his corn and they looked just like those crop circles he'd seen on the news. By lunchtime, the story had taken on legs and now everyone in the village was on the lookout for glowing objects in the sky and swirly space men patterns in their fields.

* * *

While Joe waited at the end of the lane for Tilly to appear, he was completely oblivious to the village gossip that had been ignited by Pippa's rampage the night before. All he could think of was his chat with Sam and spending a day at the beach. When he saw her appear at the gate, waving happily as she ran towards him, her dark hair swinging in a ponytail and her flowery sundress floating in the breeze,

Joe's heart flipped and he admitted to himself that he'd really got it bad!

If Tilly thought she was going to have Joe all to herself on the ride to the beach she was wrong, because the camper was almost full. Owing to the fact that Louise had appeared, there had been a reshuffle where transport was concerned and, along with Sam, who was driving, they were accompanied by Melanie, Jules and Ross who were thrilled to bits to be travelling in the back of the bus. Summer always stuck like glue to Jeannie so joined the grown-ups in the people carrier, along with Pippa who was coming along for a swim in the sea.

Joe, ever the gentleman slid across the bench seat and let Tilly sit next to the window and once everyone was secured and belted in, they set off to rendezvous in the village with the others.

It was going to be quite a crowd, Zofia and Dominique and two of the people they cared for were joining the convoy to St Marc so there was an excited buzz inside all the vehicles as they tooted their horns and began their journey.

Well, two out of three vehicles had a happy vibe because in Phil's car, there was a bit of an atmosphere once again down to Lady Louise not knowing when to keep her mouth shut.

Anna could definitely feel a tension headache coming on and they'd been on the road for less than five minutes. It had started with the picnic inquisition and almost ended with a game of musical car seats and the cold-blooded murder of Louise.

Most sensible, worldly-wise, normal members of the sisterhood knew only too well that to interfere in another woman's kitchen is dicing with death, a notion that seemed to have completely passed Louise by. And so it was that at 8am that morning, while baguettes were sliced (with extremely sharp knives), eggs boiled and the picnic box rammed with drinks, salad cream, and anything else that twelve hungry people may desire, Louise continually picked, criticised, compared and asked stupidly annoying questions like—

'Why do you need so much food?'

'Why are you making sandwiches? The French never make sandwiches!'

'Do you really need all these bags of crisps?'

'I hate boiled eggs, they smell awful and who eats salad cream these days?'

'Are you making me a salad?'

The answers were as follows—

'Sam!'

'Because we're English and that's what we do!'

'Yes!'

'We do!'

'No!'

When Anna went to the drawer and brought out her meat cleaver, staring at Louise with a glazed look in her eye, Melanie got the giggles and pretended to be washing up until Jeannie took matters into her own hands and yelled,

'Why don't you just sod off and stop bloody interfering and while you're at it, do something useful like getting the kids ready!'

This thankfully prompted a huffy but swift departure from the room followed by a few giggles and a smattering of swear words.

Once everything was stowed (rammed) in the car and camper and the kids had all been for a final wee, the afore-mentioned seating performance began. Daniel had volunteered to drive the people carrier because he knew the way to the beach with his eyes shut so Phil took the co-pilot's seat in the front, as was male tradition. It was then that Louise announced in a whiny voice that she needed to sit next to her father due to her propensity for car sickness.

Just as Anna made a wish, she heard Jeannie mutter something very unladylike, causing them both to stifle a giggle. However, Anna's wish wasn't granted because Louise didn't spontaneously combust, and as for Daniel, he just stood there, forlorn and mute.

Daniel was reminded of schooldays, when the teacher moved your best mate and forbade you to sit next to him on a coach trip, leaving you next to the school swot or worse, a girl!

Within seconds an uncomfortable silence descended around the car as everyone got shuffled about. He knew Phil had taken the huff and now sat with Anna who had Pippa squashed in the middle. On the up side, for once Jeannie had remained silent and was otherwise occupied with Summer, colouring in a Barbie book. He then did his best to act like he didn't want to push his own flesh and blood onto the middle lane of the autoroute, especially when she reclined her seat, pulled down her sunglasses and went to sleep.

To make matters worse, while he attempted to make conversation with Phil over his shoulder, and avoid Anna's glare, he had spotted Tilly in the front seat of the camper-van, snuggled up close to Joe and then the vein in his head really began to throb. The omens weren't good. Daniel knew full well that Anna was mistrustful of Tilly and now, he had the distinct impression that despite all their preparations and anticipation, it was going to be a long and very trying day.

Daniel for once, was pre-empting his daughter's every move and from the moment they arrived at the beach, did everything he could to keep his tense partner, calm and happy and Louise under control. He knew exactly where Anna liked to sit, just under the rocks on the animal friendly side of the beach. The second Louise began to complain, Daniel's patience ran out.

'Why are we sitting here? It's too far away from the children's play area.'

'Louise, stop moaning. The kids will only want to bounce on a trampoline once, it's too bloody warm for a start.' Daniel was hot, tired and sick of hearing her voice.

'But look how far we are from the restaurant, and the lifeguard. This is not a safe place to sit, anyone can see that.'

'Louise for crying out loud, we are all adults and quite capable of paddling without the need for mouth to mouth resuscitation and if you haven't noticed, we have *two* boxes of food so don't require a waiter!'

Daniel instantly regretted his words because this resulted in a mammoth Sulkathon and once she'd smothered Jules in sun cream, Louise grabbed a parasol then moved as far away from the group as not being ignorant would allow, and began to read her book.

Once they had set up camp to her specifications, Anna began to relax and chose a spot at the opposite end of the line of bodies where she had no contact with Louise. Zofia and Dominique had taken Alain and Patrick for a walk and were already almost out of sight. After plucking up courage and daring each other to brave the Atlantic Ocean, the four big kids had gone for a dip in the sea and the three smaller ones were collecting shells and looking for crabs. Allowing any tension to drift away, Anna listened to the sounds of the resort, children playing, the gentle lap of the tide as it hit the cluster of rocks nearby, the seagulls screeching overhead and Jeannie's gentle snoring.

Looking to her side, she couldn't help but smile at her snoozing friend. Jeannie was like a fluffy comfort blanket and her personal knight in Teflon-coated armour, all rolled into one. Whenever she was around, Anna felt safe and protected. It had always been that way, ever since they were at school and after so many trials and tribulations where Jeannie had always come to her aid, she wouldn't swap her mad friend for the world.

Every now and then, Anna thought it was a good thing to take stock of your life and had she enough self-discipline, would have tried mindfulness, apparently it was all the rage. Failing that, all she had to do was look around her and be grateful for her blessings, none more precious than her family who, apart from her crazy mum, were scattered all around her. She loved them so much and just the thought of them could always be relied on to make her weepy, even Enid.

She was brought back to the here and now by Jeannie who had woken from her nap and spotted Anna wiping her eyes.

'Are you okay, has someone upset you?' She was now lying on her side, eyeing Anna suspiciously and waiting for a reply.

'No, I'm fine. I think I've got sun cream in my eye and it's stinging a bit. Come on, let's get the picnic organised. The deep-sea divers will be back any minute and I'm a bit hungry myself. Your snoring is getting worse you know, it must be old age. It sounded like a camel had made its way onto the beach. For a minute there I thought I was in the Sahara!' Anna smirked and sat up, shielding her eyes to the sun as she surveyed the waves for her brood.

'Cheeky. If you carry on like that I'm going to be best friends with Tilly or worse, go off with Louise and leave you crying in this very big sand pit, so watch your step!'Jeannie threw a pebble at Anna then shuffled nearer to the cool boxes.

'Quick, pass me a sarnie before they get back, I'm starving, and while we're at it, let's open a bottle. Surely it must be wine o'clock by now? Look, I can see Dominique and Zofia on their way back… they must've read my mind.'

'Okay, okay, you win…' Anna smoothed down the blankets and waved at Daniel and Phil, miming that it was time to round the kids up and have something to eat while Jeannie knelt in the sand and began rummaging around in the picnic bag for food and glasses.

For a moment, Anna's thoughts flicked back to Enid and she reminded herself to ring England as soon as they got home, for now, she had mouths to feed and sandy, salty children to dry off, and a certain interloper to keep a close eye on. Not to mention misery guts Louise, over there.

It was only 1pm and unbeknown to Anna, the drama had only just begun because it wasn't Louise she should be worried about, or Tilly. Soon, it would be naughty Pippa's turn to take centre stage and in her own special way, hog a bit of the limelight.

CHAPTER TEN

Tilly was having a brilliant time. In fact, she actually felt like a completely different person. Had she been so inclined, she may have been mildly concerned about her ability to morph into a carefree, happy young woman and vanquish all her woes without so much as a hint of guilt. Perhaps she was borderline schizophrenic! Maybe she could use that as a reason not to get married? Her evil alter ego could turn up at the *Maire's* office wearing a blonde frizzy wig, red lipstick and a silver bikini and be so obnoxiously vile to Luke that he'd run a mile and everyone would assure him it was a lucky escape from a nutcase. So many schemes and scenarios had flickered before her eyes over the past few months so another little fantasy wouldn't do any harm. There was no getting away from it though, the main reason for her euphoria was Joe, followed closely by his family (Anna not included) and finally, the fresh air, sea breeze and not having stopped laughing from the moment she'd parked her bottom on the seat of the campervan.

Melanie was funny and clever and the constant butt of her brothers' jokes and teasing, it was all done in jest and completely harmless and you could tell she loved it. Sam was just bonkers combined with being completely natural and down to earth. He exuded a calm strength that she imagined would encourage others to follow his lead and want to be around him.

Then there was Joe, who despite being the eldest, seemed in awe of his confident younger brother, but definitely not jealous. He was happy to let Sam make plans, come up with mad ideas (like climbing a really treacherous looking rock and jumping into the frothy sea below) and importantly, Joe knew when to say no!

Joe was more spiritual, sort of deep and principled and she imagined prone to self-doubt with a tendency to over-think situations, a bit like herself. He was so good-looking but not vain at all, slimmer than his muscle-bound brother, yet still perfectly toned and healthy. Tilly adored him. There were no two ways about it. Had they been on holiday in Ibiza, or anywhere in the world, she knew that they would definitely have been together by now. As it stood, she could look but not touch and had to make do with a platonic relationship, as much as it was killing her.

After they'd eaten their mammoth picnic, Mel and Sam decided they wanted to sunbathe so Joe suggested he and Tilly took a walk along the cliff path. The kids were making sandcastles and the grown-ups were starting to nod off. Pippa looked on, content in *her* sun tent which she had commandeered the minute it was erected and from there, was keeping an eye on the proceedings.

By the time they'd climbed the stone stairs to the top of the white, craggy cliff top, Tilly and Joe were hot and out of breath so they found a shady spot and took in the view. The path was dotted with swaying cabbage palms, eucalyptus and flowering trees, which provided them with a private place to talk, settled beneath their boughs. Once they found a secluded patch of grass, both leaned against the trunk of a sturdy cedar and enjoyed the cool breeze from the Atlantic and the shade from the fluttering leaves. Below, they could see their little gang camped around the rock that jutted out and separated the two sections of the beach. Out at sea, a container ship made its lethargic journey towards some distant land and, nearer to shore, speed boats zigzagged between the waves, flipping their occupants from side to side as they manoeuvred between coloured buoys.

This was one of the things that Joe liked the most about being with Tilly, the companionable silence that didn't have to be filled with idle chit-chat or deep and meaningful conversation. Sometimes, it was just nice to sit, look, and think, while knowing you had someone by your side who was quite possibly sharing the same thoughts, or at the very least, was on your wavelength.

Eventually, Tilly broke the silence. She was tracking the course of the container ship while letting the sun warm her legs and the wind cool her face.

'This is *the* most perfect spot. I could stay up here forever. Do you ever wonder where those ships are going to, and don't you think it's weird that I never want to know where they're from? It's much more fun to imagine some exotic destination and far-off port on the other side of the world.' Tilly kept her eyes on the sea as she waited for Joe to answer.

'Where you start from is the boring part I suppose, but I know what you mean and no, it's not weird. I often do a bit of daydreaming when I see the shipment notes at work. Some of our consignments go to Asia and now and then we have ones bound for Russia. There's a port there called Archangel and I'd love to see what Murmansk looks like. It's probably grey, grim and freezing, then there's Yokohama in Japan and Ho Chi Minh City in Vietnam, how cool do those places sound?' Joe looked wistful as he stared out across the ocean.

'I always look at the departure board at the airport and check out the names of all the unusual destinations and wish I was on one of those flights. Ignore that, I sound like a right ungrateful cow, don't I? Some people never get to go on holiday so I should think myself lucky to be going anywhere.' Tilly decided to change the subject because a certain grumpy fiancé was creeping into her consciousness and he'd been banished for the day.

Joe, however, had other ideas. This was the moment he'd been waiting for and it was now or never.

'Tilly. Can I ask you something? I'm not prying… well, I suppose I am really, but something's been on my mind since we met the other day and it's doing my head in not asking you. Tell me to mind my nose if I offend you, okay?' Joe's heart was beating a little faster and he suspected he'd gone red, but Sam would think he was a wimp if he bottled out now, so he forged ahead.

Tilly was looking slightly worried and nervous, however, seeing as she hadn't replied, he took it as a green light to continue.

'I totally get that Luke doesn't like travelling further afield and all that, and it's a major blip in your relationship, but do you get on with him in general, you know, about other stuff? It's just that you hardly ever mention him or seem to want to talk about him so I was wondering if maybe you'd had a row before you came over, or that you were, well, a bit sick of him all round?' Joe felt incredibly foolish after his little speech.

Yes, he'd plucked up the courage to ask her and now, all he had to do was wait for the axe to fall and the moment when she told him he was out of order and she loved Luke to bits and he'd got the wrong end of the stick.

There was a deadly silence as Tilly stared ahead. Joe assumed she was trying to work out how to tell him to mind his own business, when she sucked in a great big breath and exhaled slowly. Her head was leaning back against the tree and as she turned to face him, she looked into his eyes and he knew there and then that he was going to hear good news. Call it intuition, whatever you wanted, yet something just told him she was glad that he'd asked.

.   .   .

Tilly had been taken aback by Joe's direct approach but rather than run a mile, she knew it was time to stand her ground and get it over with.

'Joe, if you only knew the half of it. No, we don't really see eye to eye on other stuff or have the same interests, but we haven't had a huge row either, which is mainly because we are never together long enough to argue. I'm glad you asked though because I've wanted to talk to you about it for days, only there never seemed to be the right time. I don't hate Luke okay, but I don't love him anymore either. We just sort of plod along in our separate worlds and come together when needs must. The whole relationship has got out of hand and I don't know how to stop it without hurting him and other people. I feel like the worst person in the world admitting that to you because more than anyone, I don't want you to think badly of me, but it's all true.' Tilly felt so strange and wanted to cry, but she wasn't sure why.

After instantly feeling relief at saying the words, a cold wave of terror washed over her because now it was real and she knew for certain she would have to do something about it. Worse than that, she still hadn't told Joe about the wedding, but that was coming next.

Joe interrupted. 'Don't be daft. You're not a bad person, Tilly. I don't think that at all. I reckon I'm lucky because I've never had to end a relationship, well not a grown-up, important one anyway. I don't reckon dumping Fiona Miller at the school swimming gala counts, even though I still felt bad because she was so upset, she lost her race and was sick in the pool, right in front of everyone. It was so gross, have you ever seen floating sick and the panic when everyone tries to get out of the water? After that the PE teacher hated my guts because he had to fish it out with a net. I suppose I should've done the deed after she'd had her turn, but I was only fourteen and didn't think. I just wanted to get it over with and spend the school holidays playing football with my mates in the park, not holding hands with Fiona. So I just said it. Since then it's always been me that gets dumped, probably bad karma or something like that.' Joe was rambling but at the same time sounded deadly serious. He also looked slightly taken aback when Tilly began laughing, which made him smile too.

'Joe, you're on another planet sometimes, but you make me laugh so much. If making Luke sick in the swimming pool was the worst that would happen, then I would gladly ring him here and now and tell him it's over.' Tilly was being serious while trying to control the giggles.

Without thinking (for once in his life) Joe grabbed Tilly's petite hand and gave it a squeeze. Her skin was as soft as he imagined it to be and her fingers were fine and slim and almost completely enveloped by his grasp.

They sat there in silence as he took in the enormity of her confession.

Joe was over the moon, giddy and nervous. His prayers had been answered and now, all he had to do was tell her how he felt. He owed her that after she had bared her soul and remembering Sam's advice, he decided to tread carefully, not go all hearts and flowers on her, more considerate and supportive – see how she reacted to that first.

'Well, I just want you to know that if there's anything I can do or if you need someone to talk to, I'm your man. I could tell something wasn't right, especially because he's in England and you're over here. If you were my girlfriend I wouldn't let you out of my sight, not in a creepy way though. I'd just want to spend as much time with you as I could.' There, he'd said it. Not too full-on but hopefully she'd got the hint.

When Tilly burst into tears, which quickly turned into proper, full-on sobbing, Joe had no option other than to put his arms around her and give her a hug. Boy, it felt good to hold her tight and he could smell peach shampoo mingled with the sea as his chin rested on her head. He let her cry, relishing the feel of her arms as they clung on while he whispered that it would be okay and everything would sort itself out. Once the sobs subsided and she wiped her eyes, Tilly sat up and apologised for making a scene.

'I'm sorry, Joe. The last thing I wanted was to have a meltdown and ruin your day. I'm okay now and it means a lot to me, what you said about being there if I need someone to talk to. These past few days I've spent with you have been the happiest I've felt for ages, even if you did almost squash me. I wouldn't change it for the world. I always hoped I'd bump into you again but not exactly like that. Perhaps it was destiny and that mad deer was a sign... or an Indian spirit guide. I believe in stuff like that so you never know, maybe the gods want us to be together, but just like making it hard for us.' Tilly reached out and squeezed Joe's hand.

They didn't speak for a while.

Joe was preparing to go one step further and declare his true feelings. Tilly had more or less said that she had wanted to see him again so she wasn't averse to the idea of them being an item. Well, he might as well go for it, in for a penny and all that.

'I thought about you too. I wished I'd got your number that night at the festival but even if I had, it would've been wrong to contact you because my motives wouldn't have been at all honourable. When I saw it was you in the ditch, even though you looked like something the cat dragged in, I was really happy.'

Tilly whacked Joe on the arm then laughed.

Before he lost his bottle, he carried on. 'Look, I get it that you're with Luke and you know how I feel about being faithful and all that, but I just want to say that if and when you are single again, well, I'll be waiting with my rucksack and we can run away together and see the world. Anywhere you fancy, just name it, we could start with Blackpool. I've always wanted to go there!' Joe held on tight to Tilly's hand, just in case she was appalled at his suggestion and wanted to make a break for it.

.   .   .

Tilly threw her head back and laughed out loud. 'Okay, it's a deal. Blackpool here we come. We'll do the lot, the Pleasure Beach, the Tower, buy some rock and then have a ride up the beach on some poor donkey. No, cancel that, it's cruel. Unfortunately though, before we can go mad on the golden mile I need to face up to my mistakes and grow a spine.' Tilly was so frustrated, it was like being on the verge of freedom yet the chains that held her captive were weighing her down and fastened too tight.

She turned to Joe and spoke, pent-up anger and irritation in her voice. 'Oh, Joe, why does everything have to be so complicated? I've been telling half-truths to my mum and dad and I feel really bad about that. Luke has no idea at all where I've been or who with, not that he's particularly interested and then there's your mum who, despite what you say, I can tell she doesn't like me. But apart from that, there's so much more I need to tell you about me and I'm scared that if I do, then you'll take back everything you've just said and push me off this cliff.'

Tilly was on the verge of tears and throwing herself over the edge anyway, and even though her heart was beating like the drummer from Black Sabbath, she forced herself to carry on. She couldn't just say 'I'm getting married next week' so she thought it would be easier to build up to the awful truth by explaining how she came to be in this situation.

Glancing down at her left hand, Tilly acknowledged the irony of her jewellery-free state and knew that had she been wearing her engagement ring, she wouldn't be in this predicament in the first place. The offending article was at the jewellers being made smaller, along with her wedding ring which Luke was going to collect and bring with him. Over the past few months, Tilly had shed pounds and her diamond ring had become loose and uncomfortable, hence, her finger was now bare. Dragging her eyes away from the absent truth, Tilly looked up at Joe and began.

'I suppose it'd be best to start at the beginning or somewhere near, and then you might understand why I'm in such a predicament. Last year, before I met you at the festival, Luke and I had split up for a while because I found out he'd been cheating on me. I was devastated and I thought I'd lost him forever. When he came back and asked me to forgive him and swore he'd never do it again, I was so relieved and grateful that I stupidly took him back.' Tilly chanced a nervous glimpse at Joe who looked slightly shocked, so she got on with it while she was on a roll.

'My best friend Stacey thought I was totally mad and my dad wasn't too pleased either. The thing is, when you lose someone, some kind of warped human nature wants them back, to reclaim what you thought was yours and get one over on the person who pinched them from you. It sounds childish saying it like that but I was so hurt and I honestly thought I couldn't carry on without him, which seems a bit pathetic now.' Tilly hated talking about that period in her life but it was necessary in order to paint a picture for Joe of the needy, emotional wreck she had once been and why she stupidly accepted Luke's proposal, which she was working up to next.

'Tilly, no way are you pathetic! Not at all. If anyone should feel like that it's him for cheating on you in the first place. Sorry, I'm interrupting. Go on. I'll stop butting in, I promise.'

Tilly swallowed the huge lump that had formed in her throat and grasped Joe's hand and wrapped it inside both of hers, clinging tightly so that he couldn't run away once he heard the next instalment in the car crash that was her life.

'Thanks. If I could rewind the clock or travel backwards in time, I assure you I'd give myself a good talking to or a really hard slap. Anyway, back to our holiday. Luke was doing his best to make things up to me, treading on eggshells and trying to prove he'd changed, that's why he agreed to come here and stay with Mum and Dad, even though he was bored out of his head. It was hard to forget what he'd done and get over my insecurities. Mum and Dad were so relieved I was happy again and somehow, I convinced myself everything was going to be okay.' Tilly thought she'd done a good job of setting the scene and giving Joe an insight into how her head and her heart were working just before the grand proposal.

Here goes, she thought, this is it.

At the precise moment she opened her mouth to continue her damning speech it was interrupted by ear piercing screams and angry shouts from the beach below. Joe jumped up, concern etched on his face. Tilly recognised Anna's voice and the name that was on everyone's lips so ran to his side as they peered over the wooden fence. They could see Sam, Mel and Daniel followed by the three children, frantically chasing Pippa across the beach. Just a hair's breadth in front was a small terrified dog, sprinting for its life and running amok amongst the sunbathers, scattering bemused onlookers in its path as both animals sped past.

'Come on,' said Joe, 'we'd better go and help, that dog can be a real pain in the arse sometimes.'

And with that, all thoughts of Tilly's big confession were forgotten as Joe grabbed her hand and they ran down the cliff steps, towards the drama unfolding below.

Anna was mortified and could only stand by, frozen to the spot with her hands over her mouth as her family and her dog laid waste to the calm and tranquil beach scene that they had all been enjoying, right up until Pippa spotted the little dog. In her defence, Pippa was normally over-friendly and loved meeting new canine pals and due to her docile and attention-seeking nature, completely useless as a guard dog, preferring to be cuddled and petted by anyone she met, even the postman. The reason she had gone potty was the result of being taken by surprise and more than likely, thought the events that unfolded were a huge game laid on for her entertainment.

Pippa had remained in *her* tent for most of the day and was quite content to have a fresh bowl of water brought to her while regally surveying the scene. All the children were now forbidden to enter the sea as the red flag was up and the swell from the choppy waves made swimming dangerous. After being fed titbits from the picnic box and having a wet tea towel placed on her head (just in case she was a bit sweaty) Pippa had nodded off. She eventually opened one of her extremely tired eyes just as a new family arrived and placed themselves a few feet from where Anna and her gang were camped.

Neither Pippa, nor anyone else for that matter, was aware that the picnic basket which Papa was carrying contained more than a bottle of Sancerre and a couple of wine glasses. Suddenly, and without warning, the wicker lid flipped up and out popped this 'thing'.

Pippa spotted it instantly and gave a surprised, warning woof. It really wasn't like anything she'd seen before. The thing in the box had something shiny stuck on its head, causing Pippa's ears to prick up as she stared intently, waiting and watching. After all it was her job to keep everyone safe, especially the kids who were playing in the sand close by. Then it happened. The little dog sprang from the picnic box, her pink bow jiggling about on her head, which really put the wind up Pippa who leapt from inside the tent, barking loudly to warn all her family that there was something wrong. And that was that. Mademoiselle Le Chihuahua took flight. Game on!

Everyone thought Pippa was a bit of a slow coach, when in fact she could have given a whippet a run for its money as she gave chase and pursued Le Pooch across the beach. All that could be heard were horrified screams from Mama and Papa as they watched the English beast pursue their petite Gigi, as sunbathers and picnickers were trampled by crazed dogs and panicking humans who apologised profusely as they gave hot pursuit, Pippa was having the best time. Not only was the little thing a jolly good sport, but now, all her family were joining in the game too. Pippa just wanted to catch it up, have a sniff and a good look at what it was, and then they could play.

Jeannie was in hysterics, wiping away tears so she could see properly while Phil videoed everything, convinced that £250 was in the bag and Pippa would soon be on *You've Been Framed*.

Daniel was puffing and panting and doing what Louise described as his 'comedy, dad run,' which Anna would've probably found rather funny at any other time.

The little kids were trailing behind, laughing their heads off, waving their buckets and spades and loving every minute, especially when Sam did a cool rugby tackle and finally captured Fatty.

For a minute or two, peace and quiet was restored, apart from Mama and Papa who were shouting loudly at Anna, saying her dog was a crazy monster while Louise (who came in useful for once) was assuring them that Pippa was as gentle as a lamb and only wanted to make friends with petite Gigi. No matter what she said or how much everyone apologised, they were having none of it and angrily packed up their belongings, huffing and puffing in a very dramatic, Gallic way, before stomping off up the beach to find more civilised, French company.

Joe and Tilly arrived just as Sam had wrestled Pippa to the ground and while they all stood panting and gasping for breath (Pippa most of all) Anna raced across and began to berate her exhausted dog and praise her son for capturing the sweaty rascal. Once Gigi had disappeared from view, Sam released Pippa from where they had come to rest, which was at the shoreline, close to a huge lump of volcanic basalt that jutted from the sea.

Earlier in the day it had provided a mini-nature reserve for Jules, Summer and Ross from where they had collected an array of shells, seaweed and crustaceans which lurked in the rock pools, dotted around the base of the giant rock. Now, the rippling ponds were swirling, gurgling holes that had filled with seawater and unfortunately, when Pippa sauntered over to have a sniff and a paddle, were a lot deeper than she or anyone expected.

Anna, who was extremely hot and very irritated by her naughty dog, shouted for her to come to heel, just as a huge wave rolled in and in the blink of an eye, completely engulfed Pippa and swept her away. One minute she was there, her tongue dangling and her tail wagging, the next she was gone.

Anna screeched and called Pippa's name as Sam, Mel, Joe and Tilly sprinted towards the sea. The three smaller children instantly burst into tears as Jeannie and Phil raced over to comfort them.

Daniel also waded into the swell, desperately trying to spot their dog and silently praying for her to surface soon.

Joe shouted for Tilly and Mel to stay where they were. 'It's too rough, go back in case you get dragged under too. Go on, before you lose your footing.'

Sam ran headlong into the waves followed closely by his brother and before they knew it, they were waist high, frantically searching with their hands or diving under water, scanning the ocean floor through burning eyes.

Tilly couldn't just stand there and watch. She saw the look of fear in Anna's eyes, could hear the heartbroken sobs from the children and instinct just took over. Wading in, she waited just behind where Sam and Joe were swimming and diving. As she watched cautiously for the next angry wave to roll in, she crouched low and spread her arms as wide as she could; feeling for a soft, furry body while her heart pounded in her chest and fear prickled her skin.

As the crest appeared and frothy seawater broke, Tilly spotted something. Screaming at the top of her voice for Sam and Joe to look, she heaved herself forward into the fast-moving wave and forced her body towards what she knew was Pippa. It was all over in minutes really, from the moment that she was swept away to the second the four stone, sodden lump that was Pippa hurtled into her, knocking Tilly to the seabed and almost drowning her in the process. Utilising every ounce of strength she possessed in her winded body, Tilly wrapped her arms around Pippa, holding on for dear life as salty water invaded her nostrils.

Tilly couldn't breathe. She was submerged and had swallowed a large mouthful of sea water. The weight of Pippa held her down and as panic began to rise, her mini-nightmare came to a swift end when she felt the great burden being removed from her arms and strong hands heaving her from the water. Tilly gulped the air as it filled her lungs and then coughed and spat what felt like a whole bag of salt from her mouth. As she wiped her eyes, she saw Sam running towards the shore carrying Pippa in his arms, while another set of limbs enfolded her shaking body and guided her towards the beach.

But something was wrong. Anna was crying. The kids were really hysterical now and being quickly shepherded away by Jeannie. Tilly's heart sank as she knew instinctively that Pippa was in trouble. Breaking free from Joe's grasp, she sprinted to where Sam had laid the motionless dog on the sand. Gently, she pushed everyone aside and knelt down beside Pippa.

'Let me see her, she might need CPR. Please, Anna, let me look.'

Anna was distraught and shouting at Pippa to wake up.

Daniel moved Anna's hands away and firmly told her to let Tilly help.

Opening Pippa's mouth, Tilly saw that her gums were slightly blue which meant a lack of oxygen. Her chest wasn't rising or falling either. After checking inside her mouth for an obstruction and once she knew her airway was clear, Tilly lifted Pippa's chin to straighten out her throat. Clasping her muzzle, she held Pippa's jaw shut and placed her mouth over her nose and blew gently. Nothing happened so she tried again. When she saw her chest expand ever so slightly, Tilly waited until she saw the air leave Pippa's lungs then blew again, continuing every three seconds, counting silently and praying for the listless dog to respond.

The whole beach had fallen silent and even the disgruntled sunbathers from earlier held their breath, crossing themselves as they tentatively observed the unfolding drama.

When Pippa belched loudly and spat slimy seawater into Tilly's mouth, she didn't know whether to laugh, cry or be sick. Next, Pippa's big brown eyes opened and her chest began to rise and fall by itself and Anna let out a cry of sheer relief.

Sam, Joe and Mel hugged each other as the gathered beachgoers cheered and clapped respectfully. Once Louise, Jeannie and Phil realised that all was well, they ran over with the sniffling children to join their family and fuss over a rather bemused-looking Pippa.

The second Anna regained her composure and was sure that Pippa was going to keep on breathing, she was the first to thank Tilly and leant across to give her a grateful hug.

'Thank you, Tilly, thank you so much. I don't know what I would've done if I'd lost her. You were brilliant, you really were.'

Anna's voice cracked again with emotion as Tilly assured her she was just glad to have been able to help and that Pippa was okay.

'Right, let's get her over to the tent and dry her off. I think this one needs to relax and we all need to calm down. Do you think she'll be okay now, Tilly, should we carry her or let her walk?' Daniel's nerves were completely shot and to add to his discomfort, he was completely knackered after all that running about!

Once Tilly assured Daniel that the soggy dog would be able to walk now she was breathing by herself, they all made their way slowly up the beach with tired arms and legs but lighter, almost jubilant hearts.

Joe was beyond proud of Tilly. The way she had taken

command of resuscitating Pippa had elevated her to even higher ground, let alone actually being the one who spotted and rescued their dog. As they followed the rest of the weary group, he fondly placed his arm around her sunburnt shoulders and kissed the top of her head in thanks.

Tilly didn't pull away, instead she just looked up and smiled at him, then wrapped her arm around his waist and squeezed him back.

Joe didn't care who saw or what they thought and was sure his heart was going to burst from sheer happiness, which is sad really because soon, it would be broken and snapped in two.

CHAPTER ELEVEN

Freda was fed up. All her plans for the day had gone to pot and she was now at a loose end and rather bored, thanks to the dreaded virus that was sweeping recklessly through their village and had affected most of her pupils. Consequently, instead of an afternoon teaching, she was faced with the prospect of being home alone. There wasn't even any cleaning to do as they had scrubbed every inch of the house the previous day, so rather than sit in the sun watching grown men go into combat with their little silver balls, Freda decided a wander around the market at Saint Suplice might cheer her up.

As she drove through the dusty lanes that were, as usual, completely deserted, the only signs of life were the hawks that perched on telegraph poles, surveying the fields with beady eyes and ready to swoop if so much as an ear of corn flickered. Even the farmers had prolonged their long lunch and sought sanctuary in their homes, leaving their toils until later when they wouldn't fry inside the glass cabs of their tractors. The day was unbearably hot, fuelled by an unforgiving yellow glowing orb, heating everything below from its place in a cloudless, cornflower blue sky. Today, planet earth seemed so still and peaceful, which helped Freda relax and re-evaluate her current predicament.

Maybe an afternoon to herself wasn't such a bad thing, Freda mused as she opened all the car windows to let in any chance of a breeze. Soon, she would be inundated with family and wouldn't have a minute to herself so instead of feeling abandoned and neglected, she would be uncharacteristically spontaneous and indulgent. First of all, she would treat herself to an iced coffee in the bar on the main square then, once she'd cooled down a little, would buy whatever she fancied, even if she didn't really need it. Retail therapy could always be relied on to do the trick.

An hour later, Freda was thoroughly refreshed and meandering between wooden stalls laden with strings of garlic and cured sausages of every type, hanging in netted bunches from the eaves and counter displays. Alongside were traders selling a vast assortment of cheeses and a colourful variety of fruit and vegetables, all grown locally and probably not long out of the ground or plucked from a tree. A nice chunk of pungent cheese or a wedge of homemade pâté always went down well at home so before long, Freda had amassed a handful of carrier bags containing a gourmet treat for everyone. Further ahead, she spotted the crates of chickens that were soon to end their days on someone's plate and knowing the sight of them always made her feel rather guilty and sad, Freda veered off and pointed herself in the direction of the clothing stalls.

Nothing really took her fancy and, in truth, some of the fashions on offer were slightly bizarre and not exactly what one could call haute couture or, in some cases, even from this century. The household section came next where Freda perused the usual display of pots, pans and sweeping brushes, then continued on to the second-hand stalls where, in the past, they had unearthed the odd gem or unusual piece of bric-a-brac which now adorned her home. As Freda approached a table containing an assortment of vases and old-fashioned pottery, she spotted a familiar face amongst the shoppers. It was Olivia, a relative of Rosie who owned the hotel where the wedding reception was taking place, and further along was Henry, who had his nose in a book.

They had all met the previous winter during one of Rosie and Michel's themed evenings in their restaurant. Once a month, they served cuisine from other parts of the world, which enticed, not only the ex-pat community who missed their chicken tikka masala or a spicy enchilada, but the more adventurous French villagers too. The evenings had been a huge success and a great way to meet new people, which is how her and Howard ended up being seated next to Olivia and Henry while they enjoyed bangers and mash followed by spotted dick and custard. It is also how Freda came to book the venue for the wedding.

Since then, they had bumped into each other at other events such as the *Kermesse* (the village school fête) or in the local supermarket and on each occasion, Freda had warmed to the very posh but genuinely friendly couple. They were now firm friends. As Freda approached, Olivia looked up from examining the base of a pretty figurine.

'Freda dear, how wonderful to see you. Henry, Henry, look it's Freda, do put that tatty book down and come and say hello.' Olivia turned from her henpecking of Henry to focus on Freda.

'Fancy bumping into you here. How is Howard, and Tilly? I expect she's all of a dither. I'm so looking forward to the wedding, are you all ready for the big day?' Olivia was in full throe as Henry ambled over, still clutching, what appeared to be, an atlas.

Once the hellos were dispensed with, Henry wandered off and continued rummaging through a large cardboard box stuffed with books. Obviously bored with antiquing, Olivia suggested they both rest their feet and escape from the searing heat. Once she'd informed Henry of their intentions, they left him to his happy foraging and headed for the nearest bar, anywhere would do so long as it was cool.

Olivia wasted no time in ordering drinks, fresh orange for Freda and a large G&T for herself and while they waited, they had a catch-up. By the time the waiter returned, they were onto the subject of the wedding.

As the conversation progressed, even though Freda appeared to be fizzing with excitement at her daughter's upcoming nuptials, Olivia sensed something verging on trepidation at the imminent arrival of her sister and Tilly's soon-to-be mother-in-law.

'I take it you don't get on too well with her then? I'm an only child so have no experience at all of sibling rivalry. I do have many friends who either love or loathe their brother or sister, or have a tenuous co-existence where one tolerates the other. As for the in-laws, I was perhaps in the fortunate position of having my son and his wife all to myself.'

When Freda sighed and shook her head, Olivia smiled kindly. 'Well, it looks like I've hit the nail on the head. I must say I'm rather intrigued so if you feel like unburdening yourself I'm quite happy to listen, but perhaps we need a top up first.'

Freda was feeling a bit sorry for herself and glad to share. 'I don't hate my sister, or Hazel for that matter, it's just that being around them makes me incredibly uncomfortable and to be honest, I really can't be bothered dealing with Marianne's dramas or the other one's high and mightiness. I haven't got the energy. They both make me feel either on edge or inferior.'

It was true, that's exactly how they affected her and now their arrival was looming, Freda was having trouble pushing them to the back of her mind.

'So tell me, what exactly is it about them that bothers you? You always seem like a happy, relaxed lady who is comfortable in her own skin. What's brought this on? Don't be shy, I'm quite thick-skinned and a good listener, tell Aunty Olivia and you never know, maybe I can help.' Olivia gave the waiter a jolly wave and a cheerful smile, signalling they'd like another round then she settled down to listen.

By the time she'd finished, Freda wasn't quite sure if she felt unburdened or a bit of a moaning, nasty old cow, either way, she'd had Olivia enthralled. The looks on her face had ranged from sympathy to outrage to surprise, yet at no time did she admonish, disagree or make Freda feel as though she was in the wrong. Then again, perhaps Olivia was just being polite and had now formed a completely alternative opinion from earlier, and Freda felt it was bound to be negative.

And that, according to the wise owl sitting opposite, was the trouble in a nutshell.

When Olivia delivered her verdict, apparently it was all quite obvious.

'Freda my dear, it happens to the best of us because as the confidence we once possessed starts draining from every damn pore in our bodies, we start to form a low opinion of ourselves and lack self-esteem. Believe me, Freda, there was a time when I thought I was going potty and it's no joke, which is why we have to use every trick in the book to survive it. And as for your gentleman doctor, tell him to shove his herbs where the sun doesn't shine and if you think HRT is right for you, then go for it. In the meantime perhaps you need a teeny rocket to give you a boost and guess what? I am just the person to do it.'

'Well, that's very easy for you to say but, for a start, just look at me. I've actually managed to lose some weight but that's more bad luck than good management. My sister inherited the slim gene and I reckon the last time Hazel ate anything was in 1976. I'm going to look fat and frumpy on the big day and I really wanted to turn Howard's head and wear something special. The wedding photos will be plastered all over the wall for the rest of my life and I'll stick out like a sore thumb because for a start, my dress is hideous and I hate it. I bought it in sheer panic and desperation at the end of a long day of trawling the shops in England. We were due to come back here the following morning, so I just had to find something. I was on my own because Tilly was at work and to be fair, I think she was sick to death of standing outside the changing room door while I had a tantrum because nothing fit or looked right. Sorry, I'm being a grumpy old bag, aren't I?' Freda wished she wasn't driving because she quite fancied one of those G&Ts.

'Last-minute purchases made in haste, especially when flying solo, are always fraught with problems and almost always result in exchanging the offending article. Is it really that bad? And why on earth didn't you buy something wonderful from France? I can recommend some lovely boutiques and not everything here has a designer price tag. I've found some little gems in Nantes.'

'I convinced myself that it would be far cheaper to buy something in England and truthfully, I didn't have the confidence to go into a boutique on my own, they all look so fancy and intimidating here. In the end it was false economy because I've ended up with something I don't like that wasn't exactly cheap either.' Freda wanted to go home right this minute and set fire to the floral monstrosity.

'Right, well there's no point crying over spilt milk so let's drink up and you can take me to see this abomination and then we can decide what to do next. I can spot a lost soul a mile off and I promise, all you need is a push in the right direction and a touch of va-va-voom, in your life. Now, we need to hunt down Henry and then we will follow you to your place, if that's not an inconvenience. Do you have other plans?' Olivia swirled her drink and downed the remainder in one.

Freda was slightly taken aback, but got the impression that once Olivia made her mind up about something it was probably best to do as you were told. Following suit, she finished her orange juice and began to gather her bags.

'Really, Olivia, are you sure? There's no need to drag Henry away from his shopping. I feel awful now, going on like Mrs Doom and Gloom. You must have plenty of other things you could be doing this afternoon rather than rectifying my fashion faux pas.'

'Nonsense! What are friends for?' Now stop worrying, and we need to save Henry from himself. Really, that man is a terrible hoarder so it's about time I reined him in otherwise we'll be taking a pile of tat home again.' And with that, she smoothed down her linen jacket, hoisted her Chanel bag onto her shoulder and set off in search of Henry.

In the end, after a dismal start to the day, Freda had a lovely time. Once Olivia had been shown the frocky horror, to which her only reaction was simply 'Oh dear,' they made plans to hit the shops in Nantes on Saturday morning, bright and breezy. Olivia was going to take Freda to her favourite boutiques where she assured her they would find something to knock everyone's socks off.

They had left Henry and Howard in the garden, admiring the vegetable patch so once arrangements were made, Freda suggested an aperitif. Her recently purchased delicacies were brought out to share and Howard returned from foraging with ripe, misshapen, black tomatoes, fresh green salad leaves and a punnet of his rambling strawberries. The late afternoon heat stretched into a warm, breezy evening where the diners were bathed in an orange sunset as they broke bread and swapped tales.

Olivia was such good fun and despite having an accent to rival the royal family, was down to earth, self-effacing and immensely likeable. Henry was adorable, rather academic (on a *University Challenge* scale) but not a know-it-all either. Freda thought he sounded like a World War II fighter pilot, exceedingly posh but extremely nice with it.

By the time they said their goodbyes and waved them off, Freda felt uplifted. She had a shopping trip planned with someone who epitomised style and good taste, so surely this time she would come home with something half decent. It then occurred to Freda that if she could hold her own with Henry the Boffin and The Queen's long-lost cousin, then she could certainly handle Hazel and Ken.

* * *

Joe didn't want the day to end but as they neared Tilly's house, he had to face the fact that one of the best days he'd had for ages (apart from the Pippa drama) was almost over. Nevertheless, he comforted himself with the knowledge that he had made progress and finally learned the truth about Tilly's feelings towards Luke. Now he had hope and something to work on. Not only that, he could set his mum's mind at rest and was convinced that once she heard Tilly's side of the story, Anna would feel some form of kinship or at least have a *bit* of sympathy for her.

Things were definitely looking up since Tilly had saved Pippa's life, and it was obvious that his mum had cut her a bit of slack and was quite nice to her for the remainder of the day. She'd even gone so far as to invite her to join them on Saturday when they were driving to the Vendée for a day out at Puy du Fou, a historical theme park set in an old renaissance castle.

Tilly had seemed pleased to be invited but said she would have to check what her parents were up to, they might be put out if she disappeared again. Still, it had been a good day and instead of feeling miserable because it was almost over, Joe focused on the good parts and smiled at all the memories they'd made.

Up ahead in the car leading the convoy home, Anna was also pondering the day's events and her change of heart where Tilly was concerned. Pushing away the more frightening images as she stroked the rather salty fur of her precious dog, Anna closed her eyes and welcomed some happier thoughts.

* * *

Once Pippa had been dried off and the sand washed from between her paws and wherever else it had become lodged, she did what she was best at and fell asleep inside the tent. As the tension drained from Anna and her party, they began to relax and settled down to enjoy the late afternoon rays. The big kids lay side by side listening to music and chatting while Louise took the smaller ones in search of yet another ice cream and of course, an extra one for Pippa.

Anna positioned herself beside the tent so she could keep an eye on the little mermaid. No matter how hard she tried to push it out of her mind, Anna couldn't get the image of her poor dog being swept away. Thank God for Tilly, that's all Anna could think, because had she not spotted Pippa then the last words she would ever have said to her beloved dog would've been in anger, and how could she have lived knowing that?

Anna racked her brain trying to think of a way she could repay Tilly without it seeming false or cringy. Then it dawned. The best possible gift would be one of friendship and humility. Perhaps she should put all her suspicions to one side and give the girl a chance instead of the cold shoulder. It would also make Joe happy into the bargain. She would buy Tilly a ticket and include her in their plans for Saturday, and why not ask her parents over on Sunday for the boys' farewell meal?

Once that matter was laid to rest and her conscience salved, Anna was able to enjoy what was left of the day. This included a game of rounders, girls versus boys, and then football which ended up being male only, mainly because they took it all far too seriously and the females just couldn't be bothered.

When the tide was well and truly out, Dominique and Zofia led them towards the rocks and on the hunt for oysters, which the children loved. Those who were brave sampled them fresh from the sea and after an hour or so, they returned with their haul, which was stashed in the cool box. As the beach began to empty and everyone started to flag and tingle slightly from the effects of the sun and the stiffening sea breeze, they unanimously agreed to pack up and head for home.

All in all it had been a good day, no falling out or tantrums. Even Lady Louise had shown a softer side and was full of concern when Pippa had her accident, placing a tentative, gentle hand on Anna's arm afterwards before asking if there was anything she could get, like a brandy from the restaurant or a rubber ring from the beach shop for Pippa. The showing of kindness and even cracking a joke signalled to Anna that maybe they were making some kind of progress, or failing that, Louise did actually have a heart.

The sandy, sleepy kids had buckets crammed with shells and dead things while the adults had a box full of oysters, plus bridges had been built and glimmers of hope were breaking through clouds of doubt. Everyone had full tummies, happy memories and a funny video to watch later, not to mention a living, breathing dog; sun-kissed skin, freckles and most importantly, no burny bits. As the sky glowed fiery red and the sun went to sleep, they drove home in their mini convoy and Anna smiled to herself as she cuddled Pippa, who was squashed onto the back seat, and no doubt looking forward to eating her leftover pizza as soon as they got home.

Tilly was in the most terrible quandary. As she sat between Sam and Joe on the journey home, her conscience hadn't given her a minute's peace. Her troubled heart was waging a bloody battle with her righteous head and she knew it would be a fight to the death, because both thought they were in the right. Only one would get its own way.

Her tormented, love-struck heart was flooded with joy, knowing that it had finally met its soulmate who had not only declared his true intentions, but was prepared to wait until the time was right so they could be together. Joe had said as much and even if he hadn't, Tilly would have known just by the way he looked at her. The spark of electricity she felt every time their bodies collided or a centimetre of skin made contact simply confirmed it.

Her frantic, exasperated brain was furious and insisted on reminding her that she had made a dreadful job of explaining her situation and now, poor Joe not only felt sorry for her, she had given him false hope where there was none. Well, not at the moment anyway.

In her defence, Tilly argued that she *was* actually working up to telling Joe about Luke's proposal and it wasn't her fault that Pippa's drama had interrupted her mid-flow. After that, the opportunity to be alone hadn't arisen and she could hardly whisper it in his ear, especially with his family just a few feet away.

Tilly also reminded her brain that she had done nothing since to encourage Joe, no hand holding or kissing, apart from a peck on the head and a grateful squeeze, so she hadn't behaved like the village harlot. On the other hand, her heart ached to be held by him, to experience the thrill of their first kiss and some moments of passion that her life with Luke so clearly lacked.

She could see the lights from her parents' house glowing in the distance and as they grew brighter and closer, Tilly looked into the back of the camper where Ross and Jules were snuggled together under a blanket, dribbling away, mouths wide open and enjoying the untroubled sleep of happy, shattered children.

Melanie was nodding too, her head resting against the window, the hood of her sweatshirt pulled up to stave off the chill of a summer's night. Tilly liked Melanie and it was entirely possible that they could've become good friends had fate been kinder. Soon, Melanie would hear what a sly, untrustworthy person Tilly was and no doubt be livid that her big brother had been led up the garden path.

Then there was Sam, who'd also nodded off after delegating driving duties to Joe. Even though he was the joker of the family, laid-back almost to the point of stopping, and the voice of reason or riot, Tilly imagined he'd have plenty to say on the matter once he heard the truth of her situation. She would love to be part of this family and nurture friendships with them all, even Louise who was cast as the main villain but had seemed almost pleasant over dinner.

Once the rest of the passengers had fallen asleep, Tilly enjoyed the companionable moments of silence that rested between her and Joe, interspersed by bursts of conversation or scenic observations along the route home. Still, she didn't have to be a mind reader to know that Joe wanted to continue their conversation and pick up where they left off. There was no way they could talk about personal stuff in the van, they might be overheard and what she needed to say had to be done in private.

Tilly had already told Joe that Friday would have to be a 'parents' day' which he seemed okay with. He was going with Sam to buy supplies for their trip south on Monday morning. She would let him know about Puy du Fou once she'd spoken to her mum and then there was the issue of Sunday lunch, which she already knew was a non-starter, especially after Joe had casually mentioned that it was going to be a great afternoon and she'd love the other guests, especially Rosie and Michel, the owners of the hotel in the next village. On hearing their names, Tilly nearly threw up all over the retro dashboard.

That's when a plan began to form in her mind, born out of sheer panic and a diversionary tactic instigated by her heart, whose sole intention was to avoid Rosie and Michel, allow one more day with Joe and ultimately prolong the moment of truth.

Tilly and her mum were due to meet Rosie at the hotel on Sunday morning to go over the menu and tweak any last details for the reception. Presumably, once they were gone, Rosie and family were going to make their way over to Anna's later in the afternoon. That gave her a couple of hours to meet Joe and explain everything. Worst case scenario, he would hate her and that would be that, best case, he would understand, forgive her subterfuge and agree to wait until she'd managed to sort out her life.

Hopefully, she could persuade him to leave her to it while he was out of the way, surfing with Sam. Under no circumstances would her parents be dining at Anna's, of that, Tilly was sure. The very last thing she wanted was her mother banging on about the wedding to anyone who cared to listen.

Just when she thought she'd got it all in the bag her conscience chipped in and reminded her of one very important point and a major flaw in her grand plan. Even if she did manage to make Joe understand her course of action and then by some miracle, he agreed to toddle off into the sunset and leave her to sort things out, what exactly did that mean?

Was she going to sit her parents down and explain what a terrible mistake she had made and pray they'd forgive her? Would she then ring Luke and break it to him over the phone, or perhaps fly straight back to Bristol and do it face to face? Those were her options and whilst quite sensible, they didn't fill her with determination or resolve, leaving her with another, less explosive alternative. The sane section of her brain felt the onset of a panic attack, because surely she wasn't mad enough to actually consider carrying on with her charade *or* for that matter, expect Joe to turn his back while she went through with this farce of a marriage? She wasn't, was she?

CHAPTER TWELVE

Friday jogged by unremarkably. Louise was spending the day putting a dent in Tomas's bank balance while everyone else did their own thing.

The aforementioned, exasperated husband had spoken to poor, beleaguered Daniel earlier in the day, enquiring after Jules and the current mental state of Louise, who wasn't taking his calls or replying to numerous messages.

Daniel assured Tomas that Jules was happily sliding down the water chute at the open-air pool and completely fine, but as for Louise, who could tell?

Tomas then informed Daniel that he would be arriving in Nantes on Monday evening and fully intended visiting his son. He also made it quite clear that if Louise thought she was being clever by disappearing before his arrival and continued to play games, then he would have no other alternative than to speak to his solicitor.

When Daniel ended what Anna could tell was a very uncomfortable conversation, he became lost in a world of his own. Following Jeannie's advice, she left him to ponder on his daughter's behaviour and work it through by himself. If Daniel required her input, all he had to do was ask.

He finally came to the conclusion that Louise was a carbon copy of her mother and behaving in exactly the same petty, childish, self-centred way that Carys went about ending their marriage. However, this time he wasn't going to stand by and do nothing, or for that matter, let Jules be hurt or have Tomas disrespected, either.

Anna thought this was a fair and accurate analysis of Louise's spiteful mother (based on true and undisputable facts), however, where Louise was concerned, maybe she knew she was in the wrong and had no way of backing down. From what Anna knew, accepting fault didn't seem to be in her nature. Anna's best advice to Daniel was not to take sides because if he chose Tomas, Louise would feel backed against a wall and come out kicking. Not only that, she might deem it as a grand betrayal.

In the end, Daniel agreed to pass on the message and let Louise stew on her husband's words while giving her time to work things through in her own way.

If push came to shove and they feared that Louise was planning to flee, Anna suggested that Sam could temporarily disable her car, thus preventing her escape and ensuring husband and wife came face to face.

No sooner had she patted herself on the back, Anna's wisdom was once again tested and put to good use when Joe bounced enthusiastically into the kitchen to tell her something *really* important about Tilly.

Hand on heart, once she heard Joe's story, Anna felt truly sorry that Tilly had been treated badly and understood completely the psychology behind her decision to give Luke a second chance, how could she not? It was also conceivable that sometimes, reconciliations sound good on paper but don't work in real life. The only glitch that Anna could foresee was that Joe would be blamed for splitting Luke and Tilly up, not only that, how and when was Tilly going to let Luke down gently? Whatever way it was brought to a head, it wouldn't be easy or painless.

All in all, Anna had been appeased by Joe's revelation and now understood why Tilly had been behaving in a way that had made her suspicious. Anna also thought that it was a good thing Joe was leaving on Monday and putting some distance between himself and Tilly, that way they could have a cooling-off period. After all, this could turn out to be a holiday romance. Anna warned him that he should be prepared for Tilly changing her mind or bottling out of ending things with Luke, because let's face it, she hadn't exactly been pragmatic so far, had she?

Joe calmly addressed each of her points and concerns and left Anna in no doubt that it was not a holiday romance, it was the real thing. Even though Tilly hadn't said she was going to do the deed immediately, it was a foregone conclusion and yes, he agreed completely that if he was out of the way she could sort her life out. Joe said he would definitely miss Tilly but owed it to Sam to continue with their plans, although now, he wouldn't be chasing any of the beach babes his brother had assured him were *everywhere*.

By the time they'd finished their debate, Anna was a fully paid up member of Team Tilly, at the same time as feeling a bit sorry for Luke, but he was a cheater and perhaps deserved to be dumped. As long as mud didn't stick to Joe, Anna said she was fine with the whole situation. To be honest, she was really quite pleased for Joe because he was glowing (if boys glowed) and had now reverted back to her first impression of Tilly.

Poor Anna, if only she knew!

* * *

Tilly was getting on Freda's nerves. No matter how much she tried to draw her into conversation she was met with a blank, disinterested stare. So much for having that Friday feeling! Even Howard had noticed – which was a miracle in itself.

He rarely ventured from the bottom of the garden to take an interest in anything other than his green beans, rugby and *pétanque* so the fact that he had finally picked up on their daughter's tetchy, belligerent behaviour led Freda to believe that something was seriously wrong and it was about time Tilly told her what it was.

Honestly, it wasn't like she expected Tilly to stick to her like glue for two weeks. Freda totally understood that being in the company of one's parents for a whole fortnight might be a tad boring, but the least she could do was show a bit of interest or smile occasionally, was that too much to ask? It had crossed Freda's mind as she lay awake, listening to the ceiling fan whoosh and rattle, that maybe Tilly was getting cold feet. She'd said as much to Howard just before he nodded off.

For once he seemed to agree with her summation and admitted the thought had crossed his mind too. He'd smoothed over Freda's hurt feelings on the subject of Tilly's absence, going along the humorous lines of her wanting a bit of fun and freedom before she was shackled in chains. Unfortunately, it didn't make Freda laugh and instead, gave one of her many neuroses a firm dig in the back!

Ignoring the niggling thought that Howard might feel shackled, Freda followed Monsieur Poirot's lead and examined all of the clues. It had to be said that Tilly was showing signs that all was not well in her relationship. Luke had resorted to leaving messages on their answerphone and from the tone of his voice, he wasn't too pleased about it either. To arouse Freda's suspicions further, when she pointed out to the disinterested bride-to-be that her fiancé seemed a little bit out of the loop, she was met with an irritated snort and a bored, roll of the eyes.

Freda wasn't an eavesdropper by nature (honestly) but on the occasions she had overheard their conversations or interrupted them, she hadn't been embarrassed by the whispering of sweet nothings, and certainly no indication of their longing for one another. Freda got the distinct impression from Tilly's body language and muffled yawns that she was bored to death. Not exactly what you'd call encouraging behaviour from a young couple about to embark on marriage.

Take, for instance, this morning. Freda, as usual, had been up with the lark and was enjoying her third cup of coffee when Tilly wandered into the kitchen. Glad to have some time together and a bit of company, Freda fussed around and provided her daughter with breakfast then settled down for a catch-up and the opportunity to make some plans. She was entertained by the tableau painted by Tilly of the drama on the beach and her heroic dog-saving antics, while not missing the glint in her eye and the smile on her lips when she spoke of Joe.

Was Freda being paranoid? Surely Tilly didn't have a crush on Joe, did she? Nothing improper could have occurred between them, could it? Feeling brave, Freda casually enquired as to the romantic status of both the brothers and just in case Tilly was suspicious, asked about the sister too. There appeared to be a slight ruffling of feathers when Tilly replied that they were both single and Melanie was in a long-term relationship with a French boy, then the subject was swiftly changed.

Then, when Freda explained about her shopping trip to Nantes with Olivia, the flicker of relief that flashed across her daughter's face wasn't hard to miss as she explained about the change of heart where her frocky horror was concerned. She was just about to invite Tilly along and entice her with a slap-up lunch when the flames of enthusiasm were extinguished by her daughter's next words.

It seemed that once again, the lure of the Harrison family was all too great and she had been invited to accompany them to Puy du Fou. The wonderful Anna had insisted on buying her a ticket by way of thanking her for saving the dog's life.

Seeing as she wouldn't be totally abandoning her mum because she'd be having a lovely day shopping instead, Tilly had asked if it be okay to go.

Freda almost exploded and said 'No, actually it isn't alright and I'm bloody sick of you traipsing over there every five minutes' when the simultaneous appearance of Howard and Tilly's next sentence just about saved the day. It seemed that the blue-eyed boys were heading south on Monday morning so this would be their last excursion together and after that, Freda would have Tilly all to herself. It was a promise!

Biting her lip and taking a fortifying gulp of cold coffee, Freda forced a smile and gave her consent. After all, it would probably be fun, just her and Olivia and she'd heard that the castle and shows at Puy du Fou were a wonderful spectacle, so how could she deny Tilly one last day out with the wonderful Harrisons?

Howard was eyeing Freda nervously from the other side of the kitchen, fully aware of her feelings on the matter and she could tell he was willing her to leave it be. *'Okay,'* thought Freda, *'but you don't get off that easily.'*

Pushing the boundaries at the same time as sending Howard's blood pressure through the roof, she suggested that Tilly invite the whole Harrison clan over on Sunday for something to eat.

When Tilly responded sharply that they already had plans, scraping back her chair and abruptly leaving the table as she spoke, both her parents were taken aback. After flinging her breakfast things into the sink, soapy water slopping over the side and wetting the floor, Tilly then announced she was going for a lie down and Freda took the huff, big time!

Tilly was hiding in her room. She knew her mum was upset but the surprise invitation panicked her and the uppity response was a knee-jerk reaction. Sunday was a no-go and Joe's family would not be dining here under any circumstances, final! It was obvious that her mum had been fishing earlier and would keep digging until she got to the bottom of whatever she thought was going on. Tilly felt like her head was already mashed without being interrogated by Miss Marple, so it was safer to stay out of the way.

Owing to the fact that Luke had left semi-sarcastic messages with her suspicious mother, Tilly had sent him a perfunctory text in return, just as she had every morning since arriving in France.

It should have read – Hi gorgeous, have a great day at work, don't overdo it and save your strength for our honeymoon. Looking forward to seeing you, counting the days until you make me the happiest woman on earth, miss you so much, blah, blah, blah, kiss, kiss, kiss etc, etc, etc.

Instead, it had taken Tilly about five minutes to compose a few lines that weren't misleading, two-faced or hypocritical and wouldn't arouse his suspicions or alert him to her present, semi-deranged state of mind. She reminded him to put the bin out, asked if he was eating properly and not living off takeaway food, gave a vague rundown of her trip to the beach with friends, omitting the fact that the rest of the day would be spent avoiding her parents or wedding talk wherever possible.

Luke replied promptly. His mother had fed him most evenings; he'd forgotten to put the bin out but was glad she'd enjoyed her day at the beach. He had a busy morning of seminar meetings ahead, would try to call later but had to get on. Typical!

Tilly sat cross-legged on her bed and fumed, cursed and wallowed in a pool of self-enforced misery. If they were really and truly in love, she knew full well that the brief conversations with her fiancé should have been peppered with loving, longing, romantic sentences. She would even have expected a few saucy promises from someone who hadn't had sex for over a week, well longer if she was really honest. When *was* the last time they had made love? Not even the night before she left for France! 'Well,' thought Tilly, 'that just says it all.'

Similar unhelpful thoughts rampaged around her head as Tilly flopped onto her pillows, staring at the ceiling and sending herself mad with what ifs and concocting various escape plans, all of which served no purpose at all. Perhaps she should just ask Luke outright if he still wanted to marry her. He would confess to being bored with their relationship and embrace a get out of jail free card, then they could approach their families together and explain that it was all a huge mistake, apologise for the inconvenience and waste of money then go their separate ways. That version had a lovely rosy glow to it until Tilly focused and saw the disappointed looks on the faces of her parents, jet-lagged brother and oh no, Charlotte, her giddy little bridesmaid.

'Deal with it, Tilly!' She would just have stick to her plan and burn in hell if need be. No matter what she did, people were going to get hurt so now it was merely a case of damage limitation.

Joe would be the first on her proactive hit list. Tilly remained quietly confident that if she could convince him her motives were pure and ultimately result in them being together, he'd be fine. Shocked? Definitely yes. Mildly disillusioned? A distinct possibility. Hurt but not completely rejected? An odds on bet. Despite this, Tilly was sure she could swing it.

Once he was on his way south, all she had to do was put on a brave face and go through the motions. Her wonderful parents would have their moment, her grandma and brother wouldn't have made the trip for nothing and all the guests could have a nice day out, a slap-up meal, gallons of French wine and a bit of a boogie.

Then there was Luke. As much as she knew she didn't love him enough to spend the rest of their life together, or worse, have his babies, Tilly had no desire to humiliate or hurt him either. This was definitely the kindest thing to do. Imagine having to go into work and tell everyone you'd been jilted and suffer their sympathetic, pitying looks, knowing you were the hot gossip of the week and being talked about behind your back. No, she couldn't do that to him so instead, she would protect his dignity. The next part was a little bit harder.

Tilly had to remain true to herself and her feelings for Joe which meant the unavoidable issue of consummating her marriage had to be dealt with. Not only that, once Luke arrived, how could she keep him at arm's length until after the wedding? She'd already resolved to make a solemn promise to Joe that the physical side of her relationship with Luke was at an end. If the shoe were on the other foot, Tilly would never even consider waiting for someone if they were still sleeping with their partner. The only solution was to blame Mother Nature who, after all, could always be relied on to ruin things but on this occasion, Tilly was glad to have her on the team.

Now, for the *really* scary part. Once the newlyweds were chugging down to the Côte d'Azur, Tilly would have time to formulate the final stage of her plan. She had an idea how it would go but for now, her jangling nerves and beleaguered conscience had enough to deal with on the run-up to the wedding. Tilly was going to leave the finer points for the long drive south.

Somehow, she had to pick the right time and words to tell Luke that she had made a mistake, explain sensibly and methodically her course of action and convince him she had his best interests at heart. Tilly would tell him to blame her, then tell all their friends she was a calculating, heartless cow, or worse if it made him feel better.

As doubts and fears gnawed at her brain, Tilly was completely sure of one thing – Luke would not be able to change her mind. There was no way on earth she could live a lie with a man she didn't love. She had seen a shimmer of what happiness could be and even if it turned out that her future didn't lie with Joe, then she would have to find it somewhere else. She had lived a semi-existence for so long and was sick and tired of not being able to face herself in the mirror. The path she was about to choose was going to be hard and, if necessary, Tilly would face it on her own, regarding it as a kind of punishment for any heartache she had caused. She would bravely serve her sentence and then move on.

A sense of calm pervaded her body. There was to be no more thinking – just doing. She would spend the day with her parents, go to the castle with Anna and her family on

Saturday and on Sunday, after the appointment with Rosie, Tilly would go and tell Joe the truth. With that thought in mind, she stretched her stiff legs and got off the bed. As she passed the mirror, Tilly stopped and stared hard at her reflection. She didn't particularly like the person who looked back at her, she hadn't for quite a long time now, but soon, all that would change.

One day, Tilly would have respect for her own image. It would have done its best to protect those it loved, tried hard to be honourable, faithful and true to itself. The eyes would probably have cried bucketfuls of tears by then, the heavy heart inside her chest would have ached more than usual and maybe felt some fear as her lips pronounced a sentence. Her ears would hear unkind, resentful words borne from hurt and rejection, and her hands would shake when she picked up the phone to tell her mum what she had done. In all honesty, Tilly doubted her reflection could stand the strain but it would have to find the strength from somewhere and get through what was to come.

She was weary now. Something had to give and as Tilly looked herself in the eye she knew that this was it, time for her to change her destiny and grab life with both hands. For better or for worse she had a plan and she would stick to it. No matter what!

* * *

Daniel was stressed to the max. Louise hadn't taken kindly to the news that Tomas would be arriving on Monday evening and his threats regarding legal advice were akin to showing a red rag to a psychopathic bull. She was unnervingly quiet, not quite moody, but he could tell she was gearing up for a bad spell, where no doubt someone would cop for it. The past few days had been almost normal and he had enjoyed seeing the side of his daughter he imagined her to be, rather than her very trying alter ego.

He was disappointed with his daughter on so many levels. He was also becoming extremely tired of having to defend, admonish and advise her. She really could be hard work and if Daniel was truly honest, had the potential to spoil everyone's holiday and, more importantly, his well-kept secret. The only person who was in on it was Phil. On Sunday night, in front of all her family and friends, plus his petulant, unpredictable daughter, Daniel was going to propose to Anna.

He felt it only right and yes, some might say slightly old-fashioned, but out of respect and owing to a smidgen of uncertainty, he had run things past Phil first who was convinced that it was the right thing to do and sure Anna would say yes.

Daniel on the other hand, had been worried how Anna's three children would react and whilst he'd forged a close relationship with all of them, the spectre of their father still hovered. While everyone would admit he wasn't a saint, Matthew was held in high regard by his family and for this reason, Daniel was wary of taking the next step.

Philip reassured him that they'd be fine and just wanted their mum to be happy so after slapping him on the back and shaking his hand, told Daniel to buck up and get on with it.

Daniel was nervous as hell because now he had Louise to contend with. If anyone was going to cause a fuss it would be her, and he felt the proposal hinged on the yo-yo mood of his only child. Maybe it was better that she did do a flit – it would be one less hassle to deal with. Daniel swore that if Louise spoilt things for him on Sunday, this time she would be in big trouble.

He loved Anna with all his heart. She made his life complete and he couldn't imagine the rest of his days without her by his side. After his bitter divorce he had more or less given up on women, let alone the notion of falling in love, and even though he hadn't exactly been celibate, Daniel had never come close to what he found almost instantly with Anna. Everyone said they were made for each other. Their lives had slotted together like a jigsaw.

Anna was kind and giving, selfless and unpretentious.

What you saw was exactly what you got, an honest, lovely woman who was beautiful and adored by her family and friends. Now and then she could verge on being dizzy and indecisive and, for some reason, had the odd crisis of confidence because deep down she was quite shy and unsure, which made her all the more endearing. Daniel felt blessed to have met her and call her his partner, but now he wanted more.

Regardless of his qualms, he knew he had to put his best foot forward and do the deed, otherwise Phil would call him a wimp and the perfect opportunity would pass him by. In the meantime, he would rehearse his short speech and keep his eye on Louise and hope she didn't flare up and spoil everything. Most of all though, he just hoped and prayed Anna was going to say 'yes'.

Howard was hiding in the garden. Freda was in a foul mood and Tilly was supposedly having a lie down. There was an oppressive atmosphere in the house so he had decided to take refuge with his plants where he could manage to look busy and dodge any stray bullets. He could see Freda marching around the kitchen sweeping furiously, which meant she was revving up to one of her verbal explosions. Hopefully, on this occasion, the grenade wouldn't be aimed at him. This time Tilly was going to cop for it.

Still, Howard did see things from Freda's perspective and agreed that Tilly was acting a bit weird. He'd given the situation a dose of thinking while he inspected his crops, and had decided she was either getting cold feet or had a very bad case of the jitters. To his shame, he'd been quite buoyed by the idea that Tilly might have changed her mind about her feckless fiancé, and the twinge of irony when he imagined her giving him the heave-ho.

Howard couldn't stand Luke, he'd never liked him and he never would. He'd heard the saying 'you can't choose who your children love' a million times and he still wished it wasn't true. Putting to one side that Luke had been unfaithful and almost broke his daughter's heart, as far as Howard was concerned, he was a self-centred, conceited, slimeball who lacked personality and moral fibre.

He still remembered his little girl sobbing into her pillow the night she turned up at theirs, in a dreadful state after discovering Luke's affair. Howard wanted to go straight round and throttle him, there really was no other thought in his mind. As the days and weeks went by, Tilly managed to turn hurt into anger then muster a glimmer of strength, meaning Howard and Freda were quietly confident that the worst was over and they were shot of Luke for good. Nobody was more disappointed than Howard when the worm managed to wriggle and squirm his way back into Tilly's life and he felt even worse when she announced that they were getting married.

No matter how much he rallied against Luke in private, Freda convinced him that Tilly was happy, that Luke would never do it again and had learned his lesson. It nearly killed Howard when he saw Luke again, having to welcome him back as though nothing had happened, swallow his pride and go against his better judgement. He did it though, just to keep Tilly (and Freda) happy. He even shook the cretin's hand and congratulated them on their engagement, an act that proved to Howard he'd missed his way and should've gone into the theatre.

As he snipped and plucked at whatever foliage appeared withered or spoilt, Howard processed his thoughts and weighed up his options. Should he ask Tilly outright if she was getting cold feet? After all, isn't that what dads were supposed to say in a jokey way, just before they walk their daughter down the aisle whilst praying they'll say 'no'. The thing was, Howard would be bloody chuffed if Tilly said 'yes'. He'd grab her hand and run through the lanes as fast as he could, all the way home. Sod the expense and the kerfuffle it would cause, he'd rather his girl be happy than marry someone she didn't love.

On the other hand, Tilly knew full well how he felt about Luke. He'd told her straight that the slimeball wasn't good enough for her on the night she left him. He also said a few other more unsavoury things that Freda felt were unnecessary and could get him locked up, but at the time he was infuriated. What if Tilly thought he was just trying to sway her at the last moment or cause trouble? If she genuinely loved Luke, it would sound like sour grapes and cast a shadow on her wedding day.

One thing was for sure, he had to get to Tilly before the barmy broom woman in there put her ten pence worth in. As much as he loved his dear wife, when she was in one of her strops, Freda could make a bad situation a hundred times worse. It would end in tears and tantrums and he'd be stuck in the middle. Tilly was already a bit snappy and uncommunicative and Freda felt like the fizz was being taken out of their mother and daughter time together. Freda loved Tilly and would move heaven and earth to make her happy but now and then, she needed a bit of that selfless love in reverse.

Howard balefully collected the ripest tomatoes and began stacking them in his basket. Poor Freda. He knew she struggled with so many things and despite his best efforts to jolly her along, he sometimes felt he couldn't reach the inner sanctum of her brain where the deepest insecurities lay.

Life was good, yet Freda sometimes looked lost or found it hard to fit in. Howard knew the enemy was an uninvited chemical imbalance that was playing havoc with their lives, but he wouldn't let it destroy their happiness or diminish his love for her because ultimately, Freda was his world.

He would go inside now and give Freda a cuddle and suggest they all went out for a nice meal that evening instead of her slaving over the stove, it was too hot and she deserved a treat. He would also promise to have a word with Tilly and get to the bottom of things and persuade her to leave things to him.

As he trundled up the path, Howard admitted to himself he was torn between two evils. If by some twist of fate, Tilly was actually having second thoughts, despite there being massive consequences and the equivalent of nuclear fallout, he would be rather relieved. Then on the other hand, his poor Freda would be mortified and he'd have to deal with all the emotional turbulence in the wake of a cancelled wedding. Which was the lesser evil: to see his daughter marry someone she might not love, and he despised, or watch his wife disintegrate? Howard exhaled loudly and opened the kitchen door. This was a tricky one and he knew he had to tread carefully on butterfly wings and fragile eggshells. He owed it to them both to sort things out, yet for entirely opposing reasons.

Best of luck with that, Howard!

CHAPTER THIRTEEN

J oe could hardly contain his eagerness to get the day underway or, more to the point, see Tilly again. This was like the first day of term, sitting your finals, taking your driving test and having a root canal procedure, all rolled into one.

Day one at high school was tantamount to youthful excitement, mingled with nerves as fear of the unknown fizzed through your veins. Today was no different as Joe anticipated being close enough to touch Tilly, feel her skin against his, breathe in the flowery perfume she wore and look at that gorgeous face.

Memories of exam day floated through his mind as the tinge of trepidation on entering the silent, desk-lined hall came flooding back. Joe had sweaty palm syndrome, the same that occurred as you turned over the page and read the test questions, then, with overwhelming relief, you realised that all the revision was worthwhile and you could actually do this. He'd done his homework the previous night and knew what to say to Tilly, how to behave and how not to behave, he'd rehearsed his lines and left no thought or consequence unturned.

Deep concentration was required today, the same amount involved in getting through one long, excruciating hour sitting next to a stern driving examiner, where you had to make sure there were no mistakes, take your time and think and plan ahead. Over and over, he reminded himself to just get through the trip and convince her that he was 'the one', that's all he had to do.

And finally, the pain of going through an unpleasant process at the dentist which no matter how much you dreaded and worried about it, once endured, would be worthwhile. For that reason, and as much as he hated the thought of them being together, he would drag himself away and leave Tilly with Luke so she could do what she had to. In the meantime, he would sit it out and honour his promise to Sam and continue their holiday. Simple.

Until then, following Sam's advice for the sake of their mum's conscience, during their day out there would be no smooching, snogging or hand holding! Tilly wasn't single yet and if Joe stepped over the mark, Mother Dearest would have a blue fit.

Even though it was going to kill him, Joe knew without a shadow of a doubt that Sam was on the money so instead had resolved to ensure Tilly had a wonderful day out. This would hopefully affirm in her heart and her head that the true road to happiness lay with him (and his potty family).

When he spotted Tilly waiting at the end of her lane, with whom he presumed was her dad, Joe's heart actually missed a beat. Everything about her was perfect; her scrubbed, fair, gently sun-kissed complexion; soulful, grey eyes; and her long, dark hair being blown by the breeze that drifted across the fields and skimmed the hedgerows. She wore a floaty maxi-dress, speckled with tiny flowers and had a floppy, suede tasselled bag slung over her shoulder. Joe thought she looked perfect, like a model in a perfume advert.

This image was reaffirmed when she scooted round and climbed in beside him, inhaling her scent as it filled the cab with summer flowers. The tops of her shoulders were slightly tanned and freckled from the day at the beach and as she chatted on about her burnt legs and wearing flat sandals for walking in, he thought to himself that he would never tire of hearing her voice or her infectious laugh, not to mention the feel of her soft skin as she leant against his arm.

Sam put the van into gear as they waved goodbye to Tilly's dad who was opening the mailbox, and set off towards the medieval village. And Joe thought it was high time that Luke followed suit and was consigned to ancient history, once and for all.

Tilly was having kittens and palpitations, which accounted for nervous gabbling about anything that came to mind. When her dad had offered to walk her down the lane she had to bite her tongue rather than snap at him and say 'no'. She'd only just managed to give her mum the slip, simply because she was in the shower, otherwise they'd both be at the end of the bloody lane waving her off like she was a ten-year-old going on a school trip to the museum.

The second she heard the brakes squeak to a halt Tilly had kissed her dad on the cheek and almost sprinted to the van, desperate to get away and knowing full well he was itching to come over for a quick 'Dad' chat. This would've led on to God knows what because once he was on a roll, there was no shutting him up, especially where directions were concerned.

Her dad always thought he knew the best route to most places (usually scenic and always took about an hour longer than necessary) and she wasn't prepared to sit there holding her breath, terrified he'd make some jokey comment about getting the bride-to-be back in one piece, or something equally damning. Thankfully, he stayed put beside the postbox and waved cheerfully as they moved off. She did have the grace to feel bad, and under normal circumstances would've been happy to introduce him, no matter how annoying he could be sometimes. Anyway, she'd got away with it and all she had to concentrate on was Joe and fitting as much *joie de vivre* into the rest of the day as possible. After her Oscar winning performance the night before, she thought she deserved a break from, well, just being Tilly really.

* * *

It had been quite obvious that her mum had taken the huff because she'd spent much of the afternoon sulking and noisily drawing attention to herself (and her state of mind) with the aid of various cleaning implements and cooking utensils. It was only when her dad suggested they all went out to dinner that she'd perked up a bit and scurried off to find something appropriate to wear, leaving Tilly alone and in the glare of his spotlight. When he asked her to accompany him down to the vegetable patch to get some air and wonder at the glory of his labours, she knew something was up.

As they perused his neat aisles of fruit and vegetables, she waited patiently for him to get whatever was bothering him off his chest, and when he finally plucked up the courage, Tilly was faintly relieved and surprisingly forthright.

'Look, Tilly. Me and you, we've always been able to talk about most subjects, haven't we?'

Howard fiddled with the ties on his bamboo canes and avoided eye contact as Tilly laughed, before replying.

'Dad, please tell me this isn't going to be about the birds and the bees because you're a few years too late if it is! It's not, is it?'

This time it was Howard's turn to laugh. 'No you daft beggar, nothing like that! It's just, well the thing is... and I don't want you taking the huff because it's bad enough when your mum gets the hump, what I'm trying to say is, we're a bit worried about you. I'm not prying or anything, but is everything alright between you and Luke? You don't seem your usual self and to be honest, we expected you to be a bit more chirpy and full of it, you know, about the wedding and all that. Are you getting nervous because if you are, it's perfectly normal? It can all be a bit over-whelming I suppose, and you won't be the first bride to have second thoughts. *Are* you having second thoughts?' Howard stopped in his tracks.

Tilly knew her dad well enough to tell that he had spoken out of turn and looked somewhat taken aback by his own forthrightness, which was probably as a result of being nervous and babbling, and didn't actually mean for that to come out. Now she felt uncomfortable because there was no way she could tell a real lie. If she did, then whenever she dropped the bombshell in the future, her dad would look back on today, to this very conversation and know she hadn't been telling him the truth. She was a grown-up now, not a little kid telling fibs about who'd eaten all the biscuits or blocked the loo with toilet paper. This was serious, life-changing stuff.

'I'm sorry, Dad, if I've spoilt things for you and Mum. I know I've been a bit moody but it's got nothing to do with you two, promise.' Tilly crouched down between the beds of lettuce and concentrated on the bushy courgette plants, avoiding eye contact and pretending to search for ripe pickings.

'Here, look, you've missed some.' As she twisted the stems, pulling off the stalk and then passing them to her dad, her heart was torn between right and wrong, kindness and hurt.

'I think that being here with you and Mum has given me a lot of time to think and take stock of my life. Maybe that's what all brides should do before their wedding but never get the time, whereas here, it's so peaceful and you get chance to think about stuff. Perhaps that's a bad thing, who knows?'

Tilly could feel tears pricking the corner of her eyes, so turned her back and began to search her dad's trees for a ripe pear.

When he spoke, Howard's voice was softer and hinted of concern.

'So, after all this soul-searching and thinking, what have you come up with? If it's all that business from when you split up, I'm sure Luke learned his lesson and wouldn't do it again. As much as I spoke out against him at the time, I don't think you have anything to worry about on that score, he knows what I'd do to him for a start.' Howard's tone now betrayed the fact that he hated talking about it as much as he'd hated Luke at the time.

'No, Dad, it's not that and I agree, he did learn his lesson and I have no suspicions on that score, none at all. It's more about the future, where we go from here and is he really 'the one', have I chosen wisely or rushed in. How *do* you know? Is it a feeling in your heart, like intuition, or do you have to base your decision on real life, humdrum practicalities and settle for the safe bet? Let's face it, we don't live in a fairy tale, rock and roll world and once the newness wears off, you have to have something tangible to cling on to, so what is it? How did you know that Mum was your one and only love?'

Tilly plucked a leaf from the tree and turned to face her father who was leaning against the rickety fence, deep in thought.

'Did you have doubts or worries? I promise I won't tell. Guides' honour.' Tilly had never taken the oath but held up her palm anyway, praying her dad would shine a lighthouse on her troubled soul and absolve her of any sin and set her free. She was to be disappointed.

'Dear-oh-dear, Tilly! You really are suffering with first night nerves, aren't you? Come here and give me a hug. You have absolutely nothing to worry about and what you are feeling is quite normal, honestly. I remember on my stag night, it was just me and your Uncle Norman, Tommy Sullivan and Sid Holland from work and we'd all had a few too many pints and a game of darts down the pub. I was sitting there, pretending to enjoy the game while all the time my stomach was in knots. I worried about everything from paying the bills to spending every other Christmas with the in-laws. Got myself in a right state I did. Our Norman didn't help, winding me up about balls and chains and all that malarkey and I suppose the beer got me a bit maudlin too. I took a long walk to clear my head and found myself at the end of the street where your grandma lives. It was only the thought of your mum, sitting innocently inside, surrounded by her bridesmaids getting themselves all done up for the next day that stopped me from marching up and banging on the front door to tell her it was all off. I knew I couldn't do that to her, or her mum and dad. Thank God I saw sense and went straight home because you know what? The very next day, when I saw her standing at the back of the church on your granddad's arm, she looked so beautiful that I nearly burst into tears. Not just because I was happy, but at the enormity of the mistake I could've made. I couldn't wait for her to get to the front, say the words and make her mine, and I haven't regretted one single day since then. Not even when she's on one, throwing plates round the kitchen or at my head. I thank the Lord I went straight home that night, I really do.' Howard kissed the top of his daughter's head and let his words sink in.

'I'm glad too. You and Mum have been the best parents in the world. That's why I never ever want to let you down or disappoint you, please remember that always. Promise you will, Dad.' Tilly looked up into her dad's eyes but she couldn't see him properly as her own were misted by tears.

'Hey, what's all this? You could never disappoint me, you're my little girl and I will always love you no matter what, so *you* remember that. As long as you love Luke and he loves you then the rest will fall into place. All those niggles and fears will be a walk in the park if you stick together and work it out. Marriage isn't easy, Tilly, life isn't come to think of it but when you have someone by your side who is your best friend, then everything is possible.' Howard wiped away his daughter's tears and smiled down at her, looking quite pleased with himself.

Tilly sucked in a huge lungful of air and dared herself to

ask him the question. But what if you don't love them, Dad, what if you love someone else? What if you know without a shadow of a doubt that he's not your soulmate or even your best friend? What do you do then? All she had to do was say the words, she could do it. This was her chance. She left it a heartbeat too long.

'Right then, young lady! I think I've earned myself a drink after baring my soul and dishing out all this sage advice. Are you sure you're alright now? I think you've got yourself into a bit of a lather and instead of talking to your mum about things, you've been bottling it all up. We're going to have a smashing day and I'll be the proudest dad in the world. But even when you're wed, just remember we are both here for you and always will be. Is that clear, Miss Parker?' Howard was doing his jolly 'let's change the subject before it gets too heavy and I run out things to say' routine.

Tilly knew when she was beaten. There'd be no baring of the soul tonight. No laying cards on the table then begging for forgiveness and understanding. Instead she would go inside, open a bottle, lay out some nibbles and enjoy a glass of her dad's finest wine while attempting to smooth things over with her mum. Later, she would make a special effort to get dressed up and look pretty for her parents, smile in all the right places and do her best to allay their fears. Tonight would be like a dress rehearsal and great practise for her wedding day. It was time to see just how good her acting skills were.

The one thing Tilly wasn't prepared to do was act like a giddy, enthusiastic bride, because when her parents looked back, she didn't want them to picture her that way and feel tricked. She couldn't bear that. They would question so many aspects of her behaviour but if she remained reserved and for all intents and purposes, slightly nervous, she could live with that. Who could've imagined that she would end up like this, capable of such deceit and underhandedness? Maybe this was how everyone reacted when their backs were against a wall and they just did what they had to in order to survive.

. . .

That's exactly what Tilly did. They had dined at a quaint Italian restaurant in Ancenis and laughed the night away as Tilly purposely took a long stroll down memory lane with her parents. Freda loved reminiscing and reaffirming all their good times, sealing the bond they had forged throughout their lives together. Instead of speculating or getting carried away about her own nuptials, Tilly insisted on hearing all about her parents' wedding day. She'd heard the stories many times before, they were part of her heritage. Like the cake that should've been three tiers but, because of Petra, her granddad's dachshund, it ended up only being two. Freda remembered her mum and aunts furiously buttering bread and making sandwiches for the reception buffet in the community centre, and how her bridesmaids sat up till late, helping her stick cheese and pineapple cubes onto cocktail sticks. Uncle Norman's brand-new shoes got tied to the back of Howard's mini and were lost on the drive up to their honeymoon B&B in Tenby.

While the diversion worked a treat, it served also to reaffirm that her course of action was justified in every way. They laughed and teased each other about her dad's awful eighties hairdo (he thought he looked like Bryan Ferry) and his brown suit with big lapels and permanently pressed trousers, then her mum, throwing her bouquet so high it landed on the fluorescent lights which then had to be prodded off with Uncle Fred's walking stick. Looking at them both, clinging on to each other as they relived the past, Tilly knew what they had was real love. Even though their day hadn't been a five-star affair, it was the happiest of their lives.

This revelation compounded her resolve. Her mum had done her very best to provide Tilly with all the things she probably wished for on her wedding day. How could she let all that hard work crash and burn? Not to mention the money they had insisted on forking out for a lavish, no expense spared reception. And that was why she was prepared to sacrifice her own feelings and those of Luke in order to give her mum exactly what she wanted.

Luke would hate her afterwards, she knew that. He would rant and rave and demand to know why she hadn't been honest and instead tricked him into a false marriage. He would accuse her of being fake, deceitful and calculating, just for having the sheer gall to stand before him and make promises that meant nothing. Yet she was going to do it. Tilly had never been more sure of anything in her life. The thing she actually feared most was telling Joe and then losing him forever. Accepting that simple fact flagged up one vitally important, insurmountable thing – she really didn't love Luke, not at all.

* * *

Anna had settled herself down in the back of the car and was looking forward to an enjoyable hour, watching the scenery whizz past as they made their way across country. They were minus Louise who had developed a last-minute migraine and felt too ill to make the journey. Jules didn't seem overly bothered that his mum wouldn't be coming and neither did anyone else for that matter, so once Anna had raided the medicine cabinet and assured Poorly Girl that her son would be just fine, they loaded up and moved on out.

Anna felt a bit sorry for Louise who, she suspected, needed a bit of time to herself to think things through and prepare for the arrival of her husband in a couple of days time. Maybe she did have a lot on her mind and was more than likely faking her migraine. Whatever was wrong, they all secretly knew it was better that she stayed behind rather than ruin their day, because if anyone was capable of that, Lady Louise was.

Anna loved the Loire in the summertime, she loved it all year round really, but August and September always reminded her of the first time she visited this little piece of paradise. She smiled to herself when she pictured the nervous, broken-hearted woman that precariously picked her way through the country lanes as she navigated towards her destiny. Glancing over at Daniel, who was telling Phil some tale or other, her heart softened as she recalled their first meeting and how they unexpectedly fell in love. Anna adored him with all her heart and despite their recent 'Louise troubles', she couldn't imagine life or a future without him.

Turning her head towards the window, she let the warm morning rays bathe her face while she admired the scenery on the other side of the glass. The countryside was in full bloom, the fields of maize were making the most of the sunshine, as were the rows of vines that lined the hills as far as the eye could see. Along the route, they passed signs directing you to *Caves du Vins* and farms selling their fresh produce from the other side of the hedgerows. In the lush, abundant fields, there were always signs of life and purpose, as the ever-busy farmers went to and fro, spraying the land or moving hay bales, whereas in the sleepy villages they drove through, you'd be lucky to spot the odd inhabitant on their way to or from the *boulangerie*. Anna thought that France would literally grind to a halt if the French ever ran out of bread; it was the most important food of the day and *had* to be fresh.

Melanie once told her that following the French Revolution, probably after Marie Antoinette's unfortunate comment about the peasants eating cake while most of Paris was starving, a law was declared that every Parisian should have access to bread. From then on, strict controls were placed on all bakers who had to ensure daily supplies to the citizens of France. Bread was a serious business here and they even had regulations regarding how it was prepared and kneaded, including the proportions of ingredients in certain types of loaves and baguettes. Even today, a baker was only allowed to close his shop for a certain amount of time and was required to make sure that another local bakery would be open and able to provide for his customers while he was away.

Melanie said that buying bread was like buying a piece of French history and it was snippets like that which cemented Anna's love of life here, because every time she passed her euro over the counter to the shopkeeper and accepted her baguette in return, she felt as though she had just paid into *l'histoire de France*. Vive la Revolution!

Anna chuckled when she glanced at Jeannie who was having a little nap with her mouth wide open and no doubt savouring some peace and quiet away from Summer and Ross, well Summer mainly. Jeannie genuinely loved Phil's children and enjoyed the relationship they had built, especially with his daughter who regarded her step-mum as her own private property. Anna was happy for Jeannie who was adamant that childbirth, stretch marks and sleepless nights were not for her. When all was said and done, it looked as though Jeannie had done okay out of her stubbornness. She now had two ready-made angels who she could enjoy and spoil without having to go through all the gory bits and best of all, when they got a bit rowdy and had trashed her apartment, she could send them straight home to their mother.

It was a shame that she hadn't been able to forge a similar relationship with Louise. To be fair though, the past forty-eight hours had been quite bearable and pain free. Time would tell and Anna wasn't prepared to trust her just yet. For now, she decided to put Louise out of her mind and enjoy the day with her family.

They would all be going their separate ways in a few days time, the boys to the coast and Phil and Jeannie were off to Disneyland Paris. It was a huge surprise that they planned to spring on Summer and Ross so everyone was sworn to secrecy. They would be leaving shortly after Sam and Joe to spend four whole days with Mickey Mouse and his gang, before flying home. Anna would miss them all once they drove off into the sunset, but she still had Daniel (and Pippa of course) and the three of them could have a well-earned rest and some peace and quiet. The only blip on the horizon was Louise. Fingers crossed, she wouldn't kick up too much of a fuss when Tomas arrived and, with a bit of luck, would be out of their hair by Tuesday morning.

Unfortunately, Anna was wearing her special edition, rose-tinted glasses and had also allowed a fluffy, cotton wool cloud to swathe her in a cloak of false security, because in reality, Lady Louise had absolutely no intention whatsoever of going quietly. Unbeknown to Anna, the worst was yet to come.

Back in the peaceful hamlet of La Roberdière, on the outskirts of the sleepy village of Le Pin, Louise sat all alone, plotting, festering and seething. How dare they just go off and leave her like that without so much as a second thought? Nor did they seem to consider that she was going to be here on her tod, in agony (a slight exaggeration if she was being honest) and as for her father, it looked like he couldn't wait to be gone. Jules too!

Well, so much for family loyalty! The only person who gave a hoot was the windy bulldog who was now snuggled up under the blanket beside her, snoring contentedly. As Louise stroked the warm fur of sleepy Pippa, she allowed her maudlin, self-absorbed thoughts to swallow her whole as she pondered on her isolation.

Yes, she had woken with a slight headache but that was red wine induced and had almost eased once dear sweet Anna had kindly administered two co-codamol. God that woman irritated her. She was just too good to be true and so was her perfect, goody-two-shoes family.

The golden boys could do no wrong and as for Melanie, well you'd think she ran the bloody department where she worked to hear Anna go on about her. Jeannie was a gobby cow and had far too much to say for herself. Good old Phil was right up her dad's arse. They were thick as thieves and for most of the time she felt like a spare part, surplus to requirements. Even Jules defected to *Mémé* Anna's team, apart from when he wanted clean clothes or money to spend in the supermarket.

And as for her own mother, well as usual, she was a complete and utter let down. Louise had been trying for days to get hold of her and had left countless messages but Carys was obviously having far too much fun with that sleazeball, Ed. Louise desperately needed some advice or more to the point, a reserve bolthole because she had no intention of being here when Saint Tomas arrived on Monday. Everyone was on his side and wanted them to reconcile, well, she had headline news for them on that score.

The only way she would consider going back was if Tomas came grovelling and made a full and frank apology and took back all the vile things he had said about her. How dare he speak to her like that? If the truth be known, she was utterly fed up with tagging along in his life and being the little wife who sat around waiting for him to come home, not to mention constantly hoping that one of her loved-up parents might schedule a visit in their diaries and make a token appearance in her life now and then. And let's face it they only ever came in the school holidays, so they could spend time with Jules. It wasn't as though she was the main attraction anymore – nowadays she was just part of the scenery.

Louise knew full well she had backed herself into a corner and she hated that more than anything. Maybe it had been building up for a long time, this feeling of detachment that went on to breed a deepening resentment of everyone and everything. Was it so surprising then that when Tomas made his grand announcement, it sent her over the edge? Was she now devoid of any personal ambition, so transparent and inconsequential that her life had to be put on hold indefinitely and her opinion worth so little that he had made a game-changing decision on her behalf? If only he had not been so pig-headed and full of himself she may have acted differently. If only he wasn't so sure that the life *he* thought she wanted and appeared to embrace, was enough. Yes she had a lovely home, money in her purse and Jules wanted for nothing, yet somewhere along the line, Louise had come adrift, an appendage to everyone's lives, including those of her parents.

But the worst part of all of this was Jules and because she adored him and would lay down her life for her precious son, Louise was in a dilemma. She had no idea how to solve the crisis her beautiful little boy had caused by merely possessing the innocent honesty of a child. Last night, before he went to sleep, as his big brown eyes filled with tears, he whispered that he missed his papa and actually, he really did want to live in Switzerland because he loved the snow. But it had to be with all of them, together. The easy answer would be to give in and roll over, and for the love of her child, just say she was sorry for all the fuss and for being an hysterical, snivelling woman.

Louise knew this was the easy way out and Tomas would be so relieved that he'd forgive her in an instant, but then what? She'd have to pack up and move to Geneva where, after a while, everything would be just the same. She would pencil in visits from her parents to coincide with her son's holidays, along with dinners at the institute, being charming to Tomas's boffiny colleagues and suffer jolly lunches with their dreary wives, with whom she'd have absolutely nothing in common. Other than that, there was always the mums at school to fall back on, which depended on fitting into the clique. It would be a private school and she was sure that, in Geneva, the bar would be set high and her acceptance hinged on as yet, unknown criteria. Could she really be bothered?

She might finally get a job, but doing what exactly? Tomas liked her to be at home and had so far thwarted any attempts she made at looking for something remotely interesting. Her French was good but nowhere near fluent, yet surely there must be something out there she could turn her hand to? She desperately wanted to use the business degree that was gathering dust and exercise her brain before it withered for good.

Louise felt there was no way out. It was inevitable that she would have to acquiesce but until then, she would just run. Anything was better than the humiliation of trotting off into the sunset like a good girl, especially in front of the von Trapp family who were *so* flaming perfect it made her gag. Her dad was on team Tomas, she could just tell, and as for wimpy Anna, she probably just wanted her gone anyway. This thought made Louise even more resigned to scarpering, however, this hinged on hearing from her fickle mother who she hoped would provide refuge. She would wait for another twenty-four hours then her time was up and whenever Carys did deign to phone her only child, Louise would give her what for.

She made her way into the kitchen to find something to eat, followed by her new best friend and Louise longed for her son and yes, her husband too, but until they both came back (one of them on bended knees) she was going to raid the fridge and then her dad's cave and spend the day immersed in self-pity. She would put her feet up, plan her escape and rehearse a few choice sentences, laced with long overdue home truths for each and every single person who had wronged her, got on her nerves, or in her way. And she would start with dear, devoted Anna.

CHAPTER FOURTEEN

It was Joe, offering her a boiled sweet that infiltrated her daydreams and brought Tilly back to the here and now. They had laughed themselves silly for most of the way, interspersed by Sam winding the kids up and scaring Ross half to death when he told him all about the real-life dragon they were going to feed him to if he wiped his sticky fingers on the glass, just one more time. When she reminded him that giddy kids in the back of a campervan could lead to sick covered seats, he took the hint and stopped. Since then, they had spent a peaceful, more orderly journey singing songs and playing I-Spy.

In between guessing what starts with the letter 'S' or joining in with 'Ten Green Bottles', Tilly's mind had been wandering all over the place. Some imaginary destinations were the epitome of paradise and accompanied by Joe, whereas the others were barren wastelands in which she was trapped for all eternity, with Luke.

The boiled sweet rescued her from the nightmare and as she unwrapped and savoured the sugary bonbon, Tilly forced unwelcome images from her mind and concentrated fully on what Joe was saying.

'Your dad looks nice, I felt a bit bad zooming off like

that, perhaps we should have said hello. I hope he doesn't think we're ignorant.'

'Oh, he'll be fine and I promise you, if he'd have come over for a chat we'd still be at the end of the lane right now, so don't worry about him.'

'Did you ask them to come over to ours on Sunday afternoon, Mum loves having loads of people over and from the sounds of it she's planning to make enough food to feed Sam's battalion *and* the whole village?'

Tilly glanced at Joe who was trying to surreptitiously undo a sweet without crackling the paper and alerting their junior passengers, who'd already had enough sugar and fizzy drinks to sink a campervan. The image of three puking children served as a warning not to let them hear.

'I did ask but they won't be able to make it on Sunday, they've already got plans. It was lovely of your mum to offer so maybe next time.' Tilly forced herself not to blush at her own lie.

Then Sam piped up. 'I'll tell her to drop you a food parcel off, she's got half a ton of sausages in the freezer that need eating and about ten bags of chips. I swear she's on drugs and gets the munchies when she goes shopping... she comes back with all sorts of random stuff. Remember those disgusting biscuits that tasted like cardboard and sawdust, and how can we ever forget the toffee flavoured ice cream that gave us all the runs? I was so ill. Mum's getting like our gran who buys rubbish in bulk, especially if it's on offer.'

Joe laughed out loud remembering them all throwing up and blaming the half price ice cream, and their mum for being a cheapskate.

'Don't be mean, your mum is lovely and she means well, but having said that, mine's going a bit doolally too, maybe it's an age thing. One minute she's happy as Larry then the next she's ranting about the bin men or someone on the telly. She's turned into a bit of a loose cannon lately. My dad knows when to stay out of her way but I'm just learning the ropes.' Tilly hoped she'd deflected any talk of Sunday so was happy and relieved to listen to Sam chatter on.

He told her all about crazy, Grandma Enid and her many adventures with her best friend, Gladys, especially their worrying obsessions, like binge watching box sets (they were currently on *Game of Thrones*) and their joint crush on Sean Bean. In between laughing, Tilly glanced at Joe's profile as he studied the satnav and her heart melted. She yearned for all of this to be real, to be part of his family, to be able to hold his hand in public and have the opportunity to build a life, or at the very least, have a proper relationship with someone who she knew with all her heart, was 'the one'.

Gulping down the emotions that were welling in her throat and threatening to expose her as they burst from the corners of her eyes, Tilly swiped away the tell-tale tears and took a deep breath. If she played her cards right and stuck to the plan she'd be fine. All she had to do was keep calm and carry on and with a little help from the gods, angels, destiny or the lucky euro she once threw down the well in their garden, Tilly thought she might just get away with it.

The sun shone in a cloudless sky as they made their way through bygone eras which were hidden amongst the lush forest, from where they watched artisans baking bread and blacksmiths doing their thing. Anna had been quite pleasant and seemed to be thoroughly enjoying her role as tour guide extraordinaire. Tilly had giggled when Joe rolled his eyes and whispered that his mum had methodically planned their route to enable them to see as many shows as possible. Within their hectic timetable, gratefully interspersed with lunch, they watched gladiators race their chariots in the Roman arena, then lions, tigers and leopards who threatened to lunch on a damsel in distress. There was a fearsome Viking attack on a village where a longboat miraculously rose from the water, plus medieval knights in their castle and a breathtaking falconry display where hundreds of birds swooped from the sky above the heads of a mesmerised audience.

The children in particular were enthralled as kites, vultures and pelicans, to name but a few, were within touching distance. The icing on the cake was the moment an owl landed on the top of Ross's baseball cap, then took flight before coming to rest on the arm of its trainer. Jeannie was praying that Phil had actually managed to capture something of use on his video camera because she wanted to preserve the startled look on Ross's face for eternity.

Almost everyone was moved to tears during the *Lovers of Verdun*, a show which told the tale of a young couple parted by war and set in a snow-covered trench on Christmas Eve. They actually felt the ground tremble as cannon boomed and smoke billowed in the air, bringing the plight of the soldiers in 1916 to the present day. Tilly had to wipe her own dewy eyes more than once and noticed Anna do the same, before receiving a quick, comforting hug from Daniel.

After a relaxing dinner and a welcome period in which to rest their aching feet, they made their way to the final show, the much talked about spectacular, the *Cinéscénie*. Once the burnt orange sun settled on the horizon, giving way to a balmy evening under a jet-black, star-spangled sky, the extravaganza began. Consisting of over 3000 actors and a huge cast of animals, it told the history of the region from the Middle Ages right up to the Second World War. The event was brought to a glittering end with a firework display of epic proportions, which left the audience gasping in awe at the pyrotechnic finale.

It was becoming chilly as they set off for home. Sam, being a man of the world and not one to spoil anyone's fun, offered to drive home, which left Joe and Tilly holding hands in the darkness of the cab, lost in their thoughts and content to be together. Neither had mentioned Luke or discussed any aspect of Tilly's planned uncoupling but she had sensed that Anna was keeping an eye on them. Tilly had come this far under close scrutiny and wasn't prepared to fail at the final hurdle, although it wouldn't have taken much encouragement from Joe to steal a kiss, this she knew for certain. To keep herself from temptation, she threw herself into being part of the gang and in doing so, had a thoroughly nice time, telling herself that even if it all went tits up, today would be one of her happiest memories ever.

Sam made her laugh but so did Joe, who gave as good as he got where laddish banter and making fun was concerned and she could tell he wanted to impress her, but not in a creepy, smothering, false way. He was no pushover either, he was just being himself, considerate, polite, and cheeky and so good-looking with it. Joe was a catch and she wanted him in her net, forever.

Joe was trying hard to stay awake, the motion of the van and the warm yellow headlights almost sending him into a trance. His mind wandered to their day out where he'd ignored any negative vibes from his mum and concentrated on Tilly, along with aiding and abetting Sam in his constant teasing of the kids. Joe wound Phil up when he filmed everyone's feet instead of Joan of Arc, and became his mother's slave when ice creams and cold drinks were required. During all of this, he had watched and admired his own raven-haired princess as she blended in and cast her spell on all of them. He knew this because Jeannie had given him a nudge and her seal of approval, whispering that for a small fee she could arrange to have Luke sent on a one-way trip to the other side of the world. Joe knew that his crazy, surrogate aunty could always be relied on to maximise the perks of her job, but kidnapping was probably one ask too far.

They were almost home. Joe's mind had turned the day inside out and upside down and he had come to one conclusion: Tilly was definitely the one for him, no doubt about it. Not only that, he was sure that she was going to seal the deal and tell him the same thing. During the walk back to the cars, she'd whispered that she wanted to meet him the next day, somewhere private. Tilly said they needed to make some plans and she wanted to explain a few things. His heart had gone crazy with happiness and he agreed at once. They chose to meet at the shrine in the village at 2pm where they could talk without interruption before heading over to his mum's for the giant paella eating bonanza. Joe was on cloud nine and completely confident that all would be well and soon, the girl of his dreams would be his.

Joe, have you never heard the saying about counting your chickens? You need to hold your horses, sunshine, because in your case, those eggs definitely haven't hatched, not by a long chalk!

Sunday dawned bright and cheery and as Daniel watched *Le Meteo*, he tried to concentrate on the forecast for the week ahead while ignoring the butterflies in his stomach and the death ray stares and oppressive static that hung in the air. The latter emanating from his sullen daughter who'd joined him in the lounge. The telly weathergirl was trying to put a cheerful spin on the fact that by Monday morning, the heavens were going to open and a downpour of biblical proportions was to be expected.

At least today was set to be fair which meant all Anna's planning (and his own) wouldn't be dampened and her feast could go ahead, along with his own much rehearsed proposal. He just wished that Louise would let go of being left alone all day with nobody but a windy dog for company. It was her choice for heaven's sake and by the look of her now, she'd found solace in his wine cellar and the contents of the fridge. Self-inflicted injury was what his old dad would have called Louise's hangover, and it served her right for faking illness the day before. Everyone knew she wasn't really sick enough to stay at home, which both embarrassed and annoyed him. Ignoring his daughter's mood, nothing was going to rain on Daniel's parade and without so much as a cursory glance in Louise's direction, he announced that he was taking Pippa for a walk and left the room.

. . .

Anna was in the freezer, well not literally, but she had her head stuck inside its icy depths and was extracting her haul of ingredients in preparation for her foray into Spanish cuisine. She'd always wanted to make a giant paella and had practised in England (twice) with a mini version. Nobody had died as a result, so today she was going for the 'big one'. As she made her way from the garage with her carrier bag of frozen fish bits, she spotted Daniel walking briskly towards the gate.

'Hey, who's chasing you?' she called to him as he fastened Pippa's lead.

Since her rampage through the farmer's field their little diva was being taught a lesson in obedience. Hence her disgusted expression and apparent lack of enthusiasm. Usually, Pippa would be nudging the gate in her eagerness to get out whereas now, she had plonked herself on the path and appeared to be going nowhere fast.

'Oh, nobody. I'm just keeping out of Louise's way. She's got a right face on her in there, so I'm going for a walk. I'm not in the mood for preaching to the inconvertible today. If she wants to sulk, then that's up to her. I've had enough of her attitude and it's only nine o'clock.' Daniel kissed Anna and undid the latch then pulled on the lead to give Pippa the hint.

'Right, well if that's the case I'll do the same and get on with peeling prawns. Don't let her get you down, love. We had such a fab time yesterday and I'm really looking forward to having everyone round later. If you get really desperate you can always help me in the kitchen.' Anna gave him a one-armed hug and then glanced down at her grumpy dog.

'Daniel, don't you think she's learned her lesson? I'm sure she'll be a good girl from now on, won't you, princess?' Anna bent down and kissed the top of Pippa's head then looked sadly up at Daniel, doing what most mum's do and tried to get their kids (and naughty dogs) off the hook.

'Okay, okay, I give in. But if she runs away again I'm not going in that field, wellies on or not. If you want to get bitten by a snake it's up to you.' With that Daniel bent down and unhooked the lead.

If dogs could wink, Anna was sure Pippa had just sent one her way as she trotted triumphantly out of the gate and headed up the lane.

Anna loved entertaining and as this was her last day with them all together, she wanted it to be perfect. She was extra pleased when Daniel surprised her with a crate of champagne, which they only ever had on special occasions and was touched he'd splashed out. He'd said that time with their loved ones was special, and they should celebrate being surrounded by the people that mattered the most.

That was one of the reasons Anna loved Daniel so much, because he knew exactly what made her happy. Most importantly, Daniel was part of all that. He was family too and for that she was eternally grateful. Glancing towards the lounge, Anna forced herself to include Louise in that sentiment, mainly out of respect for Daniel, but when it came down to it, the girl tried her patience, she really did.

Footsteps on the stairs alerted her that there was actually life on the first floor after all, and finally, she could begin the day so without further ado, Anna flicked on the kettle and waited for them to descend. In six hours and counting, her garden would be full of friends and family where she would enjoy the last few hours with her sons before they headed off for the coast and her paella-fest could begin. But before all that, she needed to send someone over to Rosie's to collect one of Michel's huge pans so whichever of her dear sons appeared first, they'd get the job. Looking up from the coffee cups she smiled when she spotted Joe and passing him a steaming mug, gave him his orders for the day.

* * *

Tilly was bleary-eyed and half asleep when she set off with

Freda for her meeting with Rosie. Her mother was so excited about her new outfit and wonderful day out with Olivia, not to mention the opportunity to fine-tune the wedding breakfast. Consequently, after a very quick shower, she was treated to an impromptu fashion show that quite frankly, made her want to weep.

Tilly thought her mum looked beautiful. Her day in the company of Audrey Hepburn's long-lost twin had done her the world of good and Freda positively glowed as she tried on the new outfit that suited her to a tee.

Olivia had pumped much-needed self-confidence into Freda and from what Tilly could see, the jaded, frumpy ex-schoolteacher had been vanquished. Her mum's metamorphosis had apparently begun the moment she stepped into the changing rooms of a swanky boutique, and the old Freda was replaced by a glowing, semi-retired, très chic ex-pat. Freda told Tilly all about it as she lovingly removed her new outfit from between a layer of soft tissue.

* * *

The day had begun in a small bistro where they fortified themselves with a strong cup of coffee and a delicate pastry which Freda tried to refuse, owing to her pre-wedding calorie counting. This was instantly poo-pooed by Olivia who insisted that life was short and from now on, she should embrace the French way of eating a little of what you fancied, and to hell with calories because they were sent by the devil to torment mankind. Olivia never ate large meals but she did enjoy small, delicious portions of whatever she liked, which meant she never felt deprived of anything remotely naughty and it prevented her from obsessing about mealtimes to boot.

'My dear, Freda, I was slim for most of my life and enjoyed the attention one gets from being able to slither into most things. However, life and various unmentionable bodily changes eventually take control and frankly, I haven't the inclination to constantly battle with the penalties of gravity, elasticity or any other form of expansion or contraction this ageing body imposes on me. Instead, I make the most of what I've got and languish in the knowledge that my dear Henry loves the very creaky bones of me, and would have me no other way.' Olivia delicately dabbed the corner of her mouth before continuing.

'I suggest that instead of worrying yourself into an early grave about how you wish you were, you concentrate on your assets, which in your case would be a rather enviable bosom, a glorious head of hair, wonderful legs and a brain between your ears. Stop putting yourself down for heaven's sake! You are a voluptuous, attractive woman who has had a career, two children and the wherewithal to migrate to a foreign country and rather than sit on her bottom and give up, she is now bestowing wisdom on the children of the future. Nobody handed all this to you on a plate, Freda, it's the result of study, hard work and a wise investment which allows you to live a fulfilling life and do something most women could only dream of. Need I say more?' Olivia didn't require a reply because she knew she was right and instead, with a little wiggle of her fingers, graciously alerted the waiter, with whom she was on first name terms, and asked for the bill.

'Righty-ho. Let's get this show on the road. I think we should have a little browse to start off with and get a feel for what you like and then, when we are sure we're on the right track, we'll have a try on. Once we have the perfect outfit we can do shoes, hat and bag after lunch. Now, I don't want you to be worried because I shan't go mad with silly designer price tags and I know where we can nab something just as delightful for a fraction of the price. Come along, no time to dilly-dally.' And with that, they were off.

Olivia had given Freda a lot to think about and as they pointed at mannequins in chic boutique windows, oohing and aahing over pretty summer dresses and stylish two pieces, she began to shed her old skin and embrace the words of wisdom her new friend had imparted.

Freda's personal shopper was fun, extremely witty, in a

dry sort of way, and completely honest when it came to most things, including what Freda looked good or dreadful in, yet rather than make her feel like the fault was with a part of her body, it was blamed entirely on the cut of the fabric or the shade not doing her justice. When they finally settled on the perfect outfit, Freda gazed at herself in the mirror as Olivia fussed and clapped, insisting she gave everyone a little twirl so that she shimmered in the light as the soft fabric showed off her tanned calves and sun-kissed skin.

Olivia had resisted any of Freda's tendencies towards unflattering, cover-up styles and instead they gravitated towards dresses which accentuated her curves. She also wanted Freda to stand out, be the one who you noticed on the family photos and not pale into insignificance. When her muse stepped out of the changing room in a sleeveless creation cut from silk, crepe de chine, the soft coral of the luxurious fabric enhanced her skin tone while the scoop of the tasteful neckline gently skimmed her best assets. The dress was gently fitted and its hidden bodice secretly nipped and tucked beneath the delicate fabric, allowing the cut of the dress to flow gracefully over her body creating smooth lines. The *pièce de résistance* was the perfectly matching over-coat made from a fine, intricate lace which flounced slightly towards the hem, swishing gracefully as Freda paraded up and down in a pair of very high heels, loaned by the boutique. The sleeves were straight and slimming and the turned-up collar gave a dramatic twist and an extra injection of style to the stunning creation.

Never in a million years would Freda have chosen this. From every angle she looked wonderful, not bumpy and lumpy but shapely and yes, voluptuous. After she stressed about the fact that she'd probably never wear the outfit again and whether Olivia thought it might be a bit of a waste, Freda was assured that the jacket could be worn over white linen trousers, and a pair of flat sandals would dress down her lovely frock for a more casual occasion. In a flash, Freda's conscience was appeased.

After a scrumptious lunch and a glass of champagne to celebrate, they went in search of accessories. By late afternoon, Freda was the owner of the most beautiful burnished silver shoes and matching handbag that she had ever seen. The subject of a hat, however, became a small bone of contention.

Freda insisted she didn't need one and could manage perfectly well without, once she'd had her hair done but from the look on Olivia's face, anyone would've thought she'd committed blasphemy.

Olivia happened to know that Luke's obnoxious mother had a very large hat worthy of the royal box at Ascot, making her even more adamant that Freda was not to be upstaged, whatever the cost.

One of Olivia's most endearing and charming attributes was that she was acutely aware of her fortunate position in life and would never purposely make any other human being feel uncomfortable (unless they deserved it) and had dedicated much of her life to being benevolent wherever possible. Having already spotted *the* perfect beau chapeau, and not one to be put off or denied easily, Olivia swiftly changed tack.

It seemed that during the winter months back in England, she had a few engagements planned, including a christening, an investiture and an audience with the bishop. This being the case, Olivia would require a choice of suitable head attire and the lovely cocktail hat with the swirls of silver roses would not only be perfect for Freda's outfit, but bizarrely, was just the ticket for a number of ensembles she had at home. Therefore, Olivia intended purchasing the delightful little hat and would then loan it to Freda for the wedding, how was that for a compromise?

Freda wasn't quite sure if Olivia was telling the truth but it *was* lovely and she knew that horrible Hazel would just love to have a dig at her. Freda had recognised in Olivia a woman who wouldn't give up so easily and had registered the steely glint of determination in her eye. Giving in to a worthy adversary and her aching feet, Freda wearily agreed and watched as Olivia gleefully plucked the hat from the stand and proceeded to arrange it on top of Freda's head, declaring that it was, as she knew it would be, just perfect!

* * *

The Olivia effect still hadn't worn off and as far as Tilly was concerned, her mother had been revitalised and invigorated with a new lease of life and an uncharacteristic effervescence. This fact both unnerved and pleased Tilly. That's why, when Freda stepped into the bedroom, dressed from head to toe in elegance, buoyed by her new-found confidence and looking a million dollars, Tilly's heart hurt for her lovely, excited mum and the tears that flowed were a mixture of pride, self-loathing and utter despair.

'Mum, you look a zillion dollars! Has Dad seen it yet? I just love the colour, you look fab, Mum, you really do. See you've got me all teary now.'

Tilly wiped her eyes and tried to pull herself together while Freda looked pleased and concerned all at once.

'Aw, love, don't get all weepy. Here, blow your nose, otherwise you'll get me going too. I'm glad you like it though. I would never have chosen anything like this, but Olivia had me trying on all sorts and it's given me loads of ideas of how I'd like to look from now on. After the wedding, I'm going to have a spring clean and chuck all my frumpy clothes out, then start again with my autumn wardrobe, not that I'll be shopping where Olivia does but I'm definitely going to spice up my life with a new look. What do you think, am I being a bit frivolous and vain?' Freda stopped admiring herself as she handed Tilly another tissue.

'No, Mum, you are not being frivolous, not at all. It's about time you stopped putting yourself down and focused on all your good points. You're in your fifties not the knacker's yard! Sometimes it takes another person to point out where you're going wrong and give you the courage to change. There's absolutely nothing wrong with that and nobody could ever accuse you of being vain either.'

As Freda smiled at her reflection and nodded in agreement, Tilly wondered just whose change she was talking about, hers or her mother's.

'Right, I'll hide this in your room if that's okay? I want it to be a surprise for your dad when he sees the new me. We need to get a move on and get over to Rosie's. I'm looking forward to seeing her and I want you to double check I've got everything right.' Freda began by carefully wrapping her shoes in the tissue and then placing them in the box.

'Dad thinks you're the bee's knees in whatever you wear, Mum, I hope you know that? I'll hang your outfit in my wardrobe so it won't get creased. Don't forget, I'm nipping over to the Harrisons' after we've been to Rosie's. I want to say bye to Joe and Sam and after that, I'm all yours. Is that okay?' Tilly's heart did a triple somersault the second she thought about her meeting with Joe.

'That's fine, love. Dad and I are going to take a stroll around the lake and then nip over to see one of his *pétanque* buddies for a late lunch. We'll meet you here later, then you are all mine, at least until the family turn up. Ooh, I get butterflies just thinking about seeing Scott and Charlotte next week. I miss them so much, I can't wait.'

Freda was lost in a haze of excitement and anticipation whilst her daughter was somewhat cast adrift, somewhere different entirely, in a land almost devoid of joy or absolution.

CHAPTER FIFTEEN

Joe was in a buoyant mood as he pulled into the drive of Rosie's hotel. The previous night he'd slept like a log for the first time in ages. For once his head wasn't full of niggling questions concerning Tilly. He knew from her body language, the silent looks, the tone and context of their conversations and the almost tangible electricity between the two of them that it was in the bag. Even Sam confirmed as much last night, once they'd dropped her off and were sure that Ross and Jules were still asleep.

Apparently, it was blatantly obvious to *everyone* that Tilly was crazy about him and they'd been the secret topic of conversation for most of the day and watched with much amusement by his family. When Sam called time on their conversation and began to snore, Joe drifted off to sleep with a contented smile on his face and even though it was the height of summer, he felt like a little kid on Christmas Eve.

His mum had roped him into driving to the hotel to collect a giant paella pan which apparently, Michel had ready and waiting. She also needed some smoked paprika and reminded Joe to ask if he had any, because she could only find the regular stuff in the supermarket and it was an essential part of the recipe. She'd been flapping about it since yesterday.

There was no one about when Joe opened the front door and the place seemed unusually quiet, so he made his way along the corridor in search of life. There didn't appear to be anyone in the restaurant either, so he went through the small bar and into the kitchen at the back where he found Michel, who was engrossed in wiping down his gleaming, stainless steel surfaces.

Joe hadn't seen either Michel or Rosie for ages so decided to stay and have coffee. Rosie, it seemed, was busy going through last-minute wedding details with a bride-to-be and her mother, while Michel needed to be on hand in case there was an issue with the menu. Joe settled down on one of the kitchen stools and caught up with all the news while Michel hastily prepared a tray of champagne flutes and Buck's Fizz for the wedding party, then made a pot of fresh coffee and warmed up some croissants.

Out in the garden, Rosie was explaining where the beautiful white pagoda would go and how amazing it would look when the sun went down and the fairy lights came on. They had already discussed the flowers, which would be wound around the wooden legs of the structure and match perfectly those on the centre of each table in the dining area.

Tilly had to admit that it sounded wonderful and if she was a normal bride, then right at this moment she would be bursting with heady expectation. As it was, the gargantuan effort it took to fix a smile on her face and say all the right things at the right time was almost killing her. If it hadn't been for her mum's non-stop chatter since they walked through the door, Tilly thought Rosie might have guessed something was wrong.

After the banquet, their guests would move outside and

the evening would continue under the pagoda and the stars. Her first dance with Luke would also take place here, on the flower-adorned terrace. As she inhaled the heady scent from clematis, and other assorted climbers and fragrant potted plants, Tilly cheerily confirmed the choice of romantic music, which everyone now thought was 'their song' when in truth, they didn't actually have one. What a joke!

Tilly remembered with clarity the night she received an email from Freda telling them to get their fingers out and choose some nice music that would be played during the meal, and not to forget a special song to start the dancing off. Both Tilly and Luke panicked slightly when it dawned on them that they didn't have one joint song they liked, or anything remotely suitable on their respective iPods, either.

They laughed it off and messed about for a while thinking of really stupid tunes that would send Freda into a frenzy and probably offend most of their guests, then when the joke wore a bit thin, they ignored the undercurrent of embarrassment and turned to the internet for panic induced inspiration. In the end, they chose from a list of 'Top 100 First Dance Ballads' courtesy of an online wedding site, settling for what they considered to be the least cringe-worthy option. That night, when Tilly went to bed feeling cheated and deflated, she completely ignored the writing on the bedroom wall, instead, she told herself that loads of couples didn't have the same taste in music, or a special song, it was no big deal, just a blip, get over it.

As she traipsed obediently inside after her mum and Rosie, Tilly sadly acknowledged that once again, she'd ignored the flashing neon signs. It was now menu time and the part that Freda was really looking forward to, because this was going to be the most spectacular feast anyone in her family (and hopefully Hazel and Ken) had ever tasted in all their lives.

Rosie settled them both down at one of the tables which had been set precisely as it would be on the big day, with crisp white tablecloths and elegant citrus green runners. In the centre were large goblets filled with crystals which would be festooned with fresh summer flowers. The chairs were also covered in white and embellished with matching voile, tied artfully into huge, trailing bows at the back of each seat. Freda thought they looked smashing and in turn, Rosie appeared to be genuinely pleased that her handiwork was appreciated.

It seemed she preferred Michel to explain the menu so leaving what Tilly would describe as a giddy mother and her strangely subdued daughter in peace, Rosie excused herself and went in search of her husband.

When Rosie entered the kitchen she spotted Joe and enveloped him in a big hug.

'Hello, stranger, long time no see. You look really well, has your mum been feeding you up? Look, I can't stop and talk right now, I'm fine-tuning a wedding, but we can have a long chat this afternoon. Tell Anna I can't wait to see her, and Jeannie too!' Taking the tray with the drinks, Rosie looked over to Michel.

'Come along, genius, your audience awaits. I know you think it's boring but just tell them how fantastic you are, have a quick chat about the food, then I'll let you off duty. See you later, Joe.'

Rosie winked cheekily at her husband who obediently began to clear away the coffee cups.

Joe waved to Rosie. 'I'd best get going too. Thanks for this, Michel. Mum's going to make enough to feed all of France so she obviously needs the biggest pan in Europe! Catch you later and thanks for the coffee.' Michel assured him it was no trouble as Joe heaved the giant utensil off the counter and made his way back through the hotel.

As he left the bar area, he slipped quietly past the entrance of the dining room, not wanting to disturb Rosie, when he heard something that stopped him dead in his tracks.

Rosie had been speaking, obviously telling one of her funny stories when he heard someone laugh and it was one he would've recognised anywhere, among a thousand people. It was Tilly! But why would she be here? Joe stood completely still, trying to work out what to do. Curiosity soon got the better of him as an unwelcome feeling of dread slowly pervaded his pounding heart.

Turning quickly, before he could chicken out, he made his way back to the dining room door from where he listened intently. Rosie was offering copies of the menu and then another woman spoke, saying they looked amazing. She sounded older and definitely wasn't Tilly. The next to speak was Rosie who mentioned special dietary requirements, still nothing, until the older voice asked a question and his heart simply froze.

'Tilly, are you one hundred percent sure there are no vegetarians coming to the reception. The last thing I want is poor Michel having to make an omelette or something. You might need to ring Luke later and double check, imagine if Hazel is a vegan. That's all we need. Will you do that, better safe than sorry?'

Joe thought he was going to faint, or be sick. His blood had run cold, rendering him useless, completely paralysed and welded to the spot as he put two and two together. His mind was all over the place, he was devastated, confused, bewildered and whilst instinct dared him to march in and see for himself, fear of the known prevented him from taking a look. The appearance of Michel quickly solved his dilemma.

'Hey, Joe, are you okay? Did you want Rosie? Hey, Rosie, Joe wants you.' Michel simply assumed he'd forgotten to ask her something and almost pushed Joe through the door.

Rosie, who was pouring drinks, turned to Joe and smiled brightly. 'Hi, Joe, have you forgotten something?'

Standing in the doorway, trapped like a rabbit in the headlights, holding a giant comedy pan in front of him like a shield, Joe wanted the ground to open up and swallow him whole. His mouth was bone dry and his lips were numb, his tongue had inconveniently lost the ability to move. For what seemed like hours, he just stared blankly at Rosie, too embarrassed to speak. It was Freda's surprised intervention that broke the spell and gave him a few precious seconds to recover and gather his senses.

'Oh, hello, Joe, fancy seeing you here. I've got a bone to pick with you, young man! I believe you and your brother are responsible for kidnapping my daughter over the past week. I've hardly seen her since she got here, but I suppose I'll have to let you off. Thanks for keeping her occupied while we were poorly. It's a shame you're going away because I'm sure we could've squeezed a few more in for the do, the more the merrier I say.' Freda was going at it ten to the dozen and seemed oblivious to Joe's catatonic state and that her daughter had turned the colour of a cherry.

Rosie, however, was on red alert. Amongst her many attributes, she was credited with being a people person, adept at reading signs and picking up on the merest of nuances and today, instinctively knew that something was wrong. She'd known Joe for a while and from the looks of him, he was about to pass out or burst into tears. And judging by the unflattering shade of puce that Tilly had turned, she had something to do with it. Offering Freda a glass of Buck's Fizz, hoping it would distract her and shut her up at the same time, Rosie excused herself and made her way over to Joe. Placing a firm but gentle hand on his elbow she attempted to guide him from the room, just as he found his voice which came out as a barely audible whisper.

Replying to Freda, Joe said the first thing he thought of. 'Oh, right, sorry about that. Hope you're feeling better.' Then he turned to Rosie, who seemed to be pulling him out of the door. He still couldn't bear to look at Tilly.

'Right, Joe. What was it you wanted?' Rosie was hoping he'd take the hint and leave the room but he seemed glued to the spot. *'God this is awkward,'* she thought to herself as she willed him to speak or move, anything would do.

'Paprika. Smoked paprika. Have you got any? Mum wanted me to take some back for her. I forgot to ask.' Joe had no idea how he managed to extract the words from his brain but it seemed to work. Then Michel piped in.

'Of course I have it. Wait there. I'll bring it for you. I will be very quick, *chéri*, two minutes.' And with that, he scooted off leaving Joe alone with Rosie who was steering him towards the bar.

'Why don't you wait here for Michel, I have to finish up in the dining room. I'll see you later at your mum's.' Rosie gave Joe a quick, reassuring squeeze and a worried smile. The poor lad looked dreadful and she had a very good idea why.

'Okay, thanks, Rosie. I'll stay here.' Joe had no option than to do as Rosie suggested because he seemed to have lost the use of his body and the ability to think straight.

Michel, appearing with the paprika was Rosie's cue to return to her guests, so with a quick ruffle of Joe's hair and, what she hoped was, a conspiratorial wink, she left him with Michel.

'Thanks for that. I'd best get going. Mum will be waiting.' And without another word Joe took his package and the giant pan and made his way up the hall and out of the door, leaving Michel somewhat bemused and slightly concerned.

By the time Joe reached his mum's car, his hands had begun to shake and once he'd chucked the stupid pan and the paprika on the back seat, he opened the front door and sat behind the wheel in stunned silence.

What the hell was going on?

'Don't be a complete prat, Joe! You know very well what's going on. You've been had, mate! Taken for a ride. Used. Made a fool of. Sucked in. Need I go on?' Joe's brain had kicked into action and was now making itself heard.

How could she do that to him? How could she lie, lead him up the garden path and take him *and* his family in, so completely. What kind of sick person was she?

'A complete and utter bitch, mate, that's what! She's had you running round after her all week, keeping her occupied while her parents were sick and she killed time until her fiancé turned up. And that's not all, sucker, she had no intention of finishing with him because she's getting married. That's just hysterical! And there's you walking about like a lovesick kid thinking you had it made, and she was about to kick him into touch. You are one big, fat loser!' Joe's face was burning with shame and humiliation. And then hurt arrived at the party.

It started gradually and had to fight for a place amongst the multitude of other emotions and brain searing thoughts that were fizzing around his body at that moment. Once it started to spread, it took a firm, unyielding grip and his heart actually began to feel pain as his throat constricted, forcing him to swallow and hold down the tide of emotions that were gushing from within. Joe was adamant he would not cry. No way would he give in to tears because that would make him feel even more pathetic.

Instead, he focused on the anger and disappointment that was a by-product of the scene he had just witnessed. Not wanting to spend one more second anywhere near Tilly, or her annoying mother, Joe turned on the engine and reversed out of his parking space and drove quickly onto the lane, flicking up dust and stones as he sped away from the hotel, eager to put as much distance as he could between himself and the cause of his anguish.

Tilly was in the toilet of the hotel, splashing water on her face and trying to prevent a bout of hysteria, which she knew was bubbling just below the surface of her clammy skin. If ever there was a moment to possess superhuman powers, it was a few minutes ago. She'd have settled for something simple like invisibility, anything that could've avoided the mortifyingly dreadful events in the dining room.

She was almost at the finishing line too. All she had to do was endure another hour of 'let's pretend' and then she could've hotfooted it over to Joe and explained everything. In the act of unburdening herself, Tilly had hoped to acquire a new member of her team or at the very least another human being to share her predicament, give her some advice or a shoulder to cry on. Now it was all ruined. Joe wouldn't even look at her and his poor face, she would never forget how hurt and shocked he'd looked. Worst of all, he thought he'd been betrayed, by her of all people. It was written all over him.

Tilly was also sure that whilst her mother was mildly perturbed by, but not suspicious of, Joe's swift exit and monosyllabic conversation, Rosie was definitely onto her. Freda had casually remarked that she remembered him being a bit chattier, then took a swig of her drink and got on with the more important business of reading each course of the wedding banquet, out loud.

In order to conceal her trembling hands, Tilly had clasped them together underneath the tablecloth, put her head down and focused on the words before her, which had begun to blur at the onset of tears. When Rosie returned, Tilly noticed two spots of pink on each of her cheeks and whilst she did a very professional job of looking composed, it was obvious she was flustered.

The addition of Michel around the table took the heat off for a second and once he became lost in his menu, taking Freda with him on his journey of gastronomic delights, Tilly found herself under the full glare of Rosie who was clearly scrutinising her every move. Unable to bear it any longer and unsure of her own ability to keep herself in check, Tilly had politely asked where the toilets were and excused herself from the table.

Rosie was now in a dilemma. Should she follow Tilly into the toilet and check she was okay, because it was clear that she was anything but? Then again, she hardly knew her and could be accused of poking her nose in, at the same time as alerting Freda to what was obviously 'a situation'. If her intuition served her correctly, Miss Tilly Parker, the blushing bride-to-be had formed some kind of friendship with Joe who, from the looks of him, had no idea she was going to be at the hotel today and more to the point, getting married.

Using her well-honed powers of deduction and drawing on many years of experience in the hospitality industry, she was almost convinced that what she had witnessed was a case of someone being led up the garden path. Had Joe known Tilly was engaged or involved with someone in any way shape or form, he would run a mile. Rosie knew this for a certainty. Therefore, when Joe spotted Tilly, instead of being his usual affable self and more than capable of making polite small talk with anyone, he clammed up. He had behaved like a new boy on his first day at school, or someone invited to make an impromptu speech, or worse, a man who'd just realised he'd walked into the middle of something he shouldn't have.

Poor Joe! Everything was making sense now. Add all this to the fact that since they arrived, she'd been a little put out by Tilly's lack of input or enthusiasm, however, she had presumed it may be a case of 'overbearing mother syndrome'. Yes, thought Rosie, now she came to think of it, on a number of occasions Tilly had to be prompted by Freda to give an opinion or state a preference. Now, with new, albeit tenuous information to hand, Rosie surmised that Tilly might not be quite as happy about her upcoming nuptials as one would expect.

Then it hit her. Bloody hell, what if they cancel? All Michel's planning and her own meticulous preparations would be for nothing. Rosie felt the swell of panic in her chest as she realised that her husband would already have placed orders for the lavish ingredients needed for his menu, not to mention the florist and the DJ who would be out of pocket, and she'd arranged extra waiting staff.

Rosie had to stay calm and think clearly. Panicking wouldn't do any of them any good. No, she would tie up all the loose ends quickly and then, once Freda and Tilly were gone, she would have a peep in Michel's kitchen file and see exactly where he was up to. There was no need to alert him just yet, especially because his highly strung, Gallic nature wouldn't be able to stand the stress of the threat of cancellation. Michel loved grand occasions like this and a chance to show off his undeniable culinary skills. Instead, she would proceed with caution and get over to Anna's and have a word about Joe.

Noticing Tilly on her way back from the loo, Rosie switched to professional mode and proceeded to move the meeting swiftly along and get them both out of the door as soon as possible. Across the table, Tilly appeared composed if slightly flushed, focusing on Michel and Freda, steadfastly avoiding eye contact with her inquisitor, something which further confirmed to Rosie that she was right. Miss Pink Cheeks definitely had something to hide.

Well, one thing was for sure, there was no way on earth that she would let Joe get hurt any more than he already was, or allow her husband to waste his time and energy on a non-event. One way or another, Rosie had to get to the bottom of it. The sooner the better for all concerned.

Joe drove home far too fast and he knew it. He didn't even know why he was in such a hurry as he'd already decided that he couldn't be around his family right now. There was way too much going on in his head and he needed time to think, but first, he had a delivery to make. Luck was on his side (or had taken pity on him) and as Joe pulled onto the drive, he noticed Jules and Ross kicking a football about so he wound down his window and called them over.

'Can you do a favour for me, mate, and give these to Aunty Anna. The pan is very heavy so you'll both need to hold it by the handles. Tell her I'm nipping to the shops and I'll be back in a bit.' Joe was already out of the car and dragging the pan from the back seat as he spoke to Ross who was happy to run an errand.

'Here, hold it tight and don't lose this bag of spices, okay.

I'll see you later. Thanks, lads.' And without saying another word, he tossed the packet of paprika into the pan and watched the two small boys make their way towards the house. He then quickly reversed out of the drive and onto the road before anyone spotted him.

Joe had no idea where he was going so he just drove, following the road, taking bends and sharp turns at dangerously high speeds, oblivious to his surroundings but deeply aware of how tight and heavy his heart felt beneath his ribs. Spotting the sign for the fishing lake, he slowed and turned onto the narrow track that led to an expanse of calm water that was lined with mature trees and shaded by their abundant, leafy branches. He pulled onto the car park which bordered the water's edge and turned off the engine. In the distance, Joe could see fishermen dotted around the bank, lost in quiet contemplation as they waited patiently for their lines to twitch.

This would do fine. It was isolated and peaceful. Here he could think and try to create some order in his confused, befuddled mind. Leaning his throbbing skull against the head rest, he focused on the almost motionless water. The call of a wood pigeon occasionally broke through the silence as Joe began taking apart the events at the hotel, one by one, frame by frame, reliving the moment when his dreams were shattered and his faith in love, the human spirit and an almost attainable happy ending, once again crashed and burned.

* * *

Tilly thought she would never get away from the hotel or her mother but knew she had to tread very, very carefully because any reserves of strength or tenacity she once possessed were now utterly depleted. Fragile, that's how she would describe her present state and if her mum so much as pushed the wrong button in the next few minutes, Tilly knew she would explode like an egg trapped in the microwave, or something equally as volatile and unstable.

To her credit, Rosie had wrapped things up briskly, which was a relief because there had definitely been a frostiness where Tilly had been concerned. It was as though Rosie was sending a silent warning across the table which unnerved and unsettled Tilly even more.

They were now on their way home and it had taken every ounce of self-control not to throw her mum out on the side of the road and race straight round to Joe's. Freda had suggested that Tilly should ring Luke the second they got back to ask about the 'vegetarian threat' and was only marginally mollified by the fact he was at football and wouldn't be contactable for a while. Tilly knew her tone was borderline snappy and after that, her mum became rather quiet and thoughtful, making her feel mean and acutely aware of the awkward silence in the car. Pushing these thoughts away, mainly to alleviate guilt, Tilly focused on more pressing issues. She wasn't supposed to be meeting Joe for another hour but couldn't wait that long, not now. She had to see him straight away and her mum insisting they observed the road signs and drove at the speed of a tortoise really didn't help.

By the time they pulled up at home, Tilly was actually gritting her teeth and suspected a migraine was imminent. As her huffy mother got out of the car, Tilly remained in the driver's seat and announced she was going straight out again.

'But you don't have to be at the Harrisons' for ages. I thought we could show your dad the menu and tell him all about the meeting. Do you really have to go now?' Freda looked crestfallen.

'Sorry, Mum, I just need to go now. I want to nip to the shop and buy a bottle of wine and you have to get ready for your walk. You can show Dad the menu, have a nice time, I'll see you tonight. Love you.' Putting the car into gear, Tilly drove off, not daring to look her mother in the eye or give her a chance to complain.

.   .   .

Freda stood at the gate and stared. Did Tilly really think she was that stupid? Everyone knew that the shops were shut on a Sunday and her speedy departure had sod all to do with buying wine. Howard had gallons of the stuff in the garage!

Something was going on and it had a lot to do with that Joe Harrison. Everyone might think she was going a bit scatty but you'd have to be deaf, dumb and blind not to have picked up on the weird atmosphere at the hotel, which coincidentally manifested itself the second Joe made his appearance. It was so embarrassing! What with him standing there like the cat got his tongue and Tilly turning the colour of one of Howard's beetroots.

Freda had tried to brush it off and make light of Joe's strange behaviour, but Rosie definitely picked up on it and did her best to jolly things along, especially when Tilly disappeared into the toilets. The only person who seemed oblivious was Michel, who thankfully didn't notice her daughter's peculiar mood. It was blatantly obvious what was going on and she'd been a fool to miss it earlier. Tilly performing another disappearing act did nothing to quell Freda's anxieties or allay the suspicions that niggled during the drive home. The awkward scene at the hotel earlier told her one thing, and one thing only. No matter how hard Freda tried to deny it, the expression on her daughter's face was that of pure, unadulterated guilt!

Freda had seen that look a hundred times before, not only in her own offspring when they'd been caught out over some minor childhood prank or been discovered behaving badly, but on the faces of her pupils as they tried to convince her that the dog ate their homework or when they'd cheated in a test. That word alone spread tentacles of fear through her body and gripped her heart because if she wasn't mistaken (and she prayed she was) there was definitely something going on between Tilly and Joe. This unwelcome revelation left her with one burning question. Was her daughter a cheat?

The uncomfortable car ride had given Freda time to

assimilate all the evidence and to her despair, she had come to one conclusion. At some point over the past week, during their fun days out with the bloody perfect Swiss Family Harrison, her daughter had formed some kind of relationship with Joe.

To what extent this entailed she dreaded to think, but by putting two and two together Freda had surmised that Tilly wanted to keep her parents and Joe as far apart as possible to prevent anyone giving the game away. Did Anna Harrison know what they'd been up to? She probably did, that's why Tilly belted out of the car park at the supermarket that day. Furthermore, when Freda invited them over for dinner she was instantly shot down by Tilly, and no blooming wonder! Even Howard commented that he hadn't got chance to say hello to the boys when they picked Tilly up and come to think of it, she'd always seemed very eager to get out of the house and scoot down the lane to meet him alone.

As she let herself inside the house, Freda was relieved to hear that Howard was in the shower which gave her a few minutes to compose herself and her thoughts. Throwing herself onto the sofa, she grabbed the nearest cushion and hugged it close to her chest as she processed any scrap of information or useful nugget in her quest for answers.

Freda prided herself on having an open house policy and welcomed all of her children's friends into her home, often having extra mouths to feed at dinner, sleepovers galore and another passenger in the car on days out. If their friendship was so innocent, then why hadn't Joe called in for a coffee or at least to say hello, he was supposed to be polite and well brought up, after all.

No wonder Tilly was neglecting Luke and seemed barely interested in her upcoming wedding. She had other fish to fry. Her beloved daughter had made the most of being away from her fiancé and sought the company of another man.

Freda was actually beginning to feel rather shocked and borderline incredulous at Tilly's behaviour. Just how far had it gone and just how worried should they be? From the looks of things, Tilly didn't give a fig about Luke and judging by the way she couldn't wait to get away just now, Joe was way up there on her daughter's list of priorities, even higher than her own parents. This was bad, really bad!

'Slow down, Freda, hold your horses and take a breath!' Common sense finally took the reins and halted her galloping thoughts, admonishing her for judging Tilly so harshly without proper evidence or taking into consideration the stress and anxiety involved in getting married. The waves of panic were calmed by a welcome voice of reason, easing its way inside her brain, releasing tension and loosening its grip on her heart. Just as Howard had suggested this could all be down to wedding day jitters.

Drawing on various articles she'd read in women's magazines and the few chick flicks she'd seen in the past, Freda compiled a list of worst case scenarios which she mentally ticked off, one by one.

Maybe it was just some kind of mild, harmless crush. This was Freda's preferred explanation and happened to the best of us, also, it was by far the most forgivable option.

Slightly more worrying was the possibility it was a revenge affair to banish the demons of Luke's infidelity. Freda found this to be understandable and heard it was quite common, but still not something she could condone.

The next scenario involved Tilly testing her true feelings towards Luke by pitting him against another man and comparing attributes. This was very risky and highly prone to temptation, but a potential winner and could definitely be swept under the carpet. Freda liked this option.

The thing was, Freda's brain insisted on asking the big question. What if it all came down to lust and condemning yourself to sex with the same man for the rest of your life? Maybe Tilly just fancied one last fling to see her through the next fifty years of marriage. Freda knew that if this was the case, then Tilly's marriage was doomed because it would be built on foundations of lies, infidelity and guilt.

When Howard appeared in the lounge, fresh from his shower and wondering where Tilly had got to, Freda was in utter turmoil and no better after her foray into psycho-analysis. After explaining that their daughter preferred the company of others to that of her own parents, she told Howard that she was going to get changed and stomped upstairs. In the silence of her room, Freda attempted to ignore the searing heat that raged inside her body, helpfully accompanied by thudding palpitations which only impacted her discomfort as she waited patiently for the feeling of panic to subside.

Looking despondently around the room she shared with her one true love, Freda glanced over to her dressing table which held treasured baby photographs of Tilly and Scott, but the one that always melted her heart was of her and Howard on their wedding day. Freda picked up the silver frame. She studied carefully the two young, innocent newlyweds, laughing into the camera as they stood on the steps of the church only minutes after they'd taken their vows. Hot tears gathered at the corners of her eyes as she looked upon the fresh-faced images who'd been so eager to start their journey through life together.

On that special day, they'd been completely unaware of the hurdles they'd have to jump, unfazed and undaunted by what lay ahead as they navigated their way through marriage and bringing two children into the world. Freda touched the fading photograph and sighed.

Freda's own wedding seemed a lifetime ago. The twenty-two-year-old girl in the photo was on the verge of becoming a fully-fledged woman, a wife, teacher, home-maker and eventually a mother. As she thought back to the days just before her own marriage to Howard, a flicker of something long since buried and best forgotten triggered memories and feelings that hadn't stirred for over thirty years. This remembrance of how it felt to be a nervous and confused bride-to-be brought forth a timely revelation and some welcome peace to Freda's soul. Before placing the photograph back on the dresser, Freda smiled and pressed a gentle kiss on the face of her beloved husband.

Freda knew how to get through to Tilly, let her know

she understood and that there was nothing to fear and everything was going to be okay.

Checking her watch, Freda rummaged in her make-up bag for her new lipstick and applied a fresh coat. Regarding herself closely in the mirror, she assured her image that everything was under control, she should bide her time and wait patiently for tomorrow. Whatever Tilly was doing right now was out of her hands. Steaming round to Anna's and interfering at this stage would only make things worse. Better to leave it until the morning when Joe would be gone and, once the coast was clear, Freda could set about clearing this mess, or whatever it was, up.

Taking a deep breath, she set off to look for Howard. They would take a stroll around the lake, have a nice lunch with their friends and he'd be none the wiser of today's events. Come what may, Freda fully intended to have Tilly back on track and raring to go long before the guests started to arrive.

CHAPTER SIXTEEN

Anna was busy peeling things when Ross and Jules appeared at the kitchen door, lugging Michel's paella pan and once she'd swiftly unburdened them, was surprised to hear that Joe had gone to the shops and would be back later. This left Anna mildly perplexed as they all knew that the shops were closed on Sunday and even if he found one open, what on earth would he be buying? Spotting the small parcel of paprika diverted Anna's attention and before long, she became re-engrossed in her preparations.

Louise was still in residence in the lounge and had managed to create an invisible no-go zone about her person due to the bad vibes emanating from every pore in her body. As far as she was concerned it was just another day in la-la land. The Happy Harrisons intended to have a hug-fest and entertain their bezzy mates, then give the golden boys a good send off. They were only going to the bloody seaside for pity's sake. God, Anna was pathetic! It was like a daily rerun of *Little House on the Prairie* living here, and it made Louise sick.

Had nobody even bothered to notice that her life was in

meltdown? Did anyone actually care about her anguish? Louise's stomach literally turned at the mere thought of facing Tomas when he arrived the following day. How could it have come to this, the stage where a wife was nervous about seeing her own husband? To make matters worse, Jules was so looking forward to seeing his papa.

Louise knew from the text messages she'd received from Tomas that he was losing patience and the threat of solicitors (issued via her father) proved he wasn't going to stand for much more. What also irked was that when he did turn up, it would be in the full glare of this lot and she'd have to play nicely, especially in front of her dad.

Deep down, Louise knew that she couldn't ruin her husband's career by refusing to go to Geneva or separate her child from his father. This didn't diminish the fact that Tomas was an arrogant, self-centred pig. Still, the truth couldn't be ignored, she loved him to bits and the thought of losing him was too much to bear. Despite this, it was imperative she saved face and came out the other side not looking like a jumped-up drama queen. What the hell was she going to do? For a start, she had to get through today with the Waltons, a pounding headache, and the nauseating smell of fish wafting round the house.

As she made her way upstairs to the shower, Louise heard a car pull onto the drive which instantly snapped her out of self-obsessed ponderings. What if it was Tomas arriving early? Rushing over to the window she cautiously peaked through, holding her breath before letting out a huge sigh of relief. It was only Tilly. Rolling her eyes, Louise resigned herself to another irritating goody-goody turning up to ruin her day. God, this place was just riddled with them!

Tilly was a bag of nerves as she made her way to Anna's front door. She'd spotted Louise peering out of the upstairs window and the paranoia that infested through her brain told her that she was warning Joe of her arrival. The front door, which led straight into the kitchen was open and before Tilly had chance to give a polite warning knock, Anna appeared from the utility room at the back, looking rather frazzled and carrying a basket of bread.

'Oh, hi, Tilly. If you're looking for Joe he's not here. The kids told me he's gone shopping but God knows where he'll find anything open today. The village shop shuts at twelve, I'm sure I told him. Would you like a drink while you wait? Just help yourself.'

Anna was at first oblivious to Tilly's nervous, agitated disposition, however, when she remained rooted to the spot and seemed to have lost her voice, her mum radar picked up warning signals.

'Is everything okay, Tilly? You look a bit pale, are you not feeling well?' Anna placed the bread on the table and approached her guest where she spotted tears welling in worried eyes.

'No, yes… I'm okay. I just need to speak to Joe. I was supposed to be meeting him in the village but I'm early. If he comes back, will you tell him I'll wait there? Thanks, Anna, I'll go and look for him now. And I'm sorry if I've caused any trouble, I'm really, really sorry. I've got to go. Bye.' And with that she turned and almost ran to the car.

Anna was now on red alert. What on earth was going on? What did Tilly mean, trouble? Going straight to the kitchen drawer she took out her phone and rang Joe. Her heart sank when the message said it was turned off, so she sent him a text which she hoped he'd read as soon as he switched it on again. Placing her phone on the table and checking it was set to loud, Anna went to the door and called out for Sam to come inside, maybe he'd know what was going on, if not, she'd interrogate Melanie. Surely one of them would be able to cast some light on what was upsetting Tilly and solve the mystery of her disappearing son at the same time. As she waited impatiently for Sam to appear, Anna had one of those feelings, a mild gnawing sensation that trouble was on the horizon and that today, of all days, might just turn out to be one of those she'd rather forget.

Tilly couldn't hold back the tears any longer, sobbing quietly as she wiped them from her sodden cheeks, desperately watching out for Joe as she made her way towards the centre of the village, praying all the time that she'd find him waiting for her.

She parked the car in front of the church and walked quickly towards the shrine and focused on the bench where she hoped he'd be sitting. She was disappointed. Her mind raced, turning over options and trying to come up with a sensible course of action. In the end, she settled for waiting it out. Twenty minutes and he would be here. She was convinced of it. He'd want to ask her what was going on and give her chance to explain, surely? The contingency plan was that if he didn't turn up, she would go back to Anna's and if he wasn't there, she'd wait at the end of the lane. If he still refused to speak to her then she'd damn well make him listen, one way or another.

All she had to do was be patient, take deep breaths and stay calm, which was easier said than done under the circumstances. Taking out her phone from her dress pocket, Tilly sent him a message, checked the time and settled down for the longest wait of her life.

Joe was attracting some odd stares from the fishermen at the lake as they ambled past with bait boxes or returned to their cars. He stuck out like a sore thumb in his mum's car with the English plates and they were obviously curious as to why he was sitting inside on a glorious day, staring out over the lake. The exodus signalled to Joe that it must be lunchtime, prompting him to take out his phone which he had switched off. Curiosity got the better of him and as he waited for it to boot up, he felt slightly nervous, wondering if there'd be a message from Tilly.

When the screen loaded up he saw three texts, from his mum, Sam, and the cause of his anguish, Tilly. He read them in order.

His mum's said—

Are you okay, son? Text back as soon as you get this message. Tilly called and she looked upset. She's going to wait for you in the village. Love you x

Sam's was more to the point—

What's going on, mate? Mum's stressing. Ring me when you get this.

Then Tilly's, which he saved until last, half scared to read the words, half of him too annoyed to give her the time of day—

Joe, please meet me at the shrine. I need to explain. I'll wait all day if I have to x

It was ten past one, she would think he wasn't coming which served her right, make her sweat a bit. Then a voice in his head told him he deserved some answers and it would drive him mad if he didn't find out what the hell was going on. Before he could change his mind, Joe turned the key in the ignition and fired off two texts, one to his mum saying he was fine, not to worry and he'd be back soon. Then another one to Sam saying he'd gone to meet Tilly and he'd explain later. That should keep them both happy. As for Tilly, he'd punish her a little longer.

When Tilly saw him walking towards her, the first emotion she felt was immense relief which was immediately banished by embarrassment tinged with dread. As it washed over her and chilled her bones, some insane drummer pounded away beneath her chest, increasing the erratic beat of her nervous heart to a frantic level.

Joe sat down beside her and remained silent, staring straight ahead while the gap between their bodies signified the wound she'd inflicted and how their closeness had been replaced by a chasm of mistrust.

It was clear he wasn't going to utter a word and was waiting for her to begin the conversation. The only words she could muster came out sounding weak and pathetic.

'Joe, I'm so sorry. Please believe that I never intended you to find out like that. I was going to tell you everything today and try to explain. It all got out of hand and I've wanted to tell you a thousand times, I swear I have.' Tilly still didn't dare to look at him. Instead, she let her words settle and just waited.

Joe's heart plummeted as he registered the meaning of her words. His stomach somersaulted, making him even madder, more scathing of his own pathetic self. So... it had got out of hand had it? Angry thoughts took over, steaming into battle and forming a protective layer around his heart.

You loser, Joe, you sad, gullible loser!'

By the time he found his tongue it had developed a sharp, cutting edge.

'I bet you didn't! You were having too much fun killing time until your fiancé turned up to whisk you down the aisle.' Just saying that word 'fiancé' made him want to laugh and cry at the same time. He was raging inside and before she could interrupt, Joe let rip.

'So, in all those thousands of times, what exactly was it you wanted to say, Tilly? Was it that you were a two-faced liar, a cheat or perhaps just downright false and one hundred percent untrustworthy. Does the lucky man know what a *real* gem he's going to be marrying? Because let's face it, you're very good at what you do, so I suspect he's being made a mug of, just like me.'

Joe was enraged by his own words which fuelled his anger and compounded the feeling of humiliation which was about to completely engulf him.

Tilly was hurt and horrified and almost screamed her response. She had to make him understand.

'Joe, please let me explain, listen to me, Joe. It's not like that. I swear to you everything I said about my feelings for Luke are true. I never wanted to mislead you and I should've told you straight away, I know that, but in a crazy way I wanted to pretend it wasn't happening.' Tilly forced herself to look at Joe as she pleaded. But he was closed down. His body language told her that, along with the steely look he gave her when he turned his head and stared coldly into her eyes.

'Are you completely mental or something? How the hell can you pretend that a wedding is not happening? You know what, I'm not even going to listen to this, it's just a sick joke and if you think you can convince me otherwise, you really are mad.'

Joe stood up and made to walk away but Tilly was too quick and grabbed his hand, gripping tightly as she jumped up from the bench and blocked his path.

'Please, Joe, I'm begging you. Hear me out. If I was the callous, mental case you think I am then I wouldn't be here now, would I? I'd be sitting at home forgetting all about you, not caring about your feelings, but instead, I'm standing here pleading and trying to make you understand. Just give me five minutes, Joe, that's all I ask. I've waited here for an hour, praying that you'd come so I could explain, so I could say sorry.' Tears were pumping from her eyes which she couldn't wipe away as it would mean letting go of his hands and she couldn't risk that.

No matter how much Joe tried to deny it, just feeling her soft skin clinging tightly to his and the beseeching grey eyes that were awash with tears were enough to weaken his resolve, but it was her words that finally pierced his armour and persuaded him to stay.

'Five minutes, then I have to go. I really don't know what you're going to say that will make any difference, so don't get your hopes up, okay?' Joe moved towards the bench and felt Tilly slowly release her grip.

Tilly's whole body was trembling so she clasped her hands together to keep them still. Once she was sure Joe wasn't going to do a runner, she took a deep breath and began, at the only place she could, at the very beginning.

'Remember the day I fell off my bike? Well I'd gone for a ride to clear my head and try to make some sense of the mess I was in. After I'd landed in the ditch and lay amongst the prickles trying to work out what the hell had just happened, so many thoughts pinged through my head. One of them was that if I'd broken at least two of my bones, maybe one arm, one leg, then it would be the perfect excuse to cancel the wedding. Yep, that's sad and mental, I agree, but I'm trying to give you an idea of how I was feeling that day, not to mention the many months before I arrived at Mum and Dad's.'

Tilly sneaked a look at Joe's eyes, trying to judge whether she was getting through but he remained impassive so she ploughed on.

'When I realised it was you helping me out of the ditch, despite hurting like hell, it felt like a miracle or an omen, and I want you to know this, I have never been so glad to see someone in my whole life. I know we only met once before, but I fell for you then and couldn't get you out of my mind for ages. Some people don't believe in love at first sight or that you can make a connection in such a short space of time, but I did with you, or that's how I felt anyway.'

Noticing Joe's shoulders and tightly crossed arms relax slightly, Tilly sensed she was making progress.

'The second you offered to take me to yours, I was beyond pleased. I stupidly thought I'd give myself a day off from being messed up and confused. I wanted one more chance to spend some time with you. I swear at that point, even though it seems slightly deranged, which I could blame on a bump on the head and shock, my motives were totally innocent, if a bit misguided, and I really was going to tell you on the drive home from your mum's.' Tilly was exhausted by the effort it was taking to say the right things and not break down or lose momentum.

'So why didn't you tell me? Why did you carry on lying?'

Joe had turned sideways and appeared to have softened slightly.

'That's simple. You offered to take me to fix my bike and I'd had such a lovely time with you, I wanted more. My mum and dad were sick so I gave myself a twenty-four hour reprieve. I did intend telling you the next day but things just snowballed. Do you remember how we spent hours texting each other that night? I felt like a teenager again. By the time I went to sleep I felt like I knew you. We'd just clicked. Then the next day, after we had such a nice time together, Sam invited me to tag along to the beach and later, on the way home, you told me about your mum and how she'd been hurt. I bottled out because I was scared you'd never want to see me again, so I kept quiet.'

Tilly sighed and was shocked but elated when Joe held out his hand. She took it gratefully and let him fold his fingers around hers.

Tilly continued. 'Can you imagine what it's like, living a lie and being too scared of the consequences to admit the truth? Then, after driving yourself mad trying to think of a way out and finally realising there isn't one, that you are doomed, you meet the person you've been waiting for your whole life. I just wanted to remember what it felt like to be happy and that's how you made me feel, Joe. When I was with you I could pretend you were mine. How childish and immature is that? It was just easier to push the wedding to the back of my mind for a day at a time. I've been living a lie with my parents too because they think everything's okay. It's such a mess, Joe, and most of it is my fault. Look, I know that you think I'm crazy but if you could just put yourself in my shoes for a minute, maybe you'd understand.'

Joe shook his head and pulled her close, putting a protective arm around her shoulders. Then he spoke.

'Okay, I get all that, even though you have confirmed that you really should be in the funny farm.'

Joe smiled and Tilly dared to laugh, relief spreading through her.

'But what I don't get is why you let things with Luke get this far. If you are so unhappy with him, why haven't you just told your parents and called the whole thing off? Surely that's the simple solution, a bit scary I admit but why put yourself through all this torture?'

Joe felt her take a deep breath before she continued.

'Maybe because I'm a coward and I couldn't face upsetting so many people. Look, I'll take you through the warped thought process that actually got me on the plane to France, when all I wanted to do was swap my ticket and escape to the other side of the world. The only other person who sort of knows how I feel is my friend Stacey. Like you, she thinks I've lost the plot. Anyway, just hear me out and I'll let you decide.' Tilly was drained and that was before she'd even begun to take Joe through her desperate plan.

Leaning into him and taking comfort from the warmth and feel of his body, she began.

Back at Anna's, the garden was full of hungry people and the pungent smell of paella that was bubbling away on the top of the barbeque. Under normal circumstances, Anna would've been basking in the triumph of a perfectly executed main course and looking forward to a long afternoon and a lazy evening under the stars. Now, after a very hushed and rushed conversation in the kitchen with Rosie, any hope of a fun-filled day had been left in tatters. Even Jeannie looked a bit put out and Melanie had been frantically trying to contact Joe who had turned his phone off, yet again.

Rosie had asked that they didn't mention her suspicions to Michel. Maybe she'd got it all wrong and there was nothing going on between Joe and Tilly, however, the fact that he'd gone AWOL and none of them had any idea whatsoever that she was getting married, didn't bode well at all.

Melanie went outside to discreetly reinterrogate Sam and soon returned with an update. While he was adamant that Tilly and Joe hadn't done anything that they should be ashamed of, there was definitely an attraction and they had arranged to meet up for an important conversation. Sam had confessed that Joe was hot for Tilly and she felt the same. He didn't know any more than that and was stunned, to say the least, when Melanie hit him with the news of Tilly's wedding.

After returning to the kitchen to impart her unwelcome news, the four women stood in worried, bemused silence.

Jeannie was the first to speak. 'I just find it hard to believe that she thought she'd get away with us not finding out. She's got some nerve, that's for sure. It takes someone very hard-hearted and deceitful to blatantly omit her wedding. I've heard some tales in my time but this beats most of them hands down. Poor Joe, I bet he nearly died of shock when he saw her at Rosie's. I'm convinced he didn't know. He can't have.' Jeannie folded her arms, indignant on behalf of her eldest godchild.

Melanie went next. 'I agree. He would've told Sam for a start, they're thick as thieves. I bet Tilly wanted to meet so she could tell him before Rosie turned up here. How awkward would it have been when you both came face to face this afternoon? It makes me cringe just thinking about it. Or maybe she had no intention of being here in the first place and wanted to give Joe the push then move on. I am so mad right now. I've a good mind to go and find her myself and give her what for.' Melanie was sitting at the table, tapping her fingers on the wooden surface, temper and hurt for her brother building with each passing second.

'What if it's worse than that?' All eyes shifted to Anna who was anxiously wringing the tea towel. 'If what Sam says is true and they do have secret, unrequited feelings for each other, what if they are planning to elope?'

To this dramatic scenario, Jeannie burst out laughing, it sounded ludicrous and old-fashioned. The idea was too preposterous to even consider, or was it? Realising that she was deadly serious, Jeannie fell silent when it dawned on her that this time Anna's propensity for over exaggeration might just have hit the target.

Anna threw the tea towel onto the side. 'No, I mean it, Jeannie. What if that's what she wanted to ask him? Rosie said she looked miserable as sin for most of her meeting at the hotel and was clearly forcing enthusiasm for her mother's sake. And if Tilly didn't care about being found out, why did she take it so badly when Joe stumbled in on them? I've got an awful feeling that Tilly wants a way out and Joe's it! That's what they're discussing right now. They're working out how they can break the news to us and do a runner before her fiancé turns up.' Anna could feel her cheeks flushing with the sheer enormity of her words.

'Well if they're thinking of going south with Sam, I can tell you right now he won't be pleased about it. He's looking forward to a lad's holiday not a gooseberry pie. Really, Mum, don't you think it's all a bit far-fetched? Surely she wouldn't want to hurt her mum and dad by doing a moonlight flit. She might be a bit of a weirdo, but she didn't strike me as a heartless cow.' Melanie was trying to jolly her mum along because inside, she had a feeling of impending doom.

Rosie only confirmed Anna's fears. 'No, I think your mum's right. You didn't see how Tilly was. To be honest, it only became clear after the event but now, looking back, she was just going through the motions. I've been in the company of enough brides-to-be over the years and even if their mum is running the show she's usually accompanied by Bridezilla, and Tilly was anything but that.'

Rosie looked to Jeannie for a helping hand now she'd dished out another portion of home truth.

'Look, there is nothing we can do until he turns up. We're wasting our time phoning him because he won't answer and he obviously needs to sort out whatever this is. All we can do is sit tight and when he does show, we *mustn't* overreact. Remember, this actually isn't our problem, it's Tilly's and somehow Joe has become tangled up in it. If what Sam says is true, Joe's not done anything wrong – yet. I feel sorrier for Rosie and Freda because they're the ones who are going to have one holy mess on their hands if our suspicions are proved right.'

Jeannie was hoping someone would back her up when Melanie waded in.

'I agree with Jeannie. Joe's a big boy and we have to leave

him to deal with this in his own way and once we know the truth, we can support him.' Melanie watched her mum closely and hoped she'd calmed her down, she hadn't.

'That's all well and good but what bothers me is that Joe might look like a marriage wrecker or whatever you call someone who pinches the bride before she's even got up the aisle. I just can't believe he'd do that, it's not like him and I know that one way or another he's going to get hurt. I can feel it in my bones.'

Anna looked as though she was on the verge of tears and despite their best efforts, the three other women all admitted she had a point.

None of them knew what to say for the best so when Daniel walked in on them, accompanied by Michel and asked where the ice bucket had got to, they nervously scattered and left him feeling rather uncomfortable and a bit paranoid.

Rosie briskly whisked Michel into the garden before he too became suspicious and Anna used the fortuitous arrival of Dominique and Zofia to escape the kitchen.

At the top of the stairs, Louise sat quietly and smiled to herself after eavesdropping on the most gripping conversation she'd heard in ages. Well, well, well. It looked like golden boy was about to fall off his pedestal at last and the day had gotten a bit more interesting. Louise waited until the coven had dispersed and then made her way downstairs. She was going to find herself a front row seat then sit back and watch events unfold and, for once, enjoy somebody else playing the part of the villain.

Anna was trying her hardest to be a good hostess at the same time as sorting through the myriad thoughts which were running riot in her head. Insisting everyone helped themselves to the tray of tapas, she sought out Daniel who was muttering to Phil by the drinks table. It was impossible not to have picked up on the atmosphere in the kitchen so Anna dragged Daniel away on a false errand. She needed to talk to him alone because while she valued the counsel of her closest female friends, he was the person who when all else failed, could be relied on to bring calm and sense into her world. Once they were locked in the utility room, Anna brought Daniel up to speed with the story so far, talking in a hushed, urgent tone, desperate to let him in on the situation.

Daniel was genuinely surprised by Anna's news so said the first thing that came into his head, which was that Joe was a man now and they had to let him make his own mistakes and decisions. Once they knew the facts, no matter what, they would stand by him and give him their support. Daniel reminded Anna that Joe was a decent lad but love made you do crazy things and act out of character. If all Joe was guilty of was falling for Tilly, then he for one, could forgive him there and then. It was clear that he'd got it right when Anna had almost hugged the life out of him.

Everyone made the most of the glorious afternoon sun, delicious food and the company of their friends whilst ignoring the omnipresent tension that the absence of Joe caused, thanks mainly to Louise. Anna was seriously ready to swing for her and was sure that Jeannie, Rosie and Mel felt the same way so it was probably only a matter of time before she copped for it.

At first, her commenting on the whereabouts of Joe seemed entirely innocent and a valid, if not irritating question, which was easily batted away. He had gone to meet Tilly and would be along shortly. When Louise loudly asked Anna if she should save two portions of paella for the missing guests, Anna thanked her nicely through gritted teeth and swiftly changed the subject. Her third question really riled Anna. Louise thought they were taking rather a long time too and while not wanting to worry anyone, suggested that they may have had an accident.

It was almost 4pm and there was no sign of either of them. Anna knew they were meeting at 2pm, so what took two hours to discuss? Her eyes fixed on her niece and nephew and their rowdy tribe of friends which had swelled slightly with the arrival of friends and neighbours. Rosie's two little girls, Sabine and Odette splashed around in the pool with their cousins Oliver and Lily, accompanied by Jules who chatted away in a confusing mixture of French and English. Smiling, Anna turned to Ruby, who was blooming with her baby bump and attempting to keep cool under the parasol.

Ruby was Rosie's cousin and housekeeper and had become good friends with Anna ever since she arrived in France. By Ruby's side was Dylan, holding her hand tightly and keeping her topped up with cold water laced with ice cubes. Looking at the two of them reminded Anna of their rocky road to happiness and just remembering their story and how they had been star-crossed lovers, made her wish for Joe's return. *'Please come home, Joe,'* Anna intoned silently. *'Just come back and we will sort it out. Whatever it is I don't care, I just want to see your face.'*

Maybe the power of thought is a greater force than anyone imagines because on this occasion it worked wonders and no sooner had she said the words, then Anna heard the sound of an approaching engine and then tyres crunching on the gravel.

CHAPTER SEVENTEEN

Catching the tense, cautionary looks that passed between those who were aware of the predicament, Anna took a deep breath and banished the giveaway frown from her face before she turned to welcome her son.

Joe got out of the car but instead of heading towards the garden table, appeared to be making his way indoors, not breaking his stride or showing any signs he wanted to make conversation.

Before Anna or anyone else could speak, Louise piped up.

'So... the wanderer returns. Where's Tilly? I hope you two haven't had a lover's tiff.'

As she sniggered into her glass, Daniel snapped at her to shut up. Ignoring the barb, Anna stood and calmly addressed her son.

'I hope you're hungry because I saved you some food. Do you want me to warm it up? It's in the kitchen. Come and grab a drink and I'll get it ready.'

Anna was shaken but forced her tone to remain light while she studied Joe's ashen face as he slowed slightly while stubbornly avoiding eye contact.

Around her there was a definite lull in the conversation

and Anna was aware of her allies in the background, keeping it going, desperately trying to distract attention from the scene unfolding in front of them.

Joe was angry, she could tell instantly from his body language, the set of his mouth and the barely disguised glint in his eyes when he glanced briefly at Rosie then diverted his glare towards Sam, before managing a few curt words.

'No thanks, I'm not hungry. Sorry I took so long. I'm just going to get changed. I'll be down in a bit.' And with that, he marched into the house.

Anna floundered and didn't know what to do for the best until Sam rose from the table and signalled discreetly for her to stay where she was. After casually collecting some empty glasses and plates from the table, he followed his brother inside and left Anna in limbo.

It was now obvious to everyone gathered that something was up and there was no point in dragging this charade out any longer. She also wanted to shut Louise up and prevent any further stupid comments. Moving back to her chair Anna took a sip of wine and spoke to everyone around the table.

'I'm sorry about that. I think Joe's a bit upset because unfortunately, he got a shock earlier today.' She could've left it there and implied it was a private matter, however, after a fleeting glance in Rosie's direction, received a resigned nod of the head which indicated it was okay to go on.

'It seems that Tilly hasn't been totally honest with us and somehow forgot to mention she's getting married next week, at Rosie's. That's all I know and, Louise, I'd be really grateful when he does come down if you could think before you open your mouth. We all know how much he likes Tilly so try not to make things worse by being insensitive.'

Anna could feel the anger rising and yes, she was taking it out on Louise but she deserved it, and if Daniel didn't like his precious daughter being reprimanded, well it was tough. If Anna expected Louise to put up and shut up she was wrong.

'Don't take it out on me because golden boy has spat his

dummy out. Anyway, how do you know he's innocent in all this? For all we know they could've been at it like rabbits since they met, just because you think he's perfect, *I* actually live in the real world.' Louise was furious, not only had she been told off in front of everyone by Anna, her dad appeared to have gone mute.

The switch on Anna's self-control button flicked to 'Off' and the inner rage she'd managed to keep under wraps for such a long time simply bubbled to the surface. She'd taken enough and had no other option but to let off steam, all over Louise.

'How dare you? You know nothing about it and as far as spitting dummies out, you're a pro! Do NOT criticise Joe when you are far from perfect yourself, madam. I've just about had enough of you, your spiteful behaviour and your little dramas, so shut up! And if you can't do that, do us all a favour and go to bed. You've already had far too much to drink – again.' Anna was shaking and even though she heard a gasp of shock from the object of her tirade, felt she was completely justified in giving her what for.

Louise stood up and looked straight to her dad for support.

You could've heard a pin drop in the silence as everyone waited for round three. When Daniel spoke, it wasn't quite what his daughter was expecting or hoping for.

'Louise, sit down and keep your comments to yourself because you're only making things worse. You can tell Anna's upset so leave it, okay, now isn't the time for rows. Let's all just calm down and wait for Sam to come back. Hopefully he can shed some light on the matter.'

Glaring at Louise, Daniel almost dared her to disobey him and for once, realising she was now public enemy number two and seriously pushing her luck, she did as she was told.

Throwing herself into her chair, Louise defiantly grabbed her drink and glowered at her father who had turned his attention to Anna. Louise watched him, ministering to his beloved, telling her to leave it to Sam and remember what he'd said earlier, and that Joe would be fine, they'd all stand by him.

Louise almost snorted in derision when she heard her dad's heart-warming speech. *'Pity he didn't stand by me,'* she fumed, while topping up her glass. Well, the evening had just begun and hopefully it would get even more interesting once Sam returned with the gossip, but until then, she'd keep her head down, ignore her father and the rest of the saddos around the table, and wait.

Inside, Sam hastily placed the dishes in the sink and filled it with soapy water. He was half dreading going upstairs, at the same time as being desperate to help because he knew that Joe would be hurting. Sam also felt guilty and responsible because after all, he had egged Joe on in his pursuit of Tilly.

Turning off the tap, Sam dried his hands and made his way up the stairs. When he reached the bunk room door, he took a deep breath, knocked gently and went inside, not giving his brother chance to tell him to go away or that he wanted to be alone. Joe was lying on the bottom bunk, his hands behind his head, staring intently at the wooden laths on the bed above. He didn't even acknowledge Sam's entrance.

Slightly unnerved by the silence yet resolute in his task, Sam sat on the bunk opposite and said the first words that came to mind.

'So, what's going on, mate?'

Joe turned his head slowly to face his brother and let out a huge sigh, and then told Sam everything.

Tilly was distraught. She didn't know how long she'd been sitting on the bench sobbing to the Virgin Mary, who regarded her silently from inside the shrine. The Madonna seemed to be feeling her pain and the sadness in the eyes of the statue was reflected in Tilly's tortured soul.

It had all been going so well and she was convinced that Joe was beginning to soften and sympathise as her tale progressed. He hugged her tightly and gently kissed the top of her head which she found reassuring, giving her the courage to go on. By the time she'd arrived at the present day, bringing him right up to date with their unplanned meeting at the hotel, Tilly's heart felt about two stone lighter and emboldened by his imagined support.

Maybe up until that point, he was actually on her side but within minutes, after baring her soul, divulging her most private thoughts and exposing herself truthfully, all her hard work was simply swept away. Going over it again in her head, Tilly analysed each word, wishing she'd said it differently or phrased it in another way. But who was she kidding? Regardless of her inadequate use of the English language, neither of them were going to budge and now, she was sitting here alone and Joe was gone forever. She could picture his earnest face as he turned her towards him, grasping her hands tightly and looking deep into her misty eyes.

'Tilly, please don't cry, it's going to be okay now. We can sort this out together, I promise. I know it seems like everything is such a mess, I get that, but now you've made the first step by telling me how you feel, the rest will be easier. I'll be by your side every step of the way and I'm not scared of Luke either! Your mum and dad are good people and they love you and will only want what's best for you so even if it's a shock, they'll get over it once they realise how unhappy you've been.'

Joe was about to wipe away one of Tilly's tears when she abruptly snatched her hands away and held them to her face.

'No! Joe, don't you get it? That's what I've been trying to tell you, that's why I was at the hotel today. I've got to go ahead with the wedding for all the reasons I explained. I can't hurt my family, I just can't. I wanted to explain all this to you so you would understand. They've put too much money and effort into it all. There are people coming from all over the place. My brother is coming from the other side of the world for God's sake! How can I let them all down now? It's easier to go through with it. You've got to believe me because I know I'm right.' Tilly's heart was thudding as panic returned.

'Are you having a laugh? You can't be serious, Tilly, how can you go through with it knowing you don't love him and the words you are saying are a complete lie? In front of all your family as well! And what about me, am I supposed to just forget about how you're supposed to feel about us? I can't believe you are even thinking of going ahead with this and expect me to go along with it. If you do you're totally insane.'

Joe was looking at Tilly as if she had three heads and was from another strange, unimaginable planet.

'Joe, calm down and listen. I've worked it all out, down to the finest details and I can get away with it but I need you to promise you will be patient and wait for me. But most of all, you have got to keep all this to yourself.' Tilly tried to take his hand but he pulled it away.

'What kind of weirdo are you? You'd better shut up, Tilly, because you really do sound like a calculating cow right now and deffo not the person I thought you were. You expect me to hang about while you get married do you, and then what? Go on, amaze me.' Joe looked livid and was shouting. He stood up and looked on the verge of walking away.

Looking nervously around, Tilly was relieved to see that the small garden was still deserted and the inhabitants of the village were otherwise occupied with their Sunday lunch.

'Joe, please don't shout. Sit down and I'll tell you, please, just give me a chance.' Tilly was all out of tears and any remaining emotions bordered on hysteria and desperation.

When Joe sat down she allowed herself a faint sigh of relief then continued before he changed his mind.

'I always knew you'd be going south with Sam and that's part of the reason I wanted to make the most of my time with you. It's probably a good thing because even though I'll miss you and wish I could come too, putting some distance between us will make what I have to do easier.'

Hearing Joe laugh sarcastically didn't bode well, yet she had no other option than to plough ahead.

'All I have to do is get through the next six days. I know it won't be easy and I'll be living a lie but if sacrificing my feelings saves those of my family then it'll be worth it.'

Joe was staring at her and hadn't said a word so she continued quickly.

'I'm going to wait until I'm alone with Luke and somehow pick the right time to tell him the truth, when we are as far away from here as possible. What happens after that I can deal with, all I know is that by the time I get back to England I will be single. I was going to go through with the wedding anyway, but meeting you gave me courage and the belief that I could actually be happy, but that depends on if you'll wait for me.' Tilly looked at Joe and waited, she'd said her piece.

'So, let's get this right. You're going to carry on play acting to all the people you are supposed to care about, for a whole week, then if that's not bad enough, stand in front of them all and lie to Luke's face when you say your vows. Once that performance is over, you'll have a pretend party at Rosie's... and I can't imagine what sick plans you have for your wedding night. So you think it's okay to go on honeymoon where the highlight of the trip will be the part when you dump him? Unbelievable!' Joe was becoming increasingly agitated and couldn't sit any longer. As he stood up and brushed his hand through his hair, he laughed out loud, shaking his head incredulously.

'And this is the really funny bit, in between your Oscar winning performances, where do I fit in? Am I expected just to carry on as normal while you're here in la-la land? Will you be keeping me posted on how many lies you've told that day, in between telling me how much you miss me? Hey, if I'm lucky, perhaps you'll send me a photo of you in your dress and while I think on, don't forget to save me a bit of cake, I'd hate to feel left out!' Joe turned his back on Tilly and focused on the shrine in front of him and bizarrely, congratulated himself on not swearing too much in front of Mary and her saintly friends.

'Look, I know you are angry and it might take some time to get your head round it but once you calm down, you will see it's the best option. I swear to you, Joe, that if I could think of another way out I'd take it but this is all I have.' Tilly didn't dare reach out to touch him, she prayed instead that words would suffice.

When Joe began to speak, his voice had lowered and was more measured, in control, resolute.

'No, Tilly, you're wrong. You do have another option. Just tell the truth, that's all you need to do. Getting married is the coward's way out and you know it. Don't you see what you are doing to yourself? If you go ahead with this you will lose the respect of so many people, especially me. Is that what you want?' Turning to face her, Joe delivered his final verbal blow.

'How can you expect for one millisecond that I will close my eyes and pretend it's not happening and not imagine what you will be doing next Saturday or worse, on your honeymoon? It's wrong on so many levels and I can't be a part of it. I'm sorry, Tilly, but either you come clean or we're over before we've even begun. I don't like Luke but that doesn't mean he deserves to be treated like this. So it's your call, you decide here and now how it's going to be.' Joe's blood pulsed around his body, shooting through his veins and forcing his heart to pump violently in his chest as he waited for her verdict.

'Joe, I know it will be hard and if it's any consolation, I promise I won't sleep with him. I've already thought about that and can avoid it, I swear. I know you are a good person and this is a tough one to get your head around. It's not been easy for me either, but please be there for me, help me through it by just saying you'll wait, that's all I need to hear.'

'For crying out loud, just stop! Every time you open your mouth you make it worse, Tilly. I don't want to hear that you have concocted some freak show excuse for not sleeping with your husband. It's like you are oblivious to your own deceitfulness. It's not a good look or something to be proud of and I'm beginning to think that if you can do this to him *and* your parents, then what else are you capable of? Who exactly are you because I get the feeling that the person I wanted to be with has been body snatched or something?' Despite the fact his heart yearned for his words to get through to her, Joe knew he was beaten. He knew beyond a shadow of a doubt that she wasn't going to change her mind and neither was he.

'Joe, every single word I have said is the truth. From start to finish I haven't told you one single lie. The only reason I'm acting like this is because I'm backed into a corner and that makes a person behave in ways they never imagined, can you not see that? I am still the girl you found in the ditch, I haven't changed. The only thing that has altered is finding you. Please don't throw it all away, Joe, all those things we talked about and the plans we were going to make together. I know we could be happy, I just have to sort this out first.' Tilly was spent, exhausted from explaining and dredging desperate words from a floundering brain. Her plea was over. There was nothing more to be said so she clutched her hands tightly against her chest, praying he'd agree.

'Well, go ahead and sort it out, Tilly, but you'll be doing it on your own. I mean it. This is your last chance to change your mind because I can't be part of your lies, I just won't do it.' Joe stood his ground, allowing the finality of his words to settle in the stunned silence that enveloped them.

Tilly was speechless. Not one single word came into her mind. It was blank. She felt her mouth open and then close when nothing came out. Instead she just stood there staring at him as tears began to pour from her eyes, and her body began to tremble. Even though her heart was screaming for her to do something, she knew it was too late, a lost cause and all hope had gone. The chiming of the church bell made her jump.

It was also the catalyst that snapped Joe into action because without saying one more word, he turned and walked away.

Tilly watched paralysed as he headed slowly towards his car. She knew he'd be waiting and hoping for her to call out to him, tell him he'd won, yet the words never came because she just couldn't say them. Their final scene together was played out in silence as Joe got into his car without so much as a backward glance. Instead, he had looked straight ahead, started the engine and drove away.

* * *

It was five o'clock now, the church bells told her that. Tilly had sat alone in sombre, stunned silence and talked only to Mary, who was a good listener but not much help. She knew she couldn't sit here for much longer because the park would soon be invaded by parents taking their offspring for some fresh air, or dog owners taking a few laps around the village green.

Maybe she should go home. Home. That was a word that brought with it renewed pain. There wasn't anywhere Tilly really felt was home, not right now. The house she shared with Luke was just that, four walls and a roof with things inside, not a haven or a place she sought sanctuary. Her parent's cottage wasn't her home either, but for the moment it'd have to do and would be empty, so she might as well head there. At least it was quiet and private, somewhere she could lick her wounds.

All she wanted to do was sleep. Not think or talk or cry. The simple task of driving would involve a Herculean effort but it was a means to an end. Perhaps she should ring Stacey and fill her in on this recent turn of events? Tilly already knew the answer to that so why bother? The only person that didn't answer back was her diary and the mere thought of chronicling in black and white the worst, most painful few hours of her life, made her wince.

Then, out of the blue, an unexpected thunderbolt of

inspiration struck, causing a sharp intake of breath and an injection of hope. Her diary! It held page upon page of the truth and nothing but the truth. Even though it only went back as far as January, it was still the keeper of eight months' worth of secret feelings, laying bare her anguish and exhausting every single worst case scenario or hare-brained scheme she'd come up with. Springing to her feet, Tilly made her way to the car with renewed purpose. This was the answer. If Joe could read it then he might begin to comprehend her thought process and ultimately, be able to forgive her. Surely, sharing her most private thoughts would be an indication, no, better than that, justification of her intentions.

Tilly prayed that her parents wouldn't be home. She had one last chance to make him see, one final stab at happiness so, as she drove out of the village, her heart cheered and her brain gave itself a little pat on the back for coming up with the goods, eventually.

Sam had listened patiently in silence to Joe's incredible story. Apart from eliciting a few gasps and giving the odd shake of the head in all the right places, he had refrained from passing judgement until he'd heard all the evidence. Even though he wasn't best pleased with Tilly right now, he'd decided to play devil's advocate because judging by the mood his brother was in, nothing good would come out of fanning the flames of hurt and anger that were already raging inside him.

As Sam embarked on his counselling session, he first tried going down the pity route, saying he felt sorry for her being trapped in a relationship she clearly had no desire to be in.

Joe replied instantly that if that was the case she should fess up and leave Luke, now!

Then Sam made a suggestion. 'Perhaps she was just being kind because her mum and dad have probably spent a small fortune. It'd be awful for all their plans to go to waste.'

Joe countered. 'Well if that's the case I will gladly write them a cheque to cover their losses if Tilly does the decent thing and cancels the whole fake wedding.'

Changing tack and hoping to appeal to his brother's sensitive nature, Sam did a damn good job of narrating the scene where someone delivers the bad news to all the guests. 'Imagine having to ring the gran and the in-laws, and the overexcited bridesmaid who packed her case months ago and was probably counting down the hours till she got on the plane to fly across the world. Have you really considered what a really crap job that'd be, how would you feel if you did that to Mum, or God forbid, Gran?' Sam watched for signs he was getting through and when it was clear he wasn't, forged ahead.

'Mate, it all seems mega simple when it's not actually happening to you or your family. Maybe you should consider how it would feel to walk into a room and pluck up the courage to ruin everyone's plans and look your mum and dad in the eye and ruin their day.'

The more he spoke, the more Sam came round to thinking that Tilly had some balls going through with it and instead of being a coward, he thought she was borderline brave, if not slightly unhinged but who wouldn't be under all that pressure? Warming to his theme, Sam became counsel for the defence. 'You won't like hearing this but what if one act of deceit could save a whole lot of people a great deal of hurt, even Luke? Let's face it, nobody wants to be jilted, just before or during a wedding, how embarrassing would that be?' Sam thought he'd made a damn good case until he saw Joe roll his eyes and shake his head and his will to defend Tilly began to wane.

Regardless of each valid point Sam made, Joe was resolute in his damnation of Tilly, and stubbornly refused to see things her way. To him, it was clear cut and easily resolved and he had a good mind to go round there and tell Freda and Howard exactly what Tilly was up to, and maybe Luke deserved the heads up too!

Sam knew Joe was kicking out to hide his hurt, at the

same time as having trouble swallowing his pride. Tilly had made a fool of him in front of Rosie and Michel, not to mention everyone else. Joe obviously felt like a right mug, a laughing stock who'd been following someone else's girlfriend round like a lovesick moron. After trying every trick in the book, Sam resigned himself to the obvious, he was flogging a dead horse and bowing to the abundantly clear fact that Joe wasn't going to budge, not one inch, from his standpoint, he finally gave up.

'Look, mate, I've told you what I think, not that it's done any good but don't make any hasty decisions okay, or threats, because you'll make this a million times worse if you do. Just let the dust settle a bit and you never know, by tomorrow, Tilly might've done the same and come round to your way of thinking.'

Hearing Joe's derisory snort wasn't at all encouraging.

'She can do what she wants from now on. I don't care, and anyway, she made it perfectly clear where she stands so the best thing we can do is clear off, first thing in the morning. What time do you want to leave?'

Joe had switched off and Sam knew it.

He was turning his humiliation into obstinacy and if that's what it was going to take to get him through the next few days then Sam would go with the flow. Deep down, he was also relieved that his soft-in-the-head big brother hadn't cancelled the next stage of their holiday and ran off back to England. That would have been typical Joe behaviour because when things got tough, he buried his head in work, pretending it would all go away.

'Right, if that's what you want then we'll set off about nine so we miss the traffic. I know you're fed up, mate, but at least come and show your face downstairs. Mum's worried about you and she's going to be on a downer when we leave tomorrow, not to mention having to cope with flaming Louise and her problems, so buck up and get some food. She's saved you masses of the stuff and if you don't eat it we'll only end up taking it with us tomorrow. Go on, do it for the lads!'

Joe managed the faintest glimmer of a smile, but it didn't reach his eyes.

'I'll be down soon. I need to give you time to fill everyone in on the wedding fiasco because they'll all be waiting for the gossip, so go on, best get it over with. I won't be long.'

Joe was right, they'd all be wondering, so Sam agreed to be the messenger.

It was better that he explained first, otherwise there'd be an elephant in the room and someone needed to put a gag on Louise because if she said one wrong word out there, Joe would flip and so would his mum. Getting off the bed, Sam nudged Joe's leg before making his way to the door.

'I'm going outside, okay, so let's synchronise watches. I want you down there in twenty minutes, no longer or else I'll say you want their advice and send them all up. Just imagine Mum, Jeannie, Mel, Rosie, Ruby and Zofia sitting on your bed sorting your life out. Don't say I didn't warn you.' He was hoping for a bit of a smile but Sam was left disappointed and rewarded only by a sharp nod of the head.

Closing the door behind him, Sam went downstairs in search of his mother and as he headed towards a sea of expectant faces, decided that going south tomorrow was probably for the best. Their hearts were in the right place but knowing the mood Joe was in, his well-meaning family would only end up suffocating and irritating him.

It was now a simple case of damage limitation for everyone concerned otherwise all hell could break loose, especially if Joe blabbed to Tilly's parents. Yep, the sooner they hit the road the better and Sam couldn't wait till morning, the stress was almost too much to bear. But before him and Joe made their great escape he still had a right old tale to tell his mum and then if that wasn't enough, stop her from hunting down and killing Tilly.

CHAPTER EIGHTEEN

Freda was surprised to see her car parked on the drive when they returned home later that evening. She'd fully expected Tilly to be out late at the Harrisons', enjoying her last moments with that Joe person. Trying hard to keep a check on her more sarcastic emotions, and not allowing her already suspicious mind to go into overdrive, Freda concentrated on walking in a straight line and not letting on to Howard she had gone past being tipsy and was borderline merry, very merry indeed.

It was for this reason that she felt no inclination to embark on the heart to heart she had planned with her wayward daughter and after spending a lovely evening (which went on far longer than anticipated) with their friends, didn't want the evening ruined for either of them. They had walked back hand in hand under an ebony sky, emblazoned with glittering stars and lit by a silver moon, chatting about this and that along the way, listening to the sound of the nocturnal countryside. The beasts of the fields mooed, brayed and shrieked, frogs croaked messages to one another and night birds swooped and cawed from within the forest or above their heads as they hunted for prey.

Her hand felt safe and secure inside Howard's and if she blotted out the obvious, Freda could convince herself she hadn't a care in the world. For this simple reason she was adamant that for one evening only, she would be worry-free and let the rest of the world sort out its own problems. Tomorrow was another day and seeing as they had one hour left of this one, she was going to make some supper and a nice cup of tea, which they were going to eat in bed, to hell with crumbs. During the past few years, Freda had learnt that it was best to ride the happy wave and embrace being on an upper, knowing only too well that the inevitable pebble beach was waiting on the downside.

Opening the kitchen door to silence, Freda refused to be drawn to Tilly's bedroom door to tap cautiously to check if she was okay. She had no idea that upstairs her daughter lay in the darkness of her room, unable to sleep.

Tilly's phone was glued to her hands as she stared at the screen, willing it to ring or light up with an incoming message, praying for forgiveness and understanding from the one person that mattered the most and who she'd hurt so badly. She knew there was nothing more she could do apart from wait and had only just managed to get back home before her parents after staging a vigil outside Joe's house.

* * *

Earlier, after retrieving her diary from its hiding place, she drove back to Anna's where she sat for ages trying to figure out what to do next. After leaving her car further up the road in one of the small lay-bys she'd walked back towards the house and from where she was hidden behind the hedge, Tilly could see the front garden clearly. Recognising most of the people gathered around the table, Rosie stood out the most, with her blonde hair and floaty dress, and as Tilly scanned the rest of the guests it became obvious that Joe was inside.

Her previous surge of bravado and energy had somewhat fizzled out and was replaced by nerves. Tilly was unsure of how to proceed. There was no way she could approach any of them. She just didn't have the guts to walk up there, through the gate and stand face to face with Joe's family. Perhaps Daniel might take Pippa for a walk, or better still, Sam. She'd feel more comfortable with him than any of the others. Her mind made up, Tilly walked further along the road and sat on the stone slab that held the statue of Jesus on the cross. It was similar to the one at the end of her lane and those of thousands of other homes in France, and before she made herself comfy, rearranged the flowers at the base so they wouldn't get crushed.

After what seemed like hours, with only the son of God for company, it was clear that tonight, Pippa wasn't going to take her usual stroll down the lane. It was getting dark and a bit chilly too and Tilly wished she'd changed out of her sandals and remembered to bring something warm. The lights around the parasol in the garden still twinkled but with each minute it was becoming harder to see what was going on. Her master plan was further scuppered when she heard the sound of a car engine starting up, signalling the gathering was coming to an end which sent her scurrying down the road to the sanctuary of her car. She could just about see the end of Anna's lane from where she hid, letting out a great sigh of relief when the vehicles turned right and drove off in the opposite direction.

There was only one thing for it. She would have to leave the diary somewhere Joe would find it and Tilly knew just the place. Waiting another half an hour until it was pitch black, Tilly drove her car to the end of Anna's lane and turned off the lights. Peering over the hedge, she could see the garden was now in darkness and the only lights left on were in the kitchen. It looked like someone was still up but knowing she couldn't stay here all night, Tilly walked slowly up the lane using the hedgerows of the field as cover. Her heart hammered in her chest as her eyes adapted to the darkness, the full moon casting just enough light to allow her to see her way.

At the gate, she waited and listened. Sam's camper was only feet away and she knew full well that it would be open, hardly anyone locked their cars round here and even if it was, she'd put the diary under the van, but that was plan B. Lifting the latch slowly, Tilly slipped through the gate and sprinted over to the van where she crouched on the floor and caught her breath, her blood pressure was probably through the roof and her nerves were completely shot.

Reaching up, Tilly pulled the handle of the driver's door and grimaced as it creaked open. Again, she waited and listened for signs that she'd been heard or Pippa barking to alert her owners they had an intruder. There was nothing, just silence. Tilly slid inside, keeping her body low and hidden by the front seats. Taking the diary, she stretched across and slid it under the passenger seat and wedged it between the metal runners underneath. Wiggling backwards, she exited the van and quietly pushed the door shut. She took one last cautionary moment to check the coast was clear and then sprinted towards the gate, locking it behind her and then ran like the devil was on her tail, all the way back to the car.

Inside, she fumbled for the keys as blood rushed in her ears and her heart went like the clappers. All she wanted to do now was get home and in bed before her parents turned up. As she put the car into gear, Tilly took one last look towards the house and acknowledged the pang that came from thinking of Joe, who was somewhere behind those walls. Shaking off anything negative, she pulled onto the road and forced herself to be positive.

At least she'd tried. For now, Tilly could allow herself a smidgen of hope. Perhaps it would be enough, or at the very least, a symbolic gesture which might just mean something to him. Tilly shivered and checked the clock, then concentrated on the road ahead as heavy blobs of rain began to smear the windscreen. It was going to be a long, lonely night, probably for Joe too, but with a bit of luck, by the time the sun rose, things would be clearer and they could move on, together.

* * *

Daniel was fed up. The evening had spiralled downwards and it had become abundantly clear that to go ahead with his proposal would be in really bad taste and incredibly foolhardy. How could he ask Anna to marry him when the topic of conversation revolved around a bizarre set of circumstances, all centred on a very precarious wedding? It was definitely a non-starter and even though Phil commiserated with him in private, Daniel was left feeling deflated and bloody furious with Louise.

Her behaviour had been appalling and he was beginning to think she had a drink problem to match her personality disorder, which was bad enough on its own. She would be getting a right earful in the morning whether she was hungover, nervous about Tomas or whatever other excuse she tried to palm him off with. There was always *something* with his daughter and he was sick of it! This time she had gone too far and embarrassed him in front of everyone. Thank God Jules was inside watching a DVD when she passed out in the pavlova.

* * *

They had all been looking forward to tucking into Ruby's pavlova until Louise ended up with meringue and assorted summer fruits stuck to her face. Daniel was glad to see the back of her when Zofia hauled Louise inside and put her to bed and didn't blame any of the others one bit for not offering to help, she was lucky to have left the table in one piece after her outburst. Yes, she was almost paralytic but that was no excuse, no excuse at all.

When Sam returned and began relating the 'Joe situation' he had been constantly interrupted by Louise with sarcastic snorts and lurid comments relating to Tilly's character, so when Jeannie finally snapped and told her to button it, all hell had broken loose.

Daniel hated swearing, so when Louise told Jeannie to

eff-off and mind her own business, he actually cringed. Then, when Melanie waded in and told Louise to watch her language because there were children about, she was rewarded with a sneer and a two fingered salute. At this precise moment, Dylan began to slice a piece of cake for Lily after uncovering the pavlova that was, disastrously, placed right in front of Louise, who took one look at it and grimaced. She then announced that she hated pavlova because it tasted like shite, swayed slightly in her seat and collapsed face first into the middle of the dish, scattering fruit and cream everywhere.

Daniel vaguely remembered Sam trying to suppress a fit of the giggles and the gasps of surprise from the rest of the table, then Lily wailing when she realised that cake was now off the menu. While Zofia dealt with Louise and the others cleared up the mess, Melanie went off to raid the freezer for an alternative pudding.

After he apologised profusely to everyone, Daniel decided to open a bottle or two of champagne anyway, he needed something to cheer himself up and although his proposal was doomed, there was no point in wasting it.

* * *

The night hadn't ended how Daniel had anticipated – with a redundant diamond ring. His bed was missing the person he loved because she was sitting downstairs worrying about Joe, who was just down the corridor, festering in his own pit of misery. There was a black mist hanging over the house and it would probably still be there in the morning. Daniel knew full well that once the boys headed off under a cloud of their own, Anna would be left hurt and disappointed and if that wasn't enough, he still had Louise and Tomas to deal with.

The dull sound of rain beginning to splatter on the skylight distracted him from his dismal thoughts and as the gentle shower gradually built into a deluge, pounding the roof and smearing the glass with angry rain, Daniel sighed and closed his eyes, trying hard to erase the images of the day and hopefully finding refuge in sleep.

Anna was alone in the kitchen with only her thoughts and a cup of coffee for company. Even Pippa had abandoned her and was snoring away in the next room, immersed in blissful canine innocence. Anna didn't usually go near caffeine this late, it kept her awake for hours, but tonight was an exception. She knew there'd be no drifting off to sleep for her so she may as well give in to the arabica beans and let them do their thing while she sorted out her frazzled brain.

Poor Daniel had sloped off to bed looking crestfallen after she had assured him she was fine and wanted to tidy up before turning in. Anna suspected he had things on his mind too, namely Louise, but she had no time for the drama queen's antics. First and foremost in her thoughts was Joe who she'd spoken to briefly since he returned home, and her mind wandered to earlier in the evening when they'd just heard Sam's version of events.

* * *

After the cake fiasco was over and the lush was put to bed, Joe appeared in the kitchen just as Anna was bringing in plates and her meringue splattered tablecloth. He gave her a start when she turned to see him at the bottom of the stairs and sensed he didn't know what to say or do. So she took the lead and did what mum's always do in times of trouble and offered him food. She could tell he didn't really want to eat and had only shown his face out of politeness, merely following Sam's orders.

People were in and out of the kitchen, bringing in glasses, taking out the ice cream substitute. The kids appeared, asking for crisps and drinks and then Sabine spilt hers all over Pippa who was in residence on the sofa, refusing to budge. By the time she had cleaned up the mess and dried the dog, Joe had eaten his food and washed his plate before saying he was going back upstairs and would see her in the morning. Anna knew there was no point in even attempting a conversation or following him so instead, she concentrated on her friends and remaining family.

The menfolk sloped off into the shed, which doubled up as Daniel's cave, to play darts. Once the argument over *Harry Potter* or *Frozen* was settled and the kids were installed in front of the telly, the women were left alone to pass judgement on the evening, beginning with the subject of Louise.

Rosie was appalled at her behaviour and thought that Anna had been a saint to put up with her this far.

'It seems to me that no matter what age they are, step-kids can cause all sorts of problems for men *or* women and have the ability to ruin perfectly happy relationships. I've seen it so many times before. When I worked in England, loads of my friends had stepchildren and they wreaked havoc and made them really miserable, and I'm talking all age groups here, little kids can be just as horrible as big ones.'

'I agree. There's a girl at work whose life was made a misery by her two step-kids, honestly, they regularly reduced her to tears and it almost split her and her husband up. It was like they'd tolerated her before, when she wasn't a permanent threat and then wham, the minute she got that ring on her finger, they turned into evil twins. Maybe they were worried she'd run off with their inheritance or something. I think their mother had a lot to do with it, stirring things up out of jealousy or revenge. I'm so lucky with Summer and Ross, I love them to bits and they think I'm perfect... but who wouldn't?' Jeannie as usual got a laugh then the conversation turned serious again when Rosie chipped in.

Anna spoke next. 'I must admit that Daniel is seeing another side of Louise now, but there was a time when I felt like he totally changed when he was around her, like he condoned her behaviour or turned a blind eye to it. When that happens, you feel like they're being disloyal to you and it makes you question every aspect of your relationship. I always try to keep in mind that she's his child and the last thing he wants is to fall out with her, especially when Jules is added to the mix. Louise resents me being around her son, I can tell, unless it suits her of course and then I'm allowed to be his granny for a few hours. I think he's a lovely little boy and I'd hate to lose contact with him so I can only imagine how Daniel feels. Sometimes I don't know what to do for the best.' Anna was so fed up and wondered if the night could get any worse.

'Well, you need to get tough otherwise it will go on forever. I think it's about time you had a word with Louise on your own, none of this pussyfooting around and ask her what her problem is, which we all know is the mere fact you exist on this earth and she's a jealous cow.' Jeannie was sick of Louise getting away with it and taking things out on Anna.

Melanie was sick to death of talking about Louise because she was more concerned about Joe, but they had to be careful what they said because his bedroom window was right behind them and open wide. Nobody cared about Louise who was comatose anyway.

'So what do you think is going to happen with Tilly? Maybe I should call round there and have a word with her once Joe and Sam leave tomorrow. We always got on alright and she might need someone to talk to. It's obvious her mum hasn't got a clue what's going on.' Mel spoke in a hushed tone so as not to be overheard.

Rosie was next to speak out. 'Well someone needs to get the inside track on what's going on. I can't just turn up and ask her, it'll make Freda suspicious, but I suppose I could think of an excuse to ring her and test the water. Michel is worried about all the fresh food he's ordered and the extra staff who are expecting to work next Saturday. I know we could use some of it in the restaurant but we can't freeze everything and it will go to waste and cost a bomb.' Rosie twiddled her beads nervously and waited for some advice.

'I think you should wait it out and see what happens. Sounds like she intends going through with it no matter what and she's come this far playing let's pretend, so another few days aren't going to kill her, are they?' Jeannie thought that Tilly was a bit of a tough cookie on the quiet and not to be underestimated in any way.

Ruby attempted to reassure Rosie 'We've taken a deposit and, if it all goes pear-shaped, I'm sure Michel will be able to do something miraculous with the food, otherwise perhaps we could resell it. As for the staff, I think they'll understand. I reckon Jeannie's right and it's best to wait for a few days and play it by ear.'

Anna had the interests of only one person on her mind, which seemed a bit harsh, but at the moment Tilly was the villain of the piece and her son was the wounded victim. She listened silently to the opinions of those gathered at the table and knew that jumping to the wrong conclusion was her specialty, so it was best that she waited and considered her options before making matters worse by ringing Freda.

Jeannie on the other hand took a harsher view of the situation.

'Well I feel sorry for this Luke guy, because he's being made a complete fool of. Shouldn't he know that his wedding is a farce and his fiancée is in love with another man? I know it sounds hard but maybe it'd be doing him and Joe a favour if it's all out in the open. Either Tilly's a man-mad floozy, or Luke's horrible and deserves it, but whichever way you look at it, someone is going to get hurt. I just wish it wasn't Joe because right now it seems like he's the one with the broken heart.' Jeannie loved her godson like he was her own and for that reason, probably knew something of what Anna was feeling right now.

'I think that's a bit harsh, Jeannie. From what Sam said she's only going through with it because she doesn't want to let her mum and dad down, or ruin the day for all the people who are coming to the wedding. I think that shows she's a nice person, and if she was a floozy she would've just dumped Luke and moved onto Joe. I bet it's been awful having to pretend for all this time, and now she'll think we all hate her. Just imagine what it's like to be really unhappy then fall in love with someone else just before your wedding. Nobody does that on purpose.' Melanie felt truly sorry for Joe and Tilly, and even Luke.

This was exactly the reason why Anna kept quiet. As she listened to them all have their say, each had separately voiced her own muddled opinions and raised issues that were troubling her soul. She knew how hard it was to keep a secret and the weight of that burden increased as time went by. Mel was right. Tilly must be going through hell. This led her to think that Luke must have his faults yet Tilly had decided to sacrifice herself, not him, in order to avoid disappointing her family. Perhaps, as Melanie said, this made her a good person.

Anna was sure that Tilly wasn't a floozy, as Jeannie put it. She could quite easily have got up to no good with Joe and had a last fling, then dropped him the minute he left with Sam. Anna trusted Joe and believed him when he said that nothing had happened, so therefore Tilly also had morals. For that reason it was best they stayed out of it and left her to get on and do whatever she needed to.

It was getting chilly and their conversation was interrupted by Daniel and the others emerging from the shed. All in all, despite her best intentions and meticulous planning, Anna's evening had been a complete let down, a designated disaster zone. By the time sleepy children had been loaded into their cars and the last of the clearing up had been done, most of the residents of La Roberdière were ready for bed. Pippa took the huff because she didn't get to rampage along the lane and, one by one, everyone sloped off to their rooms, leaving Anna alone in the kitchen.

Finishing the last of her coffee, Anna decided to call it a night and even though her mind would probably tick over for hours, her bones needed to lie down and rest. Tomorrow was another day and she was sure it would be as eventful as the one that was almost over. Once she'd seen her boys off, Anna was going to have a few overdue words with Louise. If that wasn't enough, they had to deal with the imminent arrival of Tomas at teatime, so one way or another, both she and Daniel had their work cut out.

Anna stood up wearily and went over to the sink and washed out her mug before checking on Pippa who was fast asleep in the lounge. Thinking she heard a noise in the garden Anna went over to the window to peep outside. It was a futile act because all she could see was the moon and the solar lamps dotted along the path and presumed it was a fox rummaging around the bins, so she locked the door and turned off the kitchen light.

Making her way upstairs, she was acutely aware of the silence that enveloped her home and couldn't erase the image from her mind of two young, confused people, one of them just yards away and probably wide awake. Both had the weight of the world on their shoulders and it bothered her that she was powerless to help.

Opening the door, she crept into the bedroom where Daniel lay fast asleep, or he was doing a very good job of pretending. The last thing she wanted was a discussion about Louise so she was glad of his snores, real or fake. Slipping beneath the duvet, Anna gazed at the moon that shone brightly through the window.

She once told Joe, Sam and Mel that no matter where they were in the world, whenever they looked up at the sky and saw the sun or the stars or the moon, that she was somewhere underneath, always thinking of them and never too far away if they needed her. As her eyes began to droop, Anna hoped that her eldest child had taken notice and remembered her words because tonight she wasn't thousands of miles away, she was just down the hall.

CHAPTER NINETEEN

Sam and Joe set off at 9am prompt, in the worst weather conditions possible, assuring Anna that they'd take their time and were driving towards the sun and before they knew it, the roads would be dry and safe.

The rain lashed against the windscreen, obscuring their vision and making the wipers work overtime as they chugged along the autoroute on their journey south. Conversation was limited, and confined to map related issues, as Sam concentrated on the road and Joe kept his eyes on the signs. By the time they'd entered the Vendée region, the rain had abated and the sun had put its hat on as predicted, much to the relief of them both. The change in weather conditions also signalled a thawing in the rather tense atmosphere inside the camper and by the time they stopped for a loo break, Joe seemed to be loosening up and Sam thought it safe to mention Tilly.

'I felt a bit sorry for Mum this morning when we left. Did you not get chance to put her mind at rest?' Sam was talking in between munching on an apple and driving one-handed.

'No, I didn't. There were too many people about and I didn't want to discuss my private life in front of everyone, anyway, there's nothing to be said. Tilly and me are over, so what's to talk about?' Joe was watching the arrow on the screen and waiting for the next junction to appear.

'Right… so you didn't text her last night then, did she contact you? I imagined you'd both be trying to sort it out well into the night.' The silence was deafening so Sam continued. 'To be honest I'm surprised you both left it like that. You should've tried to get through to her one last time, or at least ended on speaking terms.' Sam was shocked that Joe had just given in.

'Nope, I turned my phone off if you must know, and that's how it's going to stay. There's nothing I want to say to her because she made it quite clear she wasn't going to change her mind. That just shows what she thinks about me, and everyone else as far as I'm concerned. I don't want anything to do with someone who's as fake as that and can lie to the people she reckons she loves. I'm best off without her.'

Joe's voice held a lot of anger and a hint of hurt, but Sam wouldn't let go.

'I think you're being a bit harsh, mate. I know you feel like you've had a kick in the teeth and she's let you down, but don't write her off straight away. It's not the simplest of situations, is it? I think you should give it a few days and see how you feel then. You're going to have to turn your phone back on sometime, otherwise Mum will freak out if she can't get hold of you and then I'll cop for it.' Sam decided he'd said enough for now and anyway, this was supposed to be fun, and talking about Tilly wasn't remotely humorous so he'd best change the subject.

Joe was rummaging in the giant bag of food that their mum had packed and more or less ignored Sam's advice.

'A kick in the guts more like, and you seem to forget that she's made me look like a right prat in front of everyone, so thanks for that Tilly – great job! Look, let's just concentrate on the next couple of weeks okay? And I will turn my phone back on if Mum gets on your case, but for now I want to forget what's happened and have some fun. I hope you're right about all these babes that are waiting for us, or you're in big trouble, mate.' Joe opened a can of Coke and took a long swig, then concentrated on the signs up ahead.

Sam knew when he was beaten and that Joe was faking his interest in the opposite sex, still, they'd put a lot of thought into their lads' holiday, leaving him with no other option than to agree.

'Okay, I get the message. Pass me a sarnie will you and see if Mum's put any of that nutty chocolate in the bag, I'm starving and need to keep my strength up.' And with that, the subject of Tilly was closed.

* * *

Tilly had been awake since the early hours after somehow managing to fall into a fitful sleep. The first thing she did upon opening her eyes was grab her phone from under the pillow to check if Joe had replied to her messages. He hadn't. She suspected that he'd turned it off. Tilly had hoped he would reply to her final message that she typed just before giving up and going to sleep. It said simply:

Joe, the only way I have left to convince you that I'm not any of the things you said earlier and I had no intention of hurting you, is by giving you something precious that I haven't shared with another soul. Under the front seat of Sam's camper is my diary. I started it at the beginning of the year and I have written in it every day since 1st January. I've kept a diary since I was eight and can't break the habit. Inside the one I have entrusted to you are my thoughts and feelings about many things, especially Luke, the wedding and you. Please read it, Joe, because at least then you will believe me. It's all there in black and blue and a bit of red too, how I felt about meeting you again and my crazy plan. If you don't want to read it then please destroy it, I never want to see those words again. All I want to say is that I do love you, Joe, love at first sight is real and it happened to me. If you can ever find a way to forgive me for lying to you, then once I've sorted this mess

*out I'll be waiting. Whether that's the right or wrong thing to say I
don't care, it's the truth. No matter what is going on here I will be
thinking of you. Have a great time with Sam and take care of
yourself. Love always, Tilly x*

Tilly could hear her mother rattling around downstairs and
knew she would have to face her sooner or later. After
going over the next stage of her mission and fine-tuning it,
she was ready to get on with the job in hand. Having some
kind of script and role to play made it easier for her to stay
in character and stick to her lines. Now, there were no
distractions or excuses that she could use to escape what
was ahead. She needed to wipe Joe from her mind and focus
on getting over the week ahead. Once she reached Sunday
morning and was on her way to her honeymoon, then she
was in the clear, job done, and her goal achieved. All she had
to do then was find the right time to speak to Luke and
break free.

The weak link was Rosie who would be fully in the loop
and it was imperative that she didn't give anything away.
Tilly had decided to speak to her and clear the air, the last
thing she needed was anybody at the hotel slipping up, or
worse, telling her mum what they knew. Tilly was positive
that Anna and her family would want to distance themselves from her, which was a good thing, so all she had to do
was keep Freda occupied, and away from Rosie.

Tilly had an ulterior motive where keeping busy was
concerned, it would fill up her days and make them pass
quicker. Once her grandma and brother arrived on
Wednesday, and then the rest of the guests trickled their
way into France, they'd provide a welcome distraction and
the time would fly by.

She checked her phone one last time, expecting a
miracle but there was nothing. Tilly knew that before she
even looked because she'd set it to loud *and* vibrate,
hoping it would wake her during the night if he'd replied.
She wasn't going to give up hope though and had faith in

the power of the words in her diary to make Joe see sense. In the meantime, she had a mother to fuss over and a pretend wedding to prepare for. Tilly stretched her stiff limbs and climbed out of bed to face the next six days head-on. No more tears or worrying was allowed. She would paint a smile on her face and convince the rest of the world that everything was just fine. She could do this, the finish line was in her sights and whether she would get a trophy at the end wasn't down to her anymore, it was all up to Joe.

Freda was waiting in the kitchen for Tilly to appear. She'd heard the bathroom door shut and the boiler fire up, so she must be in the shower. Freda had already told Howard to have a lie in as they were up rather late and after a rather successful night of passion, he deserved a rest. In reality, Freda wanted a heart to heart with Tilly without any interruptions and owing to the subject matter up for discussion, fully expected there to be a few strong words and maybe the odd firework or two.

Whether Tilly liked it or not, it was high time Freda said her piece and her daughter stopped moping and made a bit of an effort. Not that she was going to make any accusations, merely point out Tilly's general uncharacteristic demeanour and the worrying vibes she was giving off. Freda had it all mapped out in her head and was on her second cup of tea when Tilly came down the stairs. Steadying her nerves and wishing herself good luck, Freda waited for her daughter to appear.

When Tilly breezed into the kitchen and came over to give her mum a huge hug, wrapping her arms around her shoulders and topping the gesture off with a kiss on the head, Freda was taken aback and slightly wrong-footed. Tilly made herself some toast and two mugs of tea, during which time she didn't stop chattering about the awful weather outside and Didier's dogs waking her up. After not being able to decide on honey, peanut butter or jam, she finally took a seat opposite a rather surprised Freda who had lost most of her previous conviction.

Tilly spoke first. 'Right then, Mrs Parker. As promised, I am all yours for the next three days, so I suggest we rustle up some plans then we can make the most of our time together. I'll have to share you with Grandma and Scott after Wednesday so until they get here, you're all mine. I'm going to start by taking you out for lunch, let's go somewhere really nice and treat ourselves.' Tilly was spreading strawberry jam on her toast and was oblivious to her mother's reaction.

Freda felt a bit daft now and began to wonder whether her assumptions were way off the mark and perhaps hormone related, so she changed tack and dipped her toe in the water rather than jumping in at the deep end.

'Well, I must say this is a nice change from the moody daughter who's been living here for the past week. You seem very chirpy today, what's perked you up all of a sudden?' Freda thought that was a fair analysis of her daughter and not too harsh or accusatory.

'Aww... I'm sorry, Mum, have I been a misery guts? I didn't mean it, honest, but I've been working so hard at the hospital that I haven't had any time to get nervous or think about the wedding. When I got here, I suppose it all caught up with me a bit. Fourteen-hour shifts and overtime can take their toll and I've been mentally drained. I hope I've not upset you, but if I have, then I'm going to make it right, starting from now.' Tilly winked as she opened the jar of peanut butter.

'Well there's nothing wrong with your appetite, which is a good thing, because you're looking a bit skinny and I was worried that your dress won't fit. I'm not going to lie, Tilly, I have been a bit concerned about you these past few days and I was going to ask if you were okay. But you seem fine now so maybe your dad was right, as usual, and you're a bit nervous and there's nothing for me to worry about. I haven't got anything to worry about, have I?' Freda was still unsure and didn't want to waste all the thought and preparation that had gone into her proposed tête-à-tête.

'Honest, Mum, I'm fine, don't worry. Put it down to having my last teenage tantrum, even though I'm twenty-six and should know better. Do you forgive me?' Tilly gave Freda one of her theatrical, sad looks, at the same as hoping she'd deflected her mother's concerns.

'Of course I forgive you, love. I'm just being a fusspot as usual. Anyway, enough of all that. How did your afternoon at Anna's go, I take it Joe and his brother got off safely this morning?' Freda just had one more thing to check and by mentioning his name, the subject was on the table.

Tilly didn't answer straight away and pretended she had to swallow a mouthful of toast and then wash it down with some tea before replying.

'It was nothing special, she made paella and as far as I know Joe got off okay. They left early this morning and I haven't heard from them yet.'

Tilly hoped by being vague she hadn't told any lies. She noticed Freda eyeing her suspiciously and it reminded her of when she was a child, and her mum knew she wasn't telling the whole truth about tidying her room properly or finishing her homework. It rather unsettled Tilly who thought she'd been quite convincing up to now.

'What are you looking at me like that for? You've got your tense face on, come on, what's up?'

Tilly half wished she'd not asked but she needed to throw Freda completely off the scent and to do that, she had to find out what was going on in her mum's head.

'Well if you must know, I was starting to think you'd got a crush on one of the brothers because you seemed very eager to get over there. I also picked up on the rather tense atmosphere yesterday at Rosie's when Joe walked in. Shoot me if I'm barking up the wrong tree, but you both looked really embarrassed so I put two and two together and got five, and I hope to God I'm wrong.' There, she'd said it and from the look her daughter's face she wasn't too far off the mark.

Tilly was stunned for a second and was just about to wade in with strong denials and pronounce deep offence at being wrongly accused, when Howard innocently wandered into the kitchen and scuppered their conversation.

One of those long, awkward silences followed where it was blatantly obvious to whoever had walked into the room that they weren't privy to the discussion, and those involved were trying desperately to think of something else to say. Fortunately, Tilly was ahead of her mother and dived in with a diversionary subject and a reason to leave the room.

'I was just asking Mum where she'd like to go for lunch, my treat. Are you going to come too? It'd be nice to go somewhere different, is there anywhere you'd recommend?' Tilly looked brightly at her dad who was stuck in no man's land, waiting patiently for someone to show him the way out.

'I'll have to duck out I'm afraid, love, I'm going over to Eddie's later. I promised to help him put up his new shed, but why don't you take your mum to the bistro in Le Pin, I've heard it's very nice in there. I played *pétanque* with the bloke who owns it, Sebastien, nice chap.' Howard cottoned on that whatever they were talking about was probably women's stuff, so he got on with filling the kettle.

'Right, that's where we'll go then. Is that okay with you, Mum? I'm going to ring Luke and then do something with my hair, it's gone really dry and I think it needs a treatment. I'll see you in a bit.' And with that, Tilly took her plate and cup to the sink, washed it quickly and then shot upstairs, knowing that she hadn't got away with it and before the day was out, Freda would be on her case again.

Downstairs, Freda got on with her morning tasks and made Howard a fry-up. As she cracked eggs into the pan, a feeling of unease settled on her once again. There was no doubt about it, Tilly went very pink when she made her accusation and now, there was nothing for it other than to take the bull by the horns, which is exactly what she would do while they were having lunch.

* * *

Anna felt completely miserable and a bit lost. The foul weather wasn't helping and the storm that raged throughout the night had continued to batter the Loire all morning and was only just abating. The house seemed empty and sad, which only added to Anna's maudlin mood. In desperation, she lit a small fire in the log burner to cheer herself, and the lounge, up. Everywhere felt a bit damp and grey so the orange and yellow flames went some way to warming the atmosphere that had settled, and sent most of her family to the hills, or the indoor swimming pool at Candé to be precise.

Jeannie had gone to get her hair and nails done while Daniel and Phil went to the leisure centre with the kids, leaving Anna home alone with just Pippa and Louise for company. The latter was still sleeping it off. Rather than waste one second thinking about her behaviour the previous night, Anna set the Louise problem to one side and concentrated on Joe. She had made sure she was up at the crack of dawn to make both her sons breakfast and, in the vain hope that she'd have the chance to talk to one of them alone. Unfortunately, everyone decided to get up early so it didn't happen and by the time Joe and Sam's bags were loaded into the van, the moment had passed.

Maybe it was all best forgotten. Hopefully Joe would have got over it by the end of his holiday and after spending time with Sam and having fun, his heart would be healed. Anna knew she was kidding herself. Joe didn't just shrug things off and on this occasion, she would have to let him sort it out his own way and in his own time. He was gone and it was out of her hands. Her mind then wandered to Tilly.

It was like something in a gossipy magazine or on one of those tacky talk shows, and Anna never imagined that someone in her own family would be embroiled in what could be called a love triangle. She really hoped that during the next week her path didn't cross Tilly's because, apart from it all being immensely embarrassing, what on earth would she say or do? Anna felt sorry for Freda and Howard who were in the dark and had forked out for a sham wedding, but then again, that's why Tilly was going through with it. It was all so confusing and Anna still didn't know how she felt about her, despite spending most of the morning thinking about it while she lay in bed listening to the dawn chorus and the rain.

Hearing footsteps on the stairs, Anna's heart dropped, she'd hoped Louise would stay where she was until Daniel got home but now she'd have to face her alone – cringe! The sound of the kettle being flicked on and cups rattling forced Anna off the chair. Best get it over with, she thought, and there's no time like the present! As she entered the kitchen, Louise jumped, startled by the movement behind her and flipped round to see Anna surveying her coldly.

'Anna! You scared me to death, I thought everyone had gone out. I didn't realise you were still here. Would you like some coffee?'

Louise turned to continue her task and had the grace to seem embarrassed or nervous, maybe both.

'No thanks, I've just had some. I stayed here while they all went swimming. You look like hell by the way, but I'd put that down to self-inflicted injury, and after your performance last night some people might say you deserve it.' Anna had absolutely no sympathy or patience left where Louise was concerned.

When the spoon was thrown onto the counter in temper and a petulant face turned to meet Anna's, she knew that Louise wasn't going to apologise or take the comment lying down.

'You know what, Anna? I can really do without a lecture from you or anyone else right now, and let's face it, who are you to judge me when your own son's been at it with half the village? Talk about being a hypocrite. I'm not one of your saddo children who you feel the need to control and mollycoddle so go suffocate someone else, just leave me alone. I'm going back to bed until Dad gets back. How he puts up with you and your constant nagging I do not know, but I'm not a soft touch like him.'

And with that, Louise picked up her drink and made towards the stairs but Anna was too quick and blocked her way.

'How dare you speak to me like that in my own home? And for your information, Joe hasn't slept with anybody, never mind the whole village, so get your spiteful facts right before you open your mouth. You know what, Louise? You are one of the most ungrateful people I have met for a long, long time and as for your father, I don't know how he puts up with YOU! You embarrassed him in front of everyone last night and if you were my daughter I'd be ashamed of you. But I'm so glad you've finally told me how you feel because I'm sick to death of having to mollycoddle you, so if you don't like me or my family, sod off home. In fact, you can pack your bags now and the minute your dad gets back, take your son and go, I've had enough!' Anna was shaking with rage and wasn't sure who was more surprised by her sudden outburst, Louise or herself, not that she cared because it felt bloody fantastic to finally let it all out.

'Well if that's how you feel I'll go now and when Dad gets back you can tell him you threw me out, I'm sure him and Jules will be really pleased about that.' Before Anna had chance to think of a comeback, Louise had grabbed her jacket from the hook, flung open the door and stomped outside into the torrential rain.

Anna was more annoyed that the drama queen had left the door open and now the floor tiles were soaked. She wasn't unduly concerned that Louise would get wet and neither did it bother her that she was heading for her car, because Sam had disabled it and the psycho was going nowhere fast. Instead, Anna got on with drying the floor and calming down, trying hard not to smirk when she peeped at Louise who was having a tantrum inside her car and taking it out on the steering wheel. By the time she'd chucked another log on the fire (much to Pippa's delight), the consequences of her words were beginning to sink in and a niggling worry made its presence felt.

Louise might stay in the car until Daniel returned and get her own back by playing the injured party and tell everyone she was thrown out, and what would Jules think when he saw his mum having a paddy in her car? Also, they were expecting Tomas that evening so she had to stay here, whether Anna liked it or not. Feeling her resolve dribbling away and noting the time, Anna thought it might be an idea to try and smooth things over before everyone came home, otherwise the diva out there would take great delight in causing another scene. There was also the chance that Jeannie's patience would run out completely and then they really would have a scene on their hands if she tore a strip off Louise.

Sighing, Anna ruffled Pippa's very hot fur and went to get her fleece. Opening the door to the lashing rain, she made a dash towards Louise's car, hoping on the way that she'd let her in because she would feel like a fool if she locked the doors and told her where to go. Thankfully, when Anna reached the steamed-up vehicle and pulled the handle, it opened, so she jumped quickly inside where to her surprise and with a flicker of concern, she found Louise in floods of tears.

Anna remained silent for a while and let Louise cry it out, which also gave her time to think of something to say and evaluate whether or not the tears were genuine or of the crocodile variety. By the time they had subsided and the hiccupping, snivelling stage began, Anna had deemed them genuine and felt inclined to kindness, while keeping up her guard in case Louise flipped out and bared her teeth again. Anything was possible and Anna didn't fancy being trapped in a confined space with a candidate for the lunatic asylum.

'Are you okay? I haven't got any hankies, sorry.'

Louise silently held up a scrunched up, snotty tissue so Anna took this as a cue to continue.

'Look, shall we talk about this like grown-ups instead of shouting at each other? I didn't mean what I said in there and I don't want you to leave. You have to stay to sort things out with Tomas and besides, Jules will be upset if you leave under a cloud and he's not done anything wrong, has he?' Anna was watching Louise carefully and very mindful of the fact she was, what Jeannie described as, a borderline psycho.

No sooner had Anna finished speaking than Louise set off bawling again, this time louder and on the verge of hysteria, leaving Anna no other alternative than to offer her a shoulder to cry on. Tentatively placing her arm around Louise's shoulders, rather than being shrugged away, Anna's embrace was accepted. Another few minutes passed before Louise managed to regain her composure and after blowing her nose loudly, she managed to make a hoarse apology.

'I'm sorry, Anna, I really and truly am sorry. I've messed up big time and I seem to have the knack of making any situation worse and spoiling everyone's fun into the bargain. I know I've embarrassed my dad and upset you and I'm sure all your family hate me. Don't say they don't because *I'd* hate me if I was them.'

Rather than lie, Anna remained silent and allowed Louise to continue.

'I feel like I've got this raging ball of bitterness and anger inside me and instead of sorting myself out, I just take it out on other people. The only person who still likes me is Jules and I reckon I'm pushing my luck with him too. I'm a crap mum, a nasty wife and now I'm on the rubbish daughter list. Even my own mother can't be arsed to answer my messages, that's how low I am on her list of priorities. And now I've pushed my luck with you and burned my last bridge, but I deserved everything you said in there. What am I going to do, Anna? My head's so messed up and I think I'm going mad, I really do!'

With that, Louise burst into tears again and was soon racked by heart-wrenching sobs, which Anna could tell came from somewhere deep inside of a very mixed up young woman.

'Shush now, Louise, stop this. You're going to make

yourself ill and look, you're running out of tissues. If you don't stop crying we'll be trapped between a river of snot and torrential rain, so take some deep breaths and let's see if we can't sort this out. If you bottle things up they're bound to fester and eat away at you. I always think it's best to get it out in the open and we're halfway there now, so why don't you tell me the rest. When you're ready, just tell me what makes you so angry.'

Anna had managed to elicit a weak smile with the snot remark so was quietly confident she was getting through and making some progress.

'Are you sure you want to hear all this? You'll probably think I'm a spoilt mental case by the time I've finished, then offer to go inside and pack my bags for me.' Louise looked at Anna with wary eyes that were also pleading for someone to listen.

'Louise, considering what I heard last night, and along with some of the things that have gone on in my family, I can safely assure you that I'm virtually unshockable, so take a deep breath and let me have it. We're stuck in the car for the foreseeable future so you can keep me entertained, okay?'

Anna stretched over and squeezed Louise's hand, just as a rumble of thunder could be heard in the distance and a flash of white lightning made them jump, forcing a change of plan, sharpish.

'On second thoughts, sod this! I don't think sitting inside a lump of metal is a good idea. Let's risk getting our hair wet and make a run for the house.'

As another huge bolt of lightning ripped open the sky directly overhead, they looked at each other with wide, frightened eyes, opened their doors and ran.

Once inside the relative safety of the house, and after checking Pippa wasn't worried by the storm, Anna made them both a warm drink and they settled in front of the log burner. Pippa stirred from toasting herself by the fire decided on a change of venue and hopped onto the sofa, then placed her warm head on Louise's lap and went back to sleep.

Anna often thought that Pippa had human tendencies and even though she was spoilt, headstrong and attention-seeking, she sometimes did the right thing at the right time. Maybe she sensed that Louise needed a hug, either that or a kindred spirit. Dragging her thoughts away from the sleepy dog, Anna, trying hard not to sound like an amateur psychiatrist, encouraged Louise to talk.

Louise placed her cup on the table and sighed. 'It's just hard to put into words what goes on in my head. I suppose I've felt like this for so long it's become a part of me and I got used to being bitter and twisted. See, I sound vile already. I think there's only Pippa here who likes me.'

Louise hugged the dog and looked utterly dejected. Along with her hung-over complexion, red puffy eyes and unwashed, bedhead hair, she reminded Anna of someone in a TV drama who was visiting her jaded counsellor.

'Well, start there, from the time you began to feel like this, it's as good a place as any. I promise you, Louise, I won't judge you, I just want to help.' Anna smiled and hoped it was the encouraging type and didn't come across as patronising or false, because it really wasn't.

'I know exactly when it started, when I began to change, it was when Mum and Dad split up. Before that I picture myself as a nice, smiley, happy person and then after, I only ever see myself with a frown and a bitter heart. Perhaps them splitting up changed me into who I am now. I'm not expecting sympathy, Anna, don't think that. Loads of kids have divorced parents so I'm not a special case, but you did ask.' Louise drank her tea and watched the flames in the fire flicker and sway while the storm raged on outside.

There were so many things she'd bottled up and for years now, she'd stewed in her own juice and kept everything inside. Maybe now it was time to let them out and tell someone exactly how she felt. As memories began to resurface and words she'd never said begged for release, Louise turned to Anna and decided that the kind, open face before her was the first person in a long time who had actually offered to help, or even suspected that she needed it. Placing her cup back on the table, she folded her legs underneath her and as she held on to Pippa and stroked her loyal friend's fur, Louise finally got it all off her chest.

CHAPTER TWENTY

The 'before' Louise had, what she presumed was, a happy family unit consisting of three people who, for the most part, jogged along nicely in their life. Her dad was away quite a lot but his hard work provided them all with a lovely home, foreign holidays and more or less everything any of them could wish for. That's why it came as a great shock to Louise (and her father) when Carys broke the news that actually, she wanted more out of life, and more certainly did not include Daniel.

Louise had friends with divorced parents, so the situation wasn't entirely alien and she was old enough at eighteen to understand that the ramifications wouldn't necessarily affect her too greatly and most importantly, none of it was her fault. Despite this, Louise felt as though the rug had been ripped from under her at a time in her life when she really would've appreciated a solid, stable family to run back to when uni got a bit much, or she just fancied a weekend in the fluffy cloud that was home.

Soon, she found herself in no man's land. Having to choose which parent she stayed with, and then run the gauntlet of guilt (no matter which one she chose) when she finally plucked up the guts to announce her plans. It occurred to Louise that if she'd been younger they could've fought amongst themselves for visitation rights and she would've gone along with whoever won or kicked up the biggest fuss. As it happened, she'd kept a parent appease-ment diary and constantly trod on eggshells, dreading Christmas, her birthday and term breaks. When it got too much, she would dump them both and go away with her friends instead, because sometimes it just made life easier all round.

Apart from the holiday palaver, what made her really, really angry, was her mother's blinkered self-belief and her father's weak, defeatist attitude. These negative observa-tions festered and grew over time, and eventually stained her 'before' memories and any happy events that occurred in her present life.

To start with, Carys genuinely believed she had done everyone a huge favour where the timing of her conscious uncoupling (as she insisted on calling it) was concerned. Carys had remained in a martyred, unhappy existence until Louise had finished her A levels, for which she expected applause. While Louise understood that many couples hide their discontent behind closed doors, she was also bright enough to question the fact that her mum seemed jolly enough when she was swanning about in her flash cars and jetting off around the world on holidays with her dad.

At no time did she give off unhappy vibes, or any indica-tion that things were going wrong. The clinical precision with which Carys ended her marriage only proved she had it all planned, right down to the valuables listed in her divorce settlement. To make matters worse, Louise was left in no man's land like the box of ornaments, from which Daniel was instructed to choose. Carys didn't deem her valuable, more of a hindrance or, if she was bored, some-thing to cause a scene over.

With Louise set for university, Carys had insisted that she too deserved to spread her wings, having felt trapped for such a long and miserable time, and if her daughter truly loved her, she would want her to be happy and fulfilled too. This left Louise with the unhealthy image of being a millstone around her mother's neck for the past eighteen years and it was no wonder there hadn't been any siblings along the way. If there had, then Carys would definitely have drowned.

In the end, Louise accepted that her mother had absolved herself of any sin, long before she had even begun divorce proceedings, and her blinkered self-belief was all she needed to see her through any protestations or criticism. Consequently, Carys drove off into the sunset with half of everything and threw herself into the brand-new world she'd envisioned for herself during her many hours of drudgery.

Louise and Daniel were left with the feeling that they'd been living with somebody else for most of their lives and the foundations they thought their existence was built on seemed rather precarious to say the least.

While Louise was furious with her mother, she felt equally as infuriated with her father, because not only had he somehow missed all the signs that his wife was unhappy (or a nutcase) he had just given up without a fight. Therefore, Louise regarded him as being incredibly weak and worse, a huge disappointment. She had tried desperately to drag her dad from his corner and encouraged him to fight for his marriage but he simply threw in the towel, met all her mother's ridiculous, greedy demands and scurried off to the safety of his bachelor lifestyle to lick his wounds.

Louise couldn't believe he sold the firm he'd built up over the years. It was the sole reason she'd embarked on her business degree, the intention being to work by his side. Now, because of her mother's selfish greed and her father's yellow streak, everything was gone, her home, her family and her future.

Time flashed by and she was soon a graduate working for a small investment company in London, and it was here that she met Tomas, quite by chance at a colleague's birthday party. He was a friend of a friend and over for a few weeks holiday. By the time he was due to go home, they'd fallen in love. Two years later, Louise found herself planning her wedding after which, she was going to emigrate to France and start a brand-new life with her husband.

The wedding was more like a trial than a celebration. Carys had to be involved in everything, even from a distance, and then insisted on bringing her current tall, dark and wealthy arm candy without any consideration for Daniel, who true to form said he didn't mind and could deal with it.

If Louise thought that by moving to France she would somehow take control of her life and distance herself from her pillar to post existence, she was wrong. Although she managed to avoid visits to the UK entirely, the juggling act between her parents soon became a carbon copy of her old life, just in reverse, and when Jules came along, it was even worse. Louise didn't have to pick which one she stayed with anymore, instead she had to organise and negotiate when they would take up residence with her.

Tomas was doing well as a research scientist and Louise was immensely proud of him and his work, so for a time, motherhood kept her busy and fulfilled. She was lucky that she had parents who for one, could afford to visit regularly and two, wanted to be part of her son's life. Their appearances revolved around a rota system and each grandparent took it in turns, however, where Carys was concerned her aim was one-upmanship, not a genuine desire to see her grandson.

As Jules got older, Louise seemed to pale into insignificance where her parents were concerned and their visits focused solely on her son. Even thinking this made Louise feel like the worst mother in the world, yet when she added it to the sense of insignificance in other areas of her life, as her confidence dribbled away, it was replaced by hurt and resentment.

Tomas was now one of the most respected research fellows in his field and in great demand from teaching hospitals and universities across Europe. Louise had never complained about her role in their family. She'd been happy playing the gracious hostess, who produced wonderful meals for visiting colleagues, basking in the adoration of her clever, handsome husband and her adoring, perfect son. Yet as Jules grew older and more independent, Tomas also started to travel more frequently and Louise became increasingly bored, allowing her loose ends to tie knots in her heart. She had too much time on her hands to obsess about wasting her degree and mourning her independence, and soon began to question the value of her existence on every level.

After much thought and before whatever confidence she had left evaporated, she decided she would go back to work and forge a separate identity for herself. Unfortunately, Tomas was appalled by the idea, as well as being offended and incredulous that the perfect life he had created for them wasn't enough. The row rumbled on and on for months, fuelling Louise's resentment and feelings of isolation as her life was mapped out, and what made it worse, she had nobody on her side.

On the evening Tomas bounded in and made his grand announcement that they were moving to Geneva, it really was the final straw, and, when she needed them the most, her parents were miles away. One was poncing around Peru pretending to be Lara Croft and the other was loved-up in the Loire.

Ironically, Louise wasn't adverse to the move to Geneva, it looked and sounded lovely and they could give Jules a wonderful life there. The only thing that got in the way was her stubborn streak and refusal to be railroaded into an existence similar to the one she had. The argument with Tomas had got out of hand and, once again, she had made herself look impetuous and self-absorbed, and as a consequence, hadn't a clue of how to put it right or back down gracefully.

* * *

'So, there you have it, my selfish view of life. Anyone would think I was orphan Annie the way I whinge on. I've had more than most, I know that, yet surely I'm allowed to have feelings.' Louise looked at her counsellor for a sign that she understood, because despite everything that had gone on between them, Anna's opinion actually mattered.

After listening to all of it, Anna was surprised by very little of Louise's confession. Daniel had explained how it was when he got divorced and maybe, from what she'd just heard, he hadn't handled it as well as he thought. She understood from things he'd said that there was no way of mending his marriage, Carys just wasn't interested. Perhaps, with hindsight, Daniel should've exposed his ex-wife and told Louise truthfully that, in private, her mother really was a cow, instead of protecting everyone's feelings. While he was being a peacemaker and taking the path of least resistance, he'd actually appeared weak and feeble.

Knowing she'd have to tread carefully where Carys was concerned and not daring to poke whatever scraps of loyalty Louise still had for her, Anna broached the subject of her own relationship with Daniel.

'I completely understand everything you've said and I can see why you felt the way you did when they split up, but what I don't get is why you seem to resent me so much. I'm not having a go, but from how you've described your mum's behaviour, there's no way you could possibly blame me for that, I wasn't even around. Is it because you want more attention from your dad and you feel like I get in the way?' Anna was convinced that she'd hit the nail on the head.

'In some ways that's true. When you came along, I was glad for Dad because I don't want him to be lonely, I never have. The thing is, I was jealous of *you*, of everything you stood for really. The more I got to know or hear about you, it was clear you are everything my mum isn't and it brought back my anger towards her. Even though all your kids are adults, you still manage to put them first, your life in some way still revolves around them. You don't just fit them into your schedule, you make them part of it. I'm jealous of that and because I can't take my mum's imperfections out on her, I took them out on you instead. I didn't mean any of those things I said about you mollycoddling them. I think it's lovely, the time and effort you put into looking out for your family and fussing over things. It just hurts, that's all.' Huge tears rolled down Louise's face.

Anna knew it took quite a lot of guts to be so honest and she respected Louise for that. She was also beginning to understand Louise's behaviour and why she looked incredibly sad and defeated. Leaning forward and taking Louise's hand in hers, Anna drew her attention away from the floor and looked into her eyes.

'Right, well this is where all that ends, okay? As far as I'm concerned, the worst thing you have done is bottle things up and that never does anyone any good, take it from me, I know. I forgive everything you've said and done, and I don't want it mentioned again, it's in the past and that's where it stays. That still leaves the big question of where we go from here, so tell me, what would make you happy, Louise? Go on, what is it *you* want from life?' Anna really did forgive Louise but knew that the only way to prevent a return to form was by helping her change.

'I don't deserve to be forgiven, Anna, I've been horrible to you and everyone, but if you mean it, I promise I'll never behave that way again, I swear. And if you want to know what would really make me happy, well it's simple really. I'd like to feel like part of a family again, but a real member that's involved, not just thrown the odd scrap of other people's lives when they come and visit. Mum never invites me to stay with her and Ed, and doesn't even include me when she comes to see Jules, which most of the time is an exercise in showing off and buying better presents than his other grandparents.'

When Louise finished, Anna dared to ask if she had a good relationship with her mum and confided in her, she'd always got the impression they were thick as thieves.

'We get on alright, but I wouldn't say we were best

friends either. I made out that was the case because I find the fact that we're not close embarrassing. I have some nice friends to have a moan and a bitch with but I don't have the sort of mother figure in my life that can be relied on for advice or support. Mum does exactly what she wants, when she wants, and I'd never tell her that I'm unhappy because she'd just tell me to leave Tomas, for good.' Louise looked up at Anna briefly and then continued.

'And as for Dad, well I'd like to join in his life with you and your family because he seems so happy and I'm fed up with being annoyed with him. I had a lovely day at the beach with you all. The only problem was I felt on the edge and not really part of it. I watched you all day, interacting with each other, the closeness you have and even the banter between Joe and Sam made me envious. I know it's of my own making and I've got so used to being stand-offish that I've forgotten how to join in.'

At this Anna sighed and squeezed Louise's hand even tighter.

'Louise, that's awful! I can't believe you feel like that, and I can assure you that my three won't bite, you just have to give them a chance, even Jeannie!' Anna had a lump in her throat as she spoke, which softened slightly when she saw Louise smile.

'Do you really think so? I miss my dad more than anything, you know? We hardly ever visit him in England because he's away a lot and I feel like I'd be intruding or getting in the way. I think all of your family are lovely, Anna. Despite my jealousy, I'm not stupid and can see they're all nice people who I'd like to get to know better. It would be lovely for Jules to see more of you because he only really knows his French family and it shouldn't be one-sided. Everything's been so muddled up in my head but now we're friends and I've got everything off my chest, I feel like it's a lot clearer.'

Louise did actually look as though the weight of the world rested on her shoulders, so Anna thought she'd remove some of the burden.

'Well you'll be pleased to hear that from now on, things are going to change. For a start, I would love to see more of you, and be very happy if you'd all come and stay. I know you feel awkward now, but once they see this side of you, my three will welcome you with open arms. As for your dad, he hasn't got a bad bone in his body and maybe sometimes, people mistake traits like that as weakness. I think he just knew that it was time to throw in the towel where your mum was concerned. I do think you should talk to him about how you felt back then. Just give him the chance to set your mind at rest and explain his side of the story, like you said, you don't want to resent him anymore. As for your mum, have you ever thought that even though she handled things badly at the time, everyone deserves to be happy and if she'd stayed with your dad, well it could've ruined both their lives in the long run?'

That was about as far as Anna was prepared to go in the interests of being even-handed where Carys was concerned, because deep down, she thought she was a self-centred cow!

Louise had been soaking up everything Anna said, yet sounded slightly incredulous when she replied.

'Do you really think they'll forgive me for being so awful? I'm sure Ruby hates me for squashing her cake, not to mention poor Lily, and I'm a bit scared of Jeannie, she can be quite fierce sometimes.'

Louise looked about twelve years old as she spoke with wide, concerned eyes and for this reason, it endeared her to Anna even more, and made her laugh out loud too.

'I'm sure they'll forgive you, don't worry about that, although you might have to put up with a bit of teasing for a while where the cake incident is concerned. And you should think yourself lucky that Sam didn't have his phone on him, otherwise you'd be looking at photos of yourself covered in fruit and cream for the rest of your life, and so would everyone on Facebook!'

Anna smiled and saw that Louise was happier too.

'As for Jeannie, don't mind her, she's like my own personal guard dog, mainly because the one sitting next to you is useless. She'll be fine as long as she knows we've sorted things out. Does that make you feel better?'

'I'll just have to take your word for it and prove to them I'm not all bad, but I've still got to sort things out with Tomas and I'm dreading seeing him later, which is awful because I've missed him so much. I hate that things have come to this... what do *you* think I should do?' Louise looked on the verge of slipping back into the doldrums and clearly hadn't a clue how to deal with Tomas.

Anna wasn't sure that there was going to be a quick fix for Louise's dilemma, and her husband's attitude towards his wife's career might need a softly, softly approach. What bothered Anna the most was that up until now, it appeared Louise had nobody to turn to if she needed a bit of motherly advice.

'Well, seeing that you are prepared to go to Geneva that means most of your problems are solved, however, I suggest that you use this as an opportunity to tell Tomas exactly how you feel, and any move has to be on your terms. He's landed his dream job so now he has to let you find yours. I expect his ego is at the core of his resistance so for now, why don't you meet him halfway? What if you told him that you wanted to do some voluntary work, perhaps find a charity that's attached to the university or his company? I'm sure there are lots of organisations crying out for someone to help on the administration side, it's not all about delivering parcels and working on the front line, charities must have tons of paperwork to do. It could even open doors and I'm sure Tomas will be proud to tell his colleagues about your voluntary work and his male ego won't be too dented in the process. What do you think, do you fancy doing something like that? Ignore me if you think I'm barking mad.' Anna had surprised herself with her sensible plan of action.

'Anna, that's brilliant! I just want to get out of the house and have something to talk about over dinner and let Jules know there's more to his mum than helping with his homework. I've been to loads of charity dinners and fundraisers with Tomas and I'm sure there will be more in Geneva, so now, instead of bidding on stupid things that I don't even need, I can actually get involved. But what will I say when he gets here? He's already angry with me for taking Jules away and ignoring him.' Worry was etched across Louise's face.

'Why don't you just tell him that you wanted to be with your family and talk things through with them? Simple as that! As for ignoring him, just say you needed time to clear your head and didn't want to get into any more rows over the phone. But my guess is that he will be so relieved you've decided to go to Geneva he'll agree to anything and forget all about being annoyed, well I hope that's what happens. And if all else fails, you'll just have to use your womanly wiles on him. Save that as last resort!' Anna winked at Louise who was smiling now.

'You are so wise, Anna. I feel like a great big weight has been lifted off my shoulders, I just wish I'd said all this in the first place and not wasted my time here by being a moody cow.' Louise was genuinely remorseful over her recent actions.

'Like I said, just forget about it and move on. But can I give you one last piece of advice and then I'll shut up? You might think I'm wise but I can assure you it's not always been the case. I made mistakes when I was married and if I can prevent you or Melanie repeating them, then the harsh lesson was worth learning. What I'm trying to say is don't be complacent or too comfortable in your relationship with Tomas. Never take anything for granted or assume that if temptation came his way he'd behave like a saint. I did all those things and I was caught out. No matter how hard I tried to be the perfect wife, someone managed to worm her way in and steal my husband.' Anna hated to be reminded of the past yet she felt it was important that the worst of Louise's personality traits were banished for good, and she also suspected Tomas would only put up with so much.

'I'm not suggesting for one second that Tomas would do that, but keep this in mind… if he's having a rough time at home and sees you as a nagging wife who doesn't understand him, or whatever strange thoughts go through the minds of men, there *could* be someone in his workplace on the lookout for a good catch. The last thing you want is for him to look forward to going to the office so he can be with people who flatter him or show great interest in his work, who laugh at his awful jokes and take his mind off whatever problems he has at home. It's a fine balancing act, I admit that. Somehow you have to maintain your dignity and hold on to what you believe in, while ensuring your husband thinks he has *the* most wonderful wife and the only place he ever wants to be, is at home with her. Your Tomas is a handsome, clever man who is most likely going to go far, so don't let him out of your grasp, Louise. Marriage isn't easy and you have to work at it. One day, I'll explain to you what happened with me and Matthew but for now, just take my word and concentrate on getting the balance right and I'm sure you'll be fine.'

'I understand. I know I can come across as being a nag and I do push all his buttons, but that's the old me. Just wait till he gets here, Tomas won't know what's hit him, and neither will Dad. Perhaps they'll think you've put a spell on me or I've been taken by aliens and they sent a nicer version back to earth, all in the space of a morning!'

Louise didn't realise it, but her self-deprecation was quite funny and Anna hoped her new-found sense of humour would be permanent.

'Well, they'll all be back soon and I'm starving. Do you fancy some lunch because I bet they've been to McDonald's, again?' Anna could hear her stomach rumbling and presumed Louise would need to soak up some of the alcohol from the night before.

'Me too. I could do with something really unhealthy to get rid of this hangover, let's start with some paracetamol though, and another strong cup of tea.' Louise was trying to lift Pippa's head off her lap without disturbing her.

'Right, that's a deal. I'll raid the fridge and you put the

kettle on, there's some painkillers in the medicine box, help yourself.'

And with that they sneaked out of the lounge and left Pippa in the land of nod while they attempted to fry sausages and eggs without her noticing.

By the time they'd washed up and fed Pippa the scraps from a very English fry-up, Louise was feeling more or less restored and full of beans, literally. As they munched their way through lunch, Anna suggested that Louise went to the airport to meet Tomas and from there they could go for a quiet drink and talk things through before coming back to see Jules. It would save him getting a hire car and hopefully by the time they returned, they'd be friends and everything would be in the open. Anna suspected he'd be just as nervous and tense, so if Louise held out the olive branch first, it would relax them both.

Her next idea seemed to be as equally well met. Anna invited all three of them for Christmas. After assuring Louise that they'd be able to squash into her apartment and was a firm believer in 'the more the merrier', Anna extolled the virtues of giving Jules his first English Christmas. They could all go to a pantomime and there was so much for him to see in Portsmouth docks that he wouldn't get bored, and maybe they could go up to London for a few days and then stay at Daniel's for New Year. It would be nice for Jules to see Summer and Ross again, and meet Enid too. And then there was the sea and the beach right on her doorstep, plus the icing on the cake – the Boxing Day sales.

Louise almost burst with excitement and assured Anna that it would be a non-negotiable part of her terms and conditions for moving to Geneva, explained to Tomas in the nicest possible way, of course.

When Daniel and the rest of the gang traipsed inside, fully expecting a gloomy, tense atmosphere, everyone was buoyed by the fact that it was the complete opposite. As Louise made coffee for everyone and told her dad of her plans to meet Tomas later, and whispered that they'd be coming to England for Christmas, but it was a surprise for

Jules, Anna saw the tension in his face melt away as he listened to his daughter's happy chatter.

Jeannie was admiring her hairdo in the mirror while her reflection gave Anna quizzical looks, then watched in bemusement as the 'New Louise' admired Jeannie's lovely, new acrylic nails.

While the kids set up board games on the dining room table and everyone else went about drying soggy swimwear and towels, Anna wandered over to the window, noticing that at last the sun was peeping through a white cloud and even though it was tinged at the edge with grey, it signalled better weather was on its way.

Picking up her phone she checked for messages from her sons, but the screen was blank and her heart felt sad. They'd be miles away by now and she hoped that the rain had stopped and that Sam had managed to cheer Joe up. Rosie had promised to ring her later that day and let her know if they'd heard anything from Tilly, good or bad.

For now, Anna knew there was nothing she could do but wait for some positive news. Until then, she'd obey the call of her niece who wanted to play snakes and ladders and then there was ludo and Hungry Hippos to take her mind off things. Jules was helping Ross poke the sticks into the KerPlunk game as the bag of marbles somehow escaped and rolled all over the floor and under the sofa.

Anna dragged herself away from the window and reminded her worried brain that she should enjoy the mayhem because this was the last day of having a full house; in the morning, Jeannie and Phil were springing their Disney surprise on Ross and Summer and eventually, if all went well, Louise and Tomas would be on their way home with Jules. Melanie would still be around but the house would seem very quiet with just her and Daniel. Still, maybe they needed to take a breather and have some time to themselves before the boys came back this way.

Obeying Summer who was becoming impatient and raring to go, Anna made her way over to the games table, picking up stray marbles on the way. Settling herself in a chair, she resolved to concentrate on the task in hand and put the many hours of playing board games with her three to good use. It was time she showed these kids who was the master where rolling a die was concerned and as for KerPlunk, well, little did they know but Aunty Anna was a champ!

CHAPTER TWENTY-ONE

Tilly's Monday didn't turn out to be quite as bad as she'd expected and the only blips were the two rather uncomfortable conversations she'd had to endure: one with her mother and one with Rosie. Tilly didn't want to leave the latter in total limbo and had the decency to drop a big 'don't worry' hint over the phone that afternoon. After a pleasant lunch with Freda, apart from being lightly grilled by her mother with regards to Joe, which was then topped off with a rather bizarre confession, Tilly had survived her ordeal and once the coast was clear, she rang Rosie.

As it was, the conversation fell more into the 'stilted and awkward' category, however, Tilly had managed to get the message across and allay any concerns Rosie had. She began her speech in a bright and breezy manner and went straight in with hint number one.

'Hi, Rosie. I was wondering if it would be okay to pop over on Wednesday afternoon and leave something for when Luke arrives. It's just a card for the morning of the wedding. I probably won't have chance any other time. I'll leave it at reception if you're busy.' There, that should do the trick, thought Tilly.

It seemed that Rosie wasn't too sure.

'Well I hope it's the type of card someone wants to receive a few hours before their wedding and you've not slipped a Dear John letter inside, that's all I need on Saturday, a weeping bridegroom and an uneaten banquet.' Rosie had the advantage of not worrying about being overheard and sounded polite yet firm while delivering a message of her own in return.

Tilly gulped, surprised by Rosie's tone. 'No, nothing like that. I'm just sticking to tradition and following the guidelines from the hundreds of bride magazines I've read. There definitely won't be any surprises on the day. I can assure you of that.' As Tilly said the words, Freda marched past with a pile of towels and appeared not to be suspicious.

'Oh good, so I'm to tell Michel to order the rest of the fresh ingredients for the wedding breakfast and confirm the arrangements with the extra waiters, is that correct?' Rosie was making herself abundantly clear.

'Yes, that's correct and thank you for going to so much trouble, Rosie, I'm sure it will all be worth it on the day and we'll have a lovely time. I'll bring the card over on Wednesday morning before I go to pick my brother up from the airport, is that okay?' Tilly was fed up with being interrogated today, and she didn't know what else Rosie expected her to say, especially with Freda mooching about.

'Righty-ho, I'll pass that on to Michel and I'll look forward to seeing you on Wednesday, maybe we could have a quick chat if you're on your own, but until then, have a great day.'

And with that, both women said their goodbyes and abruptly ended the call.

Tilly was rattled by Rosie's hint that she wanted a chat, while at the same time felt reassured that her secret was safe. Shaking off the bad vibes, Tilly made her way upstairs to check her phone (again) in the hope that Joe's name appeared. It was also time to unpack her dress and get the creases out, a task which had Freda champing at the bit.

So far, she had done a damn good job of putting on a brave face and making sure her mother felt wanted and appreciated, which truly was the case as far as Tilly was concerned, although she stopped short of being fake and openly lying wherever possible. Come the Day of Atonement, Tilly knew full well that apart from her wedding being a sham, the fact she had been deceitful would hurt her parents the most. For this reason, Tilly had focused all her attention on her mum, the imminent arrival of her family and friends, the favourable weather forecast and the many tasks they had to complete before the big day. In doing so, she appeared enthusiastic whilst deflecting any attention from herself. It was a good plan and for now it was getting her through missing Joe and helped her ignore the terrible ache in her heart.

Freda was so happy. Everything was going to be okay and now she'd had a little heart to heart with Tilly and cleared the air, it was full steam ahead and they could sail calmly towards the big day. Maybe all mothers should have a one to one with their daughter before their wedding. Just to make sure there was nothing bothering them and, if necessary, pass on some life skills and wisdom they'd collected over the years. It had certainly done the trick with Tilly who, since breakfast, had been most attentive and was finally showing some enthusiasm, especially about the arrival of her family.

Still, after smoothing out any perceived crinkles and reassuring her daughter on most matters, Freda had made a note to self to keep her eye on Luke in future. Going by what Tilly had said in her own defence, he hadn't exactly been brimming with *joie de vivre* or a great comfort in their everyday life, either. As Freda's mind wandered back to their chat over lunch, her subconscious prodded her sharply, reminding her of his past indiscretions and whose side she should be on.

* * *

It had all started when she returned to the subject of Joe, once their starters were placed in front of them and her daughter was well and truly pinned down to one spot.

'Tilly, I need to get something off my chest because if I don't, it will wreak havoc with my nerves and play on my mind and as we all know, I really do need my sleep. I'm not accusing you of anything I promise, but I just sense that recently you've developed some kind of feelings for Joe. Please don't be angry with me for saying it and I swear this is between the two of us, whatever you say goes no further than this table. Our secret, okay?' Freda was dying to tuck into her pâté but didn't want to risk choking if Tilly gave the wrong answer.

'Mum! What on earth gave you that idea? Honestly, sometimes I wonder where your mind wanders to when you're left on your own. Anyway, Joe is long gone and in case you've forgotten, I'm getting married in five days, so I really don't think we should be having this conversation, do you?' Tilly began chopping her melon into pieces then stuck some in her mouth to prevent a lie from popping out.

'Like I said, I'm not angry with you *or* passing judgement but I'm not blind either and it was blatantly obvious that you both looked very uncomfortable when he turned up at the hotel yesterday. I also know you well enough to see when you're upset and nervous, so come on, tell me what's going on. Why did you go the colour of those grapes while he lost the use of his tongue?' Freda knew when she was being fobbed off and had been forced to be more direct than she had previously planned, but when she noticed her daughter's watery eyes and heard the silence fall between them, she changed tack quickly.

'Tilly, can I tell you a secret of my own? It might make you realise that I'm not without faults and won't judge you for any mistakes you've made. In this life, we all mess up or push boundaries now and then, for loads of different reasons. Just eat your food and listen to your mother, okay.' Freda saw Tilly nod so she pushed her entrée to one side and they took a tentative stroll down memory lane.

* * *

Before she married Howard, Freda knew she loved him with all her heart and that the life they had planned together was what every girl dreamed of. It might not have been a castle on the hill at the end of the rainbow but the small, rented terraced house and the promise of a loyal, devoted husband waiting for her once she said 'I do' was enough for her.

The eager young woman she used to be, fresh out of teacher training college, had it all mapped out in her head. Freda was due to start work at an inner-city school at the beginning of the new term, just after she returned from her honeymoon. They planned to wait a few years until they could afford a home of their own and then hopefully, they would start a family. There was no rush, and both wanted to provide a little bit more for their kids than they'd had themselves. Not that they weren't grateful for everything that their loving, working-class families had given them but, along with strong foundations and firm roots, they hoped to push the boundaries and go one step further.

In her final week of teacher training college, Freda took the lift and not the stairs, mainly because of the huge pile of books she was carrying, and as she stepped inside and the doors closed behind her, she came face to face with Neville. Since they'd all been away at their respective placements, honing their skills with hands-on teaching practice, most of the student teachers hadn't clapped eyes on each other for almost a year. Consequently, Freda hadn't given the handsome chap who stood in front of her, a second thought.

Once he'd gentlemanly relieved her of her load, thus allowing Freda to select the floor she required whilst blushing like a teenager with a stonking crush, Neville asked polite questions and prattled on about the school he'd worked at, before asking how she'd enjoyed her placement. It was with enormous relief when the lift soon came to a stop on the second floor, allowing Freda to escape and as she retrieved her book pile, bade him farewell and wished him the best of British. As the doors closed and Freda composed herself, she felt a swell of annoyance that he'd affected her so badly, causing her to stammer and redden under his confident gaze.

What was wrong with her? Yes, Neville was lush, which was how all her single friends described him whilst swooning and vying for his attention, but Freda was with Howard, so he was strictly off limits, even where the imagination was concerned. In the past, he'd hardly given her a second glance, yet he knew her name instantly and seemed rather pleased to see her. This thought flustered Freda immensely.

By 4pm, everyone was gathered around two adjacent tables in their local Wimpy and Freda had shaken off any thoughts of Neville and his lovely blue eyes and cheeky grin. She was also looking forward to her hamburger and chips until Patty spotted a late arrival and waved them over, it was, of course, Neville. This time, Freda managed to hide behind her friends and while they clamoured for his attention, had time to appear composed. There was something definitely not right though, because try as she might to not attract his attention or catch his eye, despite Patty's flirting, Neville was definitely giving Freda the come on.

Eventually the group began to peter out and one by one, everyone headed off into the warm summer evening. Patty finally took the hint and gave up and accepted a lift home from one of the other girls. Not wanting to be left alone with Neville, Freda also made her excuses about missing buses and grabbed her bag. When he mentioned smoothly that he was heading to the bus station and would tag along, her flustered state resumed, leaving her eager to get into an open, larger space. The confines of the Wimpy bar were beginning to suffocate her.

Once they were on the street, Freda began to relax slightly and decided it was time she threw Neville off the scent and then perhaps the gooey-eye routine would cease. When she casually mentioned Howard, her fiancé, then gave Neville a flash of her ring, he didn't bat an eyelid and confessed he'd already noticed her diamond, and then asked why she was taking the plunge so young. What was a gorgeous woman with a teaching certificate doing getting married, when she had the world at her feet? To this Freda took great umbrage and spent the remainder of the journey extolling the virtues of marriage and more to the point, Howard.

When she spotted the number seventeen bus and the words, Hanham High Street, it might as well have said 'Emergency Exit' because Freda couldn't wait to get on board and away from Mr Cocky. If he so much as hinted he was getting on the same bus, Freda had silently vowed to pick the first one going in the opposite direction, even if it took her all night to get home.

Ending their one-sided conversation abruptly, Freda bade Neville goodnight and almost jumped onto the bus where she chose a seat away from the window. As the driver pulled out of the station, Freda was concerned to see Neville walking back towards the entrance, his confident gait and nonchalant air only irritating her more once she realised he had no intention of taking public transport and just wanted an excuse to spend time with her.

As the double decker trundled its way out of the city, Freda calmed down and once her personal space felt less invaded, her annoyance softened at the edges and a twinge of self-satisfaction seeped in. Freda was rather flattered that Neville had been flirting with her and then went out of his way to walk her to the bus stop. At the same time, she did feel miffed about him putting her down, and Howard too. Her mind wandered this way and that, one minute it was offended, the next it felt excitement at being pursued. Anyway, it was all harmless fun and she'd nipped it in the bud quite nicely.

Unfortunately, Neville wasn't used to being pruned back and enjoyed the chase far more than Freda had envisaged. Consequently, the following day and for the rest of the week, he kept his quarry firmly in his sights. Freda didn't know what hit her. She was bombarded with cheeky notes, surreptitiously slid inside her locker, and pulse raising, sultry looks across the canteen. He would suddenly appear in the corridor between classes, or on the way into college in the morning, monopolising every second and gradually, wearing down her resolve. Neville stood far too close in the queue for food and revelled in spotting a stray hair that needed plucking from her face or a bit of fluff that had to be brushed sensuously from her clothing. All of this could be put down to him being a caring friend and drew no attention from others yet Freda knew exactly what he was doing and to her confusion and horror, she began to enjoy the frisson of something forbidden and out of bounds.

He was charming, self-deprecating (whilst she suspected he meant none of it), funny in a wicked sort of way and so very good-looking. Freda did her best to ignore and resist him but he was getting under her skin. If he didn't appear, she was left disappointed and miserable, only to be uplifted when he finally turned up to fill the boring spaces between lectures. Neville invaded Freda's thoughts as she got ready in the morning (not that she was dressing up especially for him or anything like that) but if she was brutally honest, he was somehow worming his way between her and Howard.

One night, while they were sitting in her mum's front parlour watching telly, Freda found herself scrutinising her husband-to-be and yes, comparing everything about him to Neville, which left her feeling thoroughly ashamed. Naturally, she didn't confide any of these hidden stirrings to another soul because she couldn't bear the thought of what her friends would think. Instead, she soldiered on, enjoying the last few days of freedom, flattery and flirtation, because after Friday and the leavers' party, Freda would probably never see Neville again.

It was common knowledge that he was jetting off to try his luck in Australia and once he had his teaching certificate in those slim, manicured hands, Blighty and Freda would be far behind him and long forgotten. This alone made her feel sad and an irrational sense of time running out settled in. This is why, when the indecent proposal was made, Freda's

PATRICIA DIXON

normal, run-of-the mill life was sent into orbit and her once sensible head spent days whizzing around space.

The day of the much-anticipated leavers' party had finally arrived. It was held at the pub around the corner from college. During the evening, copious amounts of tampered with, homemade punch had been consumed as the jubilant students let their hair down, and it was here that Neville finally made his move.

Howard couldn't attend as he was on duty that night and Freda couldn't decide whether this pleased her or made her feel incredibly vulnerable. As she had envisioned and expected, Neville pursued her for the entire evening and despite her best attempts at sticking with her crowd of friends to ensure temptation was avoided, he finally cornered her on her way back from the loo. Grasping her hand firmly, Neville pulled her towards the fire escape and with a quick push of the metal bar, she found herself outside in the balmy night air and completely alone with her ardent admirer.

It was here that he told her she was driving him crazy, that he couldn't bear to spend another night without knowing what it was like to kiss her and even though he had to accept that she was getting married and he was heading for antipodean shores, surely they could both be forgiven for having one last, mad, improper fling. Even though he knew he was completely out of line even asking, he would regret it forever if he didn't. Once he had built his pitch to a crescendo, Neville asked if she would meet him somewhere more private, perhaps they could go to Brighton for the day, his friend had a flat there that they could use. If he could snatch just one day of bliss with her before he left, Neville said he'd be the happiest man alive.

Freda was shocked to the core and so far out of her depth that she was almost drowning out there on the fire escape. This was all far too much and had gone beyond flirting and daydreaming, because now the most sought after, drooled over man at college was declaring his feelings and asking her to cheat on Howard.

Why would she risk everything to go for a dirty weekend (or, by the sound of it, an afternoon quickie) with someone she hardly knew, and worse, who had the audacity to ask her to betray her fiancé for him? God, he was a jumped-up, vain chancer and in that second, Freda saw him for exactly who he was – a man who enjoyed the thrill of the chase and would go to any lengths, including spouting clichéd bullshit. All Neville was interested in was collecting a trophy once he got his own way, regardless of the hurt he could cause and the mess he might leave behind.

As Neville moved closer and locked eyes on his target, Freda's heart raced as her mind screamed no, telling her to push him away and run for her life. In the midst of her panic and just for a second, Freda thought her frantic brain was hallucinating because there was an alarming noise ringing in her ears and the sky had changed colour. From somewhere in the distance, came the familiar sound of a siren accompanied by a flashing blue light, which dragged her attention away from Neville's lust reddened face and beer laced breath, and alerted her to his wandering hands which were now clamped around her waist and pulling her near. When Freda heard voices below and the sound of a door slamming, she reacted instantly. Thoroughly revolted, she pulled away sharply from the octopus and peered over the edge. As soon as she saw the fire engine below, she knew instantly who it was.

Pushing Neville's wandering hands from her body, Freda came to her senses as the real world drew sharply into focus. She desperately needed to get downstairs. Howard was here and he'd be looking for her. Please God, she prayed, let nobody have seen us. Before Neville could protest or continue, Freda shot inside and made her way swiftly down the stairs and through the crowded, smoky pub in search of Howard, who she found laughing and chatting with Patty and her friends.

He looked so handsome in his uniform and when his eyes found hers, he smiled broadly as she pushed her way towards him. Within seconds, his strong arms were wrapped around her body and holding her tightly, and it had never felt so good. Howard and the lads were on their way back from a shout and the boss had given him permission to nip in and say hello. He felt bad about not being there and just wanted to show his face and let her know how proud he was.

Howard said he couldn't stay long as they had to get back to the station and the lads were waiting outside so Freda walked with him to the door, assuring her beloved fiancé on the way that it was the best surprise and the perfect end to her night because she was going straight home and would call at taxi the minute he set off.

True to her word, once she'd waved to Howard and the rest of his mates who'd jeered and honked the horn when he gave her a goodnight kiss, Freda went back inside. She called a cab from the number by the payphone and before any of her friends could change her mind, she grabbed her coat and bag and made her way to the door.

When Neville appeared in the doorway, before he could begin one of his rehearsed speeches or dare to touch her, knowing if he did she might just knock him out, Freda told him where to get off, not to speak to her again or even look in her direction because if he did, then she would tell Howard to punch his lights out. Seeing the taxi pull up outside the pub, Freda finished by telling him to sod off back inside and find some other unsuspecting girl to slobber over because she just wasn't interested.

Slamming the door and once safely inside the cab, she sucked in a huge breath of air before giving the driver her address. Freda's hands and voice shook, and he probably assumed she'd had a tiff with her boyfriend, but she didn't care. All she wanted to do was get home, and in the morning she'd go round to Howard's, just so she could see his face again and reaffirm her love for him, because she did love him, from the bottom of her heart and so very, very much.

The story didn't quite end there because about a month after she was married, Freda bumped into Patty in town.

They missed being able to gossip to their hearts content at college so nipped into the café on the high street and caught up. After a sticky bun and a cup of tea, Patty passed on her best bit of hot news which she'd got straight from the horse's mouth, or Hilary, the faculty secretary who knew *everything* about everyone. This juicy titbit was about Neville, and Freda prayed she hadn't gone red because for one awful moment, she thought the headline might be all about her – she was wrong!

It seemed that since the beginning of term, Neville had been seeing one of the first-year students on the sly. Her name was Gina and despite being just out of high school and barely turned eighteen, he'd only gone and got her in the family way, as Patty politely put it. Her dad was livid because it seemed that good old Neville had scarpered when he heard the news, but along with Gina's brothers, he'd tracked him down to Brighton where they demanded he do the decent thing. After dragging him back to Bristol to face the music, he hung around for a few days and then did another disappearing act and used his ticket to Australia, leaving Gina and his unborn baby behind.

Apparently, Patty always had him down as a Jack the Lad who she'd suspected had the hots for Freda. But Patty knew Freda was far too sensible to fall for a bighead like that.

All Freda could do was agree and thank her lucky stars, God, and anyone else who was involved in her coming to her senses in the nick of time. They finally said their good-byes and made promises to meet up again soon and then Patty went on her way, leaving Freda alone on the pavement. She became lost in a world of self-induced shame, and shivered, just remembering the way Neville stroked her arm and pushed a stray lock of hair from her eyes, while seductively touching her skin. It was all so well practised and fake, just like his words and crocodile skin shoes. Ugh, how could she even have wasted minutes, never mind hours, daydreaming about that slug?

Freda knew she'd had a lucky escape and for years after would shudder whenever someone mentioned that name or even a glimmer of the memories from her leavers' party invaded her brain.

* * *

Just days before her daughter's wedding, in a small village bistro in the middle of the countryside, Freda's near miss had come back to haunt her and she hoped that by baring her soul and her best kept secret, a close call from the past might have some resonance in the here and now.

'You see, love, I know what temptation feels like. I was ashamed about it at the time and if I'm honest, I still am. I was so naïve to be flattered and flirted with like that, then again, maybe it was all for a reason, so that in the future I could stop you from making a mistake too. Who knows how fate works?' Freda hoped she hadn't shocked or disappointed Tilly with her revelation but felt it had to be said and anyway, she trusted her daughter not to tell.

Tilly slid both her hands across the table and covered her mother's with hers.

'Mum, don't be ashamed of that! It's not like you even kissed him or anything. You're only human and it happened over thirty years ago so I think you should let it go now, okay? Stop beating yourself up. It all ended well so no harm done.' Tilly felt a bit sorry for her mum whose principles and conscience were getting the better of her and bringing her down, having said that, now she owed it to her to be honest in return, or something near.

'Look, cards on the table. I'm not going to sit here while you spill your guts about the olden days and then pretend I'm perfect.' Tilly winked at her mum as her own heart hammered.

Freda laughed and gave her daughter's hand a playful tap, then let her continue.

'You're right about me having feelings for Joe and I admit that over the past week, I have done exactly the same as you and compared everything about him to Luke and in most areas, unlike Dad, *my* dear fiancé didn't do so well.

Don't flip out, just eat your starter while I explain, otherwise the waiter will think there's something wrong with it and take the huff.'

Tilly watched as her mother warily picked up her knife and began to spread pâté onto her toast, clearly worried about what she might hear.

'It took me a long time to get to a point where I really felt like I'd forgiven Luke, but somewhere deep inside, the hurt still lingers and comes back to haunt me now and then. Over the past few months I felt like we'd grown apart at a time when we should be closer than ever and even while I've been here, I wouldn't say I can feel the love. We've had quite a few niggles and disagreements over the phone and maybe because of that, I've enjoyed being with Joe who is the complete opposite. He took my mind off the rows with Luke and for the past week I can honestly say I had fun, is that a crime? The thing is, Mum, where Neville turned out to be a rotten apple I can honestly say Joe isn't anything like him. We had so much in common and he is kind and considerate and made me laugh more than I have in ages, but he's gone now and I can assure you that, just like with you and naughty Neville, nothing happened. Cross my heart.' Tilly had to reign herself in before she said too much about Joe and her feelings for him.

'Well, I'm glad about that, love. I wouldn't want you being burdened by guilty feelings before you were married and to my shame, I did suspect you were having one last fling. We can put it all down to enjoying your freedom, I suppose. As for Luke, I don't want to go into all that again because Dad and I had a hard time forgiving him too, but like you said, it's in the past and should stay there. But once you are wed, I think you need to change a few things. The hours you both work are ridiculous so it's no wonder you feel like this so maybe you need date nights, or just more time together. I'm not sticking up for Luke, but he's been at that conference and his boss sounds like a nightmare, so he might be pressured to get things finished there. I reckon you've both got a touch of wedding nerves and that can make anyone a bit snappy.'

Freda couldn't resist taking a bite of her toast, she was starving and all this unburdening definitely gave her an appetite. 'Ooh, that pâté is lovely, would you like some?'

Seeing Tilly shake her head, Freda took a sip of her wine and continued.

'I'm sure once he gets here and relaxes you'll see a completely different side of him. Then you've got your honeymoon to look forward to and while you're there, you can focus on each other, not work and humdrum things. Perhaps during your holiday it would be a good time to iron out any niggles you have and find some common ground. Marriage isn't easy, Tilly, and you will have to work at it.' Freda was so relieved because even though her daughter had admitted having feelings for Joe, it was a teeny crush and no harm had been done.

There was only one thing that still played on her mind and it concerned Joe and his feelings towards Tilly. Once she'd polished off her starter and the waiter had cleared away her plate, Freda asked one final question.

'And what about Joe, do you intend keeping in touch with him or have you broken his heart? He looked very uncomfortable at Rosie's so I can only presume he has unrequited feelings for you and the thought of you being married hurt him. He does seem like a nice boy, but I think it would be best if you drew a line under your friendship, just to be on the safe side and avoid any crossed wires in the future, if you get my drift.' Freda was only being sensible and had to wear her 'parent hat'.

'To be honest, Mum, I haven't heard from him since they left and you're right, he did take it badly that I was getting married but like you said, it's for the best he's gone. I'm not too sure about the feelings he has for me at the moment. I won't cut him out of my life or ignore him though. We might bump into each other again and I'm sure we're both adult enough to behave correctly if we do, so can we change the subject now because I did promise to focus on you for the next few days, remember? Ooh look, here comes our main course. I'm starving, so shush and enjoy your food.'

Tilly was really fed up, just the mention of his name caused her heart so much sadness and she was aware of a gloomy cloud hovering above her head. She had to put Joe out of her mind, it was the only way.

'Okay, Tilly, I'm sorry. Let's just concentrate on the future and enjoy being together before the hoards descend on us. I've got you all to myself for a change. Now then, did I tell you about how Olivia's daughter-in-law met her partner Dylan? It's a lovely romantic story. This chicken looks yummy, would you like a piece and I'll try some of your fish?' With that Freda was off with the fairies and soon forgot all about the past and the subject of Joe.

As she listened to her mother's second-hand love story, Tilly forced herself to chew and swallow, raise her eyebrows and smile in all the right places while fighting the urge to take a peep inside her bag and check her phone. While her mum had forgotten all about Joe, Tilly certainly hadn't.

It was way past midnight and, as usual, Tilly and Freda lay awake in their respective bedrooms where both had completely different reasons for being unable to sleep. One was going over her list of things to do the following day and remembering how lovely her daughter looked when she'd tried on her wedding dress earlier.

The other was fuming over yet another sniping session with Luke and trying to free herself from the desolation of not hearing from Joe.

Luke had stupidly decided to revisit a previous argument that, as far as Tilly was concerned, had been resolved, or more to the point, she'd put her foot down and refused to budge on the issue. It concerned a gift for Hazel, which Luke wanted to give his mother at the reception. Freda was getting one, so he thought it was only fair. Naturally, Tilly felt nothing of the sort and pointed out that *her* parents had paid for the whole shebang and therefore a small token of the bride and groom's gratitude was deserved and proper. On the other hand, Hazel and Ken had offered zilch and seemed more than relieved not to put their hands in their pockets, so what exactly was Luke saying thank you for?

Did he want to pay homage to the blatantly obvious, like her giving birth to him or cooking his tea for the past thirty years, or maybe that she ferried him to and from school every day? Tilly pointed out that this is what mums do and they shouldn't expect a prize for it, especially on their child's wedding day.

Tilly told him straight that had they paid for just one thing, like the DJ, or the cake, or the sodding marriage licence, then she would've acquiesced but as it was, Hazel had been unsupportive from day one and for that reason alone she was NOT getting a bloody present! And that was final. That's why when Luke rang and casually asked if there was a decent florist over there, because he'd forgotten to get his mother a thank-you gift, Tilly exploded. They spent the next half hour going round the houses and ended their conversation on a very sour note. Luke thought she was being spiteful and obstinate, and she thought he was being insensitive and unfair. When he finally put the phone down on her, Tilly was more than happy to hear the line go dead.

Her attention was then drawn to the ghostly shape that hung from the wardrobe, covered in a sheet to protect it from dust and prying eyes while the last of the creases dropped out. Bowing under pressure from her mother, Tilly had tried it on and indulged Freda while she fluffed and smoothed the fabric and then they'd hung it in the bathroom with the shower on full blast so it was engulfed in steam.

Truth be told, it was probably the plainest, most boring dress in the shop. On the day they'd bought it, the poor assistant seemed glad to be rid of it and them, after Freda made Tilly try on almost everything they had, only to end up with a dress made specifically for the bride from Dullsville.

The fabric was actually lovely, white crepe de chine

overlaid with voile, very straight and simple in cut, with a strapless bodice yet graced with absolutely no embellishments whatsoever. Tilly had insisted she wanted to look understated and tasteful when in fact she was trying desperately to keep the cost of the dress down.

The one she really wanted was the cream, antique lace affair with tiny pearls sewn into the intricate flower pattern. It reminded her of something a bride from the landed gentry would wear in the thirties, floaty and elegant, oozing class and sophistication. It was the type of dress you'd see in a period drama and Tilly had adored it at first sight, but the price tag was obscene and there was no way on this earth she'd let her parents stump up for it. The plain Jane option would just have to do, even though it now looked slightly loose and might require a pair of socks for padding on the day.

Tilly yawned loudly. The house was quiet, whereas outside, in the darkness of the countryside, it was all going on. The sounds of nature and Didier's yapping dogs kept her occupied for a while but feeling her eyes droop and her body begin to relax, Tilly knew that sleep was about to claim her and for that she was grateful. Her brain and heart actually hurt and it was time she had some respite from both forms of torture.

After checking her mobile was on loud so that if Joe did send a message or ring, then she'd hear it straight away, Tilly placed it on her pillow and closed her eyes. No matter how hard she tried to brush the image of him from her mind he still lingered. All she wanted was to hear his voice and for him to say he'd forgiven her, but until then she'd just lie there in the dark, waiting and hoping for a miracle.

CHAPTER TWENTY-TWO

Freda was firing on all cylinders and her va-va-voom had returned. Her son and his family would be arriving soon, and the excited butterflies in her stomach were getting out of control. Freda couldn't wait to see them all in the flesh because Skype wasn't the same as holding your child and grandchild in your arms for real.

Charlotte was growing up, too fast really. Even though Freda and Howard did their best to be involved with her everyday life, the thousands of miles that separated them were hard to ignore. Hearing all about her day at school and her best friend's party, or clapping like mad as she held up her latest certificate to the camera wasn't anywhere near as rewarding as having Charlotte tucked under her arm while they read together.

Freda would have them for ten whole days before they left for England to stay with Susie's parents and after that, they'd be gone again, jetting to the other side of the world, far away from her.

'If you love them set them free.' Freda repeated it like a mantra. Well, it was all well and good saying the words, but the physical act was painful and so very hard. They'd promised to go over to Australia for another visit, which pleased Freda no end and would give her something new to focus on after the wedding hoo-ha had died down. Yet deep in her heart Freda knew with certainty that she'd feel exactly the same when it came to leaving Australia, saying goodbye all over again.

Realising she was being a bit of a doom-monger, Freda popped the kettle on and decided to relax and enjoy the peace and quiet while she waited for Tilly to return from Rosie's. She'd nipped over to drop a card in for Luke, which Freda suspected held a few romantic words for the big day, she also thought it was about time they got into the swing of things and showed some love and affection for one another. The card was a good sign, and as far as Freda was concerned, the sooner Tilly and Luke were reunited, the better. Otherwise she'd have to resort to banging their heads together.

Taking two mugs of tea into the garden, Freda waved to Howard who was amongst his crops and signalled for him to join her. Soon, they'd be rushed off their feet so while there was still time, she wanted him all to herself. There'd been a lot of strolling down memory lane lately and it had reminded her how much she loved the man in the tatty, corduroy gardening trousers who was making his way up the path, with mud underneath his nails and carrying a basketful of salad.

Freda watched him close the gate to his vegetable garden and smiled. *'Yes, Howard Parker, after all these years you still have what it takes to make me happy and despite the fact you've got dirt on the end of your nose and that shirt should've been chucked in the bin a long while ago, I'm so glad you chose me. I wouldn't change one single thing about you, not for the world.'*

Tilly was waiting in the lounge of the hotel while Océane went off to find Rosie. Apparently, the pretty young girl who'd opened the front door would be waitressing on Saturday and seemed very excited at the prospect, which left the bride-to-be feeling more lacking than usual. Tilly was dreading her meeting with Rosie but it had to be done.

She hadn't come this far for someone to let the cat out of the bag and slip up in front of Ken and Hazel, or worse, Luke. From the antique radio in the corner came the sounds of a violin solo, a sad lament that did nothing to lift Tilly's mood. Seeing Rosie coming along the corridor, she straightened up and tried to look confident as she was greeted warmly by her hostess.

'Hi, Tilly, would you like some coffee or juice?'

Rosie seemed friendly enough, which put Tilly at ease.

'No thanks, Rosie, I'm fine. I can't stop for long because we're all going to the airport to meet my brother and his family. Mum's insisting we're there to wave them in. She's like an overexcited child already so I should get back and keep her calm.' Tilly had no intention of dragging this out any longer than necessary.

'That's fine, I'm sure she's going to love having everyone over and making a fuss, Freda's a lovely lady. Do you want to leave the card with me, I can pop it into Luke's room the night before the wedding if you like?' Rosie held out her hand expectantly.

'Look, Rosie, can we sit down? There is no card and I need to explain things from my side. I'm not sure what you heard from Joe, or how it came across, but I want to reassure you that I've got no intention of leaving you and Michel in the lurch, and I'm not a bad person either. I could tell from our conversation the other day you're suspicious and I don't blame you. Can you spare me a few minutes so I can try to make you see?' Tilly could feel her cheeks flushing and desperately wanted Rosie not to regard her as a she-devil and maybe, she might just pass on what she heard to Anna, too.

'Okay, take a seat. I must admit we have been a bit confused and slightly worried that you could cancel at the last minute but before we start, *you* should know that I don't judge people on what others tell me. I like to make my own mind up, so stop looking so scared, I won't bite.' Rosie smiled kindly and guided Tilly to one of the sofas and then sat down opposite, waiting to hear it from the horse's mouth.

By the time Tilly had finished, not only was she in floods of tears, she also felt absolved before the sin, owing to Rosie who'd been nothing but kind and understanding. Not having left anything out, including her true feelings for Joe and all of his family, her love for her parents and her self-sacrificing plan, along with the state of affairs where Luke was concerned, Tilly hoped she'd convinced Rosie that she wasn't such a bad person after all. The unburdening had got a bit too much and as is usually the way, once given even an ounce of sympathy, barricades are broken and the gentle voice of her forgiving counsellor had allowed the tears to flow.

Rosie now felt desperately sorry for Tilly who, as far as she could see, had made one simple mistake – she should've opened her mouth a long time ago and put a full stop to this wedding. Taking into consideration hindsight and exact science, there was no point in stating the obvious so the only thing they could do now was carry on.

'Listen to me, Tilly. I don't want you to worry about anything at this end, alright? Michel and I haven't said a word to anyone, apart from my cousin, Ruby, who was at Anna's on Sunday, and that's how it will stay. At the end of the day, this is nobody's business but your own. You've made your mind up so all we can do now is support you and get you through the day. I'll be here at every step so if you have a wobble or need anything, just give me the nod, okay? I'm not going to come to the service though. I don't think my nerves could take it, and knowing the truth, well, I think I'd feel a bit uncomfortable so I'll make my excuses and wait for you here. That's the only part you'll not have me around for but I'm sure you'll be okay.'

Rosie moved over and sat beside Tilly, leaning over and holding her hand until she felt able to speak.

'Thanks, Rosie, you don't know how much that means to

me. I just hope that one day, when the truth comes out, my mum and dad will forgive me because I'm going to have to tell them eventually. I never ever want to live a lie again.'

Tilly wiped away her tears as Rosie asked a pertinent question.

'Have you heard from Joe? I know he was really cut up when he left on Monday and from what Anna told me, he hardly said a word about how you left things.' Rosie didn't want to pry but felt she owed it to her friend to ask.

'No, nothing, not a word. I think he hates me and I don't blame him. There are two things that are most important to me right now. One is not letting Mum and Dad and all my family down and the other is being forgiven by Joe. The thought of him being hurt and thinking badly of me is tearing me apart. If I had a wish, it would be that I'd met him first because I know that given half a chance, we'd be together right now. Do you believe in love at first sight, Rosie?' Tilly looked up and waited for a reply.

Rosie stared into the saddest eyes and replied honestly. 'Yes, I do believe, Tilly. And I don't think Joe hates you because that lad hasn't got a bad bone in his body, he's just hurt and confused and needs time to get over the shock. In the meantime, I think you should do your best to get through the next few days and prepare for whatever is to follow because once the wedding is over, you're not out of the woods. Put thoughts of Joe to one side for now and concentrate on plan A, otherwise you'll make yourself ill.'

Rosie watched as Tilly nodded and wiped her nose.

'Listen, Tilly, I really shouldn't be saying this, however, you've been honest with me so I think you deserve the same in return. I'd not be able to look at myself in the mirror if I didn't. You do know there is another, far easier path than the one you've chosen, don't you? You might not think so but I am almost positive that if you went home right now and told your mum and dad the truth, they'd support you. Are you sure it's not worth a try, it would save you all this heartache and pretence?' Rosie had to say it even though Michel would throw a fit if he knew.

'I've been through all the options, Rosie, and I can't. I know I should've done it a long time ago but I can't turn back the clock. I do appreciate everything you've said and I will feel better knowing you've got my back. I'm just very sorry to have put you in this predicament.'

Rosie could tell Tilly meant every word, as though she was dredging up words from the bottom of her heart and was just going to say so when her two daughters appeared.

'Mama, Odette keeps crying and wants to be with you. Can she stay here while I go outside?' Sabine, Rosie's eldest daughter was obviously fed up with looking after her sister and looked pleadingly at her mother.

'Okay, come here Odette and sit with me. Sabine, you must stay in the garden, no wandering off. I'll be out in a few minutes.'

And with that, the little girl shot off, obviously glad to be relinquished of her charge.

'Look, I'll get going, Mum will be waiting for me and is probably pacing the house. I won't see you now until Saturday but I'll be looking out for you as soon as I arrive for the reception. Thank you, Rosie, I'm so glad I came now.' Tilly stood to leave and Rosie followed suit.

As they made their way to the door, Odette clung on to her mother's hand and surprised Tilly by reaching up and taking hers too.

'Looks like you've made a friend. I suppose I'd better go and check on Sabine, she gets up to so much mischief when I leave her alone. Now you take care of yourself and ring me if you need to talk.'

Rosie picked Odette up and opened the front door, and received a peck on each cheek from Tilly who in return, was rewarded with a warm embrace from both mother and child.

As she waved from the car, Tilly's heart thudded when she realised that the next time she saw the hotel, she would be Mrs Hardy. Swallowing down a wave of panic, she drove away from the hotel and tried to focus on the next few hours, using the arrival of her brother to cheer her up and divert her attention. She would always be grateful to Rosie for her act of humility and offer of support. Knowing she had a secret ally had given her a little bit of courage and a zap of strength.

As she made her way home, Tilly managed to wipe away negative thoughts and pictured instead her little niece, who would be fizzing with excitement right now as they flew from Paris to Nantes on the final leg of their long journey. As for Joe, he lingered just out of sight and on the edge of her consciousness and no matter how much her head told her to let him go, her heart wanted him to stay.

* * *

Anna was sunbathing and trying to read, but the words just wouldn't stick in her brain, they sort of slid off the page and merged into unhelpful, unsettling thoughts about Joe. She'd still not heard from him and had to make do with second-hand messages via Sam. They were both fine apart from a sunburn related incident after a bender on the beach, which left Joe with a lobster-red back that would've needed hospital treatment had they not woken up in time.

It didn't matter how many times she reminded them, one of her son's always ended up in the wars because they'd forgotten to put cream on. What bothered her most was that Joe had been so drunk he'd fallen asleep on his stomach and was oblivious to the searing heat. She'd given Sam a ticking off and then told him to lay off the beer for a day or two, which was like talking to the wall if she was honest.

It was no good, she just couldn't concentrate. The house was far too quiet and checking her watch, Anna noted that it was seven whole hours before Melanie got home from work and, as for Daniel, she hadn't a clue what was taking him so long. He only nipped out to get some sand and cement and had been gone ages. He'd decided to build a proper brick barbecue in the garden from the leftover sandstone and remains of their renovation work. Daniel's new project had kept him occupied since everyone left on

Tuesday morning and he'd spent ages on the internet and scribbling ideas on one of the kid's drawing pads.

Thinking of the children, Anna felt slightly sad and wistful. Summer and Ross loved it here and there might've been tears when it was time to go had Phil and Jeannie not pulled the Grand Surprise out of the bag. The night before, there had been a strange atmosphere in the house, very upbeat thanks to the end of the war with Louise yet a sprinkling of post-holiday blues lingered in the air, that was until Jeannie told Summer and Ross they weren't really going straight home, they were going to Disneyland instead! Anna forgot that children could scream so loudly and how hard it was for overexcited kids to get to sleep, but seeing the surprise on their faces made the non-stop chatter and ten thousand questions worthwhile.

The other reason that peace and harmony had settled on La Roberdière was down to the joyous news that when Louise returned from the airport with Tomas, a truce had been declared and their differences resolved, much to the relief of Jules who was beside himself to see his papa. Once he calmed down, he was told that they would all be going home *together* the following day which, for him, was just as good as a trip to Disneyland.

As for Louise, the change in her was remarkable. She apologised to Melanie and Jeannie for her outburst at the table and couldn't have been more helpful over dinner, so much so that Anna caught Tomas looking at his wife in a completely different light. Louise had taken on board everything Anna had said and calmly put all her grievances to Tomas who was so glad she'd agreed to go to Geneva, that he readily accepted her demands. As a consequence, he was going to contact his colleague at the institute and ask him to forward details of charitable enterprises in and around the university campus. He also had no objection to going to England for Christmas and promised faithfully that they could book flights as soon as they got home.

Despite Jeannie's doubts and Melanie's 'leopards not changing their spots' observation, they were magnanimous when Louise apologised and actually had a bit of a giggle with her regarding the passing out in the pavlova incident. When it was time for them to leave, Louise looked slightly lost and nervous as she said her goodbyes to everyone, clinging on tightly to her dad, who felt like he'd got back the daughter he remembered. While Daniel fussed and strapped Jules into his seat, Louise stood hesitantly by the car door and held Anna's hand, tearful and reluctant to let go.

'I'll text you when we get home, if that's okay. And as soon as Tomas knows when he can take leave I'll ring you and we can arrange flights for Christmas, but if you want to come and see us before then we'd love to have you.' Louise spoke quickly, her voice held a tinge of worry and Anna sensed she was anxious that the plans they made were just hasty words and half promises which might be reneged upon.

Folding Louise in her arms, Anna hugged her tightly and reassured her that she wouldn't let her down.

'I'll be waiting for your text. I know how long it takes to get to yours so if you forget, I'll be on the phone pestering, okay? And if your dad isn't working too hard between now and Christmas, we'll nip over and see how the other half lives. I've already said it's about time he taught me how to ski so I hope there'll be lots of snow and accident and emergency departments nearby. Jeannie says there's a direct flight from Southampton so unfortunately for you, we'll all be driving you mad in the future. Sam already thinks he's an Olympic skier and I reckon he'll be your first visitor, he doesn't let the grass grow that one!' Anna gave Louise a wink and saw relief wash across her face.

'Okay, that's a deal. Give him my number, and Melanie and Joe too. Thanks, Anna, for everything. I know it's been a bit up and down but sometimes I think things are meant to happen and in a bizarre way, I'm glad I fell out with Tomas because it gave me the chance to come here and sort stuff out with you.'

Louise looked about to cry and, feeling rather emotional

herself, Anna decided it was time they went, so she gave her another quick hug and ushered her into the car.

'Yes, I do believe things are meant to be and I'm glad you came too. Now get going or you'll set me off. I'm fed up of goodbyes this week. Take care, and Tomas, make sure you drive safely and Jules, *à bientôt, je t'adore!*' And with that, the car doors closed and Anna shut up before she blubbed and made a fool of herself.

They both waved like crazy as the car drove down the lane and out of sight and once the dust settled in the garden, Daniel and Anna were left alone. Well, not quite, they still had Pippa who was currently marching along the line of sunloungers, sniffing each one. No doubt she couldn't believe her luck because now she had six to choose from – and they were all empty!

Looking to her right, Anna smiled when she saw the hound in question, lying on her side, warming her pink belly and snoring for all she was worth. Well, dogs get sunburn too, so Anna gave her sleepy friend a prod so that she turned over. The boys might not do as they're told but the last thing she wanted was a telling off from the vet if mademoiselle here got sunstroke.

There was no use in trying to read so Anna decided to go inside and prepare lunch for whenever Daniel returned. As she reached the kitchen door her phone rang. She hoped it would be Joe, instead it was Rosie.

'Hi, Anna, I thought I'd let you know that Tilly has been to see me. Everything's okay and we cleared the air but I think you need to hear what she had to say, have you got a minute?' Confirming that she had all the time in the world, Anna took a seat next to Pippa and listened intently to what Rosie had to say.

Pippa had sloped inside to cool off by the time Rosie finished going over what Tilly had told her and now, Anna was in limbo land, as usual. From the way her friend was talking, rather than being a callous, calculating, premature version of a black widow, Tilly appeared to be doing her best for everyone (apart from herself) and according to Rosie, the poor girl was at the end of her tether with the worry of it all.

'So how did you leave it, it's a huge secret to keep, won't you feel bad when you see Freda and Howard, and likewise Luke?' Anna was glad that she didn't really know any of them and wasn't in the predicament Rosie was in.

'The only way I can ease my conscience is by telling myself that it's not really any of my business. I've seen a couple of jilted brides and bridegrooms over the years when I worked in England and if I'm honest, this is much kinder than being stood up in front of everyone you know. I can't help all of them so I've chosen to be there for Tilly and if I can do anything to get her through the day, then I will. Do you think I'm doing the right thing?' Rosie sounded like she needed backup and the voice of reason.

'I do actually. You've been put in a spot and either way you won't win, so it's best to carry on as planned. I know you too well, Rosie, and you wouldn't have the heart to expose Tilly, it's not in your nature and all you can do now is sail the ship and hope for the best.'

Rosie let out a huge sigh of relief then asked Anna if she'd heard from Joe.

'Nope, not a dickie bird. I've had quite a few texts from Sam and a couple of photos of the campsite and the beach, but nothing apart from that. I presume Joe's still licking his wounds and applying calamine lotion. The pair of fools have got really bad sunburn. Anyway, back to Tilly and Joe, I'm going to follow your lead and stay out of it, he'll be in touch if he needs me and while he's with Sam, I know he's safe, sort of. Sorry to change the subject, but I need to tell you all about Louise before Daniel gets back. You're not going to believe it but we've made up and, fingers crossed, I think we've sorted out our differences once and for all. I've been dying to tell you but Daniel's always around and he hates gossip, so, are you sitting comfortably?'

Glad of having some company, albeit over the phone, Anna settled down and got on with telling Rosie how she'd put the world to rights and in the process, had earned a million brownie points from almost everyone.

* * *

Daniel was on his way back home after a very busy morning at Bricomarché where he bought sand and cement and various other barbeque related implements, Dominique had an ancient bread oven at the bottom of his garden, so he'd popped in to take some measurements.

He had it all pictured in his head now and was going to build a spectacular, all-singing, all-dancing bread oven with a barbeque attached. This way, Anna could make her own pizzas and bake as many loaves as she wanted while he got on with grilling things. Zofia had told him that most hamlets and communes had a communal bread oven which in years gone by, everyone used. But nowadays, they only fired theirs up when they had parties. All the neighbours loved it and the smell of fresh bread and pizza was amazing as it wafted around the garden.

Apart from his new building project, there was something else on Daniel's mind as he made his way along the winding lanes – his failed marriage proposal. He'd been racking his brains, trying to think of where and when to do it.

The small village of St Pierre was quite busy as he drove through, mainly because it was almost lunchtime and everyone was returning home or making their way to the bistro. Glancing over to Sebastien's place, he spotted a poster tied to a tree just outside the bistro. It was brightly coloured and eye-catching, advertising the Botanical Gardens in Angers and, lo and behold, all his prayers were answered. Laughing like a fool, Daniel pipped his horn and waved to his friend who was placing the chalkboard menu on the pavement, then put his foot down and headed for home, plotting his next move. Once Anna was occupied elsewhere, he would get straight onto the internet and check out his brilliant idea while his courage levels were on their way back up.

Yep, no matter what, Daniel was going to marry the beautiful lady who was chatting on the phone and waving as he pulled onto the drive. He'd build her the best pizza oven in all of the Loire Valley and then while she was putty in his hands, he'd propose in spectacular style and, if he was very, very lucky, she'd say yes.

* * *

Joe had never felt so ill in his whole life and if he was eight instead of twenty-eight, he'd be crying for his mum and asking to go home – fact! He'd drunk his fair share of beer while he was in New Zealand, and he'd survived shearing sheep in hotter conditions than this. So how the hell had he managed to give himself, what felt like, third degree burns? He groaned inwardly when he recalled spending the best part of the last twelve hours in utter agony, while he had his head simultaneously wedged inside a bucket. Sam seemed to be in a slightly better state and was now on the mend, whereas Joe saw no end in sight. The indignity of having half the camp site listening to you throw your guts up was almost as bad as suffocating in, what could only be described as, an airless 1960's torture chamber on wheels.

It was so hot and humid at night that they had to keep all the windows and doors open, which meant they then got bitten by hideous, flying things with spiky teeth. During the day, the only marginally cool place was underneath the van which was where Joe was now, lying on the grass, praying he wouldn't have to shuffle out and be sick again. Sam assured his brother that he'd see the funny side of it in a few days, bringing Joe to the conclusion that his sibling might be slightly deranged, because there was no way he'd ever find any of this even remotely funny.

Why did they have to pick the exact two weeks the heat-wave arrived? He'd heard the warnings on the *Météo* of the impending *vague de chaleur*, but this was ridiculous. The first night was fine and as Sam predicted, there were quite a few gorgeous beach babes knocking about and all of them were friendly. Not needing much encouragement, they'd both thrown themselves into the party atmosphere on the camp-site and the following morning, did much the same in the sea and on the beach.

If only he could wind back the clock and not try to drown his sorrows or forget to put sun cream on. Joe could hear his mum's voice now, reminding them to slip, slap, slop. She'd thought it was hilarious and they'd both cringed every time she said it, but now he'd do anything for a tub of calamine lotion and have her dab it on with cotton wool. Perhaps dehydration was causing delirium because Joe could picture himself as a child with burnt arms, trying to be brave while his gentle mum applied the cool cream to his skin. She was the best nurse, just like he knew Tilly would be... NO! Do not go there. Joe was adamant that she was not going to worm her way back into his brain, for God's sake, that's why he was in this state in the first place!

No matter how hard Joe tried to push thoughts of Tilly away, a voice in his brain dared him to turn his phone on and see if she'd text him. An image of a raven-haired girl swam amongst the memories of the camp fire the night before. He was reminded that none of the sun-kissed beau-ties with their tasselled denim shorts and bikini bodies were a patch on the one he'd left behind in Le Pin, pleading for understanding, utterly heartbroken and in tears.

'Please let me sleep,' Joe said out loud to nobody in particular, because Sam had abandoned him to search for food. All he wanted to do was erase every single trace of the various pains his body was enduring, especially the one in his heart because it ached like mad. And no matter how much beer and tequila he drank, Joe knew it wouldn't cure him of the hurt and alcohol that was running through his veins, the only possible solution was to close his eyes and pray that fatigue would get the better of him.

Joe knew he'd have to face up to what was eating away at him, and soon he'd have to turn his phone on and speak to his mum. For all her interfering and worrying, she was the best and didn't deserve to be ignored like this, she'd done nothing wrong. Until then, he'd just lie here and wait for the stinging and the throbbing and the swirling to go away, and when it did, the world might just seem like a better place. Right now though, he needed that bucket again!

CHAPTER TWENTY-THREE

When Tilly woke on Thursday morning, for a few brief seconds she actually felt quite happy, even though she had cramp and a pair of little feet in her face. Emerging from the duvet, she looked towards the end of the sofa where she saw Charlotte, sparked out, with a mass of tangled blonde hair, spread across the pillow and obscuring most of her sun-freckled face. Her niece had burned herself out the previous evening, enthusiastically spreading her time between all of her much-missed relatives.

Everyone enjoyed the attention they were receiving from the overexcited, bubbly little girl whose body clock was up the wall. Charlotte had insisted on staying on the sofa with Tilly who'd given up her bedroom to her grandma and aunty, and after talking the socks off the whole family, she'd finally conked out at around midnight.

The reason for Tilly's unusual bout of contentment was merely to do with having all of her most treasured people under one roof, something that also made her mum, in particular, deliriously happy. Freda had cried buckets when she spotted Scott and his family at the airport and Tilly had to admit she came over quite teary too, along with Susie, who, despite looking tired, had never seemed so glad to see her in-laws. Since then, Charlotte had been welded to her Aunty Tilly's side and the whole house was buoyed by the happy vibe swirling above the chimney top.

When Grandma Betty arrived just after 6pm, along with a rather flustered looking Marianne, the clan was almost complete, but for the imminent arrival of Howard's brother and sister-in-law. Freda and Tilly had aired out the touring caravan that was parked at the end of the garden, which was where her aunty and uncle would stay. It wasn't exactly luxurious, but it was cosy and clean and would save the expense of a hotel.

Tilly carefully removed Charlotte's feet and stretched her own slightly aching limbs, then relaxed under the duvet, savouring a little bit of equanimity for a change. It was 5am. The house was quiet and so peaceful, the only sounds came from Charlotte's breathing and the odd tweet of an early bird or busy farmer making his way to the fields. Her mind wandered to Joe and she tried to picture his campsite and the seaside, ignoring any images of the hot babes Sam was hoping to meet. It was impossible not to check her phone, she still hadn't heard from him. She presumed he'd found her diary and binned it, or maybe he'd read it out loud to Sam and they'd had a good old laugh at her expense.

When she looked at the screen, there were indeed some new texts, one from Stacey the night before, saying she was all packed and raring to go and another this morning from Luke, telling her he was en route and had the chief bridesmaid and best man on board. With those few words, her heart sank and the storm clouds reappeared. Tilly sighed and sent two messages back, wishing the travellers a safe trip and sticking to the diversion formula, omitting any loving or excitable sentences and went for a jokey 'I hope the sea stays flat' comment instead.

Hearing footsteps on the stairs, Tilly knew it would be her mum so she edged carefully off the sofa and by the time Freda appeared, she'd limbered up and silently followed her into the kitchen. No matter what, she was going to make sure the next few days were the happiest ones possible for her family and if that meant frying bacon and cracking hundreds of eggs, or colouring in and putting up with Marianne, then so be it. All the pieces of her plan were coming together and when Luke arrived later, even though this would test her the most, she would get through it, even if it killed her.

Freda's afternoon had been spent helping Susie unpack and trying to keep her mum nice and cool in the searing heat. Marianne appeared to have unburdened herself of her charge and was lapping up the lovely weather and a nice bottle of rosé, which suited everyone down to the ground because she was being nice. Scott and Howard were wandering around the garden and Charlotte was having her hair braided by Tilly, who seemed to be enjoying the company of her besotted niece. They were all in the garden awaiting the arrival of Luke, and whilst her daughter was doing a grand hairdressing job, it was quite clear she was a bag of nerves and on edge, and Freda knew why. That bloody Hazel managed to cause trouble even when they weren't around and now Tilly was upset after she and Luke had words about the giving of gifts at the reception.

In an attempt to smooth things over, Freda had told Tilly to let it go and if Luke wanted to pander to Hazel, let him. It was just a bunch of flowers after all and quite meaningless, so instead of getting all pent-up about it, they could have a secret chuckle at both their expense instead. It was quite wicked, but Freda suggested that Tilly should back down gracefully and offer to order the flowers – a nice bouquet of chrysanthemums. All the French guests would know that the colourful blooms were the preferred offering at funerals for departed loved ones, but they'd be far too polite to say so.

'Sod Hazel and her stuck-up attitude, just send her some grave flowers and make sure it's a giant bunch. And stick it on Luke's credit card. That'll teach them both to mess with Miss Parker and her mother!' It had made Tilly laugh and lightened the mood, however, Freda was still irked by Luke's attitude.

A car horn, honking in the distance heralded the arrival of the bridegroom, prompting the garden dwellers to get up on their feet and be ready to welcome Luke with open arms when his car appeared at the gate. The fact that Tilly was on the last braid and didn't want to let go of Charlotte's hair until she'd tied up the end meant she remained seated. Therefore Freda was left to greet Luke and do the first-hug honours until his fiancée got off her bottom and made the effort. *'Honestly, talk about dragging an argument on,'* thought Freda as she watched Tilly, more or less, stand in line to greet the man she loved.

'Just let it go and move on' was Freda's whispered advice to her daughter as she passed her in the queue, words which were met with a roll of the eyes and a less than enthusiastic, sarcastic smile.

Tilly had no intention of letting anything go where Luke was concerned. She fully intended dragging on every single minuscule annoyance or glaring sign of incompatibility, then it could be used in her arsenal of reasons why they should call it quits, along with an annulment of course.

After a very quick hug and a chaste peck on the lips, Tilly passed Luke on to Howard and Scott while she focused on Stacey and Darren, who were trying to retrieve suitcases from the boot of the car. After a more genuine hug for her chief bridesmaid and a brief touching of bodies with the best man, Tilly dragged them both into the garden and set about bringing drinks. She'd only been in the kitchen two minutes when Luke appeared, hovering about and looking as nervous as she'd felt earlier. The awkwardness between them may as well have been accompanied by red flashing lights and a wailing siren.

Luke spoke first and broke the ice.

'Hi, I came to see if you needed any help. I wondered

where you'd got to, anyone would think you were avoiding me.'

Tilly continued rinsing glasses ignoring his remark.

'I suppose you're still annoyed with me about Mum's present, is that what's wrong? Look, I'm sorry if I upset you, Tilly, but I feel like everything I say lately winds you up. We shouldn't be arguing every two minutes before our wedding, should we?' Luke looked weary and forlorn and Tilly felt awful, he was right of course, about everything, but she wasn't going to admit it, not yet.

'No, of course I'm not avoiding you but it's so hot and all we've done since this morning is make cold drinks, it's becoming second nature and anyway, I'm sure you're all parched. I *was* mad at you last night but Mum's had a word with me and put me straight, so let's forget it, okay? I don't want to argue anymore, put it down to wedding jitters and the heat, and to prove I'm cool about the flowers, I'll even order them for you, how's that? Here, this is for you, a peace offering.' Tilly held out a bottle of cold beer and hoped she'd said enough.

Luke took the beer and smiled, he looked relieved and wrapped his arms around her and kissed her tenderly on the head before taking a swig of his beer and replying.

'Thanks, Tilly. And I'm sorry too for being so busy and fobbing you off every time you rang me. I haven't stopped since you left and there was so much to finalise before I left work, not to mention that seminar which was boring as hell. Would you really sort the flowers out for me? I've left it a bit late now and I was dreading going to the florist so it's one thing off my mind. Right, give me that tray and let's go and join the others. I want to soak up some of this sun you've been hogging while I've been slaving away.'

Kissing her on the cheek, Luke picked up the tray and made his way from the kitchen leaving Tilly fuming and quite literally speechless.

It was obvious that whether she'd relented or not, he was going to go ahead and buy flowers for Hazel, so now she really was getting a whopping big bunch of chrysanths. And what was so hard about going on a course in a swanky hotel, all expenses paid? Looking out of the window, she observed him critically, irritated by the way he was playing the affable waiter, joking with her grandma and teasing Charlotte. And now he was dragging a deckchair over and positioning it in the sun so he could top up his tan, which from the looks of him, had already benefited from a good few sessions on the sunbed. Slaving away, my arse!

Walking over to the fridge, Tilly angrily grabbed a bottle of rosé which had her and Stacey's name on it and stomped outside, knowing that she needed to calm down and not let him annoy her, or at least let it show. Choosing a seat next to Susie, Tilly concentrated on pulling the cork and joining in the very jovial atmosphere, laughing along with her dad's jokes and mentioning to her mother that she'd need the number for the florist's in the village. Freda smiled sweetly and winked conspiratorially, looking pleased that her daughter was not only in a good mood, she'd also taken her advice and moved on.

Later that evening, when Stacey finally settled herself under the duvet on the sofa opposite Tilly's, they both snuggled down and faced each other in the moonlit room. The silver light cast shadows on the furniture while the warm breeze that blew in from the windows ruffled the voile curtains, giving the night a surreal feeling. Maybe it was something to do with the wine, which had numbed Tilly's senses, helping her to relax and embrace the strange sense of peace that had wrapped around her. For some reason, she felt in control, invincible and focused. Her plan was gaining momentum, her brain had switched to standby mode, her heart was less troubled and apart from the grinding sadness when she thought of Joe, the screaming voice of her conscience had been silenced for now. Maybe Luke and his unexpected outburst a few hours earlier had something to do with her absolving herself from sin and for that, she was glad.

The evening had flown by with the arrival of Tilly's aunty and uncle, which was followed by a mountain of pizza boxes since Howard forbade Freda to cook. Luke was enjoying Howard's hospitality and under other circumstances, Tilly would've reprimanded her fiancé for the amount he was drinking. But right now, she really couldn't care less and left him to it, he was playing nicely into her hands.

The issue of them sleeping together hadn't arisen during telephone conversations and if they were a normal couple, one would have assumed that being apart for over a week, a quickie before the wedding was on the cards. Tilly, however, had no intention of sneaking upstairs for a moment of passion with Luke, especially while all her family were outside. Moreover, she wanted to save her trump card for when it was needed.

By 9pm, Darren decided they should head over to the hotel and check in. With the help of Scott, they loaded Luke into the car, made arrangements for the following day and Tilly gleefully waved them off. She'd actually put Luke out of her mind until he rang her later, talking complete gibberish and whining into the phone. Some of it she understood, but the rest was nonsense and mostly to do with his guilty conscience coming back to haunt him, as he mumbled on and on about her forgiving him and that it had all been a huge mistake. She wasn't in the mood for raking over the past and told him to leave it, but he was on a roll and unfortunately for him, wouldn't shut up.

It was the bit about Hazel that wound Tilly up and resulted in Stacey grabbing the phone from her hand before telling Luke firmly, it was time for bed and not to ring again. Stacey's attention then turned back to Tilly, who was livid.

While Luke was trying to absolve his sins, it slipped out that his mother had committed a few of her own, and in the process, he'd just made everything a whole lot worse. Now, Tilly was on the verge of ringing Hazel to have it out with her and tell her a few home truths of her own since Loose-

Lipped Luke had divulged some previously unspoken facts, which in more sober moments, would've remained unsaid.

Apparently, no matter what he said to convince Hazel otherwise, she wanted him to marry someone with better prospects. Luke sort of agreed that Tilly's nursing career wasn't exactly going to make them rich and, despite his mum saying she wasn't good enough for him, he was happy with her just the way she was. The deadly hush that settled over the conversation seemed lost on Luke who assured Tilly that even though Hazel thought his bride-to-be was as dull as dishwater, it hadn't put him off and hoped that in the future, they could somehow learn to get on with each other, for his sake because he deserved to be happy!

To be fair, once Stacey had calmed Tilly down, they both began to see the funny side of it, agreeing that now they knew the truth, the gloves could come off. By morning, Luke would probably remember some of what he'd said and be mortified, so in the end, they had a giggle at his *and* Hazel's expense then spent the next hour plotting their evil, slightly sadistic, revenge.

As she lay here in the dark with her best friend, Tilly silently thanked Luke for ringing and spilling his guts about Hazel and was even more adamant that she wanted nothing to do with his family, or be married to a mummy's boy either. Stacey yawned loudly and then out of the blue, came right out and asked Tilly the killer question.

'Now that little drama is over and done with can we get down to the nitty-gritty? I've been dying to ask you something since I got here.' Stacey grabbed her phone and turned on the spotlight, shining it in Tilly's face, just in case she was faking her answer.

'Are you still having doubts... I can tell you're not exactly raring to go? I know Luke has annoyed the crap out of you tonight but apart from that, is everything alright? I've got to ask because it's part of my bridesmaid duties and obviously, I'm a nosey cow as well.' Stacey was watching her friend closely and waited for her reaction.

'Well if you must know, I'm not nervous at all. And will

you stop shining that light? I'm going to get a bloody migraine.'

Stacey switched it off but continued to scrutinise Tilly's face as she carried on.

'I feel sort of detached from everything, like I'm in a film or watching myself from the outside. I don't know if that's good or bad really, anyway, what makes you ask?' Tilly was actually being honest in her summing up and presumed she'd done well in hiding her true feelings.

'I wouldn't let anyone else hear you say that otherwise you'll end up on the psycho ward, but I don't think it's bad, you just seem like you're in a funny mood, that's all. I can't put my finger on it. I was watching you earlier and it's like you're going through the motions, sort of humouring Luke. It reminded me of when we get a really arsey patient in and no matter how rude they are or how much they annoy us, we have to be professional and get on with the job. You were behaving like you do at work and I was waiting for one of those looks you give me that tells me you want to give them a tetanus for no reason except they're a complete prat. Feel free to correct me if I'm wrong... am I?'

During the very long pause that followed, where Tilly should've jumped in and thrown cold water over her observations, Stacey raised her eyebrows, as if she knew she'd hit the nail right on the head.

'Okay then, Doctor Freud, if I told you that you're spot on with your analysis, what would you do? Pass me the syringe so I could inject the idiot where it hurt.' Tilly was trying to gauge exactly how much to confess to Stacey.

'You know I'll be your willing assistant, haven't I always got your back? I'm just a bit worried that you're making a big mistake. I haven't forgotten what you told me on your hen night, even though you fobbed me off the next day by saying it was the drink talking. I never knew fizzy pop had that effect because if it did, I'd have saved myself a few quid over the years. Come on, Tilly, tell me what's up, we've got all night and I'm going to switch my light back on and interrogate you until you tell the truth.'

'Very funny, and for your information, I didn't just drink pop, I was trying to drown my sorrows if you remember and that's why I blabbed to you. It will probably take all night to explain what's going on in my head and what I've done, and then you might not be my friend anymore.' Tilly stuck her toe a little further in the water.

'For God's sake, Tilly, just spit it out. No matter what you say I will always be your mate and I'd like to think you'd be there for me if I was in trouble. I'm no saint, am I? I'm surprised that some of my antics haven't made your hair curl by now, so go on, what have you done? What's going on in that brain of yours?' Stacey wasn't going to give up now she'd got this far, that was obvious, and would keep on pestering until the sun came up.

'Okay, so would you still be my friend if I told you that you were here on false pretences and that I had to let you waste your hard-earned money and holidays in order for me to keep up this charade? Don't interrupt because it gets better. I've decided that once I've married Luke on Saturday, I'm going to wait until we're on honeymoon and then explain it's all been a huge mistake and then dump him. Oh, and that's not all of it! I've fallen in love with someone else, who I've also lied to and probably broke his heart in the process, at the same time as offending all of his really nice family, who more than likely hate my guts. There you go, Sigmund, psychoanalyse that lot!' Tilly couldn't actually believe she'd blurted it out but it felt so good and went some way to cleansing her guilty soul.

When Stacey finally found her tongue, Tilly could hear the shock in her voice and prayed she hadn't misjudged the situation.

'Bloody hell, Tilly! I didn't expect that, what on earth has been going on? No, don't speak, I need to say something before you start. No matter what you've done or are going to do, I will stick up for you and I'm not bothered about holidays and money. I'm just glad I'm here for you and you told me the truth. You are now officially my crazy best friend. I've always wanted one and you well and truly fit the bill, so now you know where I stand, dish the dirt.' Stacey was sitting up, cross-legged and wide awake and Tilly followed suit and in a whispered, serious voice, told her friend everything.

It was 3am when they finally finished talking, drinking tea and eating toast. Stacey completely understood Tilly's thought process and as with Rosie, accepted that stating the obvious was pointless. All they could do now was carry on and make sure the day went according to plan and once it was over, Stacey promised to be there for Tilly when it all went pear-shaped.

There was no point in even discussing Joe, it seemed a bit crass to even contemplate what would happen there, although Stacey did ask to see what he looked like and after scrutinising a photo or three, agreed he was hot and then asked if his fit brother was available. Still, she advised sorting one problem out at a time, first they had to concentrate on getting through the wedding and the tsunami that was to follow.

They were settled on the sofas once again and by now extremely tired and talked out. Just before they both gave in to sleep, Tilly had one more thing she needed to say to her friend who looked comical with her bright pink hair scraped into a bunch on top of her head like a pineapple, wearing her oversized, butter-stained nightie that said HUG ME, on the front.

'Thanks for listening, Stace, and backing me up. The only other person who knows the score is Rosie, but she won't be there to keep me going. I'll never forget this you know? I owe you big time!' Tilly felt a bit weepy and was glad she was in darkness and did in fact, need a hug.

'Too right! Just remember that when I need you to cover for me at work and when it's Christmas, birthdays and Easter, because I'm due some mint pressies and a bloody big egg. Now go to sleep because your mum will be up in a bit and I need my beauty sleep. I hope there are some fit

Frenchies coming to your do because I intend to let my hair down and anything else if the fancy takes me.'

They both giggled in the moonlight and simultaneously closed their burning eyes.

The quiet of the room was interspersed now and then with tired yawns and the creak of the sofas as they tried to get comfy on the lumpy cushions, and it was then that Tilly allowed herself a small smile. It wasn't smug or out of contentment either, it was mainly relief and knowing that, despite her troubles, she was in possession of two very precious things. They would always see her through the bad times, and make the good ones, when they arrived, even better. She was lucky and blessed and even though she wasn't a very religious person, took time before she slept to say a special prayer and thank God from the bottom of her heart for her precious family and equally, Stacey's friendship.

* * *

Friday morning turned out to be a bit grey and murky, which prompted Sam to suggest they move further south and chased the weather, after all, there was no point in being young, free and the owner of a love-shack-on-wheels if they were going to stick to one place all summer. Once they'd checked the forecast, which did indicate warmer climes could be found a few hundred miles further south, they packed up and moved on.

They left Les Sables d'Olonne behind them and had been on the road for about an hour when Sam's phone rang and, as they both expected, it was their mother who insisted on speaking to Joe. After suffering a gentle ear bashing, taking the hint, and saying goodbye, Joe disconnected and retrieved his mobile from the glove compartment.

Reading his brother's mind, Sam interrupted Joe's troubled thoughts.

'Just get it over with, mate. She's bound to have texted you. I'd bet my last tenner on it so you might as well read what she's got to say. I know you keep saying you don't want to talk about it but you're gonna have to face up to the fact she's getting married tomorrow and no matter how much tequila you drink, I can tell she's on your mind. Just put us both out of our misery and turn it on.' Sam never took his eyes of the road but knew he had his brother's full attention.

'Yeah, but what if she hasn't left a message? I'm going to look even more stupid than you with your confident predictions and that daft hat. Maybe she's just moved on and after the way I spoke to her decided that Luke is the safe bet after all.' Joe really didn't want to face further rejection or humiliation.

'Joe, turn the bloody phone on! You're seriously doing my head in now. And there's nothing wrong with my hat, it's cool.'

Knowing when he was pushing his luck, Joe did as he was told and waited for the phone to come to life, which lasted long enough to see that he had quite a lot of messages, four of them were from Tilly, and then the battery died and the screen went blank. By the time they'd found a service station and spent half an hour looking for the charger, which was finally located inside one of Sam's trainers, Joe's mind was all over the place and his curiosity at its peak.

He had to admit (if only to himself) that he was glad she'd tried to contact him and all he could hope for now, was some good news. This would basically entail her telling him she'd changed her mind and the wedding was off. Once Joe had unplugged the satnav from the terminal and replaced it with the charger, Sam tactfully went in search of food, leaving his brother to read the texts in private.

The first three said pretty much the same thing, she was sorry, she needed to talk to him and please would he ring her, however, it was the fourth one that grabbed his attention and made his heart beat faster. Even though it was quite clear at the time of sending the messages, that Tilly had no intention of changing her mind, she had actually gone to the trouble of leaving her diary in the camper and this fact alone touched Joe deeply. Leaning forward, he groped about under the passenger seat and after a few seconds he found it, wedged between the metal runners.

Holding Tilly's battered diary in his hands was a humbling experience. Within these pages, her most private thoughts and feelings were written and this act alone made Joe feel slightly ashamed. He tentatively opened the first page and saw her loopy, extravagant handwriting written in black biro. It began on the 1st January and as he read the words, *Dear Diary, New Year's Eve was a DISASTER!'* Joe knew that he'd made a terrible mistake and he'd let Tilly down.

The first day of a brand-new year starting so badly, indicated to Joe that worse was probably to come and that nobody in their right mind would expose themselves in this way unless they really wanted you to know the truth. Then his mind wandered to the logistics of actually placing the diary in the van in the first place. The text was sent at 11.47pm, which meant she must've come back when it was dark and everyone was in bed. Joe knew from experience that to walk up their lane in the pitch black took some bottle, yet she had done so *and* risked being seen into the bargain. He could picture Tilly now, making her way towards the house, alone in the dark and creeping into the garden and hiding the diary in the van while he was inside, sulking and feeling sorry for himself. God, he was such an idiot!

The sound of the driver's door opening shook Joe from his imaginings and he focused on Sam who was carrying cold drinks and what he described as a snack, when in reality it looked like the entire contents of the petrol station.

'Well, what did she say? You look like you've seen a ghost, bad news?'

Sam climbed inside and began rummaging around inside his carrier bag while he waited for Joe to speak and when he did, Sam wasn't expecting the reply.

'Bad news doesn't even sum it up, mate. It's worse than that. Look, she left me her diary and I've got a feeling that when I read what's inside I'm going to wish I'd stood by her instead of acting like a complete loser.'

Joe held up the diary to Sam who seemed lost for words for once.

The remainder of the journey was spent in deep contemplation. Joe pondered his recent actions and ruminated upon the possible contents of the diary. Whatever was inside was deeply private and he'd already decided to read it when he was alone, it felt disrespectful to read it with Sam by his side.

Sam on the other hand sang along to his CD or concentrated on the road and the satnav, because his brother was lost, wandering around somewhere in a very troubled world of his own.

The coastal commune of Biscarosse was idyllic and Sam couldn't wait for the following day to arrive so they could explore. They'd found a campsite by the beach, which was bordered by lush pine forest and a stone's throw from the centre of the village. Even though he was eager to experience everything on offer, Sam admitted that after driving two hundred miles in a bone shaker he felt totally knackered, therefore he was more than happy to chill out for the evening.

He was further persuaded by the arrival of a group of campers who needed his assistance when they had trouble with their tent. The French girls were extremely grateful for all Sam's help while the unashamed flirting wasn't lost on Joe who kept a low profile and let his brother play the hero.

It was 11pm. Sam was sparked out and snoring for England, not that Joe cared because he was otherwise occupied. The campsite was quieter now as families put their tired children to bed and the louder, more boisterous residents respected one another's space and took themselves off into town, where they could make as much noise as they wanted.

Joe could still hear murmured voices from within the surrounding tents or from those sitting outside enjoying the balmy air and the jet-black, star-spangled sky. On the beach there were spots of red and orange as campfires glowed and the sound of laughter floated on the breeze. The tide had come in and during a lull you could just about hear the waves as they lapped onto the shore.

Inside the camper, Joe lay on his sleeping bag and opened the first page of the diary and flicked on his torch. As soon as he began to read, the world outside slipped away and he was immersed in the land of Tilly. It was like a window to her soul and for the next two hours, Joe lived life through her eyes, reliving good days at work and sad ones too, discovering some of her crazy dreams and wishing he'd been there to soothe her worst nightmares.

He laughed at her wicked observations and stupid mistakes, and agreed with most of her views and concerns for the state of the world. She raged at the strangest, most random things and felt sorry for almost everyone she spotted through the rainy windows of the bus on the way to work. Like the old man, struggling to walk with his shopping basket and the young boy whose school trousers were too short and showed off his white socks. Did the old man have anyone waiting for him at home? It was raining on his groceries and he might be lonely and sad. And why didn't the boy's mum alter his trousers, or worse, perhaps she couldn't afford new ones? He'd get teased at school and picked on, a thought that played on her mind all day.

Even though cycling was one of her favourite things, Joe didn't like that she sometimes rode her bike to work, it sounded dangerous, and he wanted to punch the van driver that soaked her to the skin when he purposely hit a huge puddle. Joe knew that Tilly wanted a cat but wasn't allowed one, and she would call it Jarvis, after the lead singer from Pulp. She regularly visited the local pet shop and he could picture her as clear as anything, leaning against the window, staring longingly at the kittens inside. She'd always wanted to go to Glastonbury where she'd camp out and wear patchouli oil, like her mum did in the sixties. Tilly had never tasted a truffle and hated smoked gammon, but loved Creme Eggs and wearing socks in bed. Amongst all the fascinating facts, the most important thing that Joe learned from reading the 217 pages of Tilly's diary was that she was stuck in a one-sided relationship, which left her confused, sad and lonely.

He'd seen it all, right there in front of his eyes in black, blue and even a bit of green biro. When she was really cross, the red pen would come out and she'd frantically underline the cause of her hurt or annoyance, over and over until the nib ripped the paper. Capitals and exclamation marks were saved for moments of pure rage and more often than not, Luke's name, and she wasn't averse to a bit of swearing either. By the time he reached the last entry, Joe's heart felt like a rock and it was no more than he deserved.

Tilly had told the truth. And she really was about to tell him everything on a number of occasions but each time, either a spanner was thrown in the works or she changed her mind, simply because she wanted one more day of happiness with him. Closing the diary, Joe sighed and rested the side of his head against the window. Deciding he was in need of some air, he gently opened the door and slipped out into the night, heading for the beach and the sound of the sea.

There were still people about so Joe found a quiet place on the dry, prickly grass that bordered the soft sand and as he watched the lights of a ship far out in the Atlantic Ocean, tried desperately to think of what to do. This was a big decision and even though he could wake up Sam and ask his advice, and one short text to his mum or Mel would result in an instant response, he knew he had to figure it out for himself.

Joe had no idea what would be going through her mind right now, on the eve of her wedding. Would she be thinking of him or be fast asleep? One thing Joe did know was that she wouldn't be experiencing the usual, giddy anticipation that most brides feel before their big day. How awful to be denied that? No matter how harsh his words had been on the day they parted, he was convinced now that nothing would alter her plans or her feelings for Luke.

Imagining Tilly lying there alone, dreading the following day and wondering if he'd read her diary after waiting days for a message that never came, filled Joe with remorse. She wasn't a bad person, she was quite the opposite and even though he wished she wasn't going to go through with it, he couldn't bear the thought of her facing the wedding alone. She'd asked him to wait for her, give her time to sort things out, to understand and he'd refused every single request. Tilly didn't deserve that, she deserved a friend, an ally and a chance to be happy.

He took out his phone and checked the time, 2.30am. She'd probably be asleep but he could still send her a message for when she woke up. Joe knew exactly what he had to do and say, he would be her friend and even from a distance, support her decision and wait for as long as it took if that's what she needed, it was as simple as that. His heart pounded in his chest as he typed the words, eager to make amends and start afresh. He kept it simple and to the point, and once he had typed the last letter, he quickly checked it for mistakes and pressed send. No hesitation, no second thoughts, no regrets and no going back, because he was sure. Joe meant every single word.

After watching the lights from the ship until they faded from sight, he made his way back to the van, slipped off his shoes and crept inside, shaking his head at the sight of Sam who was out for the count and oblivious to Joe's momentous decision. He would fill him in on all the gory details in the morning and then, while he waited for a reply from Tilly, Joe swore an oath to himself that he would do his best to live up to Sam's holiday expectations and stop moping about and have some fun. He also promised that he would ring his mum and Mel, who had both sent him kind, reassuring messages and they deserved a response.

There was nothing more he could do for Tilly now, she had to do what was right for her but he hoped that while she did, his message would give her strength and help her through the day. It was the first night that sleep came naturally to Joe and wasn't induced by intoxication. It also allowed him a crystal clear, semi-happy thought before he closed his eyes.

It was, as you will have guessed, of Tilly.

CHAPTER TWENTY-FOUR

Freda was beyond excitement and couldn't possibly sleep or lie in bed one moment longer. Howard was snoring gently so she slid out of bed, put on her slippers and inched the door open, just to the point where it always creaked, then squeezed through slowly without making a sound.

Downstairs in the kitchen, she flicked on the kettle and carefully spooned coffee into her mug, trying hard not to wake Tilly and Stacey. Once her drink was ready, Freda lifted a chair from underneath the kitchen table and sat alone in contented silence as she looked through the window, watching the morning mist rise above the trees in the garden and tiny birds swoop on the morning air, catching flies for breakfast.

The room was semi-tidy after yesterday's welcome party, which had gone down well, apart from Hazel and Ken putting a dampener on things by going home early and dragging Luke and Declan with them. Then there was Tilly's sour face, due in part to her fiancé's glaringly obvious hangover and his untimely comments the night before. To add insult to injury it also meant that Tilly had to drive Luke to the airport to collect a woman who thought she was dull as dishwater.

Freda had to admit that she was very put out by Hazel's comments and sort of wished Stacey hadn't mentioned it, however, this weekend she was wearing her peacemaking hat and instead of giving the cheeky cow what for, decided to rise above it and leave Olivia to sort her out.

She was also concerned about Susie who'd been a bit teary and spent a lot of time on the phone to her mother. She'd already admitted to Freda that she missed her mum dreadfully and the gaping hole that their separation had left when they emigrated to Australia had been hard to fill. Susie confessed that sometimes she struggled with her feelings and wished she could come home to England.

Freda was rather taken aback by the revelation and decided to have a word with Scott about it, probably after the wedding. Still, Susie would be seeing her parents the following week but nevertheless, Freda sympathised with her daughter-in-law because she missed all of them, so much, and imagined Susie's mum would feel just the same.

Her mind then wandered to Olivia who had turned into a female version of her very own knight in shining armour. After yesterday, Freda had nicknamed her Joan of Arc.

* * *

When Tilly returned from the airport with Luke and his parents in tow, she was in a foul mood. It was also blatantly obvious that the last place Hazel wanted to be was in Freda's garden and as a result, the atmosphere nosedived. The issue of two moody women who couldn't stand each other was further exacerbated by the appearance of a cold sore on Luke's bottom lip, which for the vainest man in a hundred-mile radius, was a calamity of momentous proportions. Stacey suggested he dabbed aftershave on it, apparently it was one of her mum's old-fashioned remedies, so they all had to sit and watch Luke, wincing and cursing every time he applied a splash of Howard's Old spice.

Freda wasn't too sure if Stacey and Tilly were just being mean and had made the remedy up, because she'd seen them both tittering every time Luke checked his lip in the mirror and dipped his cotton wool ball in the stinging liquid. Turning a blind eye, Freda focused her attention on Hazel. No matter who tried to make conversation or warm her up, Hazel's snooty attitude put everyone off so before long, she found herself marooned with only her gin and tonic for company – until Olivia turned up.

There was just something about the extremely elegant and refined woman from Cheshire who glided in, clinking pink champagne bottles together and leaving a haze of Chanel No 5 in her wake. She began hugging and kissing her way around the garden, and somehow managed to skilfully miss out Hazel. Olivia was in the loop about nasty Hazel's comments regarding Tilly and apparently her mission today was to teach the rude woman a lesson.

Olivia oozed self-confidence, exuding a mesmerising presence as she introduced herself to everyone. She just *loved* Stacey's pink hair and thought she looked very punky and was dreadfully jealous of Tilly's perfect English rose complexion. Olivia loved children and adored Charlotte who she presented with a little box of special sweeties for gorgeous girls. She then made her way over to the table heaving with food and admired every bit of Freda's splendid spread before coming to rest next to Betty. Here, Olivia spent the majority of her afternoon, holding the elderly lady's hand like that of a long-lost friend, stroking it kindly as she chatted away about the good old days.

Henry got stuck into the food and was soon chatting to Scott about the cricket and rugby. Stacey leant over to Freda and said that if you kept your back to him, it sounded like Prince Philip was at the party. Hazel's star-struck eyes widened further when Susie vaguely mentioned that Olivia was some kind of lady, or was it a dame? Anyway, she was from the very top of the Cheshire set, lived in a castle and was Freda's best friend!

From that moment on, Freda watched with amusement as Hazel did her very best to engage Olivia in conversation, and in return, Dame Olivia did her very best to ignore her.

On the rare occasions she was unable to escape Hazel's monologue, Olivia was seen to graciously stifle a yawn and looked extremely bored, but terribly polite, with it.

Freda could tell from her body language that Olivia didn't care to know about Hazel's villa in Spain, or the square footage of the garden and pool, and neither was she remotely interested in her roles on various committees and whopping majority in the council elections. She didn't seem at all impressed when she heard all about Ken's carpet shops or the fact that they were knocking down the conservatory to build a new one. Olivia certainly hadn't the inclination to swap fashion tips or sniff Hazel's brand-new bottle of perfume but yes, her dress was Dior and her shoes were in fact, Gucci.

Instead, Olivia focused on all the other wonderful guests, especially Marianne who seemed thrilled that for once, someone had taken an interest in her work. Olivia left out no one and every time Hazel rudely interjected and desperately attempted to claw back the attention, she was briefly acknowledged (out of common courtesy) then promptly silenced and filed in the drawer marked Tedious.

Naturally, Olivia was full of praise and admiration for the work that Susie did at her hospital in Australia, as with Tilly and Stacey, and commented that public service must run in the family. Along with the nursing contingent, Olivia reminded everyone of Howard's bravery during his time in the fire service and then Freda's dedication to teaching. When at long last she finally addressed Hazel directly, it was to ask her a pertinent question, or was it a thinly veiled, statement of fact? Looking her victim straight in the eye and firmly pinning her down, Olivia remarked that Hazel must be so relieved and feel extremely lucky at the same time, to know that Luke was joining such a lovely family that anyone would be proud of.

Freda enjoyed watching a nerve twitch in the side of Hazel's face when she agreed, even though it looked like it was killing her. Without missing a beat, Olivia smiled sweetly and then turned away and changed the subject. She wanted to know all about Australia, especially Susie and Scott's respective work, and then listened as Charlotte explained in gruesome detail, each and every hideous creature that lived there.

Freda couldn't understand why Olivia didn't counteract Hazel's bragging by dropping names or mentioning her castle-like home, not to mention the many awards for public service and charity work that had been bestowed upon her over the years. A quick search on the internet revealed reams of newspaper articles about her trip to the palace or the numerous good deeds she'd done. They all said the same, which was that Olivia followed proudly in her father's philanthropic footsteps and most importantly, she was much admired. It came as no surprise when Hazel eventually threw in the towel and developed a migraine, then imperiously summoned Ken from the drinks table and announced she wanted to go back to the hotel to rest.

In the meantime, Tilly was enjoying punishing Luke for his drunken outburst the night before. Despite his whispered pleas to forgive him *and* his mother, it was clear that Tilly had no intention of doing either in a hurry. Thankfully, before he left, some form of peace treaty had been agreed after Tilly commandeered him to help clear away the dishes. When they finally emerged from the kitchen after washing the pots, they'd reached a truce.

Once the outlaws left, Freda asked Olivia why she hadn't put Hazel in her place, because if anyone could have put her back in her box, the Right Honourable Dowager Duchess of Cheshire, Greater Manchester and The Pennines, surely could.

As she sipped her pink champagne, Olivia explained. 'I absolutely abhor snobbishness in every form, because those who are guilty of it have a tendency to treat others with condescension, which is unforgivable. The way I see it, snobs are basically insecure social climbers who long to be admired and are preoccupied with power and prestige, mainly because they presume an elevated position in society will compensate for all their shortcomings.'

'Well I suppose that's one way of looking at it, but people like that make me feel inferior.' Freda was referring to Hazel.

Olivia swirled her drink, watching the strawberry spinning inside the glass as she spoke. 'Ah, but snobs should never be confused with educated, well-spoken people who, through no fault of their own, have been born into wealth but remained decent and well-intentioned human beings. Everyone has the right to speak correctly, wear bespoke suits and admire or own beautiful things, as long as they don't look down on those who have a regional accent, buy their clothes off the peg and shop for furniture at Argos.'

Freda nodded, totally enthralled by Olivia who was now fishing out her strawberry but by no means finished. 'It saddens me that children who have no control over where they are born, or who they were born to, are labelled or stigmatised because of their postcode and inadequate parents. This is why I make it my special mission to do whatever I can for little ones. I have a very dear and special person in my life who once fell into that category and owing entirely to their own strength of character and tenacity, they survived, however, others aren't quite so lucky. I've met my fair share of art snobs, music snobs, and every other type you care to mention, and I know from experience that the only way to deal with them, is to ignore them entirely. There's no point in trying to outdo a snob because they would just poo-poo your opinions or try to better anything that you have done or own, which is tiresome and utterly draining. It's much more fun to seek conversation with others, lavish praise where it's due and be interested in their lives. There are so many fascinating, lovely people in the world that time shouldn't be wasted arguing with, or being irritated by fools who look down their noses at those less fortunate than themselves.'

Freda could tell that Olivia meant every word she said, especially about Freda's family who she thought were divine and welcome at her Cheshire home any day of the week. She did feel the need to tell them that it wasn't actually a real castle, it was the nickname that Oliver, her grandson, gave it when he was little. Her house had turret-like structures at each end, and to a small child it resembled something from a story book. That said, it *was* rather large with vast gardens and far too many rooms for just her and Henry, whilst being an ideal location for hosting balls and charity functions.

Susie, who had been silent throughout Olivia's speech, then asked if they had staff. Olivia laughed and admitted wistfully that they used to have a full household, she even had two wonderful nannies when she was a child but nowadays, they managed with a gardener and a housekeeper. She had a twinkle in her eye and a mischievous look on her face when she whispered to Susie that she didn't require the services of a butler because darling Henry catered for her every need. And with that, she winked, picked up her glass and then glided off in search of more champagne and another hot dog.

Stacey sighed and said she could listen to Olivia speak all night, and even Charlotte thought she was totally awesome because she wasn't a bit scared of creepy-crawlies. Tilly said she was just relieved to be praised for being an English rose but might have a quiet word later on and see if Olivia agreed with the dull as dishwater bit, just in case.

As for Luke, it seemed that Tilly had finally agreed to let him off the hook, mainly because his constant begging for forgiveness and whining voice was beginning to grate on both mother and daughter. Freda felt he deserved his punishment by way of menial servitude and watched with amusement as he obediently followed Tilly's terse orders, washing glasses, scraping plates and frantically scrubbing a very greasy pan and once he'd emptied the bins, they let him off the hook.

Luke had looked so relieved as he pulled off his yellow rubber gloves, which he insisted on wearing to protect the man-icure he'd had back in the UK. As he swept the floor, Luke told Tilly he couldn't stand the bad atmosphere, it was going to spoil the wedding for everyone so he promised faithfully to defend her in the future. When Tilly explained all this to Freda, confirming they'd hugged and made up, Freda said it all sounded a bit Victorian and chaste but owing to the cold sore predicament, let it go.

On the other hand, where the outlaws were concerned, Hazel's cards were well and truly marked, and so were Luke's.

* * *

It was 6am and Charlotte would probably be up soon. Once she was awake, the rest of the house would follow suit, so Freda began to set the table and refilled the kettle. They'd been checking the *Météo* all week and as expected, the clouds were dispersing and a blue sky was emerging from above. It was going to be in the high seventies by 2pm when the wedding would take place and was set to get hotter as the afternoon progressed. Freda smiled happily as she gently set bowls onto the table and tried not to rustle the packet of croissants as she arranged them on a plate.

The only thing left to do was a visit to the salon, then she could get all dressed up and help the bride into her gown. Today was going to be perfect and she could foresee nothing that would spoil all her planning and preparation. Tilly's wedding was here at last and Freda couldn't wait for everyone to wake up and the day to begin.

The terrible cramp in her stomach woke Tilly from a deep sleep and as soon as she opened her eyes, she was aware of a swirling, nauseous sensation, causing her to gag. Lying very still, she waited for it to pass and took deep gulps of air and tried to work out what time it was. Reaching out for her phone, she edged it from the coffee table and focused on the screen. The second her eyes began to work properly, the hour became totally irrelevant because there, in black letters on the white background, was Joe's name.

Tilly's heart flipped and she felt her cheeks flush with

nerves and wasted no time opening the message. Tears swam in her eyes before she even read the words. Every pent-up emotion that had so far been silenced, now ran amok as they were freed from her tormented heart and head. It didn't occur to her that it could contain bad news and he was simply saying goodbye, or it was his final pitch and last vain attempt to get her to change her mind. She just wanted to know he was still there, somewhere on this earth and he hadn't forgotten her. To know that he didn't hate her would have been enough. Tilly was therefore in for quite a shock when she read the message.

Hi Tilly, I'm sorry it's taken so long to get in touch. I turned my phone off and I've only just read your message about the diary. There's no easy way to say this so I might as well go for it – I have been a complete idiot and I'm sorry and I hope you can forgive me. I shouldn't have snapped like that and left you alone when you were upset and needed a friend. The way I behaved is unforgivable and my only defence is that I was hurt and shocked. I'm over that now and after reading your diary I understand why you are doing this, and I want you to know that I have no right to judge you or tell you how to run your life. I promise that I will support you, even if it is from a distance and when you have sorted everything out I will be waiting for you, no matter how long it takes. I fell for you that night at the music festival but I know for sure that during the week we spent together, you sealed the deal and got me hook, line and sinker. I won't contact you today as it's not appropriate, so I'll wait for you to get in touch with me, that's if you still want to. I'm sitting on the beach in the dark at the moment and I expect you're asleep, so when you wake up, I wanted you to know this – I think that what you are doing is brave and so was giving me your diary, but most of all – I LOVE YOU. And I promise to buy you all the kittens in the pet shop, I'll take you to Glastonbury where we'll eat truffle butties every day and the most important thing of all, is that I like Marmite too! Please look after yourself, Tilly. I'll be thinking of you every minute. I miss you loads. Love from Joe xxxxxx

. . .

Tilly laughed and cried at the same time. Wiping tears from her eyes, she read the message over and over again. He had forgiven her and would stand by her decision, and even more importantly, he said he loved her, it was there in black and white. She hoped she wasn't dreaming all this because it would be the worst nightmare she'd ever had. Tilly's hands were trembling as she typed a message back, eternally grateful to the person who invented texts and mobile phones and enabled people in love to get the most momentous messages to each other in seconds. Hers said simply:

Dear Joe, you will never know how much your message means to me. Just seeing your words will get me through today, and knowing you will wait for me is all I need. There's nothing to forgive and I am so sorry things turned out the way they did. I will be in touch tomorrow, I promise. Until then, you should know that I only need one cat, YOU, and perhaps two tubs of Marmite. I love you too, Joe, and I have missed you every day since you left. Tilly xxx

PS Please take care and don't go wandering about at night on your own – you nutter.

After checking her message and then worrying if she should've said more, she pressed send and lay back on her pillow. A smile so huge had spread across her face and Tilly imagined she looked a bit mad as she read and reread Joe's message.

Tilly lay there for another hour, going through everything in her head whilst trying to ignore the nervous cramps which were becoming more frequent. She'd heard her mum come down but wanted some time to think, but now she was rattling about in the kitchen and getting organised, so it was time to put in an appearance and offer to help.

The pain in her stomach returned and this time, it was really painful. Tilly held her breath and waited for it to pass, but when the swell of nausea began to rise in her throat and her bowels rumbled, she knew that a dash to the loo was imperative. She flew into the hall, startling her mother as she dashed inside the downstairs toilet, Freda didn't have time to ask if everything was okay because the retching sound coming from behind the door told her all she needed to know.

An hour later, wedding day nerves had been firmly crossed off the list and it was clear to Freda and Stacey that Tilly had caught the dreaded bug that had been sweeping the area. According to the chief nurse and bridesmaid, it definitely couldn't be food poisoning and all the clues pointed to the sickness virus and a potential disaster was looming.

By the time the rest of the house was awake and had been checked and cleared of any symptoms, Freda began to flap, whereas Tilly was passed caring and trapped in the loo with her head stuck down the toilet. While Stacey sat on the other side, trying to give comforting, encouraging advice as she trawled the internet for possible miracle cures, Howard, Freda and the rest of the family held an emergency meeting.

It was ten thirty and Freda and Betty were due at the salon in the village at eleven, however, the big question remained unanswered, was there any point in going to the hairdressers and should they ring Luke and make him aware of the situation?

Marianne stepped in and suggested they carried on as planned until Freda returned from town, that way, if by some miracle Tilly had improved, they would all be ready to go. On the downside, if by the time they got back Tilly was still poorly, they would have to cancel the wedding.

On hearing these words, both Charlotte and Freda became tearful and Howard did his best to instil positive thoughts and chivvy them along. Tilly was tough as old boots and might just have a milder form of the bug which could soon pass, so anything was still possible.

Unfortunately, when Freda and Betty returned looking glamourous but tense, they were given the news they both expected and as Stacey so delicately put it, the only way she'd get up the aisle was if she was wearing rubber knickers and had a bucket strapped round her neck.

Freda wanted to weep there and then, all her plans crumbled into dust while at the same time, her heart ached for Tilly who probably already knew that today was going to be a non-event.

Seeing Howard come down the stairs, Freda met him at the bottom and allowed herself to be hugged, which infused some much-needed strength before she made her way upstairs to comfort Tilly who was now holed up in their bedroom.

Meanwhile, Howard's mind was working overtime as he watched his wife slowly take each step, and once she was out of sight, got on with making some calls.

Closing the door behind her, Freda crept over to the bed and sat gently on the edge.

Tilly had her eyes closed and appeared to be dozing but opened them when she heard her mum. She wanted to say she was sorry but instead the tears that flowed down her face spoke for her. Instead of words, she sobbed into the rolled-up toilet paper that was scrunched in her hand and let Freda stroke her head, just like she did when she was little and couldn't sleep after a nightmare.

'Shush now, don't cry, sweetheart, you'll make yourself worse. Dad's on the phone to the *Maire* right now and he's going to see if he can postpone the service until next week, all's not totally lost, you can still marry Luke. It's not the end of the world.' Freda knew she'd said the wrong thing when Tilly began to sob even harder.

'I'm sorry, love, I know that's not what you wanted to hear and I'd give anything to make this alright but we've just got to make the most of a bad situation. Come on, don't take on so. Look, I'm going to nip downstairs and get you some ice, you're burning up and it's so warm in here. Be brave, Tilly. I'll be back in a minute.'

Freda could feel the heat radiating from Tilly's head and knew she needed to cool down. Seeing her daughter nod and sniffle, Freda took it that it was okay to leave her alone and quietly made her way out of the room.

When the door closed, Tilly convulsed into uncontrollable sobs. She felt so bad, not for herself, but for her mum and the whole of her family and friends who had made such an effort to come to the wedding. She could deal with the stomach bug, she'd had them before and knew that the worst would be over in twenty-four hours. What she couldn't handle was the disappointment on her parents' faces.

After all her scheming, this was exactly what she'd hoped to avoid. Life was just a sick joke and now she was right slap bang in the most dreadful comedy of all. She'd come so close to making them happy and now it was over, just like that. Feeling the familiar whirl in her stomach, Tilly grabbed the bowl at the side of the bed and waited for the virus to do its work. Downstairs, she knew her dad would be halfway to wrecking everyone else's dreams and giving fate a golden trophy.

When Freda walked into the kitchen it was quite clear she'd interrupted, what appeared to be, a secret and very hurried conversation, the giveaway was when Howard spun round and looked rather sheepish. Her family who were gathered behind him looked slightly uncomfortable and on edge too. Naturally, her first instinct was that they had more bad news, though it was beyond her what could be worse than this. Seeing as all her kin were standing before her, the death of a relative wasn't an option.

It was Charlotte who broke the ice and nudged her granddad as she spoke.

'Go on, Granddad, tell her. We're all waiting so hurry up.'

Charlotte looked impatiently at Howard who had gone slightly pink while Freda became more and more nervous as the seconds passed.

'Charlotte, be quiet love and let Granddad speak. Mum, just listen to what Dad has got to say. He's come up with an idea that might just save part of the day but it's a bit crazy so go with it, okay?'

Scott sounded slightly worried and his eyes were definitely pleading with his mum as Howard jumped in.

'Right, well I've spoken to Luke who is on his way round. He was really shocked but took it quite well, I suppose. I've spoken to Michel because Rosie wasn't there, it seems that their little girls have this bug which is probably where Tilly caught it, so that's one mystery solved. I told him not to panic as I have a plan so he's waiting for me to ring back and so is the *Maire*.'

Betty took this opportunity to cough loudly and with a sharp nod of her head, hinted that he should get on with it and cut to the chase.

'Sorry, yes, I'm rambling. Anyway, the point is, while I was waiting for you to come back from the hairdressers I had a fairly good idea that Tilly wasn't going to make it to the service and it got me thinking about all the people who were here and the reception and the food and the flowers.'

He was then interrupted by Marianne who was losing the will to live and had been keeping an eye on the clock.

'For God's sake, Howard! Spit it out, man, before we all die of old age and anticipation. Get on with it before it's too late.'

Everyone jumped and then nodded in agreement.

'Bloody hell, Marianne, I'm doing my best. Sorry, Charlotte, I forgot you were here.' Howard had gone very pink now and his ears were glowing, which they did when he was very nervous or excited.

Moving towards Freda, he took both her hands in his and stared deep into her eyes. It was so perfectly quiet and it seemed like they were the only two people in the room, then he took a very deep breath and spoke.

'My dear Freda, I know you are badly disappointed about today and I wish that none of this had happened, but it has. The thing is, just because Tilly and Luke won't be tying the knot today, it seems a shame to waste all your hard work and everything. So I was thinking… seeing as all our friends and family are here and it's such a beautiful day… I was wondering if you would do me the great honour of marrying me again and renewing our vows?'

Howard looked as though he was going to burst into tears from the emotion of it all, and the tension in the room was unbearable as they all waited for her reply.

Freda removed one hand from Howard's and placed it against her right cheek which had gone incredibly hot. She felt confused, excited and emotional all rolled into one. Looking around at the anxious faces of her family, her voice trembled.

'Howard… I don't know what to say, what about Tilly? It seems wrong when she's upstairs feeling so sad, isn't it a bit cruel? I'm just a bit confused. I'm not sure what to do.'

It was Stacey who bravely spoke up and saved the day.

'Freda, please don't think I'm poking my nose in but I know Tilly, and she's up there right now driving herself mad with the guilt of it all, even though it's not her fault. I think you're being kind, not cruel if you accept Howard's proposal because it's probably the only thing that will make Tilly smile today. We all talked it through and we wouldn't say it if we didn't think it was a great idea and the right thing to do. All we're doing is swapping the bride and groom and then the rest of the day won't be ruined. And think of all the work Michel has done. Howard said the *Maire* is going on his holidays to Morocco tomorrow, so he can't marry them next week, either. I'll stay here and look after Tilly, and Charlotte can be your chief bridesmaid, can't you, princess?'

Charlotte nodded enthusiastically, looking excitedly at her grandma and pleading with her eyes.

'Anyway, I've said enough, it's up to you now.'

Stacey hoped she hadn't overstepped the mark but the

sound of Scott and Susie agreeing, along with Norman and Caroline, made her feel justified.

'Come on, Freda, say yes and we can all nip down to the village and watch you say "I do", and then we can have a proper knees-up afterwards, just like at your first wedding but a bit swankier, what do you say?'

Norman was definitely up for it and Betty was nodding in agreement.

'Well, if you really think they won't mind and it's not bad taste or anything… then Howard, I'd be honoured to marry you again, you daft old fool. Come on, what are we waiting for? Let's get this show on the road!'

Freda hugged and kissed Howard as a huge cheer went up. The kitchen was filled with an excited atmosphere that quickly descended into panic as lots of people dashed about in different directions.

First, Freda insisted on them both going straight upstairs to double check with Tilly that it was okay and then, once they had the thumbs up, and only if she looked genuinely happy about it, Scott and Stacey could ring everyone and tell them the news. Everyone was convinced that Tilly would be fine so Susie scurried off with Charlotte while Marianne and Betty decided they needed a cup of tea to steady their nerves. Well one of them wanted a brew, the other helped herself to a large glass of wine.

Norman and Caroline disappeared down the garden to get ready in the caravan, just as a car pulled up with Luke inside. He was dressed in his suit, with a striped tie dangling from his pocket and one of his shoelaces was untied. Luke went straight inside, looking concerned, mingled with a barely perceptible tinge of irritation.

Stacey was waiting to give him the news about the alternative wedding and spotted the look straight away. She was good at reading people and Luke, for one, had never been able to convince her he was a nice bloke. Knowing that her best friend had just been spared the ordeal of actually marrying the jerk who stood before her, Stacey gave him a graphic description of just how sick Tilly was, before hitting him with the new arrangements.

Upstairs, Freda was sitting next to Tilly who, despite looking wiped out and exhausted, was holding her mother's hand and this time, crying for a completely different reason. Howard was in the hall, speaking to his friend, Edouard the *Maire*, and confirming that they were going ahead with the idea he'd discussed earlier.

Once he got off the phone, he explained to Freda that in France, if you were already married then there was no need for all the paperwork and legal whatnots, therefore it was relatively simple to renew your vows or have a civil ceremony. Edouard was going to prepare the service and Scott was already on the phone to the hotel and the rest of the guests. Freda still felt dreadful. It was impossible not to, and the underlying sense of disappointment for her daughter was hard to ignore.

'Tilly, are you really sure that all this isn't going to upset you even more? Please be honest with us, I'd understand completely you know, it's such a huge shame and deep down I feel awful for you and Luke, I really do.' Freda helped Tilly sit up slightly and plumped up the pillow behind her so she could take a sip of water.

'Mum, Dad, you do not know how relieved I am, which sounds mad but it's true. I couldn't bear the thought of the day being ruined for you, and everyone being sent home. Now I can lie here with my head in that bucket and actually feel happy. Charlotte gets to be a bridesmaid and Grandma hasn't come all this way for nothing, not to mention Scott and Susie, so please, go and get dressed up and have a lovely day. As long as you make sure there are lots of photos and videos for me to watch later, I'm sure I'll survive.' Tilly replaced the glass of water then let her body sag against the pillows, she was utterly exhausted.

'Okay, I believe you. I'd best get my finger out, hadn't I,

otherwise we'll be late. You look washed out, love, so try and rest for a bit. I'll come and see you before we go, now relax and sip that water, slowly.' Freda gave a jerk of her head, a signal to Howard they should leave her in peace.

'Yes, Mum, I am a nurse and I think I know what to do. I'll be fine.'

'Sorry, love, old habits and all that.'

'Can you ask Stacey to come up? I want her to go with you. There's no need for her to stay with me, and I'd like her to have some fun and a nice meal, she's been looking forward to it and I'll never hear the last of it if she doesn't get to eat Michel's food.'

'Course I will, love, and I agree about Stacey because Luke can stay and look after you.'

'Is he here yet? I need to speak to him. How did he take it, Dad, was he annoyed?'

Tilly actually felt sorry for Luke, which was two-faced and a bit bizarre at the same time.

'He sounded shocked and concerned once he found his tongue. I think he was just lost for words at first. I heard a car pull up outside so he should be here in a minute. I'm sure you both need some time on your own.'

Tilly knew her dad was trying hard to do and say the right thing.

'You're right, Dad, best get it over with.' Apart from him being disappointed, Tilly knew in some ways she'd done Luke a massive favour because now they wouldn't actually have to get divorced. There followed a fleeting notion that she was turning into a hard-hearted bitch, or was she just being honest and practical? Hearing a gentle tap on the door her heart plummeted and when his head popped into the bedroom, Tilly cringed inside and decided the best way to play this was to say as little as possible and milk being poorly, for now.

'Hi, is it okay to come in? God, Tilly, you look rough.'

Turning to face Freda, Luke gave her a hug then shook Howard's hand as he congratulated them both.

'I'm glad you've managed to salvage the day, everything

went into meltdown at the hotel after you called but they'll all be glad when they hear the news. I'll stay here and look after Tilly, you get off and enjoy yourselves and I'll hold the fort.'

Luke seemed genuine enough but Tilly was already dreading being cooped up in a room with him and was doing her best to look very sleepy and drained. Even if by some miracle she was cured in the next ten minutes, she was staying exactly where she was.

After her parents had fussed and fretted, they discreetly left the two of them alone and more than likely, imagined a sad but loving scene was being played out behind the closed door. They were wrong.

CHAPTER TWENTY-FIVE

L uke came over and sat at the end of the bed. Tilly had the impression that he was hoping to avoid infection as he tentatively stretched out and took her hand in his, giving it a quick squeeze and receiving a weak one in response. Tilly wasn't exactly firing on all cylinders and feared that the cycle of sickness and diarrhoea was only ever a moment away but remained in control of her faculties and sensed that Luke was nervous or annoyed, or both. She also got the distinct impression that he was awaiting an apology which irritated her immensely, for that reason, she stayed silent and let him make the first move. Tilly wanted to know how he was feeling and thinking first.

'Well, I never expected today to turn out like this. How are you feeling now? I wonder if you're still contagious. I felt a bit queasy this morning and couldn't face breakfast, maybe I'm getting it too.'

Tilly rolled her eyes. 'That's probably more to do with all the beer you've been throwing down your neck since you got here and let's face it, thanks to your minging cold sore we've hardly been pashing it up. If you've caught something, it's not from me.' Tilly was only stating the obvious and couldn't resist mentioning his unsightly blemish because, as usual, Luke was thinking about himself so she closed her eyes while he droned on, ignoring her critique.

'What do you mean by that? Who else would I catch a bug from?' Luke sounded indignant.

'I was only being sarcastic, Luke, chill out.' Tilly kept her eyes shut, swallowing down bile and irritation.

'I couldn't believe it when your dad rang me and for a second I thought he was winding me up. Mum was in a right state, she was all dressed and ready to go when I found her in the bar. Dad's been great, he's apologised to our lot for the inconvenience but at least now they'll be able to have a bit of a party and a nice meal, so it's not been a complete waste of a journey. I'll nip back down in a minute and ring them, just to make sure they got the message it's all back on, for your mum and dad I mean.'

Tilly opened her eyes and fixed him with an angry stare.

'If that little speech was supposed to make me feel better, you failed miserably. When are you ever going to see that it's not always all about you, or your bloody mother? For your information, this day was about us and for the record, it was my parents who stood to lose the most and they'll be disappointed too. I think it's really brave of them to make the best of this shambles when deep down they probably feel like shit, which if you must know is exactly how I feel right now.' Tilly closed her eyes to hold in the tears which were borne mostly of rage.

'Tilly, I know that, I was just saying… never mind. Look, you're overemotional and I know how cranky you get when you're ill, so I'm not being drawn into a row when you feel like this. I do appreciate what your mum and dad have done and I agree that it can't be nice for them, knowing in the back of their mind our day is ruined, but I reckon they'll have a great time in the end.'

Luke was flogging a dead horse and must have sensed that Tilly was riled, so bravely risked infection and grabbed her hand.

'Now, will you at least give me a smile and be friends, okay? Am I forgiven for being insensitive, again?'

Luke gave Tilly his best hangdog expression, which he'd bored her with so many times before and under most circumstances had no effect whatsoever.

Tilly couldn't be bothered smiling and just about managed to reply, after exhaling the longest, most exasperated sigh she could muster.

'Yes, I forgive you and even though I didn't do it on purpose, I'm sorry for being ill and ruining everything, now can you pass me that bowl because I'm going to be sick.'

There was no more to be said, not that she had any choice in the matter. No sooner had Luke passed her the bowl, he was edging away from the bed and telling her he'd fetch Stacey.

As the insides of her stomach swiftly departed her body, Tilly swore she was being punished for her evil ways and willingly accepted her sentence. By the time Stacey entered the room, the worst was over and Tilly lay exhausted and dripping with sweat, her whole body felt weak from the exertion of retching while her watery eyes begged for sleep.

'How you doing, mate? Here, give me that bowl. Mmm, it's just bile so maybe the worst is over, not that I'm going to admit that to anyone.' Stacey paused while Tilly took a sip of water.

'Your mum says you want me to go to the wedding but don't you think it would be best if we got rid of Luke instead, let's face it, he's not much use, is he? The way he came down those stairs I thought the devil was after him and now he's scrubbing his hands in the sink like you've got the plague. The bloody freak!' Stacey placed her hand on Tilly's head and checked her temperature, tutting when she felt how hot she was.

'I'm okay, Stace, just a bit knackered to be honest. Are you alright? Mum said it was your wise words that convinced her to say yes to Dad.'

Stacey was fussing about straightening the sheets then wiped Tilly's face with a wet flannel before sitting down on the bed, brushing the stray, tangled hairs from her damp face.

'I had to say something. It was the perfect get out clause for you, and I couldn't let them just give up and sit around all day weeping and wailing so I told her what I thought.'

'Well thank God you did, you're a star, Stace, and I owe you one, again.'

'Nah, this one's on me but I gotta say, Tilly, you really must have a guardian angel watching out for you. I know you feel shit right now but talk about a lucky escape! To say you've got perfect timing is an understatement. Even though you've been throwing your guts up, not to mention blocking the drains, I reckon this is better than actually saying "I do", or "oui", or whatever it is you say in France, don't you?' Stacey was being careful to keep her voice low, just in case they were overheard.

'Course I do. Getting this bug had actually crossed my mind when Mum and Dad were ill and I'd even considered faking it, so you're right, having your head stuck in a bowl and your arse glued to the toilet seat is a very small price to pay.'

Both girls managed a bit of a giggle then Tilly glanced at the door and whispered to Stacey.

'Thanks though, for sorting it all out because now a tiny bit of my conscience is clear. Anyway, pass my phone, quickly, it's over there on the dresser. I need to show you something before anyone comes back. I've not had time to tell you but I got a message from Joe. He's forgiven me!'

Tilly couldn't help smiling, especially at Stacey and the fact that her drawn on eyebrows had raised about two inches in surprise.

Once the phone was in her hands, Tilly found the message and passed it to her friend who began reading. Stacey's expressions as she scrolled through the text made Tilly smile. She had a funny habit of silently mouthing the words of anything she read and even though it was private, Tilly wanted a second opinion and trusted her friend with her life. She also knew that Stacey would be honest and point her in the right direction.

Passing the phone back to Tilly, Stacey gave her verdict.

'That was a really nice message, mate, but what the hell are you going to do now? You need to take things slowly for a start. I don't want you making a mahoosive mistake and getting your knickers in a twist again. This Joe seems like a really nice bloke but I think you should concentrate on ending things as best you can with Luke before you run headlong into another relationship. You'll only look bad, you know. I really don't give a toss but other people will judge you, so take it a step at a time.'

'You're right, I don't want Joe getting the blame for anything and everyone will just say I'm on the rebound when it's not like that at all. Anyway, I need to get through today and I wish Luke would sod off to the hotel if I'm honest. From what you said it sounds like he's shit scared of getting this bug so he's going to be no use here and it's not like I can't look after myself. I'm nowhere near as ill as Mum and Dad were so I'll survive a few hours on my own. Do you think I could talk him into leaving me here?' Tilly couldn't bear the thought of making small talk or being ill within a hundred yards of Luke, it was all just so embarrassing and frankly, too much like hard work.

'I think he'd be glad of an excuse to get pissed again, it seems like his main aim at the moment. Right, I'm going to wash this bowl then I'd best get my frock on, I need to look sexy for all these Frenchies at the party.' Stacey smoothed down the duvet and picked up the sick bowl on her way to the door.

'Just have a good time, Stace, you deserve it. Thanks for being there for me. I don't know what I'd do without you.' Tilly was getting teary again and meant every word.

'You'd still have sick on your chin, that's what. Try to chillax. Back in a bit.' And with that Stacey closed the door, leaving Tilly in silence.

Her stomach felt as flat as a pancake and she prayed that her bowels were just as empty, because she really didn't want to make another trip to the loo. As long as she kept herself hydrated without it unsettling her insides, she might just get away with it. She could hear frenzied activity outside on the landing as doors opened and closed and feet pounded up and down the stairs while her family got ready. Her eyes were beginning to droop when she heard a tap-tapping on the door and then a little Australian voice call her name from the other side, it was Charlotte.

'Aunty Tilly, are you okay? Can I open the door? I'm not allowed inside cos Mum says I might get sick and you've got to rest, but I wanted to show you my dress and tell you I'm really sorry you're not getting married. I know you'd have looked just beautiful but don't be sad though, cos I promise that when I get married, I'll let you be my bridesmaid. If you save your dress, you can still wear it on my wedding day. I'll bring you some cake back and if there's any balloons and sweets I'll get you some for when you're better. Grandma Freda is very excited about being the second-hand bride so it's all gonna be okay.'

Tilly could barely speak but managed to tell Charlotte to open the door. Very slowly, a gap appeared, and on the other side stood a little princess, beaming and waving from the hall. Tilly brushed the tears from her eyes so she could see better.

'Oh, Charlotte, you look beautiful. Have a lovely day, sweetheart, and don't worry, I'm not sad because seeing you has made me very happy.'

'Okay, will do, Aunty Tilly. I've gotta go now, Mum's shouting me. I love you, Aunty Tilly.'

Then she was gone, following the sound of Susie calling her name.

Tears pumped from Tilly's eyes and she couldn't prevent a sob erupting from deep inside her aching chest, already damaged by her wounded heart and the strain of retching. She wasn't crying for herself, it was for the others, her lovely family who were rallying round, putting smiles on brave faces and jollying themselves along. She loved them all so much and Charlotte's simple words, along with the innocent thought that cake and sweets made all things better, had somehow managed to leave her feeling incredibly sad, but hopeful at the same time.

One day, many years from now when all this was sorted out and forgotten, she'd be in the middle of a new life, whatever that entailed, and maybe she would find herself at her niece's wedding. She'd laugh, remembering Charlotte's words and the thought of wearing her plain white dress and being the oldest bridesmaid in town. Tilly hoped and prayed that her niece's day would be happy and turn out nothing like this one, and that the innocent little girl would find true love and happiness the first time round. As she wiped the tears from her eyes and blew her nose, Tilly made a silent promise to be there for Charlotte with a huge bunch of balloons and a bag of sweets in her pocket, just in case.

Tilly's heart had literally melted when, one by one, they'd all come to the bedroom door to say goodbye and tell her how sorry they were about her big day. She told them all they looked fab, each and every one of them, dressed to the nines with a lovely rose pinned to their new clothes. Susie and Aunty Caroline looked a bit teary when they blew kisses and promised to make sure Freda and Howard had a brilliant time, and Scott made a heart sign with his hands, probably because he couldn't speak.

When her mum appeared in the outfit she'd chosen with Olivia, Tilly nearly blubbed again but somehow managed to rein it in and clap with delight as Freda did a quick twirl in front of the mirror.

Tilly had been quite brave, right up until her grandma entered the room looking radiant in her pale lemon suit and white hat with the little net veil. After ignoring Freda, who didn't want Betty catching the bug, she announced that it was too late now and she was going to give her granddaughter a hug, and nobody was going to stop her! When Grandma Betty plopped herself down beside Tilly, opening her arms wide before folding them around the fragile, weary body in the bed, she let her cry it out, unaware that the tears weren't actually out of self-pity, they were just a result of loving her family so much. Betty held Tilly close and shushed her until she calmed down and then promised to come back later, once her dancing legs had given in and then she'd keep her company and give Luke a break.

The idea of being alone with her thoughts appealed to Tilly far more than spending an evening with her sullen fiancé, so she'd tried in vain to get him to go whereas her mother insisted he stayed, much to her and Stacey's annoyance. Talking of Stacey, Tilly thought she looked amazing in her fitted, knee-length dress, which did in fact match her hair and showed off her ample chest. It was impossible to hide her bumpy bits, but who cared?

Finally she was alone, until the return of Luke, so making the most of a few precious moments, Tilly closed her eyes and forced her brain to rest.

* * *

Everyone was waiting at the foot of the stairs for Freda to come down and when they saw her, they all gasped, then chorused their approval at the sight of the blushing bride, apart from Howard, who was too full with emotion to speak. He had never seen his wife look more beautiful, he probably had if the truth were told, but right now, he couldn't think of one single occasion and just wanted to rush up and grab her, then hold his prize in his arms forever. Having been married for twenty-nine years, Howard knew he must resist – an act of affection such as this would be the kiss of death. No woman wants to be fondled, kissed or ruffled when they are made up to perfection, with not a single hair out of place and wearing their perfectly pressed, best outfit. Instead, he just stood and gazed at the vision of loveliness who was all his.

Once they were all rounded up by Scott, they piled inside their cars and set off into the village, first stop the *Mairie*.

Whilst there was a happy, excited atmosphere amongst the

wedding party, the same couldn't be said for the one inside Freda and Howard's bedroom, where Luke was waiting for Tilly to return from another mad dash to the loo.

When she appeared at the doorway looking ashen and bedraggled in her crumpled, sweaty pyjamas, Tilly found Luke gazing silently out of the window, lost in a world of his own and oblivious to the fact she'd entered the room. He was dressed in his grey morning suit trousers and crisp white dress shirt and from where she was standing, she was able to admire his broad back, muscled arms and firm footballer's legs. Despite the fact he was handsome (even from the back) and although he was most young women's fantasy, Tilly knew that Luke's appeal was lost on her forever.

She'd been leaning against the doorframe and after gathering her strength, she padded across the wooden floor on very weak and wobbly legs before flopping onto the bed, which finally alerted Luke to her presence. There was silence for a second or two until Tilly managed to think of something to say that wasn't too deep and meaningful.

'Didn't Mum look absolutely beautiful? And Charlotte really was like a fairy princess with her diamond tiara, all she needed was a wand.' Tilly pulled the duvet over her legs and tried to get comfy.

'I think she'd need more than a wand and a spell to mend today, but you're right, Freda looked great and your dad scrubbed up well too. I've never seen him look so smart, he's usually covered in mud or in his tatty shorts. I don't know what Stacey was thinking of when she bought that dress though, the only positive thing about it was that it matched her hair! Has she put weight on since you bought it because she was popping out all over the place.' Luke stayed by the window and turned his back on Tilly the second he'd finished speaking.

Why did he make every sentence sound like a jibe, especially where her family and best friend were concerned? Yes, her dad was always in his scruffs but he was a working-class man who liked to get his hands dirty and didn't feel the need to dress up or wear the latest trends, what was wrong with that?

'Why don't you go downstairs and watch telly? I'm going to try and get some sleep. There's no point in you staying up here is there?'

'Nah, I'm not in the mood and anyway, I daren't leave the room in case Freda finds out and bites my head off.'

'Luke, stop being a whinge, you're always feeling sorry for yourself! Mum didn't bite your head off she was just making sure I was okay. She'd never have gone out of the door unless you promised to stay so now she's gone, why don't you just make your way to the hotel and meet them there. Tell her I'm feeling loads better or just say I'm fast asleep. It's supposed to be your reception too and it's not fair that you miss out on a lovely meal. Anyway, you should be with your family, not stuck here all night. Please, Luke, just go. Get me a fresh jug of water and then leave me to it. I know how to look after myself.' Tilly sensed he wanted to go and even though her mum would go mental it seemed a bit hard-faced to ban him from his own wedding reception.

'Are you sure? I could do with checking on Mum, she was a bit tearful earlier and she'll be worried about me. I suppose I should go over and show my face and say hello to our guests. That reminds me, what are we going to do about all the presents and the honeymoon? Do we open them or what? It seems a bit of a cheek when were not actually married but if we give them back, they might take offence. Bloody hell, Tilly. What a mess!' Luke slumped on the chair in the corner and put his head in his hands.

'We can worry about all that tomorrow. I'm sure nobody is going to be insensitive enough to mention presents and as for the honeymoon, let's see how I feel in the morning. As it is, I can't see myself being able to make the journey without having an accident, so could we make a decision when I feel a bit better?' Tilly's head was mashed enough without having to worry about gifts and honeymoons.

'Okay. I suppose you're right, but I don't want to cancel the holiday. It cost a bloody fortune and I bet I won't get the money back, so even if we turn up a few days late, I still want to go. I deserve this holiday … we both do especially after this and I was really looking forward to it.' Luke looked up and from the look that Tilly gave him, gleaned he was being insensitive, again. 'Right, I'll get you some water then nip over to the hotel. If your mum kicks off I'll come straight back, otherwise I'll be in the doghouse again.'

Luke made his way to the door while Tilly bit her lip, hard.

'Like I said, let's see how I feel in the morning, now you get going and check on your mum and say hello to everyone for me, tell them I'm sorry.'

'I will. Give me two ticks, I'll go and fill this up' Tilly watched Luke pick up the jug and head for the bathroom.

It had occurred to her while he was worrying about presents and the honeymoon that not only did he seem more concerned about missing his holiday and upsetting people, he didn't really need his arm twisting about the reception either. All this was being stored in her box of ammunition to be used against him when she imparted the final shot. When and where that would be, was another matter entirely. For now, she just wanted some peace and to be able to puke in private, was that too much to ask? There was also something else that needed to be done and while she wanted to contact Joe and put him out of his misery, she was acutely aware that propriety was holding her back.

Right now, it seemed wrong to send a text, let alone speak to him while Luke was feeling like he did. How could it be worded so that she didn't sound happy and gloating, or cruel and hard? If Tilly was honest, she felt a bit weird right now and the only comfortable, vaguely acceptable emotion she could admit to, was relief. It was for that reason that she left the phone where it was, underneath her pillow. Once Luke had returned with the water and gladly absolved of the need to kiss her goodbye, she didn't want a cold sore and he didn't want the lurgy, he shot off in the direction of the hotel and his mother, leaving Tilly alone at last.

* * *

Freda was observing the scene from her place at the top table. The hotel looked superb and was festooned with garlands of the most beautiful summer flowers, which hung from the walls, tied with gauze ribbons to match the soft lime green of the table runners that complemented the floral table displays.

The scent from the blooms was heavenly and circulated naturally by the breeze which blew in through the open French doors that led out onto the terrace. It was here they had enjoyed welcome drinks and canapés under the pagoda and, as Freda savoured each delicate morsel, she tried to store them in her memory so she could recreate them at home, because to taste them only once would be a crime against food. The silver platters held a combination of delights, smoked salmon, apple and a dash of crème fraiche on handmade bruschetta, seared melon wrapped in prosciutto, tiny pieces of duck breast stuffed with chives and cream cheese, petite foie gras toasts with a marmalade topping and mini sausages glazed in wholegrain honey.

It was perfect, just perfect and Freda was convinced that this was as good as anything the royal family had at weddings. She was already ten nil up on Hazel who looked sick with envy when she clapped eyes on the replacement bride as they all arrived at the *Mairie*.

Despite her smug exterior, Freda had to fight hard against the demons in her head who insisted on reminding her that all this should have been for Tilly. From the words that Edouard had spoken in the *Mairie* to the glass of bienvenue champagne with the delicate little strawberry floating on top to the entrée, which was being served from silver trays bearing a sumptuous feast for everyone to enjoy. It should have been Tilly's reward for being the best daughter in the world and, for one special day, Freda wanted to bathe her in luxury, sprinkling her wedding with the nearest thing to gold dust, so that when it was over, she'd be left with memories and images like this.

If it hadn't been for Howard's brilliant idea and Stacey putting her straight, everything would have gone to waste. Yes, maybe they still would've served up the food for the guests, but ultimately the day would've been left flat. Freda certainly couldn't imagine anyone wanting to have partied or danced, whereas now, they could all have a little bit of fun, and talk about their ceremony which was warm and quite moving. They would make the chef happy by eating his food and later, they'd drink a toast to the absent bride and the very present, rather annoying, groom who was already making the most of the table wine.

Freda was livid when she spotted Luke. He sauntered in and immediately began chatting to his mother and father, accepting a glass of champagne before wandering off with Darren who was half commiserating, half joking (rather too loudly) about making a lucky escape. The moron! Luke lapped up the attention, playing the disappointed, magnanimous bridegroom to a tee, and it left Freda fuming. This was Tilly's starring role, not his. Her precious daughter had missed out on being a princess for a day and to top it all, was now lying in bed, all alone, chucking her guts up.

The newly remarried bride and groom were seated at the top table, which was raised slightly on a plinth to give them a bird's eye view of their guests, which Freda found a bit embarrassing and uncomfortable. Fortunately, Howard felt no such thing and was revelling in being in the top spot. He also had to be restrained from picking the decoration off the croque en bouche, the magnificent conic tower of handmade, fondant filled choux balls, adorned with wisps of spun sugar, edible pearls and flowers, and studded with tiny, artisan sweets.

Rosie had told Freda that Michel would spend hours making the centre piece for the top table, which was the French alternative to a traditional English wedding cake. It was truly stunning and everyone had admired the sugary masterpiece when they entered the room.

As the waiters and waitresses made their way around the tables, Freda spotted a couple of faces she recognised from her visits to the restaurant, however, on this occasion André and Wilf were busy serving food. Freda chuckled to herself as she watched Olivia and Henry become engaged in a conversation with André, who seemed to spend more time chatting to his friends from the village than actually working. He was a lovely man, as was his partner Wilf, and together they roamed Europe in their camping car, returning frequently to see Rosie, who André regarded as his adopted daughter.

Poor Rosie, thought Freda, there's another one who's missing out and after all her hard work, she was at home caring for her little girls who had more than likely passed the virus on to Tilly. Michel had conveyed her apologies and assured them that Ruby was in charge and would ensure everything went perfectly, and as far as Freda could see, it was. Howard broke into her thoughts by giving her a nudge and pointing at her plate.

'Come on, tuck in. Michel has done us proud here, this beats egg and cress sarnies and a pork pie. And the best bit is, you've not been up all night making it yourself, so stop worrying about Tilly and relax. If you don't eat up, I'll have yours, it's bloody lovely.' Howard winked and Freda smiled back.

He knew her so well, but having said that, there was nothing wrong with egg and cress and even though this was a five-star, all-singing, all-dancing upgrade, she wouldn't change wedding number one, not for anything.

CHAPTER TWENTY-SIX

The starter of roasted beetroot and goat's cheese salad was served with fresh figs and vinaigrette. It was sublime and accompanied by a Sancerre Sauvignon Blanc and, according to Michel, one of the best Loire wines to eat with chevre. As Freda took a sip, the clean, crisp fruity acidity cut through the richness of the creamy cheese and cleared the palate in anticipation of another bite. Hazel, who was sitting just a few people away, was not impressed in the slightest – it appeared that goat's cheese wasn't her thing. Thankfully, Hazel seemed to be in the minority because all the other plates around her looked empty and the rest of the guests were eager for the next course.

After a little rest, because the French never, ever hurry a meal, the fish course arrived in delicate white china bowls. Inside was bourride with lemon aioli; three scallop sized chunks of halibut, steamed in clam juice until they were light and fluffy, then rested in a creamy, lemon and garlic sauce, infused with saffron, bay leaves and orange, decorated with sprigs of fresh chervil. Resting on the side plate were two slivers of homemade toasted baguette. To accompany the rich sauce, André produced a Rosé d'Anjou and with great flourish, proceeded to fill everyone's glasses.

It had been a risk to include a fish course, and Freda had been worried that it wouldn't go down well, however, on the day they chose the menu, she bowed to Michel's exceptional taste and experience, along with being scared to death he might blow a gasket if she rebelled. Now, as she tasted the sauce and let the flakes of fish combine with the garlic and lemon, the aromas transported her to a seaside restaurant in the South of France.

It was clear to Freda and Howard that Luke had no intention whatsoever of ringing Tilly or eating any of the wonderful food, which he left almost uneaten in favour of throwing glass after glass of wine down his neck. Instead, Susie did the honours and checked up on her, reporting back that she was doing okay and just wanted to sleep.

Charlotte looked adorable and was basking in the attention that being on the top table affords you. She was fascinated by the different accents and languages being spoken around her. Charlotte had stood next to Freda during the ceremony at the *Mairie* where the bride passed her the bouquet of roses, proud as punch to have played a special role in the day. Charlotte was mesmerised and drank in every word that Edouard spoke, even if it was in French, and then listened to it once again in English when his assistant repeated the vows for the non-speakers.

During the gaps in the courses, many of the guests took a little stroll to say hello to Freda and Howard and compliment them on the reception, which narked Hazel to the max. The wine had finally softened the edges of Freda's anxiety and allowed her to enjoy herself, although she fastidiously stuck to one glass per course otherwise she'd end up being overemotional and blubbing.

The sight of the waiters entering the room heralded the arrival of the main course and any straggling guests immediately returned to their seats. There followed a difficult choice between magret de canard infused with lavender and complemented by a honey and fig sauce, or rack of lamb with pancetta, red wine and rosemary. Both dishes were accompanied by minted peas, honey roast carrots, green beans in lemon butter and roast potatoes with thyme and garlic. Naturally, the wine required a change of colour and soon the diners were sipping a medium bodied Pinot Noir, chosen to tantalise the palate and aid the digestion of the rich meats.

Freda was beginning to think she'd never manage the next course so sampled a small portion of everything, which was a damn site more than Hazel had eaten. On the up side, Ken was happily filling his boots, so at least one member of the Jackson family had been fed. Luke didn't like French food and had bemoaned that fact on each visit, that's why Freda hadn't factored him into the equation when she chose the menu, otherwise they'd all be eating at Burger King. From what she could see, he seemed to prefer a liquid lunch, so she left him to chew on the assortment of artisan bread from the baskets scattered liberally along the tables.

All of Tilly and Luke's friends and colleagues were very merry and having fun after being squashed into a mini bus for hours. They'd all arrived at the *Mairie* on time and were dressed to the nines, only to be told the news that the real bride was ill and couldn't make it; within minutes were asked if they would mind being witnesses to Tilly's parents tying the knot again.

Freda's attention turned once again to Luke, who was thick as thieves with his leery, defunct best man. Darren appeared to be ogling Tilly's female friends, much to the amusement of Luke. When he accidentally caught Freda's eye she gave him a look of death, causing him to visibly shrivel. Yes, he was definitely starting to get on Freda's nerves and after totting up all the bits and bobs that Tilly had let slip over the past few days, she decided that Luke was pushing his luck!

Betty couldn't stand him and was all for having him strung up when he'd cheated on Tilly although, along with everyone else, sort of forgave him, but only for her grand-daughter's sake. Freda's mother had never taken to Luke from day one and always said that his eyes were too close together (whatever that meant) and he was spoilt and too fond of the beer (which was true). When Luke finally took out his phone and appeared to be checking for a message from his sick fiancée, Freda watched him scathingly as he tried hard to focus through wine-fuzzed eyes and typed something back. 'Hallelujah,' muttered Freda through pursed lips, her narrowed eyes registering his sheepish glance in her direction.

It was taking a while to clear the tables after the main course and in the meantime, Susie shuffled along from where she'd been chatting to one of Luke's aunts and made her way into Howard's recently vacated spot. Freda loved Susie with her mad, curly blonde hair, freckled skin and sunny personality, but now she came to think of it, since her arrival she'd seemed less glowing and, most of the time, appeared to be miles away. While there was a lull and her mum radar was on full beam, Freda thought she'd check that all was well with her daughter-in-law and have a quiet chat.

'Are you having a nice time, love? You still look tired to me. We can all have a few lazy days in the garden after this, no more rushing about and then you can get your energy back before you go and see your mum and dad. I wish they could've come over. I'll make sure we save some cake for you to take when you go.' Freda patted Susie's hand and despite her chatter, didn't miss the sad look that flitted across her daughter-in-law's face when her parents were mentioned, or the watery look in her eyes.

'I'm fine, Freda, I've just got a lot on my mind, you know with Dad being poorly and even though he's battling it, I know in my heart he's not going to get any better. We can give him a few more years and pray for new treatments but the chemo takes it out of him already, and I wonder just how long he's really got. Anyway, we shouldn't be talking about this now, not on a special day. Where's Howard gone?' Susie was changing the subject, but Freda had other ideas.

'Don't be daft, Susie, you can talk to me anytime and when do I ever get you on my own for long enough to have a serious chat? Charlotte's always in and out and we've got a houseful, but that doesn't mean I haven't got time for you. I'm always there if you need me, love, you should know that.'

'I do, Freda. I just don't know where to start. This trip is really important, you know? I was so happy for Tilly when she told us about the wedding but I was more happy for me because it meant I could come home. I might as well tell you the truth… I'm not enjoying it in Oz, I haven't been for a while and Scott knows I've had enough. I want to come home, not just because my dad's poorly, even though that's a huge part of it, it's everything rolled into one. Oh no, I've upset you haven't I, are you annoyed with me?'

'Well I'm a bit shocked, but I'm certainly not annoyed or upset. I'm a little confused though, because you always seem so happy and full of beans when I speak to you, and Scott hasn't mentioned anything. How does he feel about it?'

Freda had felt her heart lift at the prospect of them all being back on her side of the world, but knew that if her son wanted to stay in Australia, there was going to be trouble.

'He wasn't happy about it at first, he really likes his job but I can be a midwife in England or anywhere, and it's not like Scott is underqualified, he'll easily find work. The thing is, even though Charlotte has a lovely home by the sea and lots of friends, she misses out on one really important thing. And that's simply having her grandparents about. At weekends, her mates are always off to stay with their relatives but we don't have any. I know how close Scott and Tilly are to Betty and I was always at my gran and granddad's house. I practically lived there when I was little, whereas Charlotte has to make do with chats on Skype or a visit once in a blue moon, and it's just not enough. I want another baby too, but there's no way I'm doing that on the other side of the world. I want you and my mum to be there to help me and be part of its life too. So if I can't come home then there'll be no more babies and Scott knows it.' Susie's voice had replaced emotion with determination and common sense.

Freda got the feeling she'd been storing up for ages.

'Well, I'd be a liar if I said that our long-distance relationship with Charlotte hadn't crossed my mind now and then. And especially where your dad is concerned, I agree that time is precious and it would be lovely for her to know him properly. The thing is, Susie, I don't feel I can give you impartial advice. I could give you a list of positives as long as your arm, but half of them would be purely selfish on my behalf, so for that reason, I will stand back and let you and Scott make your own mind up.' Freda felt so sorry for Susie who she knew was hoping for an ally.

'I appreciate that, Freda, but you did ask and it would have come out over the next few days anyway. Scott will do it for *me*, I know he will, but at the same time I feel so guilty, like I'm being selfish and spoiling it for him. We never said Australia was forever, so I suppose I'm just cutting the adventure short before it's too late. My mum is going to need my support one of these days, when Dad gets really poorly, and I don't want the next trip back to be for his funeral either. I want it to be for good reasons, family ones. As long as you're not annoyed with me for ruining things for Scott, that's fine. You know I'd never hurt him on purpose, don't you?'

Susie was filling up and Howard was on his way back to the table, so Freda had to reassure her quickly.

'Of course I know and I'm definitely not annoyed with you. Deep down, I'm chuffed to bits and I'll be your silent supporter until you've made your final decision, so stop worrying, I think everything's going to turn out fine.' Freda squeezed Susie's hand just as Howard arrived to reclaim his throne.

Freda had to hand it to Michel. He really knew his stuff and the main course had settled nicely when the cheese course was served. They had never seen a selection like this, however, today there was a rare addition to the offerings which may have raised a few eyebrows amongst the French contingent, well, those who had never dined at Freda's house, anyway. On this very auspicious occasion, along with the bread and cheese, the guests would also be eating English crackers!

No matter what Michel thought or said, Freda had stuck to her guns and insisted that they were on the table, the simple reason being that there was no point in offering the best fromage in the world if the English had nothing, apart from bread, to put it on. It was what they were used to and the beautiful selection of gourmet cheeses would just go to waste. That's why, after each trip to England, Freda returned with a bag full of the finest crackers she could find, sprinkled with God knows what and in every variation she could lay her hands on. To be fair, Michel had accepted defeat gracefully, and being married to a strong-minded Brit may also have had something to do with it.

Once Howard had munched his way through the whole of France, he took a breather and relaxed in his chair, giving himself a minute to take in the scene and allow himself a contented smile. It hadn't turned out the way anyone expected but when all was said and done, they'd certainly had their money's worth out of the little nest egg that had paid for all this, and it was just grand. Freda had done them proud with all her lists and planning and he was glad that she'd still got some benefit out of it, even if it was at the expense of Tilly. Then an awful thought occurred to him, if they had to stage a rerun for Tilly and Luke, there was no way they'd be able to cough up for another posh do like this! Howard pictured his last bank statement and the balance at the bottom, which caused a mild touch of panic to set in, prompting him to test the water and drop a few hints to Freda.

'I've got to hand it to you, love, it all came together just perfect, are you pleased with everything? I know you're still a bit down about our Tilly but one way or another we'll find a way to make it right... but do you think they'll be expecting all this, because it's going to be a bit of a stretch if they do?' Howard was watching Freda, watching Luke, and for a moment he thought she hadn't heard him, however, she replied almost immediately whilst keeping her eyes on the defunct groom.

'No, love, I'm sure Tilly wouldn't expect it, not for a moment. And anyway, if me-laddo over there wants a swanky do, this time, his parents can get their hand in their pockets and cough up. Between me and you, I'm beginning to see another side of Luke. Sometimes he acts like a big, stupid kid, not husband material.' Freda turned away from the object of her irritation and placed her hand over Howard's.

'Just look at him, not straight away, Howard, for God's sake, he'll know I'm talking about him! Wait a minute, then just watch and you'll see I'm right. He's not made any effort to speak to my mum or Marianne, or the other guests who've introduced themselves and said hello. All he cares about is his family and friends. He has no manners at all and it's always about him. He knows I've got my eye on him and I swear he's pretending to text her, just to keep me in my box.'

As Freda took a sip of water, Howard obeyed and stole a glance at Luke.

He wasn't really that bothered if Luke was acting like an arse. Maybe there really was such a thing as fate or destiny, but whatever had intervened today had done Howard a favour. One thing was for sure, Freda was bang on the money and there wasn't a cat in hell's chance he'd be stumping up for another wedding.

'Just ignore him for today, love. As far as I'm concerned, the whole family are a bunch of wazzocks so let's not spoil things, eh? Anyway... have I told you enough times yet that you look bloody gorgeous in that frock, I nearly passed out when you came down the stairs. I think you should go shopping with Olivia more often because you look a million dollars, and best of all, you're mine.' Howard leaned over and gave Freda a smacker on the lips and didn't care who saw.

'Yes, my love, you've told me about ten times but don't hold back, a girl can never get enough compliments and by the way, you wouldn't be saying that about Olivia if you knew how much this lot cost, I assure you.'

Seeing Howard's worried expression made Freda giggle, then he waved his hand, telling her it was only money and worth every penny. She also knew that it was the lovely wine doing the talking and he'd be checking his balance first thing in the morning. It was time she took her own advice and gave Tilly a call, it would set her mind at rest if she heard her voice and not just the word of the other's.

It took a few minutes to make her way from the room because her hand was constantly grabbed by guests, telling her they were enjoying the day or saying how lovely she looked. Freda also noticed Hazel and her sister stomp by, noses in the air.

Freda finally managed to make it to the lounge and perched herself on the edge of one of the sofas, she didn't want to crease her dress, even though she was dying to flop into the squashy cushions and relax. Removing her phone from her bag, she tapped Tilly's name and waited for it to connect, however, when it did, it went straight to voicemail. Maybe she'd turned it off and was sleeping, which was a good thing. Freda tried once again but it was the same so she left a message, assuring Tilly they were all okay and having a lovely time but missing her lots, then asked if she'd let her know how she was feeling when she woke up. There was just enough time for a quick wee and a make-up check. As Freda pushed open the door to the ladies she heard a familiar voice inside.

'Never mind feeling sorry for Tilly, what about my Luke and the money we've all wasted trudging over here? If he'd have done what I said and told her he wanted a proper wedding at home then none of this would've happened. This whole place is riddled with germs and from what I hear, everyone's been ill and now I bet we all get it. That's another reason why I'm not eating that French muck, it's probably got salmonella crawling all over it so if you're sick as a dog tomorrow, don't go blaming me. I can't wait to get back on the plane and as far away from here as possible. Hurry up in there will you, I'm bursting out here?' Hazel was in full flow while Freda was riveted to the spot, and on hearing the chain flush, waited curiously for the sister to reply.

'Well, I thought the food was lovely but I see what you mean about it all being a waste of time. And how fortunate that Tilly's parents took over the day? They're obviously so tight they wanted to get their money's worth and hijacked their own daughter's wedding, now that is sad.'

Hazel cackled loudly from inside the cubicle in response to the snide comment.

Freda was livid and actually shaking in her shoes and just about to go inside and massacre them both when she heard Charlotte calling her name. The door was still open, so the women inside were now aware that someone was there, however, Freda didn't want Charlotte to witness two spiteful women being verbally abused then skinned alive, so she stayed where she was, and answered in a loud voice.

'Hello, princess, do you want me? I was just listening to how much everyone is enjoying the wonderful party that *I've* paid for. What's up, are you missing me?' Freda knew they'd heard her because there was now a deathly silence.

'Yes, come on, Grandma, the cakes are here, you should see them, they're just gorgeous. Granddad told me to fetch you because he's going to eat yours if you don't hurry up.' Charlotte grabbed Freda's hand and began dragging her towards Howard and dessert.

By the time she was seated, Freda had composed herself, mostly due to Charlotte's infectious enthusiasm, the rest was down to play acting. How dare Hazel say that? She should've gone in there and given her what for, the cheeky cow! Just wait, she'd make sure they were sorry for the spiteful things they said and give them a few home truths into the bargain, then she'd wipe the sour smiles right off their obnoxious faces! A zillion thoughts pinged through Freda's head as she tried to show enthusiasm for the plate of perfection that had been placed before her, because the dessert truly was a mini work of art.

Michel's finale consisted of a pear and chocolate tart, panacotta with mango sauce and a skewer of fresh fruits dressed with mint and lime. Howard was already halfway through his and eyeing up Freda's puddings in the hope that his wife might be too full to eat them all.

Freda kept the fruit for herself then sliced her two remaining desserts in half and slid them onto Howard's plate causing him to wink and whisper that she really was the perfect wife. Freda had so much information rushing about inside her brain, Susie's plans to return, Tilly all alone at home, Luke the fickle lager lout and not to mention the toilet witches who had really iced the cake with their barbed comments.

In an attempt to fend off any negativity, Freda scanned the room where her eyes settled on Charlotte who had made friends with the *Maire's* granddaughters. They were having an intercontinental giggling fit because Edouard was oblivious to the blob of crème in his beard and they were gleefully watching it bob up and down as he spoke.

Just the sight of Charlotte warmed Freda's heart and it was hard to ignore the image of summers with her and Howard, and Christmases shared with Susie's family. To know that she was a couple of hours away and she'd be able watch her in school plays, not on a video, and take her shopping for clothes when she was a teenager, not just make do with vouchers or money in the post, well it would be wonderful.

Nothing would ever be the same as living in the same town or up the road from Scott and his family but the short distance from here to Bristol didn't feel anywhere near as daunting as the huge gap that the other side of the world represented. It was like a chasm, and Freda remembered that when they first went, she'd had awful dreams where she was stretching out her hand to her son but could never reach him. Their fingertips didn't even touch. What if he needed her? It took so long to get there, spending hours on a plane, trying to reach the other side of the world as quickly as possible would be torture.

If Susie got her way, Freda would be able to reach out to all of them and grab their hands, be there in a flash, not stuck on a plane, wishing it would go faster. She could get home in the time it took some people to commute to work and knowing this would make her sleep easily at night and fill the future with hope and exciting prospects. Maybe she should intervene, bat for Susie's team and tell Scott she missed them all so much. Remind him that having your family close by when they needed you, and you them, was more important than all-year sunshine and barbies on the beach.

Howard's voice broke into her musings and provided her with a welcome break from worrying about her family.

'What shall we do about speeches and all that... do you think everyone will be expecting me to say something? Perhaps I should just thank everyone for their support and say we're sorry about Tilly and Luke's big day being spoilt. What do you think?'

Freda knew full well that Howard had been dreading making his father-of-the bride speech, especially as he'd had to do it in French and English.

'I don't know, love. I've got the feeling that whatever you say about Luke and Tilly, certain people will take the huff or pick holes and I'm not in the mood for sarcasm or snidey looks. I suppose you should just say thank you for coming and all that, just out of politeness. Will you be alright with the French? Don't worry if you make a mistake, most of the English probably won't realise so just keep it short and simple and you'll be fine.'

'I take it you're referring to Luke's family, has something been said?'

'Yes and no, not directly. I overheard Hazel and her

sister having a bitch fest in the toilet. I'll tell you later because I've just managed to calm down. Don't you dare be nice to them in your speech though, in fact, try and leave them out altogether and when you switch to French, tell everyone that the Jackson family are a bunch of arseholes and our daughter might have had a lucky escape today!' Freda could feel the anger rising again and Howard could see it in her face.

'Bloody hell, Freda, she has riled you! Don't worry I'll keep it simple and just for the record, my lover, I can't help agreeing with you. Maybe our Tilly has been given a reprieve today, only a thought mind, so let's not get our hopes up.' And with that, Howard gave Freda a peck on the cheek and a crafty wink.

No matter how hard she tried to ignore it, her heart ached for her daughter and if she was honest, she just wanted to go home and look after her. The whole day had unsettled Freda, despite Howard's best efforts to save it, she couldn't shake away the feeling there was an unpleasant undercurrent caused by the Jackson family. Would the niggles still have been there if the real wedding had gone ahead? Would she have noticed Luke's drinking or over-heard Hazel's spiteful comments?

Freda would never know but one thing was for sure, once Tilly was up and about they shouldn't rush to organise an alternative wedding. No, this time she would wait and see and in the meantime, she'd be telling Tilly exactly what she thought about her joining the Jackson clan and then leave her to it. She might take the huff, or agree, but Freda knew she had to speak out if there was even a slim chance that Tilly might just take a different path and, if they were lucky, it would lead to nicer people than the Jacksons.

Tilly's stomach ached and her muscles were sore but she'd gone a whole two hours without a visit to the loo and her best friend, the bowl, was also taking time out. She was flicking through the photos that Scott had sent her and despite feeling weak and tired, the sight of her mum and dad and little Charlotte managed to lift her spirits and make her smile. She'd looked through them about five times and now, unlike the first time she saw them, they didn't make her cry.

Scott had innocently sent a few of Luke who seemed to be enjoying himself, surrounded by their friends who all looked lovely in their wedding outfits, beaming happily into the camera. Their faces gave her genuine cause to smile, but she purposely averted her gaze from Luke, the last thing she wanted to see in there was sorrow, because even though she didn't love him, she still had some compassion. It was easier not to look, not to go down that road and definitely best to avoid pity which might weaken her resolve and give him a second, second chance.

It was 5pm and Tilly's thoughts now turned to Joe who, in between visits to the loo, she'd managed to text. Even sending the message took about an hour's worth of thinking through, composing the words in her head so as not to say the wrong thing; she stuck to the bare facts about the wedding. She owed it to him. He'd have been imagining her making vows to Luke.

Joe had texted back immediately and as with her message, she sensed he was exercising reserve, keeping things matter of fact, not wanting to gloat or raise hopes. Seeing his words made Tilly feel lonely and in need of human company, not letters on a screen, so she listened to her heart then threw caution to the wind and rang him, eager to hear his voice.

'Hi, are you okay?' Joe spoke before Tilly had chance to speak.

'Well I've had better days but I'm getting there, how are you?' Tilly was smiling, picturing his face.

'I'm fine, just worried about you. Are your mum and dad alright?'

'I think so, they looked happy enough on the photos my brother sent.'

'Oh good... I'm glad you rang, Tilly, I've been dying to hear your voice.'

'Snap... it's cheered me up. Look, Joe, I'm going to have to go soon, I just wanted to hear your voice too... I'll be in touch okay?' Tilly felt the return of a familiar swirl in her stomach.

'That's fine, I understand but ring me if you need me, to talk or anything, promise you will.'

'I promise... I'll have to go... I don't feel too good, take care, Joe.'

'Take care, Tilly, get better soon.'

Tilly disconnected the call and ran to the bathroom, all thoughts of Joe's sun-kissed face forgotten, for now.

Later, messages had been exchanged. Their chat remained practical, within boundaries, a check-up of sorts and once they were sure that the other was okay and assured of love and support, reminded that they were only a text or a call away, they left things there, for another day when their heads were clear and their hearts were sure. Until then, one went off in search of frites and the other made another mad dash along the landing. Despite being miles apart and unsure of what the next few days would bring they had one thing in common, Joe and Tilly could now hold tightly on to hope.

CHAPTER TWENTY-SEVEN

Joe and Sam were chillaxing (a word they'd forbidden their mother ever to use, it just sounded wrong) and drinking beer outside the van whilst doing a bit of star gazing. They'd had their fill of the surf and the local restaurant so decided that before they hit the showers and then the centre of town, they'd have a bit of a tidy up. The camper might have been small, but it was surprising how much mess two men could make within the confined space, and there was definitely something a bit whiffy lurking underneath the piles of T-shirts and trainers. Once they'd made a small degree of difference, which basically entailed stuffing all the dirty clothes in a bin liner and the half-eaten food and containers in another, both thought they deserved a rest. It was imperative they conserved their energy for the rest of the night, which would stretch on into the morning and more than likely find them watching the sunrise from the beach.

Sam was glad Joe had cheered up and, after being sick for a couple of days, was now raring to go. He knew a lot of it had to do with the news from Tilly earlier that day, along with reading the contents of her diary, which had appeased his fragile heart and allowed him to see sense and forgive her. Even though Sam was pleased that, in a roundabout way, Joe had got his wish and the wedding hadn't gone ahead, he'd warned him not to get his hopes up. No matter which way they looked at it, Tilly had yet to pluck up the courage to tell Luke it was over.

Sam really hoped his words had sunk in while at the same time, knew the dreamer in Joe believed in true love and destiny and all that crap, so he let it go and left him in the land of happy ever after. Just because *he* didn't believe and preferred to exist in the here and now, shouldn't mean that Joe had to. But Sam had seen too much horror while he was overseas to invest any faith in fate.

He knew only too well that if you put one foot wrong, in either direction, destiny had no soul and took no prisoners, so he wasn't going to be caught out or leave his future in anyone's hands but his own. It was better that way, for everyone, and it helped him keep a clear head and focus.

His mates had made plans that were ruined, and then they had to deal with their dreams being shattered. Sam remained convinced that his way was best and as long as his mum and the rest of the family were okay, then he'd look after himself. But who was he to put a downer on things for Joe? They came at life from opposite angles and wanted different things entirely. At least now, they could get on with their holiday without feeling like he was dragging an abandoned puppy around with him. Sam intended to have some fun and he also needed a wingman, so Joe had better step up to the mark and get into the swing of things.

After they'd sniffed their half decent looking T-shirts and sprayed them with deodorant (just to be on the safe side) the brothers headed off into the night. Joe felt like his heart was as light as a feather and admitted that it was ages since he'd felt this alive and carefree. That said, there was no way that he'd be taking Sam's lead and spreading some love. Joe was happy to go with the flow, have a few laughs and do as his mum had advised, which was to keep his head down and make the most of being with his brother, because times like these were what memories are made of.

When he'd sent his mum a text earlier, briefly bringing her up to date with the state of affairs and trying to avoid a protracted, deep and meaningful 'Mum Conversation', she'd replied instantly and, like Sam, had advised caution and to allow things to play out without his interference.

For now, he'd been appointed squadron leader to the wing commander up ahead, so he'd better get his finger out and support him, not that Sam needed much help but there was no harm in soaking up the party atmosphere and the company of their new friends. His mum was right, times like these were precious and Sam had always stood by him, so now he'd return the favour and make sure he didn't end up face down in the sand (again) and when they got home, they'd both have a bank full of shared, if rather blurry, memories.

* * *

Sunday morning started just like many others had, except this time Freda was a newly remarried bride, living in a house that looked like a bomb had hit it. The mad rush to get ready yesterday had left the kitchen and lounge strewn with unwashed bowls and dishes, clothes scattered every-where and what looked like the remains of an abandoned hair salon dotted around most of the surfaces. As she sipped her coffee, Freda's eyes fell onto the bowl that held Tilly's bouquet of white roses and beside it, one of the fresh table arrangements that Freda had brought home as a reminder of the day. The rest of them had been given to their nice guests to take home, which meant Hazel and her sister got nothing.

Charlotte and the other children went away with hand-fuls of balloons and purses full of glittery stars and sweets, not to mention little boxes of wedding cake. Despite the happy faces as they waved goodbye, along with the heartfelt thank-yous she received at the end of the night, Freda couldn't help feeling deflated and sad. The anticlimax was compounded by the stark fact that in the end, it had all been for nothing. No matter how hard she'd tried to jolly herself along or throw herself into making the most of it, there had been a lump of something gloomy weighing heavily in her chest and even now, she couldn't rid herself of it. While she gently stacked pots in the sink and squirted cleaning fluid onto the worktops, Freda's mind wandered back to the previous day.

* * *

Once the food had been eaten, Michel had made his customary entrance into the restaurant and as was tradition, the diners gave him a huge round of grateful applause and he took a gracious bow. Howard insisted on him having a seat and sharing a drink with them while he made a toast and a very short speech. He thanked everyone for coming, expressing his sorrow that his beautiful daughter was so poorly and even though their plans had been dashed, he had somehow benefited from the unfortunate turn of events. He told the hushed gathering that he had been honoured that Freda said yes the first time round, but to be able to marry his one true love again and affirm the vows that had bound them together, made him the happiest man alive.

After the cheers and wiping of tearful eyes, Howard announced that he had a little gift for a special girl and asked Charlotte to come up to the front, where Freda passed her a beautifully wrapped box, which she claimed excitedly and whizzed back to her seat to open. Next, he called on Stacey who he thanked for travelling all that way to support Tilly and for her little rallying speech in the kitchen. She accepted her hugs and gift box then made her way back to her seat (strategically chosen by Freda) right next to Claude, the *Maire's* rather handsome son who was on leave from the navy. Howard then gestured to Luke that he should come up to the front and take over, which was a mistake because it was quite clear that standing was a big ask and when he staggered around the tables, holding on to the backs of chairs for support, Freda cringed and wanted the floor to open up on his behalf.

He finally made it to the front where Howard passed him the gift that was meant for Darren, however, for some reason, Luke thought was for him and stuck it straight in his pocket before slurring something which sounded like thank you. Howard loved every minute as the unworthy buffoon who'd once broken his daughter's heart, swayed precariously in front of him. Smiling broadly, he then handed Luke a very large pot of red chrysanthemums who slowly, set off on legs made of elastic, trying to focus and reach his mother's table, this time, unable to hold on to anything due to his cumbersome floral arrangement. Everyone was made to feel uncomfortable yet equally engrossed by the spectacle of Luke as he bumped into the backs of chairs, then took a wrong turn and had to retrace his steps as he gazed drunkenly about the room in search of his parents. When he finally located Hazel (who looked suitably ashamed) he ungraciously thrust the flowers into her hands before shuffling to his seat and semi-collapsing in a chair.

There was a ruffle of embarrassed clapping from the English contingent as the bemused French guests looked at one another quizzically, then everyone made their way onto the terrace for some fresh air. While the locals subtly asked amongst themselves as to why the groom had given his mother flowers of death, the dining room was cleared and the DJ made his preparations, and Freda finally managed a word with Olivia who looked most amused.

'My darling Freda, how glad you must be not to have been given a potted funeral plant *and* how glad am I that we had our little shopping spree? You look absolutely divine and I couldn't have picked a more beautiful outfit for your wedding day if I'd tried. You look superb, the belle of the ball and it knocked spots off Hazel's outfit, not to mention her ridiculous hat. Anyone would think she's entered the

Easter bonnet parade. What was she thinking?' Olivia was holding Freda's hand as she spoke quite loudly, not caring who heard her.

'Thanks, Olivia. The flowers were mine and Tilly's idea of a little joke, but I think that Luke is turning out to be the prize fool today. But as for my outfit, you know that's all I could think of as I got ready. What on earth would I have looked like in that awful dress? I swear I'd have said no to Howard for that reason alone, but as it was, I felt like a million dollars. Howard loves it and thinks I look amazing, which is all I needed to hear really. And don't even mention that awful Hazel to me, she's a spiteful cow and so is her sister.' Freda could feel two hot spots on her cheeks and had to force herself not to swear in front of royalty.

'Why, what on earth has she said? Come on, let's go for a little stroll and you can tell me all about it while I get some air. All that champers is making me sleepy and I believe we're going to have a bit of a dance soon so I need to wake up, here, heave me off this chair.' Olivia stretched out her hand and Freda pulled her upwards, then they set off, arm in arm towards the garden.

Needless to say, Olivia had assured Freda that all the guests were full of admiration and compassion for both her and Howard and fully understood why they'd taken their course of action. Olivia had also been observing the Jackson clan and had come to the conclusion they were an unhappy bunch, incapable of generosity, whether it be emotional or financial and were blatantly envious of everything Howard and Freda stood for.

Olivia surmised that in England, the only functions they attended were in a professional capacity in order to crawl their way up the social ladder and they probably never got invited to private affairs because they were just too obnoxious. For that reason, it would've irritated the hell out of Hazel to see all of Freda's friends congratulate her on the beautiful reception and as for the comments about the food, well that was just plain ignorance speaking.

By the time they'd done a circuit of the hotel, Freda felt

cleansed and was going to take Olivia's advice and not confront Hazel. It was better to let them stew in their own poisonous juices while you got on with life in a nicer world, one where your son doesn't get drunk and show you up in front of a group of strangers for a start! Freda laughed and agreed, apart from one thing. She would be having a word with Luke about his drinking. The last thing she wanted was Tilly being saddled with a drunken, two-timing, self-obsessed waste of space. And if he didn't like it, he could lump it!

Freda had stayed until the dancing was underway and then used her mother as a perfect excuse to retire for the night. Once they'd said their goodbyes, the bride and bridegroom left the building and took Grandma Betty home for a cup of tea and some wedding cake. Even though Betty looked tired, she was on fine form as she described the whole day in great detail to Tilly who was enthralled.

Freda took comfort in seeing true happiness in her daughter's eyes, that was until Betty got on to the subject of Luke and his drinking habits.

'I'm telling you now, Tilly Parker, that lad has got problems... you mark my words. And if he carries on in his ways, then you'll be wed to a drunk, and that's no fun for anybody, my love, and you deserve better. I know of plenty of men like that, throwing ale down their throat afore they turn nasty and it's always the lass that gets a thump. I don't want that for you, so you'd best have a word afore me or your mum does it for you.' Betty drank her tea and helped herself to some more cake, she never minced her words especially when something as important as Tilly's happiness was at stake.

'Was he really that bad, Grandma? He doesn't drink that much at home, but he does go a bit silly if he's out with his mates and always comes home really drunk, but by then I'm in bed so it doesn't affect me. Don't worry yourself though, as soon as I get the chance I'll be having words with Luke about that and a few other things, one of them being his mother. And just because Mum let her off with the awful things she said, I won't, I can promise you that.' Tilly saw her grandma nod and was livid that Hazel had disrespected her mum.

Freda yawned. It had been a long day. 'Well, I expect Luke and his hangover will turn up tomorrow at some point so you can save telling him off till then. You look a bit better than you did, anyway. I think you got off lightly compared to me and your dad. Are you sure you don't want some toast or cereal, you must be starving?'

'Not a chance! The only thing passing these lips will be water and the thought of food still makes me want to throw up. I'll be fine, Mum, honest. I just need some sleep and I've still got cramps in my stomach so I'm not risking it.' Tilly was exhausted and knew her parents and grandma were too, and no doubt she'd be woken by the returning party-goers at some point so was happy to lie on the sofa and rest until they turned up.

'Right, well if you're sure, I think it's time we all called it a night. Come on, Mum, I'll help you up the stairs. Howard, I'll leave you to wash the pots and can you get Tilly some fresh water. Night, my love, sleep well but shout me if you feel poorly again. I doubt Stacey will be fit for much when she gets in so I'm here if you need me.' Freda gave Tilly a bear hug and a kiss on the forehead then shepherded Betty from the room.

Tilly was left alone with Howard who was in a sombre mood.

'You've been very quiet, Dad. Is everything alright or have you overindulged too and don't want Mum to know? I won't tell, I swear.' Tilly winked at her dad who seemed thoughtful.

Howard was on the verge of saying something when they heard the back door rattle then voices in the kitchen.

'I'm fine, love, just a bit tired that's all. Don't you worry about me.' Before he had chance to say anymore, they were joined by Scott, Susie and Charlotte, all eager to share the highlights of the day, no matter how tired or infectious Tilly might be.

Howard made a swift exit before he ended up making more tea and coffee and hoped that someone else would wash the pots, otherwise Freda would have his guts for garters in the morning. What he had to say to Tilly could wait. There was no rush, it would take time to organise another wedding, big or small and by then he hoped that she'd see sense and get rid of the little creep once and for all. There were plenty more fish in the sea and Tilly just needed a bigger net to catch someone decent, because as far as he was concerned, the one she had now should have been bashed on the head and chucked over the side a long time ago.

* * *

Tilly was stuck right in the middle of a really awkward situation and hadn't the foggiest idea how to get out of it. It was mid-afternoon and after a big lie in and lazy morning, the Parker family were enjoying one of Freda's French style, mezze feasts and preparing to say bon voyage to Stacey and Darren who were getting a late flight home. Tilly had managed some bread and was sticking to water so as not to aggravate her stomach. It was a pity that the same couldn't be said for her brain because Luke was seriously grating on her and had been ever since he arrived in a taxi earlier.

The topic of conversation had turned to plans for the future and when Marianne mentioned rebooking the wedding, wondering when and where it was likely to be, Tilly wanted to lean over and ram the balls of croque en bouche right down her throat. Her dad rode to her rescue by joking that he'd have to start doing the Lotto or sell one of his kidneys, which everyone laughed off.

When her Aunty Caroline brought up the honeymoon, Tilly looked to Stacey for backup but having already heard her views she understood why her best friend remained neutral and silent. Still, a teeny bit of support wouldn't have gone amiss because Tilly was desperately trying to think of a bona fide excuse why she shouldn't go away with Luke.

Stacey, forthright as ever, had brought the subject up that morning while they lay under their duvets and even though the mention of it made Tilly squirm, it was something that had to be faced before long. Soon, Luke was going to turn up with his cases packed and expect to head off into the sunset with her by his side.

To everyone gathered around the garden table it was a foregone conclusion that she and Luke would just pick up where they left off and head south for a week in the sun. After all, they both deserved a holiday, now more than ever, even though they should already be on their way.

Freda was urging Tilly to set off as soon as possible and not waste time, mainly because after yesterday's disappointment, she wanted her daughter to relax and be pampered at the luxury hotel by the sea. Howard said nothing at all which clearly irritated the hell out of his wife, while Marianne thought Tilly was being a wimp, assuring her she'd be fine because the virus was almost gone and if she felt ill she could always be sick out of the car window, simple.

Even Grandma Betty wanted her to get some sea air – apparently it cured everything, apart from the after-effects of binge drinking, a remark which was accompanied by a look of pure disgust and aimed in Luke's direction. Stacey and Susie tittered at the slight and then Charlotte asked loudly what a binge was, only to be told to be quiet by Scott who was trying not to laugh at his grandma's barbed comment.

Tilly was in a dilemma. The last place she wanted to be was with Luke in the sodding bridal suite or worse, trapped in a car with him for five long hours on the journey down. Her only alternative was to end it right here and now, today. They weren't married so she had no need to carry on with the charade, therefore she could just take him to one side, sit him down and say she wanted a cooling-off period, time to think and find herself, that type of corny rubbish. It was more or less what she was going to say when they were on their honeymoon, she'd just bring forward the moment of doom.

The only sticking point was her well-meaning family. Imagine the hoo-ha when Luke announced to them all that he'd been dumped the day after his wedding had crashed and burned. They'd all feel sorry for him and she'd look like the bitch queen from hell, besides, all his family had left and he'd be alone with no support.

Maybe Stacey was right, as usual, and she should endure the drive down by pretending to be asleep for most of the journey then, at some point, and let's face it there'd only be five days left by the time they got there, she could cause a row about something and nothing then get it over and done with. It all sounded so manipulative and at the same time, relatively simple and tempting. As she looked around the table Tilly knew she'd have to go, there was no way she could dump him here in front of the bloody Waltons.

'I suppose you're right. I feel ten times better than yesterday, so I might make it without any accidents in the car and not infect you, at the same time. We could set off first thing in the morning if you want. It's your call, Luke.' Tilly thought it was worth one more shot and that the image of sick and poo on his leather upholstery might put him off once and for all.

'I reckon if I'm going to get it, then it's in my system now and I might as well be ill in five-star luxury than stuck at that bed and breakfast place, or at home. Anyway, it cost me a bomb and I won't get my money back so I think we should get going as soon as possible. Why don't we drop Darren and Stacey off at the airport later tonight then carry on driving for a couple of hours? We can stay in a motel then set off early, that way we'd be there by lunchtime. Do you think you'll be up to it by this evening?' Luke looked hopeful.

To Tilly's annoyance, he received unexpected support from Freda who added her ten pence worth.

'That's a great idea, what do you think, Tilly? You've

managed to keep your bread down so maybe you'll be fine, and it would be so nice to know you were heading off for a little holiday and I'm sure Luke will take extra special care of you, won't you, Luke?'

There was definitely an ominous threat hidden somewhere amongst Freda's question, which wasn't lost on the rest of the family or Luke, who wisely took the hint.

'Course I will, Freda, she'll be in good hands I promise. So, is that a deal, babes?' Luke seemed sincere, however, Tilly knew full well that he was capable of charming the birds off the trees in order to get what he wanted, and she really hated him calling her babes – the prat!

'Yes, that's a deal. I'd best get cracking and sort out my suitcase, do you want to come and help me pack, Stace? I won't be long, Mum, then I can spend some time with you all before I go.' Tilly was unable to continue because for some reason her neck felt tight and her eyes were misting over with hot tears and she knew she was going to cry.

Freda spotted her daughter's face immediately and jumped out of her seat and came to her aid, folding her in her arms and trying to soothe her as best she could.

'Now, now, Tilly, there's no need for tears, you're just overemotional and worn out, come on, let us girls go inside and help you pack and make sure you're organised. It's been a funny twenty-four hours, love, and I'm not surprised you feel like this.' Freda let go and wiped away Tilly's tears.

They were soon surrounded by Grandma Betty who did the arm rubbing thing while Susie hugged Tilly tightly and soon, she was being led inside, followed by Charlotte who considered herself to be one of the big girls. The men found themselves left alone at the table where a strange and uncomfortable silence had settled, which Scott felt duty bound to break with a weak joke about hormones, swerving the ball and chain and escaping the in-laws.

Everyone laughed along, apart from Howard who remained silent and was fighting the urge to march in there and demand a quiet word with his daughter who quite obviously didn't want to go on holiday – or anywhere – with Luke.

Could nobody else see that? Was Freda blind or just so racked with guilt and disappointment that she presumed a week by the sea would make everything right? And as for Luke, all he cared about was topping up his fake tan and not losing out on a holiday he'd actually forked out for, which was a bloody first!

Well, it was all agreed now and there was no point in him kicking up a fuss and getting an ear full from Freda, but something was definitely up with Tilly, he just knew it! Howard slid back his chair and announced he was going to get himself a beer, he didn't offer to bring anybody else one and once inside, took himself and his bottle into the lounge for a bit of peace and quiet where he indulged in a well-earned, great big man-sulk.

* * *

Joe was doing his best not to let his imagination run riot, or allow the demons in his head to unsettle him and wreak havoc with his heart. He would just sit here and work it through and try not to jump to conclusions.

When Tilly's text came through, his heart had almost stopped when he read the message which was short, factual and apologetic. It could have been worse, but at least she hadn't changed her mind, yet the fact remained that instead of getting it over with and ending things, she'd actually stuck to her original plan and set off for Juan les Pins.

Joe's pessimistic theory was that she felt sorry for Luke but this scenario only conjured up unhelpful and quite frankly distressing images of them both in the honeymoon suite, consummating their non-marriage, which left him shaking with rage. It was sheer torture but he had to endure it and be patient. For now, all he could do was sit there and watch the screen like an idiot, waiting for it to light up.

He chastised himself for being so gullible. He was sick and tired of riding the waves, up one minute, then down at rock bottom, the next. All he wanted was a nice, simple life, work hard, play hard (but no where near as hard as Sam) maybe find somewhere of his own to live and someone to share it with. How difficult did it have to be for God's sake and why was life so unfair?

He'd tried to do what was expected of him. He never got in trouble and flogged himself to death at the haulage yard to honour his dad's legacy. He looked after his mum and family and never treated any girl badly or cheated on them, apart from Debbie Jones in year eleven but she soon got over him and was married to a Southampton footballer now, so was probably glad in the end.

Joe knew he was obsessing but prepared a 'being let down and not giving a toss speech' as a contingency, when his phone buzzed, bleeped and flashed all at the same time and nearly gave him a heart attack. He grabbed it off the floor and had swiped the screen within milliseconds, eager to read the message.

Hi, are you awake? I'm so sorry it's taken ages to get in touch but I had to wait till he was asleep. We are in a Formule 1 just outside Bordeaux and before you worry, I'm on the bottom bunk, he's on the top. I swear he is terrified of catching my bug so I suggested he slept up there, and YES, I've played my get out of jail card so he won't be coming anywhere near me, okay!! I know you are wondering why I came with him but it was too cringy to get out of, everyone was saying we deserved a break and I just couldn't dump him with my family around. Just try and imagine being in the same situation, try to understand. It was better to get away and deal with it alone. We should arrive at the hotel around midday so if you don't hear from me don't worry. I'll make contact, I promise. If I were you, there'd be loads of stuff going round in my head but please, Joe, you have got to believe that it's you I want to be with and I will sort this out. Just trust me. I'm going to sleep now. I don't want him to catch me talking to you. I hope you're okay and I really miss you so much. I'll speak to you sometime tomorrow.

Night night, love you, Tilly xxx

. . .

Joe smiled like a fool as he reread the words then sent a quick message back.

Hi, I was worried but I trust you and understand now why you had to go. I hate it that you seem to be moving further away from me, not closer. I know it's hard for you so I'm not going to pressure you in any way. Ring me if you need me and I don't give a shit if he finds out about me – we can deal with it together. Anyway, I'll be thinking of you 24/7. You get some kip and I'll wait for you to get in touch. Love you too – night xxx

PS Have you got any penicillin in your nurse's bag cos I think Sam might need a shot before we go home?

Tilly giggled quietly and even though she should try and sleep, couldn't resist texting back. Joe was right, they did seem to be moving further away and knowing he was there, connected by some magic world of binary and the internet, made her feel safe and happy.

Instead of sleeping, from their respective beds, Tilly and Joe spent the next few hours sending messages back and forth, one from their mobile home by the sea and the other from under the covers of a motel bunk bed.

By the time the morning came and Sam wandered back to the camper, bedraggled and ready for a well-earned rest, all was well in his brother's world. Along with affirming their belief and feelings for one another, Joe and Tilly had compiled a joint bucket list of things to do and places to see. It was comfortingly harmonious and symbolised that finally, despite the strangest of circumstances, they had both found 'the one'.

CHAPTER TWENTY-EIGHT

Rosie was exhausted but *so* glad to be out of the house where she'd been trapped for the past forty-eight hours. It was exhausting caring for Sabine and Odette who had both succumbed to the virus that had lain waste to her weekend, most of their bed linen and about ten rolls of toilet paper. It couldn't have been helped and even though it drove her mad thinking of what was going on at the hotel, her first priority was the girls and they needed their mama more than the guests and the bride did.

When she took the call from Ruby saying that it had all gone belly up because Tilly was ill, Rosie's heart sank and her suspicious mind went into overdrive, wondering if, in the end, she hadn't been able to go through with it. Then came the second call, saying it was back on and the parents of the bride were getting married instead so it was all systems go. Rosie was over the moon and relieved that Michel would get to serve up his feast and their staff wouldn't have to be sent home.

The girls were much better now and Rosie felt comfortable enough to leave them with her mother-in-law and had escaped to the hotel. Mondays were always busy. She'd just finished clearing away the remains of breakfast and was re-laying the tables for later that evening, completely lost in a world of her own, when Océane, her faithful helper popped her head around the door. A few minutes later, they were seated at one of the tables enjoying fresh coffee and a break from their chores, when Rosie requested a blow by blow, female version of the wedding day events, because Michel's was so boring, gossip-free and all about the food.

'Did you enjoy it then, even though it looked like it was going to be a disaster at first? Ruby said it all went according to plan and you'd never have known, apart from the bride and groom had been swapped.' Rosie was so grateful to have such a dedicated team around her.

'Yes, this is true but I think it was a good thing that the real bride had the maladie because if Tilly had married that awful man, her life will be ruined forever.' Océane may have only been eighteen but she spoke with certainness and an air of worldly wisdom.

'Why, did you not take to him then? I only met him a couple of times and that was very briefly. He wasn't rude to you, was he?'

Rosie was responding to Océane's dramatic expression and raised eyebrows, who then looked from side to side, just to check they couldn't be overheard before continuing in a hushed, serious tone. As she did, a sense of foreboding overcame Rosie.

'No, he was not rude to me, but his horrible friend had the hands of le poulpe, if you know what I mean. I had to give him the hard warning on the end.' Océane wore a disgusted expression as she spoke.

'Well, as long as you put him in his place, and I've had my fair share of octopus hands while I've been waitressing, I assure you. Oh, and it's the *hard word* and *in the end*, just so you know.'

Rosie was under strict orders from Océane to always correct her English whenever she made a mistake, a favour she regularly returned when Rosie spoke incorrect French.

'But apart from his friend being a creep, why would

Tilly's life be ruined if she married Luke, I don't understand?'

Océane pulled her chair a little bit closer and leant over the table, towards Rosie, and whispered conspiratorially while enjoying being the bearer of first-hand, hot gossip.

'Normand has told me a big secret which is very shocking! He was working at the bar on the day that Luke and the octopus arrived, and in the evening they drank so much beer that their tongues became loose in their mouths, like the wagging dogs! Luke's phone was ringing all the time but he did not answer at first, then his friend tells him he should speak because it was going on his nerves. Luke went outside and when he was gone the octopus told Normand that the person on the phone is the girlfriend of Luke, he has been having the affaire!'

When Rosie gasped, Océane paused for dramatic effect then continued.

'The octopus thought it was a big joke and when Luke came back, they were both laughing and saying very rude things. Luke had photographs on his phone and he showed them to Normand and all I can tell you is this woman has no pride and obviously, no clothes! They were so drunk that they told Normand everything. Naturally, because he is a man he had a good look at the pictures of the naked woman, but still, he thought it was very shocking. He told me all about it on the day of the wedding while we were having our rest. I have been waiting since then to see you because I think Tilly should know and *you* will have to tell her. We cannot let her make a big mistake with this horrible man.' Océane looked at her boss expectantly, waiting for her to rise to the challenge and defend Tilly's honour.

Rosie was completely dumbfounded and having trouble gathering all the thoughts inside her frazzled brain. Once over the initial shock, she managed to ask Océane if she was completely sure of all the facts and that there was no possibility that Normand could've got it wrong. When her informant imparted the gory details of what Luke had told Normand, in particular an explicit summary of her attributes and acrobatic prowess in the bedroom department, it was apparent that Normand couldn't possibly have made it up, but then again, why would he?

Part of Rosie suddenly wished she had stayed at home with the girls and gone stir crazy because now, she was in the possession of explosive information and no matter how much she tried to ignore the evidence she would have to pass it on. The question was, to whom? There was no way she could just ring Tilly up, she didn't have the bottle and the same went for Freda who'd already had enough drama and disappointment for one weekend. This would be the last straw.

Océane then informed Rosie that when he checked out, the octopus mentioned that Tilly and Luke were heading south for their 'honeymoon'. What a mess!

Then it occurred to Rosie if nothing else, Tilly had a cast iron reason to dump Luke once and for all and the revelation might be a blessing in disguise. She felt so sorry for the poor girl who had gone to hell and back, worrying about letting everyone down and now it turned out that it was for nothing. Her fiancé was a two-timing scumbag.

There was no doubt about it, Tilly had to know and Rosie didn't fancy doing the deed, or telling Freda so in the absence of hearing it from her own mother, who could be relied on to say it kindly? Then it came to her. She knew exactly who to tell and how to get a message to Tilly, in a way that might just kill two birds with one almighty stone.

* * *

Anna and Daniel had just returned from a long walk and were now enduring the silent treatment from Pippa. She was sitting in the garden by herself, just like she'd been all afternoon following her unnecessary and downright cruel abandonment!

Anna peered out of the window at her moody dog and

418

spoke to Daniel. 'Honestly, I swear that animal is part human and knows how to push my buttons. Anyone would think she'd been dumped at the dog's home the way she carries on, here, give her some of this ham on your way past otherwise she might ring Dogline and report us.'

Anna passed Daniel a large slice of Jambon de Paris as he laughed and rolled his eyes, even he felt awful whenever they left her but it was far too hot to take Pippa on a long hike. 'She'll soon come sloping in when she smells food cooking, she might be stubborn but she's not daft! I'll go and find us a bottle of something special to go with our dinner then see if I can coax her in, and you ought to ring Rosie. I can tell you're dying to find out what her urgent message is… so am I if I'm honest.' Daniel gave Anna a peck on the cheek before wandering into the garden to make peace with a huffy bulldog.

Anna closed the fridge door and picked up her phone. She was intrigued by the missed calls and the text, urging her to ring Rosie as she had something REALLY important to tell her. As Anna pressed the button and let it ring out, she hoped it wasn't about Tilly's cancelled wedding because she already knew that. She'd received a short, restrained message from Joe who had probably danced a jig when he'd found out.

When Rosie picked up, she sounded relieved then asked if Anna was sitting comfortably because she had a bit of tale to tell her.

'What a mess! The poor girl. And I take it she's still none the wiser and has gone on honeymoon with a total shit who is still carrying on with this woman? What are we going to do? She needs to know, Rosie, somebody has to tell her.' Anna was incensed and her heart went out to Tilly who was undoubtedly heading for a second dose of embarrassment and heartache.

'Well, that's where you come in… I'm not going to do it. It's not like she's my best friend or anything, she's really just a client. I don't think it's my place to ring her up and dish the dirt.' Rosie waited for Anna to mull it over.

'I agree, it's not the type of thing anyone wants to hear or pass on for that matter, but what do you mean, where I come in? I can't tell her! You should ring her mum and dad.' Anna's voice had gone up a notch and her cheeks were burning with the stress of it all.

'No, I wouldn't dream of getting you to tell her, but Joe could. We both know the situation there and he's the closest person to her, apart from her mum and I really don't think it's fair to distress her at this stage. It's a private matter for Tilly to sort out. If you told Joe, maybe he could ring her and break it to her gently then let her deal with it her way. Not only that, he'd be a shoulder to cry on at the same time... do you see where I'm coming from?' Rosie was glad she'd unburdened herself of the secret and had passed the responsibility on to Anna and perversely, paved the way for Joe.

'Yes, I think you're right. Joe could tell her kindly, if that's even possible, and then when she's got her head round it and in her own time, she can confront Luke or speak to her mum and dad. You are so wise, Rosie. I'd have got my knickers in a twist about all this and not known what to do. I'll ring him now and tell him. That poor girl, she's going to feel so humiliated, you know? I've been there and got the T-shirt and it's awful. I just wish she was here and with her family who could look after her, not in the bloody South of France with that toerag.' Anna's mind was delving into the past and her heart, as always, felt the aftershock.

'I know that, Anna, and that's why I knew you'd want to help and not let Tilly be made a fool of any longer. Joe's a sensible lad, he's kind and in love with Tilly so I'm sure he will do what's right in the best way possible. Make the call and then leave it in his hands.'

'I will, and I'll let you know what he decides to do and all that. I'll just explain to Daniel what's going on and check he thinks we're doing the right thing. You know I don't like to make rash decisions and I'll be up all night worrying about it otherwise. You relax and leave it with me, I'll ring you later.' Anna saw Daniel pass by the window so after saying her goodbyes, hung up and went into the kitchen to meet him, hoping he'd agree and not say they were interfering, which was usually his retort.

Daniel said it was a no-brainer because Tilly had to be told, no matter how much it was going to sting. He wavered a little at first and toyed with the idea of telling her parents but in the end, they both tried to imagine how awful they would feel having to tell their own children something like that, and agreed that a third party was probably the gentler option. As Daniel opened the dusty bottle of wine he'd brought from his cave, Anna went back into the lounge and picked up her phone.

By the time Anna had explained the reason for her call, Joe's heart was hammering in his chest once again as his blood pumped furiously through his veins. His brain was scrambled by a million thoughts, most of them murderous, some of them sad and incredulous, yet he couldn't ignore those that were elated and running away with the possibilities the situation now presented.

'Mum, are you completely, one hundred percent sure you've got this right? There is no way I can risk telling Tilly any of this unless it's all true. Can you imagine what will happen if it's a load of bollocks? She will hate me forever and Luke will probably kick my head in!'

'We are as sure as we can be, love.'

'I can't believe he's done it to her again, and it's like he's really making a fool of her this time, bragging about it the night before the wedding. The guy is unbelievable. I don't think I can tell her, Mum, I'll feel so bad just saying it.' Joe was in turmoil, half of him wanted to ring Tilly there and then and give her the bullet for the gun, while the other half imagined her lovely, innocent face and how her heart would feel once he'd said the words. She would be humiliated.

'I know, love, being the messenger is always tricky, but if

you really do have feelings for Tilly, then you owe her the truth. Why don't you think about it? If you need to talk, we'll be here, is that okay?'

'That's fine, Mum, Sam's on his way back now so I'll talk it through with him and get back to you soon. Thanks for telling me, I know you mean well and only want to help. I'll get off now if that's okay? Love you, Mum.'

'Okay, catch you later, say hi to Sam for me. I wish I could give you a hug, Tilly too for that matter. Bye, son, take care, love you.' Anna heard Joe say he loved her too, and then he was gone.

Sam and Joe were sitting on the terrace of a beach front bar, waiting for their food to arrive. They'd talked through the 'Tilly Situation' and both agreed that she needed to know about Luke, still the question remained, how should Joe tell her?

'What you've got to do is put yourself in her shoes and imagine how you'd feel if someone gave you the same news, would you want to be told verbally or sent a text? Maybe a message would be the best option, then she might not feel so stupid, you get me?' Sam spotted the waiter on his way over with their meal and picked up his knife and fork in anticipation.

'If I got a text like that, there'd be a million questions I'd want to ask, so I suppose I'd want a phone call. I think I'll ring her then I can reassure her the facts are right because she still might not believe it.'

'Oh, I think she'll believe you alright, he's got form and let's face it, she's got a cracking reason to dump him now. I reckon you're giving her the golden ticket to freedom. Trust me, mate, she will know he's guilty and I can guarantee that you won't have to do much persuading.' Sam was sprinkling salt onto his frites and squirting tomato ketchup everywhere.

'In an ideal world I'd rather tell her face to face, then at least I'd be able to comfort her if she got upset.'

'Yeah, I bet you would.' Sam gave Joe a cheeky grin then stuffed chips into his mouth.

'I meant that I'd make sure she knew I wasn't gloating or anything. Don't get me wrong, I'm sort of glad the creep has been found out but I still don't like the thought of her being feeling sad and isolated. I know I would.'

Joe set about stabbing his chips in a half-hearted fashion and felt totally miserable, until Sam came up with a crazy idea.

'Well, if that's how you'd rather tell her, then let's go and give Tilly the news straight from the horse's mouth, we can go on a road trip... where exactly is she, is it far from here?'

Joe looked up quickly from his plate and gave his mad brother a quizzical look before replying.

'Yes it's far away, she's in the South of France. I think it's near Nice. There's no way we can drive all that way in the van, it'd probably explode!'

'Get the route on your phone, go on, have a look and see how many miles away it is. How big is France anyway? It's not like we're in America or Russia... you do the maths, I'll eat my chips.'

Sam winked at Joe who wasn't sure if he was kidding or not, but pulled out his phone and got on with Googling the route.

'It's flaming miles away, look... eight hundred kilometres. That's at least a day's drive in the van. What about the train, that'll be loads quicker?' Joe had turned the screen to face Sam who was nodding in agreement with a mouth full of bread.

After a few seconds of surfing, Joe discovered they'd have to change trains a few times and it would take seventeen hours, so the TGV was a non-starter. However, if they caught a plane from Bordeaux airport, they could be in Nice in one hour twenty minutes. It was a no-brainer.

As usual, Sam was up for an adventure and already weighing up the advantages of a cheeky trip to the Côte d'Azur. 'Well, I'm up for it if you are, but you can cough up for the tickets. It's about time you spent some of that executive wage you've got stashed away and if I'm riding shotgun, I need danger money too. I can use it at the casino in Monte Carlo.' Sam was smiling and rubbing his hands together in glee.

'What do you mean casino, we're going on a serious mission here so where does Monte Carlo and gambling fit into the plan?'

'Come on, amigo, lighten up, this is stage three of our lad's holiday and I must say it's all working out brilliantly. We can't go all that way and not make the most of it. Once we've dished the dirt, we can hole up in Monte Carlo or Nice and check out the babes who I swear are like supermodels. I've seen them on the Grand Prix and I'm talking well FIT! Then we can see the sights and have a gander at all the flash cars and try our hand in a casino or two, come on, mate, it'll be a laugh. We only need to stay one night and I reckon we can pack quite a bit of partying into twenty-four hours, we don't even need to get a hotel, who needs sleep? We can leave the van at the airport then pick it up when we get back... are you feeling this or are you on the verge of wimping out. You're going to bottle it aren't you?'

Sam had clearly convinced himself by this point that it was a class idea and was raring to go, whereas Joe still looked a bit unsure.

'You do realise that if we actually manage to find Tilly there is a strong possibility we might bump into Luke as well and he ain't going to be pleased to see us, that's for sure. Especially when he finds out why we're there. He's a big bloke you know, what if he gets violent?' Joe was being serious and didn't fancy a punch up. Fighting wasn't his style.

His brother, however, had no such qualms and looked totally unfazed by the prospect.

'Mate, take a look at these beauties.' Sam flexed his biceps (which were enormous) making Joe laugh and relax a little.

'You've got your very own personal bodyguard trained by none other than Her Majesty's Armed Forces, so what's there to worry about? I'm not scared of Luke, take it from me, I've dealt with bigger, uglier blokes than him, so take a chill pill and book the flights… you know you want to!' Sam waved, trying to attract the waiter's attention while he gave Joe time to man up.

'Okay, let's do this! Mum's going to freak when she finds out, do you reckon we should tell her before or after we get there?'

Sam replied instantly. 'After!'

Joe began tapping away at his phone, eager to get the flights booked and now he was fired up, didn't care if the cheap tickets on the low-cost airline actually cost a bomb because as long as he found Tilly and rescued her from Luke, they'd be worth every penny. It only took a few minutes and by the time Sam had ordered three giant ice cream sundaes, they were both booked on the midday flight the following day. After a bit more research, they discovered that Juan les Pins was about half an hour from Nice airport and Monte Carlo was the same distance in the opposite direction. If all went well and they both didn't end up in jail, or A&E, they could spend a night posing with the in-crowd. While Sam turned his thoughts to practicalities, like the fact that neither of them had any clean clothes and a mad dash to the launderette was required, Joe was off with the fairies.

He wasn't exactly wearing a suit of armour and riding a trusty white steed into the sunset, but you get the picture. When he pulled himself together, he told himself not to expect miracles or count on getting the girl there and then. He was going to deliver a message and offer support, nothing more. He also suspected Sam might not be too pleased to have a third member of the gang tagging along, so the best thing was to play it by ear and see how things unfolded.

The most important thing was to get some clothes washed and dried by morning and then try to work out what the hell they were going to tell their mum, who would not be happy with their plan. Not happy at all.

CHAPTER TWENTY-NINE

Joe now understood what it meant when they said in the movies that someone was 'wired' because an incredible energy was pumping through his veins, crackling like electricity and powering him on. He hadn't experienced a shred of nerves since they jumped into a taxi at Nice airport and as they raced through the midday traffic, the thrill and momentum were making him feel sort of invincible.

Sam was loving every minute of their adventure and in truth, was the brains of the duo and had orchestrated much of their plan of action, priming Joe on what to say before he rang Rosie. All he had to do was keep the conversation light and ask if she knew the name of the hotel where Tilly was staying. Their luck was in. During the many conversations Rosie had with Freda, the proud mother-of-the-bride had divulged where the honeymooners would be heading, extolling the attributes of their luxury destination as she the flashed photos on her phone.

When Rosie became suspicious of his line of question-ing, Joe crossed his fingers and stuck to the script. He'd been trying to get through on Tilly's mobile but it was switched off, so he was going to contact her via the hotel even though he knew it would be risky. Rosie bought the fib, hook, line and sinker and said she'd keep her fingers crossed then wished him the best of British.

As soon as he disconnected, Sam and Joe high-fived and set about finding the hotel on the internet, apparently it was necessary to get an idea of the layout so they could plan their escape route if it all got a bit physical. Joe paled slightly at the thought, knowing only too well that their mum would go mental if they got locked up. He also had the impression that Sam was getting a bit carried away with his James Bond mission and might need to be reined in if things became tense.

Sam got the taxi driver to stop just before they reached The Marine Hotel which was the grand and opulent jewel in the crown of the seaside town of Sainte Valérie. Their intention was to spend some time doing reconnaissance and if they were lucky, get a visual on the target without breaking cover. Once they'd ascertained the location of the enemy (Luke), then Joe would be free to approach the target (Tilly) and carry out the hit.

Joe was sweating slightly and kind of unnerved by Sam's military turn of phrase, hushed tones and stealth-like movements. They had cautiously made their way around the side of the hotel, past the pool area, which was almost deserted at lunchtime, then onto the beach, which was similarly empty.

After taking cover behind a fishing boat, Sam instructed Joe to text Tilly, just to say hello and ask how she was doing and if she was enjoying herself. Fingers crossed, her reply might give them a clue to her present location. Unfortunately after ten, very long minutes of sweltering in the afternoon sun, there was no reply. After scratching their heads, they assumed her phone really was turned off or she couldn't reply because Luke was in the vicinity.

In stark contrast to Tilly's lack of contact, their mother was driving them mad and had sent both undercover agents simultaneous messages. They knew full well that the more they ignored her, worry, suspicion and curiosity would peak and then result in an irate phone call, so both had wisely switched to silent mode. There was only so long they could stall her so they needed to get on with it, which prompted them to venture inside the hotel in the hope of spotting the target in the restaurant, even if it meant running the risk of the enemy being there too.

Joe's wiring had gone a bit haywire and his bursts of fearlessness were interspersed with moments of hesitation, or a fit of nervous giggling, which was entirely Sam's fault. He was currently hiding behind a huge potted plant and peering through the palm leaves, trying to get a glimpse inside the restaurant. They had wandered into the foyer of the grand hotel, via the rear entrance which led in from the beach. Neither of them stood out too much in their shorts and T-shirts as most of the guests were similarly attired, albeit in Gucci and Prada, not Primark and Top Man. When Joe spotted one of the receptionists giving them strange looks, he tugged at Sam's shirt and told him to pack it in or they'd get chucked out.

'Maybe they've gone out for the day and it's just been a total waste of time, they could be anywhere, and unless Tilly answers her phone we could be wandering round looking like a pair of weirdos for hours. Come on, let's go and get some food. There's a café opposite and we can keep a lookout from there. It's making me edgy being in here and you look really dodgy, see, she's staring again. That receptionist is deffo on to us.' Joe had completely lost his nerve and wanted to get the hell out of there.

'Stop whining. We're not doing any harm and for all she knows we could be guests looking for our mates, you need to act casual like me. See, she's waving back, totally harmless. She probably thinks I'm hot and let's face it, who can blame her?' Sam was flashing the receptionist a wicked grin and waving cheerily, completely unfazed.

'Are you ever off chick-patrol? Come on, let's go. I can't take the stress anymore and stop flirting, we haven't got time.' Joe grabbed the straps of Sam's rucksack and began marching across the polished marble floor towards the entrance when, without warning, he was dragged sideways and pulled down onto one of the plush, leather sofas that dotted the foyer.

'What the hell?' Joe looked at Sam as though he'd gone mad.

'Shut it! Here, hide behind this.' Sam hissed his instructions, thrusting a glossy magazine into Joe's hands before covering his face with another, then began peeping over the top and nodding in the direction of the escalators.

Joe did as he was told and hid behind Vogue, then followed Sam's gaze, realising instantly why they were acting like a pair of comedy spies. There, only a few yards away stood Tilly and Luke, embroiled in a heated if not hushed debate. From the angry looks they were giving each other, along with their body language, things weren't going too well. Joe could hardly breathe and he thought his heart was going to pop while Sam whispered for him to remain completely still as sudden movements might blow their cover.

Whatever they were arguing about was over relatively quickly as Luke raised his hands as if to admit defeat or signal he wasn't listening anymore, to which Tilly turned sharply and stormed off, leaving the enemy glaring in her direction before flouncing towards the exit.

When they allowed themselves to breath, Sam and Joe lowered their camouflage and let out a huge sigh of relief. Sam glanced towards the receptionist and her colleague who were now shaking their heads and laughing, clearly bemused by the strange men on the sofas.

'Shit, that was close! We nearly walked straight into them. Can you imagine how awkward that would've been? Come on, those two think we're nutters so we'd better get out of here. I think Luke's gone so let's follow Tilly, she looked like she was heading for the beach.' Sam stood and dragged Joe up and off the sofa then waved casually to his admirer, treating her to a cheeky wink for good measure.

Wasting no time, they scurried outside and after the

cool, marbled surroundings of the hotel interior, they were hit by a blast of searing heat. The midday sun forced them to squint as they scanned the beach for their quarry who was nowhere to be seen. Undeterred, they put on their sunglasses and tramped along the row of loungers and palm tree parasols which lined the sand, hoping they weren't heading in the wrong direction as the row of sun worshippers stretched for miles along the coastline.

When he spotted Tilly, Joe's heart skipped a beat and then melted just at the sight of her. He grabbed Sam's arm and silently pointed in her direction. She was trying to find a suitable position under the shady branches of the palm and was having difficulty manoeuvring the heavy wooden steamer chair in the soft, golden sand. Her dark hair was tied in a ponytail and she wore a bright blue bikini top with a floral sarong tied at the waist, her flip-flops had been abandoned and rested on the bed along with her bag and beach towel. Joe noticed her wipe her forehead, the exertion was obviously making her hot and the urge to run over and help was thwarted by an attack of nerves and trepidation. What he was about to do caused Joe to falter and pay attention to his brain, which was now riddled with self-doubt and second thoughts.

It was Sam's firm, calm voice that brought him to his senses and gave him the courage to carry on. 'Look, mate, don't bottle it now, just go over and say hi. She's going to freak out when she sees you so the first thing you have to do is calm her down and let her know you're not here to cause a scene, well, not yet anyway. I'll be right here keeping watch and I promise, nobody will lay a finger on you or Tilly so don't be scared of Tango man, I'll deal with him. Just go and tell her, get it over with then you can move on and so can she, you're doing the right thing, Joe. I promise you, mate, it's going to be okay.'

Sam gave Joe a gentle push who returned a nervous look and a weak smile then stepped forward and set off across the sand.

. . .

Tilly was fed up, frustrated, in a foul mood and she wanted to smash this stupid sunbed into smithereens and then use the pieces of broken wood to do the very same thing to Luke's head. God, he was so selfish, and during the past twenty-four hours it had taken her all her self-control not to push him off the balcony or smother him with a pillow. See, he was turning her into a bloodthirsty maniac and she really didn't think she could stay the course.

They had hardly spoken one word on the journey down, mostly as a result of Tilly pretending to be asleep and Luke feeling sorry for himself because he had to do all the driving. Well it served him bloody well right for being a prize pillock and booking a hotel in the South of France and being too much of a tight-arse to pay for flights. Had he not even bothered to look on the map or find out how far it was to drive? The moron! He'd already been whingeing about the drive home, so she was dreading the return journey which would be nothing more than a psychological endurance test.

Once they'd checked in, Luke had headed straight outside and into the sun, desperate to make up for lost time and get his money's worth while she settled for a lie down in the air-conditioned room. When he finally returned, not only did he resemble a lobster, he wanted to get all dressed up and go for a fancy, first night dinner and was openly irritated by her preference of something simple as her stomach was still a bit delicate. This resulted in a huge huff, room service for her and an all-night session in the cocktail bar for him, plus the obligatory hangover in the morning.

Tilly had left him to it and enjoyed a leisurely, light breakfast alone and then took a walk into town from where she'd spoken to Joe who was his usual upbeat, supportive self and had cheered her up no end. It was a shame he had to cut the conversation short, but it was probably for the best because it was hard to hear him. He sounded like he was somewhere busy, there was a lot of noise in the background – maybe the supermarket or a service station. Anyway, once she'd sorted this stupid sunbed out she was going to send him a text. Her battery had gone flat and she was terrified of Luke seeing Joe's name flash up, so had left it on silent and hidden under the bed while it recharged.

Talking of her delightful fiancé, once he'd recovered from his excesses, Luke hadn't taken too kindly to her sightseeing plans, which caused further tension. He knew her fair skin burnt easily and there was no way she was going to spend the next few days sitting by the infinity pool. Luke hated the beach because the sand got everywhere and the sea air dried his orange skin, whereas Tilly loved being close to the sound of the waves. After sarcastically mentioning she didn't relish the thought of being surrounded by oiled-up posers who were obsessed with spending the day like sweaty humans on a rotisserie, they'd argued the toss all the way down in the lift.

He refused to even consider a trip to Nice where she hoped to take a tour on the open top bus and visit the Matisse and Chagall museums, or the monastery and Russian Cathedral, so she said she'd go by herself which she preferred anyway. As revenge, Tilly said he could stick a boozy night at the casino in Monte Carlo right where the sun doesn't shine which was why he stomped off to the pool on his tod!

In truth, any niggles and arguments that occurred meant he was playing right into her hands and when she felt the time was right, she was going to let him have it, all guns blazing, tell him she thought they were incompatible and it was time to call it a day. Having said that, he bugged the hell out of her 24/7 and it was hard to imagine them getting to the end of the day, never mind the end of their holiday, without blood being shed.

Tilly pushed these thoughts away as they only wound her up more. She had totally given up on the sunbed and set about laying her towel on the mattress when a shadow fell across the sand and for a second, her heart dropped, expecting it to be Luke who'd come to say he was sorry. When she looked up, her heart did actually stop for a moment, then began beating like the whole percussion section of an orchestra. By the time she finally found her tongue, the voice that accompanied it came out high-pitched and incredulous, her brain went into warp speed as her hands and insides began to tremble.

'Joe, what are you doing here? Is something wrong... has something happened... is it Mum and Dad, or Grandma? Look you've got to go... Luke might see you and I've not had chance to tell him yet, he's going to go mad if he comes back.' Tilly was clutching both hands together, panicking and rambling as she looked nervously towards the hotel in between snatching wary glances at Joe.

'Tilly, calm down. It's okay, nothing's wrong. I just needed to see you. I'm not going to cause trouble and Sam's here too. He's keeping a lookout.' Joe turned and pointed towards his brother who was standing with his arms crossed like the proverbial bodyguard, who in this case was wearing dark glasses, a bucket hat, Stone Roses T-shirt, tie-dyed shorts and sandals.

'I don't understand, why couldn't you just talk to me on the phone, why did you need to see me, and how did you get here anyway?' There were so many thoughts running rampant in her head and there was no time to get answers, she was scared out of her wits that Luke would turn up and then all hell would break loose, she just knew it.

'Come with me, we can walk along the shore and get away from here and then if he does turn up it'll be harder to find you. I've got something to tell you, it's something I found out and couldn't say on the phone, so Sam suggested I did it face to face. It was a spur of the moment thing and I thought he'd lost the plot at first, but then I knew it was the right thing to do, so we booked a flight yesterday and here we are.'

'What have you found out? Are you ill or something... please don't say it's that? You're really scaring me now, Joe, just tell me what it is.' When she saw Joe shake his head, the fear in her heart released its grip just slightly.

'Walk with me and I'll explain, come on, you've just got to trust me.' Joe was edgy too and wanted to get away from the hotel so took a few steps towards the sea, welcoming the huge rush of relief he felt when Tilly nodded in agreement, picked up her bag and followed.

They made their way to the water's edge in silence and walked on for a few minutes until they passed the curve in the beach which obscured the hotel from sight. As they reached the wet sand, Joe turned to see Sam following discreetly only a few yards behind.

'I can't tell you how much I want to hold your hand right now or put my arm around you... but I know it's the wrong thing to do so I'm going to have to restrain myself. I want you to know before I start that I'm not taking any pleasure from this... and I wish that I didn't have to tell you because you're going to be hurt and I never, ever want to cause you pain. And please, Tilly, don't shoot the messenger.'

Joe was beginning to ramble so when Tilly stopped in her tracks and faced him with an angry look in her eyes, he took the hint and got on with it.

'Joe, just spit it out... what is it?' Tilly's voice had a hard edge and there was fear in her eyes.

'Luke's been cheating on you. I don't know who with but he's been in contact with her recently, actually, on the night before the wedding and as far as I know it's still going on. I'm sorry, Tilly... but he's a liar and a cheat and he doesn't deserve you and I thought you had the right to know.' It was a bit weird to see someone with sun-kissed skin go deathly pale and for a moment, it looked like Tilly was going to faint, or scream or punch him.

After what seemed like an eternity, she responded and when she did, Joe was aware of nothing else, his focus was entirely on her, silhouetted against the gently lapping azure sea which met a clear, cobalt sky on the horizon.

When his words finally penetrated Tilly's stunned brain, the shockwaves rippled through her body, wreaking havoc and giving chaos a free pass. Whatever strength she had in reserve, any last dregs of fight or remnants of pride that she'd squirreled away and saved up for the moment when she ended her relationship with Luke, finally evaporated, abandoning her when she needed them the most. All her barriers came tumbling down, the dam that held in her tears burst its banks. The spine that had held her up, crumpled, leaving her legs weak and her arms reaching out for support.

Joe intuitively did the only thing he could, he held her tight and let her cry. He wasn't really sure what or who her tears were for, but it didn't matter and he didn't care, because she hadn't rejected him or called him a liar and told him to go. While Tilly sobbed, he looked around for Sam who gave him the thumbs up and pointed to a small café on the edge of the beach, indicating that he'd be there, to which Joe nodded slightly and watched his brother pick up their rucksacks and walk away.

The sun hid behind a cloud and the heat seemed less harsh as they stood locked together on the sand. Maybe it was his imagination, but the rays felt gentle, calming, or was it the breeze from the sea that blew against their skin, cooling and tender? Whatever it was, it worked and before long, Tilly's sobs faded and her tears slowed, leaving his T-shirt soggy and stuck to his chest. When she finally spoke, her voice was hoarse and broken, timid and sad.

'I want you to know right here and now that I wasn't crying because I'm devastated. I know once and for all that he doesn't love me and I'm glad, because I hate him, I really hate him. What's getting to me is the waste. Everything has been a sham and I've spent almost a whole year being unhappy and worrying while my parents paid for the best wedding they could afford and all that time, he's been cheating on me. The worst part is that I've been lying to everyone and acting like a massive fake. I hate myself as much as I hate him for not having the guts to end it ages ago... I'm so pathetic, it's all just *so* pathetic.'

Tilly's voice cracked again and her lip began to tremble which gave Joe another excuse to hold her, which really was the best feeling.

'Hey, stop this, *do not* blame yourself. He's a big-time loser and like I said, he doesn't deserve you and you certainly don't deserve to feel this way. All you did was try to protect your family and do the right thing. You're not pathetic, Tilly. I think you're really brave and honourable and if anyone says otherwise they'll have me to deal with. Shush now, it's going to be okay, I promise. You've just had a huge shock and it's going to take time to get your head round everything, that's all.' Joe kissed the top of her head and tried to soothe her, holding her tight and once again waited for her tears to subside.

'I can't believe he's done it again. I'm such a fool! How gullible can one person be? It's bad enough the first time round but the second time is even worse. I feel like a right mug. I bet half of our friends know and they're all laughing behind my back.' Tilly pulled away then regarded Joe, her stare was intense and the anger in her voice was clear when she asked the obvious question.

'Anyway, you haven't told me how you found out, who told you?' Tilly wiped her eyes as she waited to hear more damning news.

Joe released her from his grasp and realised he'd only done half a job and now he had to tell her the gory details, or the ones he knew about. Before he had chance to begin, he spotted Sam making his way towards them carrying bottles of water which he offered to his brother and their red-eyed friend.

'Here, I thought you'd be thirsty, it's boiling out here. Are you okay, Tilly? I'm sorry about the news and for what it's worth, you *so* need to get shut of him... look, I'll wait over there. You two need to talk, alone.' Sam turned to walk away when Tilly stopped him.

'No, don't go, Sam. I'm sure you know all the sordid

details already. It's obviously not a secret so stay, let's go and sit in the shade though, I'm burning to death in this heat.' Tilly sounded flat and dejected.

Sam looked at Joe for confirmation that he wasn't going to be in the way, when his brother nodded in agreement, all three wandered slowly off the beach. They found a spot on the promenade wall and sat under a row of sturdy palms, gratefully drinking their water in the shade before the talking began.

Tilly was flanked on either side by her bodyguards and it occurred to her that if Luke turned up right now, it would be him needing their protection, not her.

'Go on then, get it over with. Tell me what you know, and don't miss anything out or give me an edited version to spare my feelings. I want to hear it all, okay? I don't feel half as brave as I sound though, and I'm half dreading, half dying to know what Luke had been up to.'

When he'd finished explaining the chain of events that led to the discovery, Joe gave Tilly time to process the information before she began to fire off questions he had no answers for. Nobody knew the other woman's name or where she was from, Joe had no idea what she looked like or how long it had been going on, whether it was a serious relationship or just a fling and if any of her friends were in on it. He felt like a bit of a fraud now, he really had turned up with half a story. His conscience told him that he could've given her these meagre snippets of information over the phone and admitted to himself that he'd have used any excuse to see her again after parting on such bad terms. Luke's indiscretion had provided the perfect opportunity to do just that, so when Sam's voice broke into his guilty thoughts, he pulled himself together, ignoring his inner voice and listened to what he had to say.

'The only person who can answer all of your questions is Luke... whether he'll fess up is another thing though. Do you reckon he'll try and wriggle out of it or admit to what he's been up to? You're gonna have to play clever if you want to get him bang to rights. I know, why don't you try and pinch his phone and see if you can find the photos, or the texts at least. I don't suppose you want to be looking at pictures of her flashing her bits, but at least you'd know what she looks like, if she's actually showing her face on them, which when you think about it, I don't suppose she is.' Sam's summing up was sensible and honest.

Joe on the other hand thought he was being slightly insensitive. 'Okay, Sam, she doesn't want to be reminded of all that, but you are right, Tilly needs to confront him and I think we should stick around, just in case he gets arsey.' Joe was genuinely concerned and trying desperately to string out his time with Tilly for as long as possible.

'No, it's okay, Joe. And actually, I'd love to see those photos so the images are imprinted on my brain. They'll be a permanent reminder of what a shit he is and what a fool I am. Come on, I need to get back. No time like the present. I want to get this over with.' Tilly stood up and waited for Sam and Joe to get a move on.

'Do you want us to come in with you or should we wait outside the hotel? He won't be pleased to see us you know. It might make matters worse if we're there when you confront him so maybe we should keep out of the way.'

Sam was being practical whereas Joe's heart was in complete control of his brain.

'I'm not going anywhere until I know Tilly's okay... we'll stay close in case she needs us.' Joe recognised a hint of panic in his voice and felt slightly foolish, desperate even.

'Thanks, Joe, but this is something I need to do by myself. I'll go and find him and even if I did get my hands on his phone, there's no point in pinching it because it's always locked and now I know the reason why. No matter what he says or how many lies he tells, it's over. I've had enough and the sooner I can get away from him the better. He can try and bullshit his way out of this as much as he wants, I won't be listening. Come on, you can walk me up to the hotel then I'll be okay on my own. I'll let you know what's happening… where are you staying, anyway?'

Taken aback by Tilly's steely determination and her no-nonsense approach to the situation, Joe couldn't help but acknowledge the feeling of rejection that was creeping up on him.

'We hadn't planned to stay anywhere, it was all a bit of a rush job and Sam wants to head back to Monte Carlo and see the sights but I'm quite happy to stay here and wait for you.' Joe didn't dare look at his brother who was most likely a bit put out by this statement and disloyal change of plan.

'No way! You've both done enough and I don't want to spoil things for you. I'll be fine, honest. I can't drag you into my crap relationship as well, so if I'm going to do this, it's got to be because of what Luke has done and believe me, he'll do anything to blame things on us, I know what he's like. Monte Carlo is only a taxi ride away so if I need to, I'll ring you.' From the tone of her voice, Joe knew for a fact that Tilly had made her mind up, and the last thing he wanted to do was irritate her or add to her problems so he resigned himself to leaving her behind.

As they marched back up the beach towards the hotel, Joe could tell by her purposeful stride that Tilly meant business and that Luke was in for a huge shock when she clapped eyes on him.

When they reached the stretch of blue and white stripy sunbeds, which indicated the section of beach owned by L'Hôtel Marina, they wove their way towards the spot where Tilly had left her things, all three relishing the cool shade afforded by the palm tree parasols overhead. Spotting her beach towel and flip-flops resting exactly where she'd left them on the mattress, Tilly was momentarily relieved that her belongings hadn't been stolen or removed by one of the attendants. Within seconds, any feelings of calm were replaced by those of dread when she spotted Luke, scanning the crowds and looking angry.

There was no time to divert or alert Sam and Joe, apart from stretching out her arms to stop them in their tracks by which time they had reached the foot of the sunbed. Here they came face to face with Luke, who looked shocked and confused, an expression which turned quickly into one of suspicion.

Before Tilly could speak, Luke's voice bellowed, laden with accusation, breaking into the tranquil afternoon and disturbing the elegant sun worshippers surrounding them.

'Where the hell have you been? I've been ringing you for ages! You've waltzed off with my room key and more to the point... what's he doing here?' Luke nodded in the direction of Joe, his eyes were angry slits of pure dislike, motivated by a brain that was rapidly putting two and two together.

In the meantime, Tilly had gathered her wits and found her voice. 'Never mind what Joe's doing here, and don't speak to me like that, who do you think *you* are? But seeing as you asked, they came to bring me some good news... about you. Seems like your dirty little secret is out and everyone knows you've been shagging some scummy tart behind my back, *again*! And you know what? It's given me the best reason in the world to end what we laughingly call a relationship, to go with a list as long as my arm of things I despise about you. Is that a good enough answer... or shall I tell all these lovely people about the delightful photos on your phone, you pervert?'

Luke appeared to have been struck dumb as Tilly pointed and jabbed her finger in the direction of his ashen face whereas her voice was calm and clear, yet laced with unadulterated rage.

'What the hell are you talking about, you've lost the flaming plot, just shut it you silly cow? And what gives you two the right to come here talking shit and causing trouble. Why don't you piss off and mind your own business?' Luke was fuming and barely able to control his temper and when he stepped forward, clenching his fists and looking like he was going to swing for Joe, Sam flew into action.

'I wouldn't if I were you, mate... not unless you want your nose spread across that pretty-boy face. Just calm it down, you're upsetting these nice people and there are kids about.' Sam placed himself between Joe and Luke. He'd also spotted two security guards who were paying close attention to the fracas and talking into their radios.

'I'm not scared of you, mate... and I'm not discussing my personal life in front of this lot so if you want to talk, I'll meet you in the room, just give me the key.' Luke had turned his attention from Sam to Tilly who he regarded with a look of pure disgust.

'I'll leave you with your boyfriends, which one is it or do you prefer them both at the same time? Don't try and throw mud at me when you've clearly been a busy girl while I've been away. Who'd have thought it, eh? I bet Mummy and Daddy haven't got a clue what a dirty slapper you really are.'

Almost before the words and left his mouth, Tilly sprang forward and began punching Luke who, taken by surprise, suffered a smack in the eye before raising his arms to protect himself from the blows.

Joe and Sam were also caught off guard and now the security men were running towards the scene, so before she got arrested, they waded in and dragged Tilly off, while Luke cursed and cowered as horrified onlookers gasped in shock.

By the time the two burly men arrived by the sunbeds, Tilly had been restrained and was in floods of hysterical, angry tears which gave the guards the impression that she was the one who'd been wronged, despite Luke's swollen eye and dented pride.

Joe did his best to explain that there was no need for their concern and that everything was under control, not that they believed him and insisted the rowdy group left the beach immediately. They herded Luke away first, eyeing him suspiciously as they smiled and reassured the rest of the astounded guests that the show was over. Once they reached the entrance to the hotel, Tilly rummaged in her bag and when she found his room key, hurled it at Luke.

'Here, take this and get out of my sight. I'll be back in a bit to get my stuff and then I'm going home. I never want to see you again, you disgust me! You can stay here and rot for all I care, just make sure you're not around while I pack my stuff, do you hear me?' Tilly glowered at Luke as she waited for his reply.

'Oh, I've got it all right. And don't think I'll be begging you to come back either. As far as I'm concerned I'm well shot!' Luke sounded braver than he looked as he scrabbled about on the floor to retrieve the key, keeping a wary eye on Sam and the security guards.

Joe knew they'd all pushed their luck with the hotel staff so he gently rested his hand on Tilly's arm and told her to ignore him, a suggestion which she thankfully took notice of. As Luke gave them all one last look of disgust then walked away with as much bravado and pride as he could muster, the guards hovered, observing the parting of the ways. Once he was out of sight, they both looked at each other and smirked before telling Tilly that even though she had an excellent right hook, they'd be keeping an eye on her and suggested she behave herself from now on, otherwise they'd have to call the gendarmes.

Suitably ticked off and shamefaced, Tilly apologised for her behaviour and promised faithfully that there would be no more trouble and for good measure, assured them she'd be gone by the end of the day. As they sauntered off, the fight suddenly left Tilly, causing her to slump against the wall of the rockery that bordered the immaculate lawns. Covering her face with her hands, she wailed in horror at her actions.

'Oh my God, what have I done? I can't believe I behaved like that. You must be so ashamed of me.' Tilly looked up at Joe and Sam, the latter spoke first.

'Why would we be ashamed, he deserved everything he got. Look, why don't we all go and get a drink and calm down then decide what you're going to do. Did you really mean that about going home because if you did, then we need to check out flights or find somewhere for you to stay because there's no way you can stop here tonight?'

'Sam's right. Look, you're shaking. Come on, you need to think about your next move and not do anything rash.' Joe was emotionally drained too and he suspected that Sam would be starving, they hadn't eaten since early that morning and if he knew his brother, his stomach would be rumbling by now.

Tilly stood up and sighed. Then she grabbed her bag off the floor telling them in a resigned voice to lead the way, knowing full well that if she went within a foot of Luke right now there was a chance she'd throttle him. He knew how to wind her up and was too much of a coward to admit what he'd done, it was far easier to blame her. It would come out in the wash eventually, no doubt the jungle drums would start beating once she got home and if she didn't manage to extract the truth from Luke, someone would slip up or be eager to tell her what she wanted to know. For now, she just wanted to get as far away from him as possible and put all this behind her.

Haphazard plans zapped through her head, at some point there would have to be a long conversation with her parents which she dreaded, but this time there'd be no holds barred and she was going to tell them the truth about everything, then start afresh. She had to find somewhere to live, he could have the house and everything in it as far as she was concerned. Maybe Stacey would help her out, she needed to ring her too and somehow, she was going to pay her parents back, every single penny they had wasted.

As her brain worked at a million miles an hour, Tilly silently followed Sam and Joe towards the centre of town. There was a breeze blowing in from the sea and she was aware of well-dressed pedestrians passing her by, like extras in a silent movie in which she had the starring role. Tilly felt detached from reality, which was a nice change. Her surroundings were tranquil and refined and seemed to soothe her, or was it that with every step she took in the opposite direction from Luke, she became someone else, someone new. Without warning and in complete contrast to how she felt just a few minutes before, a strange sensation passed over her. It was a kind of peace, and she noticed that the cold hand that had gripped her heart for so long appeared to have let go. Tilly had been liberated, she was light as a feather and burden free.

Even though the road ahead wasn't clear and there'd be bumps along the way, something told her she'd be fine, this was still the best route and even if she had to walk the whole way in bare feet, then that's the direction she would take. For now, she would treat her guardian angels to a slap-up meal and trust them to keep her safe and sane, then help her get as far away from Luke as possible.

Tilly had no idea how things would turn out with Joe, or whether they really did have a future together but that was too much to contemplate right now. Her head was mashed and she had practicalities to sort out before jumping straight into another relationship. However their story ended, she would never regret meeting him again and be eternally grateful for his spur of the moment decision to fly to her aid and, in the end, love her enough to set her free.

BOOK 2

CHAPTER 1

Anna was on the way back from Angers after a wonderful and surprising day out with Daniel when she received the photos from Sam. He was with Joe and they were outside the Casino de Monte Carlo, smiling and giving her the thumbs up. The next photo was of them posing by a swanky yacht in the harbour and when she assimilated the photographic clues, she was struck dumb. After going hot and cold, Anna carefully read the text underneath, mouth wide open as her hand rested nervously around her neck.

It was straight to the point, apologising firstly for ignoring ten thousand messages and a million missed calls (Sam was being his usual sarcastic, over-exaggerating self) but they didn't want her to freak out and worry about their spur of the moment joyride, so decided to tell her once they'd arrived and everything was sorted. Anna couldn't believe that they had actually flown to Nice to tell Tilly in person. Had they gone mad? Sam casually assured her that all was well and now their mission was accomplished they'd decided to enjoy the sights and would give her a ring later to fill her in on the best bits of the story.

Anna speedily related all this to Daniel who was driving and seemed amused by their antics, whereas she was having none of it and took matters into her own hands. After firing a message straight back, Anna knew her words had hit home because within seconds, she saw Joe's name appear on the screen. Sam had obviously passed the buck and Anna was amused by the notion that her youngest son wasn't quite as tough and cocky as he thought he was!

It was simpler to put Joe on speakerphone so that she didn't have to deal with Daniel interrupting throughout the conversation or the irritating inconvenience of having to relay the gist of things in the midst of telling them both off. Once Anna accepted that her chastisement was falling on deaf ears, and that nobody had been beaten up or arrested, she climbed down from her soapbox and let Daniel get a word in edgeways. After he told the boys he was proud of them, they gleaned that Tilly was winging her way back to England as they spoke, and that Sam and Joe were going to spend the evening in Monte Carlo before catching the midday flight back to Bordeaux the following day.

However, before they signed off, Daniel told Sam and Joe that they had a bit of news of their own. He nodded to Anna who looked a bit nervous before speaking to her faraway sons.

'You'll never guess where I've been today... Daniel took me to Angers and we went up in a hot air balloon, it was amazing, even though I was a bit scared at the beginning and I wasn't that keen on the landing, if I'm honest.' Anna was silenced by the sound of her sons being impressed and amazed that she'd had the bottle so when they let her get a word in, she continued.

'And that's not all, while we were up there, floating about in the clouds and drinking champagne, guess what? Daniel proposed and I said yes!' As the words tumbled out, Anna was aware of the deafening silence and in the seconds it took for Sam and Joe to take them in, she prayed that they'd be happy for her.

When the sound of whoops and laughter came down the line, her heart leapt with joy and relief.

Sam spoke first. 'Nice one, that's ace, well done, Daniel,

I'm really happy for you mate and you too, Mum… that's a brilliant surprise, hang on, Joe wants to say something.'

'Congratulations… I'm made up for you both. Have you told Mel yet? Look, we'll do something nice when we drive back up to yours, I'll take everyone out for a meal or something. We'll make arrangements later on in the week if that's okay?' Before they got chance to reply, Sam butted in.

'Mum, Mum, can I be a pageboy? I've never been one and I'd like velvet pantaloons and a frilly shirt, and those shiny shoes with a buckle, please pick me first, I'm the cute one… Joe's too old and boring and he won't be able to carry it off.' They were all laughing when Anna told him he was barmy, but promised he'd got the job.

By the time they disconnected, both Daniel and Anna were floating in a happy bubble and decided that they'd enjoyed spreading the news so much that they'd call in and see Rosie and Michel on the way past, but first, they were going to pull over and ring Melanie and Louise, and then Enid of course.

* * *

Many miles away, Sam and Joe were making their way to the taxi rank, buoyed by the surprise news and the happiness they'd heard in their mum's voice. It had been quite a day and if he was honest, Joe was exhausted and half tempted by the idea of a night in a motel, but as usual, Sam was raring to go and determined to win at least a million Euros on the roulette table.

Secretly, Joe's head was all over the place and whilst showing enthusiasm for his brother's final escapade, his heart was flying north with Tilly, who once again, was moving farther away from him instead of coming closer.

He had the awful sensation that even though he had valiantly released her from a life with Luke, he had somehow inadvertently loosened the hold he had on her heart at the same time. The connection they once had was in danger of being severed now she was on her way home and, their affair, if it could even be classed as one, was about to be consigned to the holiday romance section of his life.

* * *

There had been no promises given or arrangements made before she entered the departure lounge and waved bravely from behind the glass, and this had unsettled him. He'd kicked himself for not being bolder, even though it wasn't the time or place to make a show of affection, Joe was left feeling cheated and short-changed. Joe couldn't help sensing that Tilly, whilst being grateful for all his help, seemed closed down and switched off emotionally. For this reason, he had to make do with a long hug and a kiss on the cheek before she walked away.

Sam had assured Joe that he wasn't a complete mug, or a loser and doomed to be single for the rest of his life. He reckoned Tilly's cool behaviour was natural after being told her fiancé was a cheat and a liar, and she still had to tell her parents and sort her life out once she landed in England. No wonder her brain was scrambled and she was acting a bit weird. Nobody wanted to be the other half of a rebound relationship.

That sentence sent Joe's head to spin mode. What he had with Tilly wasn't like that. They were in love before all this so surely her feelings couldn't change within the space of a few hours, could they?

The whole thing was driving him mad but as they made their way out of the airport, Joe accepted he had no alternative than to wait until the dust had settled. He resolved to taking Sam's advice not to push his luck, and leave Tilly to sort herself out.

All of which had left Joe completely deflated and slightly adrift, *and* he'd also splashed out on ridiculously expensive flights from a supposedly low-cost airline *and*, to add insult to injury, was now stumping up for his bodyguard's extortionate expenses on his big day out!

Perhaps he had MUG written across his forehead, either that or just tired, grumpy and frustrated and to coin one of Sam's phrases, acting like a big mard arse. They'd reached the front of the queue at the taxi rank by the time he'd pulled himself together. He even managed to laugh at his brother, who was weighing up the very glamorous women who were parading about or zooming past in their sports cars.

Sam didn't stand a cat in hell's chance in his crinkled floral shirt and chinos, not to mention the tatty rucksack on his back. Nothing about either of them screamed sartorial elegance. Nevertheless, Sam was giving flirting his best shot and when a taxi screeched to a halt, waved for his brother to get a move on.

Within minutes, they were speeding along the circuit of the Monte Carlo Grand Prix and Sam's infectious enthusiasm began to rub off on Joe. Despite his worries, he was just as thrilled as his brother to be entering the actual, real-life tunnel that Lewis Hamilton had once raced through, appreciating the tightness of the hairpin bends and close proximity to the pedestrians and buildings on either side. Sod it, thought Joe. He was fed up with being the serious brother all the time and he'd done all he could where Tilly was concerned. He would do his best to switch her off, have some fun and leave the rest to fate.

It was his only option really. He'd soon find out if the words from all the cringy sayings he'd ever heard really did come true. He'd let her fly away and if she was his, then she'd come back because, after all, patience was supposed to be a virtue and good things apparently came to those who waited around like lovesick puppies. He just hoped he didn't end up with fried egg on his face, because in his case, and for most of the time, life really was a bitch.

CHAPTER 2

Tilly was utterly exhausted and emotionally drained. She was also praying that nobody came and sat beside her on the plane because the last thing she wanted was a nice chat during the flight home, not even if it was Tom Hardy. She was done talking, probably forever. A numb sensation had enveloped her. She was closing down, folding up like a flower petal at the end of the day and switching off any unnecessary emotions, placing her heart on standby mode and conserving her energy. Maybe it was an inbuilt defence mechanism that clicked into action when your body had just had enough. Whatever this was, it allowed her to explain the whole sorry state of affairs to her astounded mum, without histrionics, shedding one single tear or drawing attention to herself as she waited patiently to board the plane.

Anyone who was sitting in the departure lounge wouldn't have had the faintest inkling that the girl in the corner was in the process of blowing her parents' world apart, albeit in a cool and collected manner. Or explaining methodically why she had no intention of running back to them and was headed for England.

* * *

Tilly couldn't face her family, or the questions they'd want to ask, not right now. Going back to her mum's to lick her wounds and be fussed over wasn't going to be productive in any way. Nothing they could say or do would change what had happened. She needed to be clinical and proactive, and that meant going back to the UK where she intended to extricate herself from her existence with Luke before he could get home to make things difficult. Tilly fully expected him to remain at the hotel and get his money's worth but just in case Hazel or Ken poked their noses in, she was making a pre-emptive strike.

At least her parents understood. They'd conducted their conversation through loudspeaker, two birds felled with one great boulder. Her dad had been angry but supportive, her mum teetered on the verge of tears throughout their discussion which left Tilly racked with guilt, and for that reason alone, she was glad to end the call.

Once that ordeal was over, she rang Stacey and gave her a more floral account of events, which did raise a few eyebrows amongst the passengers sitting nearest to her. Well, she had to let off a bit of steam after holding it in while she spoke to her mum and dad. Stacey was horrified and then using her best swear words, explained exactly what she was going to say to Luke the next time she saw him. Once she'd got that off her chest, Stacey promised to be waiting at the airport, and offered the spare room at her flat before Tilly even had chance to ask.

There was one tiny drawback to her semi-catatonic state, it had prevented her from giving Joe what he wanted when they'd said au revoir, which was a promise or some vain shred of hope for the future, maybe even a meaningful kiss.

He deserved to know where he stood if nothing else. He'd been so brilliant and taken care of everything while Sam devoured almost the entire menu at MacDonald's. Joe had booked her onto a flight when, due to what she suspected was delayed shock, her hands began to tremble, meaning she couldn't even hold a cup of coffee, let alone type in her debit card number to pay for her fare.

It was obvious he wanted her to stay close and even suggested she flew back to Bordeaux with them, then hitched a ride up to her mum's, but she refused. Tilly's sole aim was to get back home and take her things before Luke got back. Tilly was sure that Stacey would put her up until she got herself sorted, otherwise she'd ask her grandma if she could stay with her.

Once Sam had finished his McFlurries, they headed back to the hotel where Tilly prepared herself for the eventuality that Luke might be waiting for her in their room. In the meantime, her loyal knights waited in the foyer, one was tense and nervous while the other had spent his time wisely, chatting up the receptionist.

Tilly had marched haughtily into the large, opulent room where she was met by silence, leading her to believe she was alone until she spotted the voile curtains blowing in the breeze and the open, patio door. Knowing intuitively that Luke was outside, some of her bravado abandoned her, causing her to flounder momentarily and draw in a deep breath.

Luke was leaning against the balcony, gazing out to sea, completely unaware of her presence and from where she stood, Tilly could see he had a drink in his hand, which unnerved her even more. Knowing that the alcohol could make him brave or angry, it certainly made him stupid on most occasions, she knew that the quicker she got out of there, the better.

She wasn't scared of him, not one bit, but her thirst for the truth or an opportunity to rip him to shreds, verbally or otherwise, had dried up. All she wanted now was to get away without hearing his vile accusations or having to look at his sneering face, or there being a drink fuelled punch up and the police being called. With one eye on Luke, she quietly retrieved her suitcase from the stand by the door then slowly slid back the mirrored glass and set about removing armfuls of her clothes from the wardrobe, flinging shoes and whatever other belongings she could lay her hands on inside.

Tilly was on her way out of the bathroom, loaded up with toiletries when Luke turned and spotted her and, for a second, remained impassive before swaying slightly and stepping through the patio doors into the bedroom. She literally quailed under his scrutiny then tried hard to look braver than she felt, wishing some of the anger from earlier would return, because right then, his stare was intimidating and the door to the hall seemed a long way off. The only thing she could do was brazen it out and hope he hadn't sussed that she was nervous, not scared exactly, more unsure.

She needn't have worried because in the end, he let her go without putting up a fight and Tilly accepted that he was probably glad to see the back of her. This revelation alone had a humiliating edge to it, knowing that he couldn't even be bothered to beg her forgiveness or plead with her to stay. Instead, he remained true to form, incapable of taking the blame or being man enough to say he was sorry.

'So, this is it then. I take it you're running off with lover boy? Well I hope he makes you as miserable as you made me. I'll give it five minutes before you bore him to death, and tell him from me he's welcome to you, he's done me a favour. Thank fuck I didn't marry you. Getting the shits was the best thing you've ever done, so go on, piss off then I can have some fun.'

They were spiteful words which one day, wouldn't hurt anymore, but, in that pivotal moment, they had caused the raw wounds that lashed her heart to sting like hell.

As she fastened the clasps on her case and slung her bag over her shoulder, the rage she felt earlier began to surge and bubble, temporarily overriding the hurt his bitter words had caused. Angrily pulling the case from the bed, Tilly dragged it towards the door then pulled it open before turning to face Luke for what she hoped was the very last time, and fired her parting shot.

'You really are pathetic, Luke, do you know that? And

just for the record, I'm just as glad this joke of a relationship is over. I actually despise every single thing about you *and* your vile, obnoxious family. Yes, I was going to marry you but it would all have been a sham, every single word would have been a lie because I fell out of love with you a long, long time ago and have been going through the motions ever since. The only reason I didn't call it off was so I wouldn't hurt Mum and Dad and this is the hilarious part, I was going to dump you right here on our so-called honeymoon. So high five to Joe for giving me the perfect excuse, that's if I actually needed one.'

Tilly could hear her own voice which sounded manic and from the look on Luke's face, he was waiting for her head to spin round and a fountain of green sick to spout from her mouth.

'Oh and by the way, the feelings you have for me are mutual and whoever *she* is, she's so very welcome to you because, believe this, Luke, puking in a bowl for a day was worth it to avoid being your wife, even if it would've only been for a few, hideous days. At least I was spared the embarrassment of admitting to anyone you were my husband and the expense of divorcing you.' Tilly was trembling as she tried to hook her bag over her shoulder.

'Well thank fuck for small mercies, and the feeling is entirely mutual, just so you know.' Luke sneered then swigged his drink, which wound Tilly up even more.

'And this is the really hilarious bit, we could've even got an annulment because I've even been lying about the reason I can't sleep with you. See, the truth is, you make my skin crawl. I can't bear for you to touch me so I'll let you chew on that little nugget while you're off having fun, by yourself, you slimy cretin. I'll be well gone by the time you slither back to Bristol and before you start panicking, you can have the lot, the sooner I'm away from that house and everything that reminds me of you, the better. You can shut your gob now... you really do look more stupid than usual. Ta-ra!' And with that, she slammed the door shut and marched away.

Tilly's legs were like jelly as she sped down the hall. She hadn't the patience or the nerve to wait for the lift so she took the stairs instead, bouncing her case down eight flights until she appeared in the foyer, flushed and searching desperately for Joe's face. The second he saw her, he was on his feet, striding across the polished floor looking concerned and relieved before taking her case and then her arm, guiding her gently towards Sam who took the hint and hastily said goodbye to his admirer before all three of them scarpered.

There was a fifty–fifty chance that once her words sunk in, Luke would snap and chase after her, he hated not having the last word and for that reason, Tilly didn't allow herself to feel safe until they were in the taxi and heading towards the airport. Only once the hotel was out of sight did she allow herself to breathe and relax into the seat. The adrenalin levels in her body began to drop and her heart-beat returned to normal as she leaned against Joe who was holding her hand tightly. He didn't let go for almost all the time they were in the airport, apart from when she checked in, not that she minded the feeling of his hand wrapped around hers. It made her feel safe and protected. It was a chaste kind of contact, appropriate and within any bound-aries that a recently separated, slightly shell-shocked ex-fiancée is expected to observe.

The three companions waited until the last moment to say their goodbyes and, once Sam gave her a bear hug and the thumbs up, he wandered off giving them some space. Joe made her promise to ring him the minute she landed and if Stacey couldn't pick her up, to call him from the taxi. She could tell he was desperate to make plans and offer to come and see her as soon as he got back to the UK, and she wanted to invite him over, but something inside her prevented even the simplest of tokens, it just didn't seem right. Instead she hugged him tightly and thanked him again for coming to her rescue, promising to keep in touch every day and let him know where she was staying once she'd sorted something out.

Her final kiss on his cheek was long and lingering and he reciprocated in an identical way. Tilly assured and comforted herself with the knowledge that nobody wants a snogathon in broad daylight, right in front of passport control, a thought which appeased her conscience and allowed her to walk away without feeling too bad.

* * *

The plane was full of passengers and ready for take-off. Although Tilly's prayers hadn't been completely answered, she did at least find herself sitting next to a very uncommunicative man who had already plugged himself into his phone and was tapping his hand to whatever music was playing. Thankfully she had a window seat and wouldn't be bothered by the toing and froing of the other passengers on the way to the loo, because it was her intention to spend the whole flight plotting her next move and making mental lists of all the things she was going to need from the house.

The revving of the plane's engines and the powerful roar as they sped along the runway made Tilly's skin tingle, this was how it had to be from now on. From somewhere in her psyche, she remembered a Hebrew word they'd learned in RE at school. Kadima. It meant forward. That would be her motto from now on, no looking back, no regrets, no more excuses, this was her time to spread her wings and as the plane lifted above the clouds, Tilly smiled and closed her eyes, then flew into her future, alone.

CHAPTER 3

I
t was 8pm and Freda just couldn't stop crying. No matter what anybody said to try and cheer her up it had absolutely no effect whatsoever. The flood barriers inside her body were down and an uncontrollable tidal wave of tears just kept pumping away, spilling from her eyes and showed no signs of abating. The image of her precious daughter, sitting alone in the departure lounge at Nice airport was too much to bear. Freda pictured Tilly, broken-hearted and dejected, her face pushed against the window of the plane as she took a solitary flight back to the UK. It made Freda want to scream with rage. Much worse was the guilt that had begun to torment her and, despite what anyone said to the contrary, she had to take responsibility for part of this calamity. Freda knew deep in her heart that she had ignored so many signs and still ploughed ahead regardless.

Flashbacks from the weeks before the ill-fated wedding haunted her, everything about Tilly was screaming, 'help me', but instead, Freda had focused on her grand plans and carried on, displaying an epic example of tunnel vision.

Once they were aware of the situation, Howard had been simultaneously vindicated and incensed, blaming himself for not speaking up sooner and giving Luke a black eye a long time ago. After he'd said his piece, he stomped off and took refuge in his vegetable garden, where he was currently being counselled by Norman with the aid of endless cups of tea made by Caroline, who firmly believed that a nice brew eased most types of suffering.

At least Howard had recognised their daughter's distress, whereas in Freda's case, even when she suspected something was wrong, she had been far too happy to brush things under the carpet for the sake of her perfect summer wedding.

Susie deflected most of the blame onto Luke's shoulders (which wasn't hard) and was also brave enough to apportion a slice of responsibility to Tilly, who she felt should've been honest with everyone and saved her family all this heartache.

Freda didn't take kindly to anyone having a go at her daughter, even if it was true, and loyally defended Tilly because, no matter what, her motives were completely righteous.

Scott stuck up for Susie and countered his mother's semi-blinkered and biased appraisal by raising the issue of Joe. He pointed out that Tilly hadn't exactly been without fault, an opinion that was unfortunately shared by Marianne.

On hearing this, Freda literally blew her top and set off crying again, giving Grandma Betty no option than to step in and sort things out.

The senior member of the family soon restored order. 'Right you lot… listen to me. What's done is done, and no good will come out of taking the whole sorry mess apart and trying to work out who did what and why. The facts are plain and simple. Luke is a lying, spineless cheater and a lush, which means our Tilly has actually been given a lucky break for which we should all be glad about. We all know and love her for being a good girl who always thinks of others, so it's not so surprising that she wanted to protect us and sacrificed herself and no small amount of pride in order to do so.' Betty waited for her words to settle as those around her nodded in agreement.

'And as for her having feelings for Joe, she's only human and humans make mistakes, Luke being one of them. So can any of us blame Tilly for reaching out and grabbing a bit of happiness while she could? If the lad gave her courage or strength or even if he just made her happy, then hats off to him. This Joe thought so much of our Tilly that he went all that way to help her and that shows character, a good one at that.'

Betty finished by addressing her own daughter. 'And, Freda my love, instead of feeling guilty, do something positive, like packing a bag and getting over to England where you can be of use, instead of sobbing into a hanky and making matters worse. There's no reason why you can't hitch a lift in the car with me and Marianne, or go over with Scott and Susie, whatever you think is best.'

Scott spoke next. 'Grandma's right, Mum, you need to be with Tilly now. I think it will make you feel better, so why not wait till morning and then give her a ring and decide then. It makes a lot of sense all round.'

'Yes, I suppose so... and maybe once your dad has calmed down he might want to come too. My head's all over the place at the minute but I do want to see Tilly, as soon as I can so I can make things right.'

Betty leant over and held Freda's hand, one last piece of advice still left to impart. 'Freda, love. There's nothing to put right. All you are really guilty of is loving Tilly too much and wanting her to have a perfect day. Now, we have to give Tilly our support, that's all she needs and the sooner she puts Luke behind her, the better, because life is too short for regrets – life is for living.'

CHAPTER 4

The December rain battered against the windows of Anna's apartment. It was aided and abetted by a howling wind which lashed everything in its path as it blew in from the Channel, roaring up the Solent before it hit land and began battering everything in its wake. They had been expecting the storm for days and the coastal residents were prepared, however, if they thought this was bad, Anna wondered how the people in the north of England were coping after Storm Deirdre wreaked havoc over the weekend.

Anna thought the Met Office had missed a trick where the actual picking of names was concerned because Barney, Steve and Wendy didn't exactly strike fear into the hearts of anyone watching the *News at Ten*. She would've gone for Lucifer, Cruella and Vlad, who sounded much more menacing and come to think of it, who the hell chose Deirdre?

The foul weather had also ruined Anna's plans for a brisk walk along the seafront into town. She had intended posting all her Christmas cards, but didn't fancy being drenched and was quietly confident that Pippa felt exactly the same way.

In the meantime, she decided to occupy herself by wrapping some presents while Daniel was out of the way. He thought all this lovely shiny paper and glittery bows was a waste, but Anna's gifts always looked spectacular and in her opinion, verged on artistic masterpieces. The kids made fun of her every year when she went around salvaging bows, gift bags and ribbons from the pile of ripped up paper on the floor, which she stashed in the cupboard and recycled.

Anna began to rip open the cellophane wrappers that bound the wrapping paper and thought wistfully of the upcoming holidays. She was really looking forward to Christmas, especially after last year's performance with Louise in France. Talking of her soon-to-be stepdaughter, it was a pleasure to talk to her these days after she'd turned over a new leaf and into a nice person, much to the relief of the whole family. She'd even seemed genuinely happy about her dad's surprise engagement and was looking forward to the wedding.

The only person to be slightly put out by everything, was Carys, who wasn't used to not being in the limelight *or* at the back of the queue where her daughter was concerned. It transpired that she had kicked up a bit of a fuss when Louise announced their impending trip to Portsmouth for Christmas, which was ironic, all things considered.

It was clear from the excitement in her voice that Louise was really looking forward to her visit even though she'd been rushed off her feet since the summer, arranging the move to Switzerland and the letting of their home in France. Tomas had settled into his new job and Jules loved his school and, most of all, skiing. Louise had met a few of the other mothers who seemed very welcoming and, after having so many worries and reservations, was hopeful that their new life in Geneva would be a happy one. She'd already told Anna that her New Year's resolution was to find some part-time work and was keeping her ears and options open, especially during the many events they were due to attend on the run-up to Christmas.

Anna's wrapping up had come to a halt as she was at a bit of a loss as how to disguise a snowboard, a gift for Jules.

Placing it on one side, she decided to wait for more parcels from Amazon to arrive and hopefully, one of the boxes would be big enough to cover it. The poor delivery drivers probably cursed Sam who had an aversion to actually going into a real shop, and bought almost everything he needed online, all year round. Christmas was no exception and his bedroom looked like a mini warehouse facility.

Anna chortled to herself when she imagined Sam's despondent face when it dawned on him he'd actually have to wrap them all up, a performance he repeated every year just before trying to bribe her or Melanie into doing it for him.

Somewhere amongst Sam's ever-growing pile was a Portsmouth FC shirt, plus a ticket for the home match on Boxing Day, for Jules. Anna was slightly dubious about whether or not the youngster would embrace a cold after-noon on the stands listening to grown men rant and rave, not to mention hearing a few ripe swear words about the ref. On the other hand, she knew that for her own sons, the raucous banter had been one of the highlights of the game and as they got older, a free pass to shout the odd obscenity without being told off.

It was going to be a very full house when everyone arrived, and they'd have to do a bit of shuffling about, but Anna was sure they would manage, especially now that Joe had moved out. It still made her feel a bit peculiar when she remembered the day he announced he was going to buy a place of his own. Even though he had been away before, at uni and then off to New Zealand, this time it felt a bit too final, like the end of an era.

To Anna's delight, it had all turned out quite nicely because when Joe eventually moved out at the beginning of November, he hadn't strayed too far and bought an apart-ment, one floor below in the same block. When she rang Joe one morning to say there was a sign going up on the railings of their forecourt, she was utterly convinced it was divine intervention. Needless to say, the cogs of Anna's mind and her indomitable enthusiasm were on full throttle and by the end of the day, she had the keys in her hand and an offer was on the table before the agent could get out of the door.

Joe did actually like the apartment which he said ticked all his boxes and if nothing else, gave him a leg up onto the property ladder. He had also joked that it landed him back in Anna's good books and simply resigned himself to what possibly *was* the hand of God whom he suspected of being in league with his mother.

Anna's heart had been worried for Joe since the summer and the Tilly business. He'd always been unlucky in love and as far as she knew (from the snippets she'd dragged out of Sam) the romance with Tilly hadn't exactly fizzled out, it was more of a slow burner, which she suspected might be a portent of doom.

On the other hand, Joe had been extremely busy with work and his feet hadn't touched the ground since he returned from France, giving him much-needed focus and something to occupy his mind. She was so proud when he'd jetted off to China as part of a trade delegation hoping to woo big business from Asia. All those dinners at the Guild Hall and conferences at trade fairs finally paid off when he was approached by local government to be part of the group representing transport.

Maybe over Christmas she would have the chance to delve a little and enquire about Tilly, or should she just leave well alone? Sam let slip that they'd kept in touch, but both were busy with work and it had been difficult for them to hook up as often as he'd have liked. Anna didn't swallow this for one moment and reverted back to her original, doomed analysis of the relationship.

It was a shame really because Tilly was a nice girl and Joe could do much worse, still, she would try to keep out of it and hope instead that somewhere out there in the big bad world was his perfect match. She just wished whoever it was would hurry up and come out of hiding.

Anna wondered whether all parents spent their time

treading on eggshells and waged an almighty battle to extract even the tiniest bit of information, which was of no consequence to her kids, but meant the world to her.

For example, when they started nursery and school, all she wanted to know as they walked home hand in hand was who they'd played with in the yard and what they had for their lunch. Things hadn't changed much and even though she'd tried to curb her annoying habit of questioning every aspect of their daily lives, still asked if they'd had something proper to eat or met anyone nice at work. What a saddo!

Anna felt a bit guilty too, while Joe was in limbo she had everything to look forward to, like arranging her own wedding and honeymoon for the summer, which was going to be her number one priority in the New Year. For now, that and other people's problems would have to wait because she had more pressing things on her mind, like how the hell she was going to wrap up Ross's scooter. Perhaps Daniel was right, and all this fussing was a waste of time and she should just stick it back in the Argos bag and whack a tag on it.

Looking up, she noticed the rain had eased off and a chink of sun was peeping through the grey-white clouds, and her eyes were hypnotically drawn to the stack of cards. Abandoning her task, Anna made an executive decision and shouted for Pippa to wake up, they were going to brave the wind and head outside.

Five minutes later, they were both marching along the seafront towards the post office. Anna looked like a woman possessed in her pink wellies and bobble hat, clutching a carrier bag stuffed with cards and accompanied by a reluctant, naffed-off bulldog wearing a Santa coat embellished with very jingly bells.

Happy Christmas, Pippa!

CHAPTER 5

Freda was warming her feet by the fire after a morning stroll through the beautiful Cheshire countryside with Olivia. The terrible storms of the previous week had abated and the even though the fields and lanes were a little soggy underfoot, the air was bracing, and the views of the rolling fields were spectacular. Howard had disappeared off somewhere with Henry, and she suspected their destination would be the tiny pub in the centre of the village. Its creaky floors and timbered roof were as much of a draw as the cask real ales, leaving her husband in picture-postcard heaven.

Olivia had bustled off into the kitchen to have a word with her housekeeper, Mrs Wallace, about the catering for tonight's party which Freda was extremely excited about. It was a gathering of Cheshire's remaining glitterati, not footballers and their wives, the old guard consisting of Olivia's dearest friends. It had come as a wonderful surprise when Olivia and Henry invited them to stay at 'The Castle' and Freda didn't have to be asked twice. They had flown up to Manchester from Rennes and after a few days in Cheshire, they would be heading down to Bristol on the train to stay with Betty for Christmas. Olivia and Henry were flying south to be with Ruby and the rest of the family.

Freda was looking forward to spending time with her mum and better still once Boxing Day was done with, Grandma Betty would also be flying back to France to see in the New Year.

It seemed that following the 'Tilly situation,' Betty decided to take her own advice about living her life and had surprised them all by being proactive in other aspects of her life. She began by taking a firmer approach with Marianne, which surprised and delighted Freda in equal measure. After enlisting a painter and decorator, she had the whole house done up, inside and out. Then Betty ordered a new three-piece suite and with help from Tilly, chose a fancy telly for the front room.

Marianne had been a trifle concerned that her mother was getting a bit carried away and her savings would be dwindling rapidly, whereas Freda was over the moon that at last, some of her parents' hard-earned cash was being spent on making one of them happy, instead of gathering dust at the bank.

There was an ulterior motive to Betty's plan. She wanted to spruce up the house for when Scott and Susie came home in early February. It would take time for them to find a new home so once the decision was made to leave Australia, Betty offered them her house for as long as they wanted.

It was her intention to be nipping back and forth to France and just the thought of her mum visiting regularly and Charlotte being back in England, brought a huge smile to Freda's face.

As for Susie, she was so relieved to be coming home and was eternally grateful to Betty for providing them with somewhere to stay while they all got settled in jobs and school. Most importantly, it took the stress out of the situation with her poorly dad. Yes, Betty had come up trumps and, with her new lease of life, was making a lot of people happy in the process.

The only cloud seemed to be hovering above Tilly who hadn't bounced back as quickly as Freda would have liked and for want of another expression, seemed to be treading water.

* * *

Betty had been absolutely right when she suggested Freda should go to Tilly's aid. It had given her the chance to apologise for not realising what was going on in her heart and her head. Even though Tilly refused to accept any wrongdoing on her mother's part, it set the tone for how their relationship would be in the future. Freda was going to listen more and not jump the gun while Tilly swore she'd be open and honest. It was clear that Tilly wasn't going to sit around weeping and wailing because she meant business, which entailed wiping the memory of Luke from the face of the earth.

Within twenty-four hours, Tilly had removed all her personal belongings from their home, then in a few clicks and with the aid of internet banking, relieved Luke of half the money they'd been saving for a deposit on a house. Freda panicked a bit when Tilly made the transfer, saying it could be regarded as stealing or fraud and he'd have her arrested, whereas her daughter didn't even bat an eyelid. As far as Tilly was concerned, she'd paid for half of everything in their luxuriously furnished home and was leaving it all behind, so she was taking the money and if he didn't like it then he could sue her, she'd see him in court.

Freda had just about got her head around Tilly acting like Bonnie Parker when she surprised them again, by reimbursing them for the wedding fiasco. Howard and Freda kicked up a right old fuss and insisted she take it back, and in return, Tilly told them to go on a cruise or whatever they wanted but if they gave it back, she'd donate it all to the Dogs' Home. The mood Tilly was in, Freda and Howard believed her and took heed of the threat and left it in their deposit account for a rainy day or an emergency.

The thing was, even though she'd kept her side of the bargain and had left her daughter to go her own way in whatever direction she wanted, until a few days ago, Freda hadn't a clue what was going on in her daughter's head or heart. Tilly had moved in with Stacey and instead of moping, had thrown herself into working long shifts and volunteering for overtime whenever she could.

During one of their weekly telephone conversations, sometime in early October, during which Tilly stuck to the basics about work and a visit to the cinema with Stacey, Freda had boldly asked if she'd heard or seen anything of Joe. The tension crackled down the line, at which point, after a moment of silence in which she knew Tilly was deciding how much to say, or not as the case may be, Freda gently reminded her daughter of her promise to be open.

Tilly sighed and allowed Freda into her head, just for a short time, and confirmed that they were in touch regularly by text. Joe had sent her some amazing photos from China and Manchester, where he'd been hobnobbing with the Chancellor, but apart from that, they'd both been so busy with work that they'd found it hard to meet up. Then, in the very next sentence, she stumped Freda by announcing that Joe was driving over to Bristol that weekend and, during this time, Tilly was going to test the water where her feelings for him were concerned. Hopefully by Sunday evening, she would know once and for all if their time in France was a flash in the pan, holiday romance or, could be something more.

Freda praised Tilly for being sensible and taking her time and hoped that whatever they both decided was for the best and, no matter what the outcome was, she would have her mother's support. Tilly then succinctly closed down the conversation and moved straight on to the new boots she'd bought online.

Nothing more had been said until she received a message from Tilly letting her know that the weekend had gone really well and that Joe was planning a return trip the following weekend. As she'd read the words and tried to fathom what was going on between the lines, Freda wondered whether all parents have the same hurdles to jump in order to find out what the hell was going on in their kid's lives? Even when they were teenagers, Freda remembered thinking carefully before asking either of them where they'd been or who was on the phone. She sometimes thought that Scott and Tilly had been recruited by MI5, both were masters of evasion, and if she was honest, not much had changed since!

Since then, Freda had managed to extract a few juicy nuggets. Tilly said her feelings for Joe were definitely more than a holiday romance, but they had both agreed to take things slowly.

* * *

As far as Freda knew, Tilly would be seeing Joe just before Christmas as it was the only time she could get off and planned to stay at his apartment in Portsmouth. And that was it, very matter of fact and semi-subdued, until totally out of the blue, she'd rung Freda and Howard that very morning, brimming with excitement and eager to share her big news.

She had made a snap decision and knew where her life and career were headed; she was packing up and leaving Bristol to start over in a brand-new place where she could train to do the work she always dreamed of.

Everyone knew Tilly wanted to be an ophthalmic nurse and her burning ambition was to go to India or China and do volunteer work on one of the Hospital Trains which travelled across the continent. They performed life-enhancing operations on those who couldn't afford treatment or lived so far from civilisation that finding a cure was impossible. She would be spending Christmas in Bristol with all the family and then she was off, and from the sound of her voice, Tilly's soul had been cleansed and her head was definitely on straight. All being well, she was going to begin the next chapter of her life with a clean slate and was raring to go.

Olivia, entering the room carrying a large tray laden

with sandwiches and cake, brought Freda back to the present and drew her eyes away from the mesmerising flames that were sending her to sleep. They were both due at the hairdressers in an hour so they could be glammed up before tonight's party. Freda couldn't wait to wear her gorgeous new evening gown and was equally excited to see Howard in his dinner suit.

Tonight was a full-on, black tie affair and after an exhausting shopping spree with the Queen of Style, Freda came home with a beautiful dress, which Olivia assured her would never date and could be worn again, especially if they ever took that cruise they'd all been talking about. Freda had a sneaky feeling that before long, Howard might be persuaded to part with their rainy-day money and within the next twelve months, the four of them would be sailing down the Nile and gazing at the pyramids.

Life looked extremely rosy right now. They had wonderful friends, her son and his family would soon be winging their way back across the world and, fingers crossed, her mother would be a frequent visitor to France. And best of all, despite her troubles, if all went according to her plan, Tilly would be happy, at last.

CHAPTER 6

Two large cases of clothes and three cardboard boxes containing all her worldly belongings didn't seem much to signify twenty-seven years of her life, yet Tilly knew they contained everything she needed for now and material possessions weren't that important. She'd become accustomed to living out of her suitcases in Stacey's tiny spare room and if all went well today, they'd be coming with her when she relocated. Tilly slung her bag over her shoulder, picked up her phone and overnight case and headed for the door knowing her days living with her best friend could be numbered. Just thinking about moving unsettled the butterflies in her stomach, but Tilly was ready to face the final stage of her reinvention head-on.

* * *

The day she posted the keys to the house she shared with Luke back through the letter box, her transformation began. Stacey had wanted to do all sorts of crazy things, like cut the legs off his trousers and sew prawns inside the hems of the curtains. Tilly just wanted to go, and rash acts of revenge weren't going to change a thing. Stacey argued that some of the stuff that Tilly had left behind was top of the range and they could've flogged it on eBay, why leave it there and make life easy for Luke who would no doubt use it to entertain his bit on the side?

Money and possessions hadn't been a huge concern for Tilly. Instead she'd worked hard since returning from France and stashed her wages so she now had a healthy sum in her account. When she wasn't at the hospital, Tilly had spent the time sleeping, watching television or reading up on training courses. She had no desire to party with Stacey, meet someone new, get wasted, or do anything really. There had been more important things on the agenda, including her relationship with Joe. She had his feelings to consider and owed it to them both to do the right thing.

They had kept in touch constantly since August, a text or a call to and fro every day, nothing heavy or romantic, just an appraisal of their lives and work, funny stories and grumbles about this and that, plus gentle teasing and hints from Joe now and then. He had been so supportive and understanding, even though she heard the disappointment in his voice when she let him down gently each time he suggested they meet up, and then the relief when she finally invited him over for the weekend in October.

Stacey thought she was being a bit harsh and would end up losing him, but Tilly insisted that there was a method to her madness and Joe's best interests were foremost. She wasn't going to be on the list of girls who'd led him up the garden path before breaking his gentle heart. Hers was fragile too and had more or less frozen over, encased in a protective, impenetrable layer. In the time they'd been apart, Joe had passed every single test she threw at him, proving beyond a shadow of a doubt that he would do anything for her and gradually, she began to thaw.

Tilly also had one more issue to overcome. She was terrified that when it came down to it, the spark they felt in France might no longer be there, if and when they met in person. The potential that it was all a silly holiday romance was too much to contemplate, so she fended off fate for as long as possible. Before long, Stacey's warnings began to chip away and then Freda started dropping hints too, so Tilly knew it was time to test the water and hopefully silence both her critics in one go.

The day of reckoning arrived and Joe turned up on the doorstep, eager to collect Tilly and whisk her off for lunch. Never in her life had she been this nervous and unsure, literally dreading their reunion while at the same time counting the minutes until he rang the bell. All the 'what ifs' hung about like annoying, unwelcome guests while the emergency excuses hovered in the background, waiting to be called on to extricate her from a tricky situation if her feelings really had changed.

Tilly had been a quaking mess when she opened the door to Joe, who'd looked so handsome and equally nervous and unsure, then within seconds, everything changed as contact was made. Who'd have thought that an act so simple, like the holding out of a hand to welcome him in, the touching of skin accompanied by a bolt of something fizzy and wildly electric would have the power to smother doubt?

Before sane thoughts had the chance to interfere with the insane way her heart reacted to his touch, Tilly was in his arms and having the life kissed out of her. She was laughing, in between wiping away happy tears that had sprung from nowhere. It was everything she had spent many hours thinking of. To be able to touch his skin, feel his body and lips as they pressed against hers, be consumed by desire and give in to it, had made the waiting, doing the right thing, worthwhile.

From that moment on, the weekend flew by in a haze of perfect harmony. They booked into a hotel, threw caution to the wind and immersed themselves in a world that contained just the two of them. The tentative foundations they'd laid during the summer allowed them to build on the purest of love that they'd found in each other, affirming hour by hour that this was it, it was real, and they hadn't imagined anything.

By the time she said goodbye to Joe on a misty, cold Monday morning after clinging on to as many minutes as they dared, there wasn't a shred of doubt in her mind that Joe was in fact, 'the one'. Since then they had managed two more glorious visits after her calling in favours and swapping shifts, while Joe made detours and hastily wrapped up meetings so they could be together.

It was all quite exciting too, driving towards each other in the rain and the fog, meeting halfway in a motel room where they locked the door on the world for a few hours, only to have to say goodbye before it got light and then head back to work.

While they'd talked about everything under the sun and revised the bucket list of adventures they wanted to share, Tilly had made it clear that she had personal goals of her own to achieve, as did Joe, who was more focused on the haulage yard than ever. Owing to their like-mindedness, Tilly had reached a startling yet refreshing conclusion. It was like a breath of fresh air to know that finally, she could realise her dream and while doing so, Joe was the type of man who would respect and support her decision as he forged ahead with his own career.

* * *

All Tilly had to do now was catch a train, make some final arrangements and hope the offer was still on the table, and if it was, she could surprise Joe with her bold move and then her plan for the future could be set in motion. It was time for Staff Nurse Parker to take a leap of faith and, after everything he'd said in the past, she was sure Joe would be pleased. She was also utterly convinced that she hadn't misread the signals and knew that the way forward was clear. Tilly Parker had to grab life with both hands and not waste a moment.

She would be the first to admit that the last year had

been just that, a waste, but in some ways it had taught her valuable lessons and painful as they were, she would learn from them. Her future would involve hard work and new challenges and a change of scenery, but compared to the dull monotony of the past, it looked quite sparkly, and Tilly couldn't wait!

CHAPTER 7

Joe was standing in the middle of the typing pool holding fairy lights while his PA, Samantha, tried to untangle them. The rest of the girls were singing along to a Christmas song on the radio while they stapled tinsel and dangly decorations to everything in their path. The room was beginning to look quite festive, but Joe still wasn't in the mood. He had a terrible feeling of doom that he couldn't shake off. It was the result of a text he'd received from Tilly earlier that day, sending him into meltdown.

After the success of his trips up to Bristol and their romantic motorway tryst, he'd invited her down to Portsmouth to stay at his place once he returned from a whistle-stop trip to Belgium. It was an offer which she'd eagerly accepted and he'd been so sure of her commitment to the idea (and him) that he'd stupidly told his mum, who seemed genuinely pleased about the whole situation.

Naturally, she'd gone into full-on Mum Mode and offered to give his apartment the once over and if he wrote a list, would stock up his fridge for when Tilly arrived. He loved his mum to bits, but she still hadn't got to grips with the idea that he'd actually moved out and saw his apartment as some kind of annexe or extension to hers.

Sam on the other hand thought he was mad because having their mum live on the floor above was a huge bonus if they ran out of bread or needed a lift into town. Maybe he'd made a huge mistake by moving so close (and giving Sam *and* his mum a key) but it seemed like a good idea at the time.

The catalyst he needed to get off his bottom and find somewhere of his own was Daniel's marriage proposal. Joe knew it wasn't a good look, living with your parents at his age, especially when he had an executive wage coming in and should already have a foot on the property ladder.

He'd attempted to be proactive in every aspect of his life, mainly to keep his mind occupied and prevent him from obsessing about Tilly, while at the same time, showing her he was an all-round good bet and not a lovesick limpet. Before long, Joe became thoroughly fed up with traipsing around unsuitable properties and his enthusiasm was waning by the time Anna spotted the apartment below going up for sale. His mother behaving like a woman possessed and basically arranging it all for him was in all honesty a bonus, so he rolled over and went with the flow.

Sam thought it was the best thing in the world to have two options when he came home on leave and meandered between both apartments, his final choice determined mainly by the time he rolled in from a night on the town or whether it was a mealtime.

Joe's intention was to have a tactful word with his brother about privacy and respecting his space, but now it looked like it wasn't needed after all. Tilly had postponed her visit that coming weekend and hadn't even explained why, saying merely that there'd been a change of plan and she'd be in touch later that day to explain.

Something was up, he could just tell, and he'd not been able to eat his lunch with the worry of it all. Sam would call him a girl (as usual) for getting so wound up over a text but why would she cancel? Their weekends together had been perfect, out of this world in fact, and since then, her messages and calls left him in no doubt of her feelings, or so he thought. His heart tried to remain optimistic while his head told it to him straight – Tilly was getting cold feet. Then something even worse sprang to mind, maybe she'd met a handsome doctor on her work's do! After seeing how gorgeous she looked when she FaceTimed him before they all went out, who could blame someone for trying to pinch his girlfriend?

Samantha's exasperated voice interrupted his dismal thoughts and his attention was brought back to the task at hand. She'd finally managed to get the knots out of the lights, which turned out to be a complete waste of time because when she plugged them in, there was a strange popping noise and then nothing. Now, the disgruntled office junior was being dispatched to Tesco to buy a new set and seeing this as an excuse to escape decoration duties, Joe scurried back to his office, closed the door and sulked in front of his computer screen.

He had tons of work to do but no matter how hard he tried he just couldn't concentrate and didn't care, either! The sound of his phone pinging made him jump and he half dreaded it being a doom and gloom message from Tilly, one which started YOU ARE DUMPED.

Instead it was from his mum who'd kindly sent a selfie of her and the dog on the beach. His mother was smiling, despite looking slightly dishevelled and when he looked closer, decided that if an animal could be embarrassed, then that's exactly the expression Pippa was wearing right now. What drug *was* his mother on these days, and why on earth would you dress a bulldog up like Santa?

Joe knew he was being grumpy, but he was allowed. Nothing ever went right for him and he was beginning to think that he was eternally cursed and fated to being dumped before or after Christmas, either way it was crap. He'd texted Tilly twice and there'd been no reply, and now her phone was turned off, which didn't bode well. It was her free afternoon, so she couldn't even pretend she was too busy with a patient.

Looking down into the haulage yard, Joe spotted Yvette,

the junior, who was trudging her way towards the exit and en route to buy new lights. She'd stopped on the way to chat to the stacker truck driver who had a roving eye and the ability to shirk for most of the day whenever possible. Joe was wondering how long Yvette could keep hold of her brolly before the wind blew it away when his phone pinged again. His head snapped immediately towards the screen, hoping it wasn't another festive dog photo.

It was actually from Tilly and the fear of what it might say caused him to hold his breath as he read the words, which didn't seem too bad and said simply – Please read this then ring me x

Joe's heart hammered in his chest, his intuition was right, and this proved something was going on, so it was with extremely low expectations and self-esteem that he began to read her message.

Dear Joe, please don't flip when you read this. I haven't got the bottle to say it on the phone or to your face so I'm going to explain everything this way because I'm a big coward. All I want you to do is be honest with me and tell me if you are happy when you hear my news. Here goes.

The reason I won't be coming to see you this weekend is because I'm going to hand in my resignation at the hospital and might have to work my notice quickly (they can be funny like that). I've just come out of a final interview and the amazing part is they offered me the job which I want to accept, but that depends on you. A few weeks ago, I spotted an advert and applied for a course to train as an ophthalmic nurse, you know it's my dream, but to do this I need to leave Bristol and work at a new hospital. There was a lot of competition but they've literally just given me a place and I think it is the perfect job for me and my life. I didn't want to tell you until it was in the bag and we'd worked out how we felt about each other. Anyway, here's the scary bit. The hospital is in Southampton which is precisely 19 miles from Portsmouth (I looked it up) so I will be loads nearer to you. In case you are totally freaking out right now, I can have a room in the nurse's residence until I get settled and all that, so I won't be a nuisance and we can take things slowly. I'm totally committed to my new job and YOU and hope you are smiling right now and not heading for the airport to escape from me. That's it really. Please ring me and put me out of my misery. I love you. Tilly xxxxx

Joe was stunned and his face hurt from smiling. His heart was going mad in his chest and he was in a bit of a state. He rang Tilly straight away and she answered immediately. Joe was sure she would be able to tell he was grinning while he spoke and he imagined she was too when she listened to what he had to say.

'Is that Staff Nurse Parker?'

There was a nervous silence before she replied. 'Yes, speaking.'

Joe heard her giggle before he continued in his correct, professional voice. 'It has come to my attention that you may be requiring the services of a man with a van in the near future and as I have a whole fleet of vehicles of various sizes at my disposal, I'd like to offer my services. There is, however, one condition.'

Joe could hear Tilly laughing at the other end.

She replied. 'Oh really, and what exactly is this condition, should I be worried?'

Joe was on a roll and deliriously happy which made him feel brave and determined.

'I refuse to deliver to the Southampton area on personal grounds and I'm only prepared to deposit you and your consignment to a very nice apartment I know of in Portsmouth – Southsea to be precise. It's got all mod cons and a sea view. Would madam be agreeable to these terms or would she prefer student digs and a communal kitchen?' Joe held his breath and hoped his cheeky gamble had paid off, because he was thoroughly sick of being apart from her.

'But what if I do your head in? It's a big step, moving in together straight away. Don't you think we should take our time? I'm touched that you asked but I'm just being honest, this is scary stuff.'

Joe wasn't in the least bit worried so proceeded to deliver the sales pitch of his life.

'Tilly, I'm tired of going with the flow and being predictable. I think it's time I was a bit spontaneous and I'm sick to death of waiting! Do you know you've almost killed me these past months? If you're going to be working crazy shifts and studying and I'm going to be away with work a lot of the time, then we need to make the most of the days we do get together and that means keeping you prisoner in my apartment. I want to wake up *and* go to sleep with you lying next to me, so living down the road in Southampton just doesn't make sense.' Joe had surprised himself with his spur of the moment offer and subsequent burst of logic.

'Well, I suppose when you put it like that I'd be stupid to refuse. I want to be with you too and we've wasted so much time being apart and miserable, so let's go for it. I'm a bit in shock with everything but I can't wait to move now. I'd only thought as far as the interview and then sounding you out, I hadn't factored living together into the equation.'

'Trust me, it's going to be fine, I promise. Anyway, what are you doing now, are you in your car?' Joe was punching the air and strutting around his office, brimming with relief and nervous energy.

'Well, that's the other thing. I came on the train and as I don't need to go back to Bristol till tomorrow, maybe I could stay the night at yours? I really should check out this amazing apartment. Would you be able to come and pick me up? I'll get a bus if you're busy there.'

Joe was actually dragging his jacket from the back of his chair as he spoke.

'I'm on my way. Just text me the address of where you are and I'll come and get you.' Joe flicked off his computer then headed out of the office, waving cheerily to a bemused-looking Samantha as he pushed open the swing doors and disappeared from sight.

'Okay, I'll send it now and, Joe... I love you so much, please drive slowly.'

'I always do... and, Tilly, I love you too.' Joe ran towards his car, passing Sam's campervan that was stored in the huge garage over winter, the sight of it made him smile and gave him an idea. His attention was then drawn to a message showing the address of the hospital, but before he set off, Joe realised he needed to send one more text.

Hi Mum, could you do me a massive favour and nip down to mine and give it the once over and check it's respectable. Sorry it's short notice but Tilly is staying over tonight and I want it to look nice. Be there in about an hour. You're the best. Love you x

P.S. Good news, she's moving to Southampton Hospital and in with me – will explain later

CHAPTER 8

Anna was just taking off her coat when she received the message from Joe and smiled as she read the words. It meant they'd finally worked things out.

After fishing the keys for Joe's apartment out of the drawer she made her way down the stairs. Curious thoughts of why Tilly was moving conflicted with images of the two of them in France, smiling and having fun. All sorts of questions and scenarios played in her mind. Was this all a bit hasty? She'd have to make contact with Freda the next time she was in France. It was only polite after all. Would they have to set an extra place at the table for Christmas dinner? Maybe Tilly would be attending Anna's wedding as Joe's partner. In this crazy world, anything was possible.

As she let herself into Joe's apartment Anna scanned the room with a critical eye. It was already quite clean and tidy but felt a bit unlived in. With a bit of luck and a woman's touch, perhaps it would soon become a proper home, somewhere full of happy memories and laughter. There was no harm in giving it a quick once over with the polish and the hoover, the cushions needed plumping too, so Anna set about tweaking the apartment. Drawing the curtains wider, she tied them back properly and while she smoothed the fabric, pondered on the fact that men never seemed to be able to make them hang right or look nice, they just dragged them open and left them uneven and messy.

Once she'd finished fussing, Anna opened the patio doors allowing a rush of brisk, salty air to enter the room. There was plenty of time before Joe returned so she took a few moments to admire the view and savour his good news.

The year was almost at an end and all in all, it hadn't been too bad. Anna had a feeling that as always, the new one would bring challenges of its own and knowing her lot, there would be some drama or another to keep her on her toes. Families were rarely perfect and hers certainly wasn't, but she loved them all dearly and whether they liked it or not, it was her job to interfere and worry about them. No matter how far away they travelled or grown-up they thought they were, each one still needed an anchor, someone to run to if it all went wrong and be proud of them when it all went right.

Shivering, Anna could feel that her nose was cold and probably turning pink, so she decided to go inside and get on with the job. Before closing the doors against the wind, Anna took one last look across the Solent and thought wistfully of her friends on the other side of the Channel, hoping they were well. She sometimes wished they lived closer and could see them more often because they had become an important part of her life, her extended family.

Anna was always making wishes and praying to her angel for one thing or another. Most of the time, the special requests were aimed at her children, while a frequent prayer for patience was usually related to her mother. In the interests of family harmony, she had also been known to ask for a favour where the football results were concerned and once asked her angel not to let Tony Blackburn win on *I'm A Celebrity*. It must have been her night off because he took the crown regardless.

Today, if Anna had one wish, she would keep it simple and ask for happiness, for all of her family. That one word encompassed so many elements of life and it didn't matter if you were rich or poor, old or young, happiness was a precious gift. And as for whatever lay ahead, she was sure they could overcome any obstacles as a team. With love, trust and respect for one another, propped up by the comfort of friendship, they could face anything the future may bring.

Glancing upwards, Anna noticed that the wind had finally banished the grey storm clouds to reveal a crystal clear, winter-blue layer of sky that stretched on for miles and miles. It struck her then that maybe this was a sign, so she lifted her head towards the December sunshine and allowed it to gently warm her face.

It was simple really. All her family had to do, was hold tightly to the bonds that bound them together, just as they always had, and they'd be just fine. Smiling, Anna closed the door and went inside.

CHAPTER 9

Tilly was seated on a bench at the pick-up zone of the hospital, waiting for Joe to arrive, her presumptuous overnight bag by her side. Her toes were cold and her bottom was numb but her heart was glowing. She imagined it as a ball of fire, swirling like a comet inside her chest. Unzipping her handbag, Tilly impatiently checked her phone for the tenth time, hoping that Joe would be there soon. It was as she went to close the zip, she spotted her diary.

Joe had returned it the first time they met up, hoping that she'd be able to fill it with happier memories than the ones it already contained. Frozen fingers crossed, her next diary would be bursting at the seams with new adventures, no red pen and angry scribbles.

Tilly looked along the road, hoping to spot Joe's car – maybe he was stuck in traffic? In the meantime, she decided to bring her battered and well-travelled diary up to date. Pulling it from her bag and taking the pen from the loop, Tilly opened the page, thought for a moment and smiled, then through misty eyes, she wrote just one simple sentence.

Flicking away warm tears, Tilly replaced the pen and closed her diary before slipping it back into her bag. As she zipped the top, then wedged cold hands between her knees for warmth, she heard a familiar chugging sound. Looking up, knowing exactly what she was going to see, Tilly's laugh was distorted slightly by emotion and the huge lump that had formed in her throat.

Springing to her feet, ignoring the odd looks from passers-by, she began waving like crazy at Joe, who was now flashing the headlights of the campervan. Despite more tears, and as he got closer, she could see his gorgeous face through the windscreen. He was smiling and waving, then pulling into the pick-up zone and leaping from the cab, looking comical in his suit and tie, instead of his summer clothes and sunglasses. Without a second's hesitation, Tilly grabbed her bags and sprinted towards Joe and into his outstretched arms. Oblivious to the rest of the world who just walked on by, she kissed him, never wanting it to end, parting only when an impatient driver honked his horn.

Laughing, Joe took her bag and once inside the camper, the familiar sound of the engine ignited Tilly's senses, memories of summer days and starry nights, like little sparks of happiness shooting around her head and heart. In between changing gear, Joe held on tightly to Tilly's hand as they pulled out of the car park and headed home, towards a brand-new future that was theirs for the taking. Stealing a glance at Joe, the man she loved so much, who had come to her rescue more than once, Tilly smiled as she thought of the few, simple words she'd written just minutes before.

Dear Diary,
Joe said yes, he's coming to get me. It's all going to be okay!

The End

ACKNOWLEDGMENTS

I hope you all enjoyed this story which took me a lot longer than usual to write owing to the devastating and untimely passing of my beloved mum. I had the great honour of caring for her before she was taken from us suddenly, and despite the huge shock, I thank God for giving us that precious, special time together. I was in the early stages of the book when she became ill and after she left us, it took me a while to get back on track. Knowing how proud she was of my writing was the only thing that spurred me on, kept me focused and made me finish the story.

The idea for Tilly evolved following a conversation with an acquaintance who confided that she had gone through with her wedding, simply because it was the easy option. After I got over the shock of her confession, I couldn't get the ramifications of such actions out of my head but I did understand her logic and her fervent desire not to upset her parents.

My parents were the centre of our family and they gave us everything – support, friendship, guidance and the most important element of all, unconditional love. I hope that this story has explored how our relationships can shift, the frailties of human nature, the interaction between family members, and ultimately, the hopes and dreams we have for our children.

There is one other underlying theme within the story – the precious gift of friendship, which conveniently leads me to saying thank you to some special people.

To my friend Angela, for everything. To the amazing team at Bloodhound and Bombshell Books and in particular Heather who has worked so hard and been my rock during the writing of this series. Thanks to Abbie for proofreading, my amazing group of ARC readers for your support and friendship and everyone who reads my books and cheers me on, thank you.

To my precious family.
Vous êtes ma vie, toujours.

And to Pearl, our bulldog.
Miss you forever, chubby chops, love you always.
xxxxxxx

Printed in Poland
by Amazon Fulfillment
Poland Sp. z o.o., Wrocław